By Nora Roberts

Trilogies and Quartets

The Born In Trilogy:
Born in Fire
Born in Ice
Born in Shame

The Sign of Seven Trilogy:
Blood Brothers
The Hollow
The Pagan Stone

The Bride Quartet:
Vision in White
Bed of Roses
Savour the Moment
Happy Ever After

Chesapeake Bay Quartet:
Sea Swept
Rising Tides
Inner Harbour
Chesapeake Blue

The Key Trilogy:
Key of Light
Key of Knowledge
Key of Valour

In the Garden Trilogy:
Blue Dahlia
Black Rose
Red Lily

The Irish Trilogy:
Jewels of the Sun
Tears of the Moon
Heart of the Sea

The Circle Trilogy:
Morrigan's Cross
Dance of the Gods
Valley of Silence

Three Sisters Island Trilogy:
Dance upon the Air
Heaven and Earth
Face the Fire

The Dream Trilogy:
Daring to Dream
Holding the Dream
Finding the Dream

Nora Roberts also writes the In Death series
using the pseudonym J. D. Robb

NORA ROBERTS

MORRIGAN'S CROSS

piatkus

PIATKUS

First published in the US in 2006 by G. P. Putnam's Sons
First published in Great Britain in 2006 by Piatkus
This paperback edition published in 2012 by Piatkus

5 7 9 10 8 6

Printed and bound by CPI Group (UK) Ltd, Croydon, CR0 4YY

Papers used by Piatkus are from well-managed forests
and other responsible sources.

 MIX
Paper from
responsible sources
FSC® C104740

Piatkus
An imprint of
Little, Brown Book Group
Carmelite House
50 Victoria Embankment
London EC4Y 0DZ

An Hachette UK Company
www.hachette.co.uk

www.piatkus.co.uk

For my brothers,
Jim, Buz, Don and Bill

None but the brave deserves the fair.
—DRYDEN

Finish, good lady; the bright day is done,
And we are for the dark.
—SHAKESPEARE

Prologue

It was the rain that made him think of the tale. The lash of it battered the windows, stormed the rooftops and blew its bitter breath under the doors.

The damp ached in his bones even as he settled by the fire. Age sat heavily on him in the long, wet nights of autumn— and would sit heavier still, he knew, in the dark winter to come.

The children were gathered, huddled on the floor, squeezed by twos and threes into chairs. Their faces were turned to his, expectant, for he'd promised them a story to chase boredom from a stormy day.

He hadn't intended to give them this one, not yet, for some were so young. And the tale was far from tender. But the rain whispered to him, hissing the words he'd yet to speak.

Even a storyteller, perhaps especially a storyteller, had to listen.

"I know a tale," he began, and several of the children squirmed in anticipation. "It's one of courage and cowardice, of blood and death, and of life. Of love and of loss."

"Are there monsters?" one of the youngest asked, with her blue eyes wide with gleeful fear.

"There are always monsters," the old man replied. "Just as there are always men who will join them, and men who will fight them."

"And women!" one of the older girls called out, and made him smile.

"And women. Brave and true, devious and deadly. I have known both in my time. Now, this tale I tell you is from long ago. It has many beginnings, but only one end."

As the wind howled, the old man picked up his tea to wet his throat. The fire crackled, shot light across his face in a wash like gilded blood.

"This is one beginning. In the last days of high summer, with lightning striking blue in a black sky, the sorcerer stood on a high cliff overlooking the raging sea."

Chapter 1

Eire, the region of Chiarrai
1128

There was a storm in him, as black and vicious as that which bullied its way across the sea. It whipped inside his blood, outside in the air, battling within and without as he stood on the rain-slickened rock.

The name of his storm was grief.

It was grief that flashed in his eyes, as bold and as blue as those lightning strikes. And the rage from it spit from his fingertips, jagged red that split the air with thunderclaps that echoed like a thousand cannon shots.

He thrust his staff high, shouted out the words of magic. The red bolts of his rage and the bitter blue of the storm clashed overhead in a war that sent those who could see scurrying into cottage and cave, latching door and window, gathering their children close to quake and quail as they prayed to the gods of their choosing.

And in their raths, even the faeries trembled.

Rock rang, and the water of the sea went black as the mouth of hell, and still he raged, and still he grieved. The rain that poured out of the wounded sky fell red as blood—and sizzled, burning on land, on sea so that the air smelled of its boiling.

It would be called, ever after, The Night of Sorrows, and those who dared speak of it spoke of the sorcerer who stood tall on the high cliff, with the bloody rain soaking his cloak, running down his lean face like death's tears as he dared both heaven and hell.

His name was Hoyt, and his family the *Mac Cionaoith,* who was said to be descended from Morrigan, faerie queen and goddess. His power was great, but still young as he was young. He wielded it now with a passion that gave no room to caution, to duty, to light. It was his sword and his lance.

What he called in that terrible storm was death.

While the wind shrieked, he turned, putting his back to the tumultuous sea. What he had called stood on the high ground. She—for she had been a woman once—smiled. Her beauty was impossible, and cold as winter. Her eyes were tenderly blue, her lips pink as rose petals, her skin milk white. When she spoke, her voice was music, a siren's who had already called countless men to their doom.

"You're rash to seek me out. Are you impatient, Mac Cionaoith, for my kiss?"

"You are what killed my brother?"

"Death is . . ." Heedless of the rain, she pushed back her hood. "Complex. You are too young to understand its glories. What I gave him is a gift. Precious and powerful."

"You damned him."

"Oh." She flicked a hand in the air. "Such a small price for eternity. The world is his now, and he takes whatever he wants. He knows more than you can dream of. He's mine now, more than he was ever yours."

"Demon, his blood is on your hands, and by the goddess, I will destroy you."

She laughed, gaily, like a child promised a particular treat. "On my hands, in my throat. As mine is in his. He is like me now, a child of night and shadow. Will you also seek to destroy your own brother? Your twin?"

The ground fog boiled black, folded away like silk as she waded through it. "I smell your power, and your grief, and your wonder. Now, on this place, I offer this gift to you. I will make you once more his twin, Hoyt of the Mac

Cionaoiths. I will give you the death that is unending life."

He lowered his staff, stared at her through the curtain of rain. "Give me your name."

She glided over the fog now, her red cloak billowing back. He could see the white swell of her breasts rounding ripely over the tightly laced bodice of her gown. He felt a terrible arousal even as he scented the stench of her power.

"I have so many," she countered, and touched his arm— how had she come so close?—with just the tip of her finger. "Do you want to say my name as we join? To taste it on your lips, as I taste you?"

His throat was dry, burning. Her eyes, blue and tender, were drawing him in, drawing him in to drown. "Aye. I want to know what my brother knows."

She laughed again, but this time there was a throatiness to it. A hunger that was an animal's hunger. And those soft blue eyes began to rim with red. "Jealous?"

She brushed her lips to his, and they were cold, bitter cold. And still, so tempting. His heart began to beat hard and fast in his chest. "I want to see what my brother sees."

He laid his hand on that lovely white breast, and felt nothing stir beneath it. "Give me your name."

She smiled, and now the white of her fangs gleamed against the awful night. "It is Lilith who takes you. It is Lilith who makes you. The power of your blood will mix with mine, and we will rule this world, and all the others."

She threw back her head, poised to strike. With all of his grief, with all of his rage, Hoyt struck at her heart with his staff.

The sound that ripped from her pierced the night, screamed up through the storm and joined it. It wasn't human, not even the howl of a beast. Here was the demon who had taken his brother, who hid her evil behind cold beauty. Who bled, he saw as a stream of blood spilled from the wound, without a heartbeat.

She flew back into the air, twisting, shrieking as lightning tore at the sky. The words he needed to say were lost in his horror as she writhed in the air, and the blood that fell steamed into filthy fog.

"You would dare!" Her voice gurgled with outrage, with pain. "You would use your puny, your pitiful magic on me? I have walked this world a *thousand* years." She slicked her hand over the wound, threw out her bloody hand.

And when the drops struck Hoyt's arm, they sliced like a knife.

"Lilith! You are cast out! Lilith, you are vanquished from this place. By my blood." He pulled a dagger from beneath his cloak, scored his palm. "By the blood of the gods that runs through it, by the power of my birth, I cast you back—"

What came at him seemed to fly across the ground, and struck with the feral force of fury. Tangled, they crashed over the cliff to the jagged ledge below. Through waves of pain and fear he saw the face of the thing that so closely mirrored his own. The face that had once been his brother's.

Hoyt could smell the death on him, and the blood, and could see in those red eyes the animal his brother had become. Still, a small flame of hope flickered in Hoyt's heart.

"Cian. Help me stop her. We still have a chance."

"Do you feel how strong I am?" Cian closed his hand around Hoyt's throat and squeezed. "It's only the beginning. I have forever now." He leaned down, licked blood from Hoyt's face, almost playfully. "She wants you for herself, but I'm hungry. So hungry. And the blood in you is mine, after all."

As he bared his fangs, pressed them to his brother's throat, Hoyt thrust the dagger into him.

With a howl, Cian reared back. Shock and pain rushed over his face. Even as he clutched at the wound, he fell. For an instant, Hoyt thought he saw his brother, his true brother. Then there was nothing but the screams of the storm and the slashing rain.

He crawled and clawed his way up the cliff. His hands, slippery with blood and sweat and rain, groped for any hold. Lightning illuminated his face, tight with pain, as he inched his way up rock, tore his fingers in the clawing. His neck, where the fangs had scraped, burned like a brand. Breath whistling, he clutched at the edge.

If she waited, he was dead. His power had waned with

exhaustion, drained with the ravages of his shock and grief. He had nothing but the dagger, still red with his brother's blood.

But when he pulled himself up, when he rolled to his back with the bitter rain washing over his face, he was alone.

Perhaps it had been enough, perhaps he'd sent the demon back to hell. As he had surely sent his own flesh and blood to damnation.

Rolling over, he gained his hands and knees, and was viciously ill. Magic was ashes in his mouth.

He crawled to his staff, used it to help him stand. Breath keening, he staggered away from the cliffs, along a path he'd have known had he been blinded. The power had gone out of the storm as it had gone out of him, and now was merely a soaking rain.

He smelled home—horse and hay, the herbs he'd used for protection, the smoke from the fire he'd left smoldering in the hearth. But there was no joy in it, no triumph.

As he limped toward his cottage, his breath whistled out, hisses of pain that were lost in the rise of the wind. He knew if the thing that had taken his brother came for him now, he was lost. Every shadow, every shape cast by the storm-tossed trees could be his death. Worse than his death. Fear of that slicked along his skin like dirty ice, so that he used what strength he had to murmur incantations that were more like prayers for whoever, or whatever, would listen.

His horse stirred in its shelter, let out a huff as it scented him. But Hoyt continued shakily to the small cottage, dragging himself to the door and through.

Inside was warmth, and the ripple from the spells he'd cast before he'd gone to the cliffs. He barred the door, leaving smears of his and Cian's blood on the wood. Would it keep her out? he wondered. If the lore he'd read was fact, she couldn't enter without an invitation. All he could do was have faith in that, and in the protection spell that surrounded his home.

He let his soaked cloak fall, let it lay in a sodden heap on the floor, and had to fight not to join it there. He would mix potions for healing, for strength. And would sit through the night, tending the fire. Waiting for dawn.

He'd done all he could for his parents, his sisters and their families. He had to believe it was enough.

Cian was dead, and what had come back with his face and form had been destroyed. He would not, could not, harm them now. But the thing that had made him could.

He would find something stronger to protect them. And he would hunt the demon again. His life, he swore it now, would be dedicated to her destruction.

His hands, long of finger, wide of palm, were tremulous as he chose his bottles and pots. His eyes, stormy blue, were glazed with pain—the aches of his body, of his heart. Guilt weighed on him like a shroud of lead. And those demons played inside him.

He hadn't saved his brother. Instead, he had damned and destroyed him, cast him out and away. How had he won that terrible victory? Cian had always been physically superior to him. And what his brother had become was viciously powerful.

So his magic had vanquished what he'd once loved. The half of him that was bright and impulsive where he himself was often dull and staid. More interested in his studies and his skills than society.

Cian had been the one for gaming and taverns, for wenches and sport.

"His love of life," Hoyt murmured as he worked. "His love of life killed him. I only destroyed that which trapped him in a beast."

He had to believe it.

Pain rippled up his ribs as he shucked off his tunic. Bruises were already spreading, creeping black over his skin the way grief and guilt crept black over his heart. It was time for practical matters, he told himself as he applied the balm. He fumbled considerably, cursed violently, in wrapping the bandage over his ribs. Two were broken, he knew, just as he knew the ride back home in the morning would be a study in sheer misery.

He took a potion, then limped to the fire. He added turf so the flames glowed red. Over them he brewed tea. Then wrapped himself in a blanket to sit, to drink, to brood.

He had been born with a gift, and from an early age had soberly, meticulously sought to honor it. He'd studied, often in solitude, practicing his art, learning its scope.

Cian's powers had been less, but, Hoyt remembered, Cian had never practiced so religiously nor studied so earnestly. And Cian had played with magic, after all. Amusing himself and others.

And Cian had sometimes drawn him in, lowered Hoyt's resistance until they'd done something foolish together. Once they'd turned the boy who'd pushed their younger sister in the mud into a braying, long-eared ass.

How Cian had laughed! It had taken Hoyt three days of work, sweat and panic to reverse the spell, but Cian had never worried a whit.

He was born an ass, after all. We've just given him his true form.

From the time they'd been twelve, Cian had been more interested in swords than spells. Just as well, Hoyt thought as he drank the bitter tea. He'd been irresponsible with magic, and a magician with a sword.

But, steel hadn't saved him, nor had magic, in the end.

He sat back, chilled to his bones despite the simmering turf. He could hear what was left of the storm blowing still, splattering on his roof, wailing through the forest that surrounded his cottage.

But he heard nothing else, not beast, not threat. So was left alone with his memories and regrets.

He should've gone with Cian into the village that evening. But he'd been working, and hadn't wanted ale, or the smells and sounds of a tavern, of people.

He hadn't wanted a woman, and Cian had never *not* wanted one.

But if he'd gone, if he'd put aside his work for one bloody night, Cian would be alive. Surely the demon couldn't have overpowered both of them. Surely his gift would have allowed him to sense what the creature was, despite her beauty, her allure.

Cian would never have gone with her had his brother been by his side. And their mother would not be grieving.

The grave would never have been dug, and by the gods, the thing they buried would never have risen.

If his powers could turn back time, he would give them up, abjure them, to have that one night to re-live that single moment when he'd chosen work over his brother's company.

"What good do they do me? What good are they now? To have been given magic and not be able to use it to save what matters most? Damn to them all then." He flung his cup across the little room. "Damn to them all, gods and faeries. He was the light of us, and you've cast him into the dark."

All of his life Hoyt had done what he was meant to do, what was expected of him. He had turned away from a hundred small pleasures to devote himself to his art. Now those who had given him this gift, this power, had stood back while his own brother was taken?

Not in battle, not even with the clean blade of magic, but through evil beyond imagination. This was his payment, this was his reward for all he had done?

He waved a hand toward the fire, and in the hearth flames leapt and roared. He threw up his arms, and overhead the storm doubled in power so that the wind screamed like a tortured woman. The cottage trembled under its might, and the skins pulled tight over the windows split. Cold gusts spilled into the room, toppling bottles, flapping the pages of his books. And in it he heard the throaty chuckle of the black.

Not once in all of his life had he turned from his purpose. Not once had he used his gift for ill, or touched upon the black arts.

Perhaps now, he thought, he would find the answers in them. Find his brother again. Fight the beast, evil against evil.

He shoved to his feet, ignoring the scream in his side. He whirled toward his cot and flung out both hands toward the trunk he'd locked by magic. When it flew open, he strode to it, reached in for the book he'd shut away years before.

In it were spells, dark and dangerous magicks. Spells that used human blood, human pain. Spells of vengeance and greed that spoke to a power that ignored all oaths, all vows.

It was hot and heavy in his hands, and he felt the seduction of it, those curling fingers that brushed the soul. Have all, have any. Are we not more than the rest? Living gods who take whatever is desired?

We have the right! We are beyond rules and reasons.

His breath came short for he knew what could be his if he accepted it, if he took in both hands what he'd sworn never to touch. Unnamed wealth, women, unspeakable powers, life eternal. Revenge.

He had only to say the words, to rebuke the white and embrace the black. Clammy snakes of sweat slithered down his back as he heard the whispers of voices from a thousand ages:

Take. Take. Take.

His vision shimmered, and through it he saw his brother as he'd found him in the muck on the side of the road. Blood pooled from the wounds in his throat, and more smeared his lips. Pale, Hoyt thought dimly. So very pale was his face against that wet, red blood.

Now Cian's eyes—vivid and blue—opened. There was such pain in them, such horror. They pleaded as they met Hoyt's.

"Save me. Only you can save me. It's not death I'm damned to. 'Tis beyond hell, beyond torment. Bring me back. For once don't count the cost. Would you have me burn for all eternity? For the sake of your own blood, Hoyt, help me."

He shook. It wasn't from the cold that blew through the split skins, or the damp that whirled in the air, but from the icy edge on which he stood.

"I would give my life for yours. I swear it on all I am, on all we were. I would take your fate, Cian, if that were the choice before me. But I can't do this. Not even for you."

The vision on the bed erupted in flames, and its screams were past human. On a howl of grief, Hoyt heaved the book back in the trunk. He used the strength left to him to charm the lock before he collapsed on the floor. There he curled up like a child beyond all comfort.

* * *

Perhaps he slept. Perhaps he dreamed. But when he came to, the storm had passed. Light seeped into the room and grew, bold and bright and white, to sear his eyes. He blinked against it, hissing as his ribs protested when he tried to sit up.

There were streams of pink and gold shimmering in the white, warmth radiating from it. He smelled earth, he realized, rich and loamy, and the smoke from the turf fire that was still shimmering in the hearth.

He could see the shape of her, female, and sensed a staggering beauty.

This was no demon come for blood.

Gritting his teeth, he got to his knees. Though there was still grief and anger in his voice, he bowed his head.

"My lady."

"Child."

The light seemed to part for her. Her hair was the fiery red of a warrior, and flowed over her shoulders in silky waves. Her eyes were green as the moss in the forest, and soft now with what might have been pity. She wore white robes trimmed in gold as was her right by rank. Though she was the goddess of battle, she wore no armor, and carried no sword.

She was called Morrigan.

"You have fought well."

"I have lost. I have lost my brother."

"Have you?" She stepped forward, offered him a hand so he would rise. "You stayed true to your oath, though the temptation was great."

"I might have saved him otherwise."

"No." She touched Hoyt's face, and he felt the heat of her. "You would have lost him, and yourself. I promise you. You would give your life for his, but you could not give your soul, or the souls of others. You have a great gift, Hoyt."

"What good is it if I cannot protect my own blood? Do the gods demand such sacrifice, to damn an innocent to such torment?"

"It was not the gods who damned him. Nor was it for you to save him. But there is sacrifice to be made, battles to be fought. Blood, innocent and otherwise, to be spilled. You have been chosen for a great task."

"You could ask anything of me now, Lady?"

"Aye. A great deal will be asked of you, and of others. There is a battle to be fought, the greatest ever waged. Good against evil. You must gather the forces."

"I am not able. I am not willing. I am . . . God, I am tired."

He dropped to the edge of his cot, dropped his head in his hands. "I must go see my mother. I must tell her I failed to save her son."

"You have not failed. Because you resisted the dark you are charged to bear this standard, to use the gift you've been given to face and to vanquish that which would destroy worlds. Shake off this self-pity!"

His head rose at the sharp tone. "Even the gods must grieve, Lady. I have killed my brother tonight."

"Your brother was killed by the beast, a week ago. What fell from the cliff was not your Cian. You know this. But he . . . continues."

Hoyt got shakily to his feet. "He lives."

"It is not life. It is without breath, without soul, without heart. It has a name that is not spoken yet in this world. It is vampyre. It feeds on blood," she said, moving toward him. "It hunts the human, takes life, or worse, much worse, turns that which it hunts and kills into itself. It breeds, Hoyt, like a pestilence. It has no face, and must hide from the sun. It is this you must fight, this and other demons that are gathering. You must meet this force in battle on the feast of Samhain. And you must be victorious or the world you know, the worlds you have yet to know, will be overcome."

"And how will I find them? How will I fight them? It was Cian who was the warrior."

"You must leave this place and go to another, and another still. Some will come to you, and some you will seek. The witch, the warrior, the scholar, the one of many forms, and the one you've lost."

"Only five more? Six against an army of demons? My lady—"

"A circle of six, as strong and true as the arm of a god. When that circle is formed, others may be formed. But the six will be my army, the six will make the ring. You will teach and you will learn, and you will be greater than the sum of you. A month to gather, and one to learn, and one to know. The battle comes on Samhain.

"You, child, are my first."

"You would ask me to leave the family I have left, when that thing that took my brother may come for them?"

"The thing that took your brother leads this force."

"I wounded her—it. I gave her pain." And the memory of that bubbled up in him like vengeance.

"You did, aye, you did. And this is only another step toward this time and this battle. She bears your mark now, and will, in time, seek you out."

"If I hunt her now, destroy her now."

"You cannot. She is beyond you at this time, and you, my child, are not ready to face her. Between these times and worlds, her thirst will grow insatiable until only the destruction of all humankind will satisfy it. You will have your revenge, Hoyt," she said as he got to his feet. "If you defeat her. You will travel far, and you will suffer. And I will suffer knowing your pain, for you are mine. Do you think your fate, your happiness is nothing to me? You are my child even as you are your mother's."

"And what of my mother, Lady? Of my father, my sisters, their families? Without me to protect them, they may be the first to die if this battle you speak of comes to pass."

"It will come to pass. But they will be beyond it." She spread her hands. "Your love for your blood is part of your power, and I will not ask you to turn from it. You will not think clearly until you have assurance they will be safe."

She tipped back her head, held her arms up, palms cupped. The ground shook lightly under his feet, and when Hoyt looked up, he saw stars shooting through the night sky. Those points of light streamed toward her hands, and there burst into flame.

His heart thumped against his bruised ribs as she spoke, as her fiery hair flew around her illuminated face.

"Forged by the gods, by the light and by the night. Symbol and shield, simple and true. For faith, for loyalty, these gifts for you. Their magic lives through blood shed, yours and mine."

Pain sliced over his palm. He watched the blood well in his, and in hers as the fire burned.

"And so it shall live for all time. Blessed be those who wear Morrigan's Cross."

The fire died, and in the goddess's hands were crosses of gleaming silver.

"These will protect them. They must wear the cross always—day and night—birth to death. You will know they are safe when you leave them."

"If I do this thing, will you spare my brother?"

"You would bargain with the gods?"

"Aye."

She smiled, an amused mother to a child. "You have been chosen, Hoyt, because you would think to do so. You will leave this place and gather those who are needed. You will prepare and you will train. The battle will be fought with sword and lance, with tooth and fang, with wit and treachery. If you are victorious, the worlds will balance and you will have all you wish to have."

"How do I fight a vampyre? I've already failed against her."

"Study and learn," she said. "And learn from one of her kind. One she made. One who was yours before she took him. You must first find your brother."

"Where?"

"Not only where, but when. Look into the fire, and see."

They were, he noted, in his cottage again, and he was standing in front of the hearth. The flames spiked up, became towers. Became a great city. There were voices and sounds such as he'd never heard. Thousands of people rushed along streets that were made of some kind of stone. And machines sped with them.

"What is this place?" He could barely whisper the words. "What world is it?"

"It is called New York, and its time is nearly a thousand

years from where we are. Evil still walks the world, Hoyt, as well as innocence, as well as good. Your brother has walked the world a long time now. Centuries have passed for him. You would do well to remember that."

"Is he a god now?"

"He is vampyre. He must teach you, and he must fight beside you. There can be no victory without him."

Such size, he thought. Buildings of silver and stone taller than any cathedral. "Will the war be in this place, in this New York?"

"You will be told where, you will be told how. And you will know. Now you must go, take what you need. Go to your family and give them their shields. You must leave them quickly, and go to the Dance of the Gods. You will need your skill, and my power, to pass through. Find your brother, Hoyt. It is time for the gathering."

He woke by the fire, the blanket wrapped around him. But he saw it hadn't been a dream. Not with the blood drying on the palm of his hand, and the silver crosses lying across his lap.

It was not yet dawn, but he packed books and potions, oatcakes and honey. And the precious crosses. He saddled his horse, and then, as a precaution, cast another protective circle around his cottage.

He would come back, he promised himself. He would find his brother, and this time, he would save him. Whatever it took.

As the sun cast its first light, he began the long ride to An Clar, and his family home.

Chapter 2

He traveled north on roads gone to mud from the storm. The horrors and the wonders of the night played through his mind as he hunched over his horse, favoring his aching ribs.

He swore, should he live long enough, he would practice healing magic more often, and with more attention.

He passed fields where men worked and cattle grazed in the soft morning sunlight. And lakes that picked up their blue from the late summer sky. He wound through forests where the waterfalls thundered and the shadows and mosses were the realm of the faerie folk.

He was known here, and caps were lifted when Hoyt the Sorcerer passed by. But he didn't stop to take hospitality in one of the cabins or cottages. Nor did he seek comfort in one of the great houses, or in the conversations of monks in their abbeys or round towers.

In this journey he was alone, and above battles and orders from gods, he would seek his family first. He would offer them all he could before he left them to do what he'd been charged to do.

As the miles passed, he struggled to straighten on his horse whenever he came to villages or outposts. His dignity cost him considerable discomfort until he was forced to take his ease by the side of a river where the water gurgled over rock.

Once, he thought, he had enjoyed this ride from his cottage to his family home, through the fields and the hills, or along the sea. In solitude, or in the company of his brother, he had ridden these same roads and paths, felt this same sun on his face. Had stopped to eat and rest his horse at this very same spot.

But now the sun seared his eyes, and the smell of the earth and grass couldn't reach his deadened senses.

Fever sweat slicked his skin, and the angles of his face were keener as he bore down against the unrelenting pain.

Though he had no appetite, he ate part of one of the oat-cakes along with more of the medicine he'd packed. Despite the brew and the rest, his ribs continued to ache like a rotted tooth.

Just what good would he be in battle? he wondered. If he had to lift his sword now to save his life he would die with his hands empty.

Vampyre, he thought. The word fit. It was erotic, exotic, and somehow horrible. When he had both time and energy, he would write down more of what he knew. Though he was far from convinced he was about to save this world or any other from some demonic invasion, it was always best to gather knowledge.

He closed his eyes a moment, resting them against the headache that drummed behind them. A witch, he'd been told. He disliked dealing with witches. They were forever stirring odd bits of this and that in pots and rattling their charms.

Then a scholar. At least he might be useful.

Was the warrior Cian? That was his hope. Cian wielding sword and shield again, fighting alongside him. He could nearly believe he could fulfill the task he'd been given if his brother was with him.

The one with many shapes. Odd. A faerie perhaps, and

the gods knew just how reliable such creatures were. And this was somehow to be the front line in the battle for worlds?

He studied the hand he'd bandaged that morning. "Better for all if it had been dreaming. I'm sick and tired is what I am, and no soldier at the best of it."

Go back. The voice was a hissing whisper. Hoyt came to his feet, reaching for his dagger.

Nothing moved in the forest but the black wings of a raven that perched in shadows on a rock by the water.

Go back to your books and herbs, Hoyt the Sorcerer. Do you think you can defeat the Queen of the Demons? Go back, go back and live your pitiful life and she will spare you. Go forward, and she will feast on your flesh and drink of your blood.

"Does she fear to tell me so herself then? And so she should, for I will hunt her through this life and the next if need be. I will avenge my brother. And in the battle to come, I will cut out her heart and burn it."

You will die screaming, and she will make you her slave for eternity.

"It's an annoyance you are." Hoyt shifted his grip on the dagger. As the raven took wing he flipped it through the air. It missed, but the flash of fire he shot out with his free hand hit the mark. The raven shrieked, and what dropped to the ground was ashes.

In disgust Hoyt looked at the dagger. He'd been close, and would likely have done the job if he hadn't been wounded. At least Cian had taught him that much.

But now he had to go fetch the bloody thing.

Before he did, he took a handful of salt from his saddle-bags, poured it over the ashes of the harbinger. Then retrieving his dagger, he went to his horse and mounted with gritted teeth.

"Slave for all eternity," he muttered. "We'll see about that, won't we?"

He rode on, hemmed in by green fields, the rise of hills chased by cloud shadows in light soft as down. Knowing a gallop would have his ribs shrieking, he kept the horse to a plod. He dozed, and he dreamed that he was back on the cliffs struggling with Cian. But this time it was he who tumbled off, spiraling down into the black to crash against the unforgiving rocks.

He woke with a start, and with the pain. Surely this much pain meant death.

His horse had stopped to crop at the grass by the side of the road. There a man in a peaked cap built a wall from a pile of steely gray rock. His beard was pointed, yellow as the gorse that rambled over the low hill, his wrists thick as tree limbs.

"Good day to you, sir, now that you've waked to it." The man touched his cap in salute, then bent for another stone. "You've traveled far this day."

"I have, yes." Though he wasn't entirely sure where he was. There was a fever working in him; he could feel the sticky heat of it. "I'm to An Clar, and the Mac Cionaoith land. What is this place?"

"It's where you are," the man said cheerfully. "You'll not make your journey's end by nightfall."

"No." Hoyt looked down the road that seemed to stretch to forever. "No, not by nightfall."

"There'd be a cabin with a fire going beyond the field, but you've not time to bide here. Not when you've so far yet to go. And time shortens even as we speak. You're weary," the man said with some sympathy. "But you'll be wearier yet before it's done."

"Who are you?"

"Just a signpost on your way. When you come to the second fork, go west. When you hear the river, follow it. There be a holy well near a rowan tree, Briget's Well, that some now call saint. There you'll rest your aching bones for the night. Cast your circle there, Hoyt the Sorcerer, for they'll come hunting. They only wait for the sun to die. You must be at the well, in your circle, before it does."

"If they follow me, if they hunt me, I take them straight to my family."

"They're no strangers to yours. You bear Morrigan's Cross. It's that you'll leave behind with your blood. That and your faith." The man's eyes were pale and gray, and for a moment, it seemed worlds lived in them. "If you fail, more than your blood is lost by Samhain. Go now. The sun's in the west already."

What choice did he have? It all seemed a dream now, boiling in his fever. His brother's death, then his destruction. The thing on the cliffs that called herself Lilith. Had he been visited by the goddess, or was he simply trapped in some dream?

Maybe he was dead already, and this was merely a journey to the afterlife.

But he took the west fork, and when he heard the river, turned his horse toward it. Chills shook him now, from the fever and the knowledge that the light was fading.

He fell from his horse more than dismounted, and leaned breathlessly against its neck. The wound on his hand broke open and stained the bandage red. In the west, the sun was a low ball of dying fire.

The holy well was a low square of stone guarded by the rowan tree. Others who'd come to worship or rest had tied tokens, ribbons and charms, to the branches. Hoyt tethered his horse, then knelt to take the small ladle and sip the cool water. He poured drops on the ground for the god, murmured his thanks. He laid a copper penny on the stone, smearing it with blood from his wound.

His legs felt more full of water than bone, but as twilight crept in, he forced himself to focus. And began to cast his circle.

It was simple magic, one of the first that comes. But his power came now in fitful spurts, and made the task a misery. His own sweat chilled his skin as he struggled with the words, with the thoughts, and with the power that seemed a slippery eel wriggling in his hands.

He heard something stalking the woods, moving in the deepest shadows. And those shadows thickened as the last rays of sunlight eked through the cover of trees.

They were coming for him, waiting for that last flicker to die and leave him in the dark. He would die here, alone, leave his family unprotected. And all for the whim of the gods.

"Be damned if I will." He drew himself up. One chance more, he knew. One. And so he ripped the bandage from his hand, used his own blood to seal the circle.

"Within this ring the light remains. It burns through the night at *my* will. This magic is clean, and none but clean shall bide here. Fire kindle, fire rise, rise and burn with power bright."

Flames shimmered in the center of his circle, weak, but there. As it rose, the sun died. And what had been in the shadows leaped out. It came as a wolf, black pelt and bloody eyes. When it flung itself into the air, Hoyt pulled his dagger. But the beast struck the force of the circle, and was repelled.

It howled, snapped, snarled. Its fangs gleamed white as it paced back and forth as if looking for a weakness in the shield.

Another joined it, skulking out of the trees, then another, another yet, until Hoyt counted six. They lunged together, fell back together. Paced together like soldiers.

Each time they charged, his horse screamed and reared. He stepped toward his mount, his eyes on the wolves as he laid his hands upon it. This at least, he could do. He soothed, lulling his faithful mare into a trance. Then he drew his sword, plunged it into the ground by the fire.

He took what food he had left, water from the well, mixed more herbs—though the gods knew his self-medicating was having no good effect. He lowered to the ground by the fire, sword on one side, dagger on the other and his staff across his legs.

He huddled in his cloak shivering, and dousing an oat-cake with honey, forced it down. The wolves sat on their haunches, threw back their heads, and as one, howled at the rising moon.

"Hungry, are you?" Hoyt muttered through chattering teeth. "There's nothing here for you. Oh, what I wouldn't give for a bed, some decent tea." He sat, the fire dancing in his eyes until they began to close. As his chin drooped to his chest, he'd never felt so alone. Or so unsure of his path.

He thought it was Morrigan who came to him, for she was beautiful and her hair as bold as the fire. It fell straight as rain, its tips grazing her shoulders. She wore black, a strange garb, and immodest enough to leave her arms bare and allow the swell of her breasts to rise from the bodice. Around her neck she wore a pentagram with a moonstone in its center.

"This won't do," she said in a voice that was both foreign and impatient. Kneeling beside him, she laid her hand on his brow, her touch as cool and soothing as spring rain. She smelled of the forest, earthy and secret.

For one mad moment, he longed to simply lay his head upon her breast and sleep with that scent filling his senses.

"You're burning up. Well, let's see what you have here, and we'll make do."

She wavered in his vision a moment, then re-crystallized. Her eyes were as green as the goddess's, but her touch was human. "Who are you? How did you get within the circle?"

"Elderflower, yarrow. No cayenne? Well, I said we'd make do."

He watched as she busied herself, as women would, dipping water from the well, heating it with his fire. "Wolves," she murmured, shivered once. And in that shudder, he felt her fear. "Sometimes I dream of the black wolves, or ravens. Sometimes it's the woman. She's the worst. But this is the first time I've dreamed of you." She paused, and looked at him for a long time with eyes of deep and secret green. "And still, I know your face."

"This is my dream."

She gave a short laugh, then sprinkled herbs in the heated water. "Have it your way. Let's see if we can help you live through it."

She passed her hand over the cup. "Power of healing, herbs and water, brewed this night by Hecate's daughter. Cool his fever, ease his pain so that strength and sight remain. Stir magic in this simple tea. As I will, so mote it be."

"Gods save me." He managed to prop himself on an elbow. "You're a witch."

She smiled as she stepped to him with the cup. And sitting beside him, braced him with an arm around his back. "Of course. Aren't you?"

"I'm not." He had just enough energy for insult. "I'm

a bloody sorcerer. Get that poison away from me. Even the smell is foul."

"That may be, but it should cure what ails you." She simply cradled his head on her shoulder. Even as he tried to push free, she was pinching his nose closed and pouring the brew down his throat. "Men are such babies when they're sick. And look at your hand! Bloody and filthy. I've got something for that."

"Get away from me," he said weakly, though the smell of her, the feel of her was both seductive and comforting. "Let me die in peace."

"You're not going to die." But she gave the wolves a wary glance. "How strong is your circle?"

"Strong enough."

"Hope you're right."

Exhaustion—and the valerian she'd mixed in the tea— had his head drooping again. She shifted, so she could lay his head in her lap. And there she stroked his hair, kept her eyes on the fire. "You're not alone anymore," she said quietly. "And I guess, neither am I."

"The sun . . . How long till dawn?"

"I wish I knew. You should sleep now."

"Who are you?"

But if she answered, he didn't hear.

She was gone when he woke, and so was the fever. Dawn was a misty shimmer letting thin beams eke through the summer leaves.

Of the wolves there was only one, and it lay gored and bloody outside the circle. Its throat had been ripped open, Hoyt saw, and its belly. Even as he gained his feet to step closer, the sun beamed white through those leaves, struck the carcass.

It erupted into flame that left nothing behind but a scatter of ashes on blackened earth.

"To hell with you, and all like you."

Turning away, Hoyt busied himself, feeding his horse, brewing more tea. He was nearly done when he noticed his palm was healed. Only the faintest scar remained. He flexed his fingers, held his hand up to the light.

Curious, he lifted his tunic. Bruises still rained over his side, but they were fading. And when he tested he found he could move without pain.

If what had come to him in the night had been a vision rather than a product of a fever dream, he supposed he should be grateful.

Still, he'd never had a vision so vivid. Nor one who'd left so much of itself behind. He swore he could smell her still, and hear the flow and cadence of her voice.

She'd said she'd known his face. How strange that somewhere in the center of him, he felt he'd known hers.

He washed, and while his appetite had come back strong, he had to make do with berries and a heel of tough bread.

He closed the circle, salted the blackened earth outside it. Once he was in the saddle, he set off at a gallop.

With luck, he could be home by midday.

There were no signs, no harbingers, no beautiful witches on the rest of his journey. There were only the fields, rolling green, back to the shadow of mountains, and the secret depths of forest. He knew his way now, would have known it if a hundred years had passed. So he sent his mount on a leap over a low stone wall and raced across the last field toward home.

He could see the cook fire. He imagined his mother sitting in the parlor, tatting lace perhaps, or working on one of her tapestries. Waiting, hoping for news of her sons. He wished he brought her better.

His father might be with his man of business or out riding the land, and his married sisters in their own cottages, with young Nola in the stables playing with the pups from the new litter.

The house was tucked in the forest, because his grandmother—she who had passed power to him, and to a lesser extent, Cian—had wanted it so. It stood near a stream, a rise of stone with windows of real glass. And its gardens were his mother's great pride.

Her roses bloomed riotously.

One of the servants hurried out to take his horse. Hoyt merely shook his head at the question in the man's eyes. He walked to the door where the black banner of mourning still hung.

Inside, another servant was waiting to take his cloak. Here in the hall, his mother's, and her mother's tapestries hung, and one of his father's wolfhounds raced to greet him.

He could smell beeswax, and roses cut fresh from the garden. The turf fire simmering in the grate. He left them behind, walked up the stairs to his mother's sitting room.

She was waiting, as he'd known she would be. She was sitting in her chair, her hands in her lap, clasped so tightly the knuckles were white. Her face carried all the weight of her grief, and went heavier yet when she saw what was in his eyes.

"Mother—"

"You're alive. You're well." She got to her feet, held out her arms to him. "I've lost my youngest son, but here is my firstborn, home again. You'll want food and drink after your journey."

"I have much to tell you."

"And so you will."

"All of you, if you please, madam. I cannot stay long. I'm sorry." He kissed her brow. "I'm sorry to leave you."

There was food and there was drink, and the whole of his family—save Cian—around the table. But it was not a meal like so many he remembered, with laughter and shouted arguments, with joy or petty disagreements. Hoyt studied their faces, the beauties, the strengths and the sorrows as he told them what had passed.

"If there is to be a battle, I will come with you. Fight with you."

Hoyt looked at his brother-in-law Fearghus. His shoulders were broad, his fists ready.

"Where I go, you can't follow. You're not charged with this fight. It's for you and Eoin to stay here, to protect with my father, the family, the land. I would go with a heavier heart if I didn't know you and Eoin stand in my stead. You must wear these."

He took out the crosses. "Each of you, and all the children who come after. Day and night, night and day. This," he said and lifted one, "is Morrigan's Cross, forged by the gods in magic fire. The vampyre cannot turn any who wear it into its kind. This must be passed on to those who come after you, in song and story. You will swear an oath, each of you, that you will wear this cross until death."

He rose, draping a cross over each neck, waiting for the sworn oath before moving on.

Then he knelt by his father. His father's hands were old, Hoyt noted with a jolt. He was more farmer than warrior, and in a flash, he knew his father's death would come first, and before the Yule. Just as he knew he would never again look in the eyes of the man who'd given him life.

And his heart bled a little.

"I take my leave of you, sir. I ask your blessing."

"Avenge your brother, and come back to us."

"I will." Hoyt rose. "I must gather what I need."

He went up to the room he kept in the topmost tower, and there began to pack herbs and potions without any real sense of what would be needed.

"Where is your cross?"

He looked toward the doorway where Nola stood, her dark hair hanging to her waist. She was but eight, he thought, and held the softest spot in his heart.

"She didn't make me one," he said, briskly. "I have another sort of shield, and there's no need for you to be worrying. I know what I'm about."

"I won't cry when you go."

"Why would you? I've gone before, haven't I, and come back handily enough?"

"You'll come back. To the tower. She'll come with you."

He nestled bottles carefully in his case, then paused to study his sister. "Who will?"

"The woman with red hair. Not the goddess, but a mortal woman, one who wears the sign of the witch. I can't see Cian, and I can't see if you'll win. But I can see you, here with the witch. And you're afraid."

"Should a man go into battle without fear? Isn't fear something that helps keep him alive?"

"I don't know of battles. I wish I were a man, and a warrior." Her mouth, so young, so soft, went grim. "You wouldn't be stopping me from going with you the way you stopped Fearghus."

"How would I dare?" He closed his case, moved to her. "I am afraid. Don't tell the others."

"I won't."

Aye, the softest place in his heart, he thought, and lifting her cross, used his magic to scribe her name on the back in ogham script. "It makes it only yours," he told her.

"Mine, and the ones who'll have my name after me." Her eyes glimmered, but the tears didn't fall. "You'll see me again."

"I will, of course."

"When you do, the circle will be complete. I don't know how, or why."

"What else do you see, Nola?"

She only shook her head. "It's dark. I can't see. I'll light a candle for you, every night, until you return."

"I'll ride home by its light." He bent down to embrace her. "I'll miss you most of all." He kissed her gently, then set her aside. "Be safe."

"I will have daughters," she called after him.

It made him turn, and smile. So slight, he mused, and so fierce. "Will you now?"

"It is my lot," she told him with a resignation that made his lips twitch. "But they will not be weak. They will *not* sit and spin and knead and bake all the damn day."

Now he grinned fully, and knew this was a memory he would take with him happily. "Oh won't they? What then, young mother, will your daughters do?"

"They will be warriors. And the vampyre who fancies herself a queen will tremble before them."

She folded her hands, much as their mother was wont to do, but with none of that meekness. "Go with the gods, brother."

"Stay in the light, sister."

They watched him go—three sisters, the men who loved

them, the children they'd already made. His parents, even the servants and stable boys. He took one last long look at the house his grandfather, and his father before, had built of stone in this glade, by this stream, in this land he loved with the whole of his heart.

Then he raised his hand in farewell, and rode away from them and toward the Dance of the Gods.

It stood on a rise of rough grass that was thick with the sunny yellow of buttercups. Clouds had rolled to layer the sky so that light forced its way through in thin beams. The world was so still, so silent, he felt as though he rode through a painting. The gray of the sky, the green of the grass, the yellow flowers, and the ancient circle of stones that had risen in its dance since beyond time.

He felt its power, the hum of it, in the air, along his skin. Hoyt walked his horse around them, paused to read the ogham script carved into the king stone.

"Worlds wait," he translated. "Time flows. Gods watch."

He started to dismount when a shimmer of gold across the field caught his eye. There at the edge of it was a hind. The green of her eyes sparkled like the jeweled collar she wore. She walked toward him regally, and changed to the female form of the goddess.

"You are in good time, Hoyt."

"It was painful to bid my family farewell. Best done quickly then."

He slid off the horse, bowed. "My lady."

"Child. You have been ill."

"A fever, broken now. Did you send the witch to me?"

"There's no need to send what will come on its own. You'll find her again, and the others."

"My brother."

"He is first. The light will go soon. Here is the key to the portal." She opened her hand and offered a small crystal wand. "Keep it with you, keep it safe and whole." When he started to re-mount, she shook her head, took the reins. "No, you must go on foot. Your horse will get safely back home."

Resigned to the whimsy of gods, he took his case, his bag. He strapped on his sword, hefted his staff.

"How will I find him?"

"Through the portal, into the world yet to come. Into the Dance, lift the key, say the words. Your destiny lies beyond. Humankind is in your hands, from this point forward. Through the portal," she repeated. "Into the world yet to come. Into the Dance, lift the key, say the words. Through the portal . . ."

Her voice followed him in, between the great stones. He locked his fear inside him. If he'd been born for this, so be it. Life was long, he knew. It simply came in short bursts.

He lifted the stone. A single beam of light speared out of those thick clouds to strike its tip. Power shot down his arm like an arrow.

"Worlds wait. Time flows. Gods watch."

"Repeat," Morrigan told him, and joined him so that the words became a chant.

"Worlds wait. Time flows. Gods watch."

The air shook around him, came alive with wind, with light, with sound. The crystal in his uplifted hand shone like the sun and sang like a siren.

He heard his own voice come out in a roar, shouting the words now as if in challenge.

And so he flew. Through light and wind and sound. Beyond stars and moons and planets. Over water that made his sorcerer's belly roil with nausea. Faster, until the light was blinding, the sounds deafening and the wind so fierce he wondered it didn't flay the skin from his bones.

Then the light went dim, the wind died, and the world was silent.

He leaned on his staff, catching his breath, waiting for his eyes to adjust to the change of light. He smelled something— leather, he thought, and roses.

He was in a room of some sort, he realized, but like nothing he'd ever seen. It was fantastically furnished with long, low chairs in deep colors, and cloth for a floor. Paintings adorned some of the walls, and others were lined with books. Dozens of books bound in leather.

He stepped forward, charmed, when a movement to his left stopped him cold.

His brother sat behind some sort of table, where the lamp that lit the room glowed strangely. His hair was shorter than it had been, shorn to the jawline. His eyes were vivid with what seemed to be amusement.

In his hand was some sort of metal tool, which instinct told Hoyt was a weapon.

Cian pointed it at his brother's heart and tipped back in the chair, dropping his feet on the surface of the table. He smiled, broadly, and said, "Well now, look what the cat dragged in."

With some confusion, Hoyt frowned, scanning the room for the cat. "Do you know me?" Hoyt stepped forward, farther into the light. "It's Hoyt. It's your brother. I've come to . . ."

"Kill me? Too late. Already long dead. Why don't you just stay where you are for the moment. I see quite well in low light. You're looking . . . well, fairly ridiculous really. But I'm impressed nonetheless. How long did it take you to perfect time travel?"

"I . . ." Coming through the portal might have addled his brains, he thought. Or it might be simply seeing his dead brother, looking very much alive. "Cian."

"I'm not using that name these days. It's Keene, right at the moment. One syllable. Take off the cloak, Hoyt, and let's have a look at what's under it."

"You're a vampyre."

"I am, yes, certainly. The cloak, Hoyt."

Hoyt unhooked the brooch that held it in place, let it drop.

"Sword and dagger. A lot of weaponry for a sorcerer."

"There's to be a battle."

"Do you think so?" That amusement rippled again, coldly. "I can promise you'll lose. What I have here is called a gun. It's quite a good one, really. It fires out a projectile faster than you can blink. You'll be dead where you stand before you can draw that sword."

"I haven't come to fight you."

"Really? The last time we met—let me refresh my memory. Ah yes, you pushed me off a cliff."

"You pushed me off the bloody cliff first," Hoyt said with

some heat. "Broke my bloody ribs while you were about it. I thought you were gone. Oh merciful gods, Cian, I thought you were gone."

"I'm not, as you can plainly see. Go back where you came from, Hoyt. I've had a thousand years, give or take, to get over my annoyance with you."

"For me you died only a week ago." He lifted his tunic. "You gave me these bruises."

Cian's gaze drifted over them, then back to Hoyt's face. "They'll heal soon enough."

"I've come with a charge from Morrigan."

"Morrigan, is it." This time the amusement burst out in laughter. "There are no gods here. No God. No faerie queens. Your magic has no place in this time, and neither do you."

"But you do."

"Adjustment is survival. Money is god here, and power its partner. I have both. I've shed the likes of you a long time ago."

"This world will end, they will all end, by Samhain, unless you help me stop her."

"Stop who?"

"The one who made you. The one called Lilith."

Chapter 3

Lilith. The name brought Cian flashes of memories, a hundred lifetimes past. He could still see her, smell her, still feel that sudden, horrified thrill in the instant she'd taken his life.

He could still taste her blood, and what had come into him with it. The dark, dark gift.

His world had changed. And he'd been given the privilege—or the curse—of watching worlds change over countless decades.

Hadn't he known something was coming? Why else had he been sitting alone in the middle of the night, waiting?

What nasty little twist of fate had sent his brother—or the brother of the man he'd once been—across time to speak her name?

"Well, now you have my attention."

"You must come back with me, prepare for the battle."

"Back? To the twelfth century?" Cian let out a short laugh as he leaned back in his chair. "Nothing, I promise you, could tempt me. I like the conveniences of this time. The water runs hot here, Hoyt, and so do the women. I'm not interested in your politics and wars, and certainly not in your gods."

"The battle will be fought, with or without you, Cian."

"Without sounds perfectly fine."

"You've never turned from battle, never hidden from a fight."

"*Hiding* wouldn't be the term I'd use," Cian said easily. "And times change. Believe me."

"If Lilith defeats us, all you know will be lost in this time, for all time. Humankind will cease to be."

Cian angled his head. "I'm not human."

"Is that your answer?" Hoyt strode forward. "You'll sit and do nothing while she destroys? You'll stand by while she does to others what she did to you? While she kills your mother, your sisters? Will you sit there while she turns Nola into what you are?"

"They're dead. Long dead. They're dust." Hadn't he seen their graves? He hadn't been able to stop himself from going back and standing over their stones, and the stones of those who'd come after them.

"Have you forgotten all you were taught? Times change, you say. It's more than change. Could I be here now if time was solid? Their fate is not set, nor is yours. Even now our father is dying, yet I left him. I will never see him alive again."

Slowly Cian got to his feet. "You have no conception of what she is, what she is capable of. She was old, centuries old, when she took me. You think to stop her with swords and lightning bolts? You're more fool than I remember."

"I think to stop her with you. Help me. If not for humanity, then for yourself. Or would you join her? If there's nothing left of my brother in you, we'll end this between us now."

Hoyt drew his sword.

For a long moment, Cian studied the blade, considered the gun in his hand. Then he slipped the weapon back in his pocket. "Put your sword away. Christ, Hoyt, you couldn't take me one-on-one when I was alive."

Challenge, and simple irritation, rushed into Hoyt's eyes. "You didn't fare very well the last time we fought."

"True enough. It took me weeks to recover. Hiding around in caves by day, half starving. I looked for her then, you know. Lilith, who sired me. By night, while I struggled to hunt enough food to survive. She abandoned me. So I've a point to square with her. Put the damn sword away."

When Hoyt hesitated, Cian simply leaped. In the blink of an eye he was up, gliding over Hoyt's head and landing lightly at his back. He disarmed his brother with one careless twist of the wrist.

Hoyt turned slowly. The point of the sword was at his throat. "Well done," he managed.

"We're faster, and we're stronger. We have no conscience to bind us. We are driven to kill, to feed. To survive."

"Then why aren't I dead?"

Cian lifted a shoulder. "We'll put it down to curiosity, and a bit of old time's sake." He tossed the sword across the room. "Well then, let's have a drink."

He walked to a cabinet, opened it. Out of the corner of his eye he saw the sword fly across the room and into Hoyt's hand. "Well done on you," he said mildly and took out a bottle of wine. "You can't kill me with steel, but you could—if you were lucky enough—hack some part of me off that I'd rather keep. We don't regenerate limbs."

"I'll put my weapons aside, and you do the same."

"Fair enough." Cian took the gun out of his pocket, set it on a table. "Though a vampire always has his weapon." He offered a brief glimpse of fangs. "Nothing to be done about that." He poured two glasses while Hoyt laid down his sword and dagger. "Have a seat then, and you can tell me why I should get involved in saving the world. I'm a busy man these days. I have enterprises."

Hoyt took the glass offered, studied it, sniffed at it. "What is this?"

"A very nice Italian red. I've no need to poison you." To prove it, he sipped from his own glass. "I could snap your neck like a twig." Cian sat himself, stretched out his legs. Then he waved a hand at Hoyt. "In today's worlds, what we're having here could be called a meeting, and you're about to make your pitch. So . . . enlighten me."

"We must gather forces, beginning with a handful. There is a scholar and a witch, one of many forms and a warrior. That must be you."

"No. I'm no warrior. I'm a businessman." He continued to sit, at his ease, giving Hoyt a lazy smile. "So the gods, as usual, have given you pitifully little to work with, and an all but impossible task. With your handful, and whoever else is fool enough to join you, you're expected to defeat an army led by a powerful vampire, most likely with troops of her kind, and other manner of demon if she deigns to bother with them. Otherwise, the world is destroyed."

"Worlds," Hoyt corrected. "There are more than one."

"You're right about that anyway." Cian sipped, contemplated. He'd nearly run out of challenges in his current persona. This, at least, was interesting.

"And what do your gods tell you is my part in this?"

"You must come with me, teach me all that you can about her kind, and how to defeat them. What are their weaknesses? What are their powers? What weaponry and magic will work against them? We have until Samhain to master these and gather the first circle."

"That long?" Sarcasm dripped. "What would I gain from all this? I'm a wealthy man, with many interests to protect here and now."

"And would she allow you to keep that wealth, those interests, should she rule?"

Cian pursed his lips. Now there was a thought. "Possibly not. But it's more than possible if I help you I'll risk all that and my own existence. When you're young, as you are—"

"I'm the eldest."

"Not for the last nine hundred years and counting. In any case, when you're young you think you'll live forever, so you take all manner of foolish risks. But when you've lived as long as I, you're more careful. Because existence is imperative. I'm driven to survive, Hoyt. Humans and vampires have that in common."

"You survive sitting alone in the dark in this little house?"

"It's not a house," Cian said absently. "It's an office. A place of business. I have many houses, as it happens. That, too, is survival. There are taxes and records and all manner of things to be gotten around. Like most of my kind I rarely stay in one place for long. We're nomadic from nature and necessity."

He leaned forward now, resting his elbows on his knees. There were so few he could speak to about what he was. That was his choice, that was the life he'd made. "Hoyt, I've seen wars, countless wars, such as you could never imagine. No one wins them. If you do this thing, you'll die. Or become. It would be a feather in Lilith's cap to turn a sorcerer of your power."

"Do you think there is a choice here?"

"Oh yes." He sat back again. "There always is. I've made many in my lifetimes." He closed his eyes now, lazily swirling his wine. "Something's coming. There have been rumblings in the world under this one. In the dark places. If it's what you say, it's bigger than I assumed. I should've paid more attention. I don't socialize with vampires as a rule."

Baffled, as Cian had always been sociable, Hoyt frowned. "Why not?"

"Because as a rule they're liars and killers and bring too much attention to themselves. And those humans who socialize with them are usually mad or doomed. I pay my taxes, file my reports and keep a low profile. And every decade or so, I move, change my name and keep off the radar."

"I don't understand half of what you say."

"Imagine not," Cian replied. "She'll fuck this up for everyone. Bloodbaths always do, and those demons who go about thinking they want to destroy the world are ridiculously shortsighted. We have to live in it, don't we?"

He sat in silence. He could focus and hear each beat of his brother's heart, hear the faint electrical hum of the room's climate controls, the buzz of the lamp on his desk across the room. Or he could block them out, as he most often did with background noises.

He'd learned to do, and not do, a great deal over time.

A choice, he thought again. Well, why not?

"It comes down to blood," Cian said, and his eyes stayed closed. "First and last, it comes to blood. We both need it to

live, your kind and mine. It's what we sacrifice, for the gods
you worship, for countries, for women. And what we spill
for the same reasons. My kind doesn't quibble about reasons."

He opened his eyes now, and showed Hoyt how they could
burn red. "We just take it. We hunger for it, crave it. Without
it, we cease to be. It's our nature to hunt, kill, feed. Some of
us enjoy it more than others, just as humans do. Some of us
enjoy causing pain, inciting fear, tormenting and torturing
our prey. Just as humans do. We're not all of the same cloth,
Hoyt."

"You murder."

"When you hunt the buck in the forest and take its life, is
it murder? You're no more than that, less, often less, to us."

"I saw your death."

"The tumble off the cliffs wasn't—"

"No. I saw her kill you. I thought it a dream at first. I
watched you come out of the tavern, go with her in her car-
riage. And couple with her as it drove out of the village. And
I saw her eyes change, and how the fangs glinted in the dark
before she sank them into your throat. I saw your face. The
pain, the shock, and . . ."

"Arousal," Cian finished. "Ecstasy. It's a moment of some
intensity."

"You tried to fight, but she was an animal on you, and I
thought you were dead, but you weren't. Not quite."

"No, to feed you simply take, drain the prey dry if you
choose. But to change a human, he must drink from the
blood of his maker."

"She sliced her own breast, and pressed your mouth to
her, and still you tried to fight until you began to suckle on
her like a babe."

"The allure is powerful, as is the drive to survive. It was
drink or die."

"When she was done, she threw you out into the road, left
you there. It was there I found you." Hoyt drank deeply as
his belly quivered. "There I found you, covered with blood
and mud. And this is what you do to survive? The buck is
given more respect."

"Do you want to lecture me?" Cian began as he rose to get the bottle again. "Or do you want to know?"

"I need to know."

"Some hunt in packs, some alone. At wakening we're most vulnerable—from the first when we wake in the grave, to every evening if we've slept through the day. We are night creatures. The sun is death."

"You burn in it."

"I see you know some things."

"I saw. They hunted me when I journeyed home. In the form of wolves."

"Only vampires of some age and power, or those under the protection of another powerful sire can shape shift. Most have to content themselves with the form in which they died. Still, we don't age, physically. A nice bonus feature."

"You look as you did," Hoyt replied. "Yet not. It's more than the garb you wear, or the hair. You move differently."

"I'm not what I was, and that you should remember. Our senses are heightened, and become more so the longer we survive. Fire, like the sun, will destroy us. Holy water, if it's been faithfully blessed, will burn us, as will the symbol of the cross, if held in faith. We are repelled by the symbol."

Crosses, Hoyt thought. Morrigan had given him crosses. Part of the weight eased from his shoulders.

"Metal is fairly useless," Cian continued, "unless you manage to cut off our heads. That would do the trick. But otherwise . . ."

He rose again, walked over and picked up Hoyt's dagger. He flipped it in the air, caught the hilt neatly, then plunged the blade into his chest.

Blood seeped out on the white of Cian's shirt even as Hoyt lunged to his feet.

"Forgot how much that hurts." Wincing, Cian yanked the blade free. "That's what I get for showing off. Do the same with wood, and we're dust. But it must pierce the heart. Our end is agonizing, or so I'm told."

He took out a handkerchief, wiped the blade clean. Then he pulled off his shirt. The wound was already closing.

"We've died once, and aren't easily dispatched a second time. And we'll fight viciously anyone who tries. Lilith is the oldest I've ever known. She'll fight more brutally than any."

He paused, brooded into his wine. "Your mother. How did you leave her?"

"Heartbroken. You were her favorite." Hoyt moved his shoulders as Cian looked up into his face. "We both know it. She asked me to try, to find a way. In her first grief, she could think of nothing else."

"I believe even your sorcery stops short of raising the dead. Or undead."

"I went to your grave that night, to ask the gods to give her heart some peace. I found you, covered with dirt."

"Clawing out of the grave's a messy business."

"You were devouring a rabbit."

"Probably the best I could find. Can't say I recall. The first hours after the Wakening are disjointed. There's only hunger."

"You ran from me. I saw what you were—there had been rumors of such things before—and you ran. I went to the cliffs the night I saw you again, at our mother's behest. She begged me to find a way to break the spell."

"It's not a spell."

"I thought, hoped, if I destroyed the thing that made you . . . Or failing that, I would kill what you'd become."

"And did neither," Cian reminded him. "Which shows you what you're up against. I was fresh and barely knew what I was or what I was capable of. Believe me, she'll have cannier on her side."

"Will I have yours on mine?"

"You haven't a prayer of winning this."

"You underestimate me. I have a great deal more than one prayer. Whether a year has passed or a millennium, you are my brother. My twin. My blood. You said yourself, it's blood, first and last."

Cian ran a finger down his wine glass. "I'll go with you." Then held the finger up before Hoyt could speak. "Because I'm curious, and a bit bored. I've been in this place for more than ten years now, so it's nearly time to move on in any case. I promise you nothing. Don't depend on me, Hoyt. I'll please myself first."

"You can't hunt humans."

"Orders already?" Cian's lips curved slightly. "Typical. As I said, I please myself first. It happens I haven't fed on human blood for eight hundred years. Well, seven hundred and fifty as there was some backsliding."

"Why?"

"To prove that I could resist. And because it's another way to survive—and well—in the world of humans, with their laws. If they're prey, it's impossible to look at them as anything more than a meal. Makes it awkward to do business. And death tends to leave a trail. Dawn's coming."

Distracted, Hoyt glanced around the windowless room. "How do you know?"

"I feel it. And I'm tired of questions. You'll have to stay with me, for now. You can't be trusted to go walking about the city. We may not be identical, but you look too much like me. And those clothes have to go."

"You expect me to wear—what are those?"

"They're called pants," Cian said dryly and moved across the room to a private elevator. "I keep an apartment here, it's simpler."

"You'll pack what you need, and we'll go."

"I don't travel by day, and I don't take orders. I give them now, and have for some time. I have a number of things to see to before I can leave. You need to step in here."

"What is it?" Hoyt poked at the elevator walls with his staff.

"A mode of transportation. It'll take us up to my apartment."

"How?"

Cian finally dragged a hand through his hair. "Look, I've books up there, and other educational matter. You can spend the next few hours boning up on twenty-first-century culture, fashion and technology."

"What is technology?"

Cian pulled his brother inside, pushed the button for the next floor. "It's another god."

*   *   *

This world, this time, was full of wonder. Hoyt wished he had time to learn it all, absorb it. There were no torches to light the room but instead something Cian called electricity. Food was kept in a box as tall as a man that kept it cold and fresh, and yet another box was used to warm and cook it. Water spilled out of a wand and into a bowl where it drained away again.

The house where Cian lived was built high up in the city, and such a city! The glimpse Morrigan had given him had been nothing compared to what he could see through the glass wall of Cian's quarters.

Hoyt thought even the gods would be stunned by the size and scope of this New York. He wanted to look out at it again, but Cian had demanded his oath that he would keep the glass walls covered, and he would not venture out of the house.

Apartment, Hoyt corrected. Cian had called it an apartment.

He had books, so many books, and the magic box Cian had called a television. Indeed the visions inside it were many, of people and places, of things, of animals. And though he spent only an hour playing with it, he grew weary of its constant chatter.

So he surrounded himself with books and read, and read until his eyes burned and his head was too full for more words or images.

He fell asleep on what Cian had called a sofa, surrounded by books.

He dreamed of the witch, and saw her in a circle of light. She wore nothing but the pendant, and her skin glowed milk-pale in the candlelight.

Her beauty simply flamed.

She held a ball of crystal aloft in both hands. He could hear the whisper of her voice, but not the words. Still, he knew it was an incantation, could feel the power of it, of her across the dream. And he knew she was seeking him out.

Even in sleep he felt the pull of her, and that same impatience he'd sensed from her within his circle, within his own time.

It seemed for an instant that their eyes met across the mists. And it was desire that pierced through him as much as power. In that instant, her lips curved, opened, as if she would speak to him.

"What the hell is that get-up?"

He came awake and found himself staring up into the face of a giant. The creature was tall as a tree, and every bit as thick. He had a face even a mother would weep over, black as a moor and scarred at the cheek, and surrounded by knotted hanks of hair.

He had one black eye and one gray. Both narrowed as he bared strong white teeth.

"You're not Cain."

Before Hoyt could react, he was hauled up by the scruff of the neck where he was shaken like a mouse by a very large, angry cat.

"Put him down, King, before he turns you into a small white man."

Cian strolled out of his bedroom, and continued lazily into the kitchen.

"How come he's got your face?"

"He's got his own," Cian retorted. "We don't look that much alike if you pay attention. He used to be my brother."

"That so? Son of a bitch." King dropped Hoyt unceremoniously back on the sofa. "How the hell did he get here?"

"Sorcery." As he spoke, Cian removed a clear packet of blood from a locked cold box. "Gods and battles, end of the world, blah blah."

King looked down at Hoyt with a grin. "I'll be damned. I always thought half of that crap you told me was, well, crap. He's not much for conversation before he's had his evening fix," he said to Hoyt. "You got a name, brother?"

"I am Hoyt of the Mac Cionaoith. And you will not lay hands on me again."

"That's a mouthful."

"Is he like you?" both Hoyt and King demanded in unison.

Wearily Cian poured the blood in a tall, thick glass, then set it in the microwave. "No, to both. King manages my club, the one downstairs. He's a friend."

Hoyt's lips peeled back in disgust. "Your human servant."

"I ain't nobody's servant."

"You've been reading." Cian took out the glass and drank. "Some vampires of rank have human servants. I prefer employees. Hoyt's come to enlist me in the army he hopes to raise to fight the big evil."

"The IRS?"

In better humor, Cian grinned. Hoyt saw something pass between them, something that had once only passed between himself and his brother.

"If only. No, I told you I've heard rumblings. Apparently for a reason. According to the gossip of the gods, Lilith of the Vampires is amassing her own army and plans to destroy humanity, take over the worlds. War, pestilence, plague."

"You can jest?" Hoyt said in barely suppressed fury.

"Christ Jesus, Hoyt, we're talking about vampire armies and time travel. Bloody right I can joke about it. Going with you is likely to kill me."

"Where are you going?"

Cian shrugged at King. "Back to my past, I suppose, to act in an advisory capacity, at least, for General Sobriety there."

"I don't know if we're to go back, or forward, or to the side." Hoyt shoved books over the table. "But we will go back to Ireland. We will be told where we travel next."

"Got a beer?" King asked.

Cian opened the refrigerator, took out a bottle of Harp and tossed it.

"So when do we leave?" King twisted off the cap, took a long slug.

"You don't. I told you before, when it was time for me to leave, I'll give you controlling interest in the club. Apparently, that time's come."

King simply turned to Hoyt. "You raising an army, General?"

"Hoyt. I am, yes."

"You just got your first recruit."

"Stop." Cian strode around the counter that separated the kitchen. "This isn't for you. You don't know anything about this."

"I know about you," King returned. "I know I like a good fight, and I haven't had one in a while. You're talking major battle, good against evil. I like to pick my side from the get."

"If he's a king, why should he take orders from you?" Hoyt put in, and the black giant laughed so hard and long, he had to sit on the sofa.

"Gotcha."

"Misplaced loyalty will get you killed."

"My choice, brother." King tipped the bottle toward Cian. Once again, something silent and strong passed between them with no more than a look. "And I don't figure my loyalty's misplaced."

"Hoyt, go somewhere else." Cian jerked a thumb toward his bedroom. "Go in there. I want a word in private with this idiot."

He cared, Hoyt thought as he obliged. Cian cared about this man, a human trait. Nothing he'd read had indicated vampires could have true feelings toward humans.

He frowned as he scanned the bedroom. Where was the coffin? The books had said the vampire slept in the earth of his grave, in a coffin, by day. What he saw here was an enormous bed, one with ticking as soft as clouds and covered with smooth cloth.

He heard the raised voices outside the door, but set about exploring his brother's personal room. Clothes enough for ten men, he decided when he found the closet. Well, Cian had always been vain.

But no looking glass. The books said the vampyre cast no reflection.

He wandered into the bathroom, and his jaw dropped. The expansive privy Cian had showed him before retiring had been amazing and was nothing to this. The tub was large enough for six, and there was a tall box of pale green glass. The walls were marble, as was the floor.

Fascinated, he stepped into the box, began to play with the silver knobs that jutted out of the marble. And yipped in shock when a shower of cold water spurted out of many flat-headed tubes.

"Around here, we take our clothes off before getting in the shower." Cian came in, shut the water off with one violent twist of the wrist. Then he sniffed the air. "On second thought, clothed or otherwise, you could sure as hell use one. You're fucking rank. Clean up," he ordered. "Put on the clothes I've tossed out on the bed. I'm going to work."

He strode out, leaving Hoyt to fumble through on his own.

He discovered, after some time and chill that the temperature of the water could be adjusted. He scalded himself, froze, but eventually found the happy medium.

His brother must have been telling pure truth when he spoke of his wealth, for here was luxury never imagined. The scent of the soap seemed a bit female, but there was nothing else.

Hoyt wallowed in his first twenty-first-century shower, and wondered if he might find a way to duplicate it, by science or magic, once he returned home.

The cloths hanging nearby were as soft as the bed had been. He felt decadent using one to dry his skin.

He didn't care for the clothes, but his own were soaked. He debated going out and getting the spare tunic out of his case, but it seemed best to follow Cian's advice in wardrobe.

It took him twice as long to dress as it would have. The strange fastenings nearly defeated him. The shoes had no laces, but simply slipped on the foot. He was forced to admit that they were quite comfortable.

But he wished there was a bloody looking glass so he could see himself. He stepped out, then came up short. The black king was still on the sofa, drinking from the glass bottle.

"That's an improvement," King observed. "You'll probably pass if you keep your mouth mostly shut."

"What is this fastening here?"

"It's a zipper. Ah, you're going to want to keep that closed, friend." He pushed to his feet. "Cian's gone on down to the club. It's after sunset. He fired me."

"You're burned? I have salve."

"No. Shit. He terminated my employment. He'll get over it. He goes, I go. He don't have to like it."

"He believes we'll all die."

"He's right—sooner or later. You ever see what a vamp can do to a man?"

"I saw what one did to my brother."

King's odd eyes went grim. "Yeah, yeah, that's right. Well, it's this way. I don't figure to sit around and wait for one to do it to me. He's right, there's been rumbling. There's going to be a fight, and I'm going to be in it."

A giant of a man, Hoyt thought, of fearsome face and great strength. "You are a warrior."

"Bet your ass. I'll kick some vampire ass in this, believe me. But not tonight. Why don't we go on down, see what's jumping. That'll piss him off."

"To his . . ." What had Cian called it. "His club?"

"You got it. He calls it Eternity. I guess he knows something about that."

Chapter 4

She was going to find him. If a man was going to drag her into his dreams, push her into out-of-body experiences and generally haunt her thoughts, she was going to track him down and find out why.

For days now she had felt as if she stood on the edge of some high, shaky cliff. On one side there was something bright and beautiful, and on the other a cold and terrifying void. But the cliff itself, while a little unstable, was the known.

Whatever was brewing inside her, he was part of it, that she knew. Not of this time, not of this place. Guys just didn't ride around on horses wearing cloaks and tunics in twenty-first-century New York as a rule.

But he was real; he was flesh and blood and as real as she was. She'd had that blood on her hands, hadn't she? She'd cooled that flesh and watched him sleep off the fever. His face, she thought, had been so familiar. Like something she remembered, or had caught a glimpse of in dreams.

Handsome, even in pain, she mused as she sketched it. Lean and angular, aristocratic. Long narrow nose, strong, sculpted mouth. Good, slashing cheekbones.

His image came true on paper as she worked, first in broad strokes, then in careful detail. Deep-set eyes, she remembered, vividly blue and intense with an almost dramatic arch of brows over them. And the contrast of that black hair, those black brows and wild blue eyes against his skin just added more drama.

Yes, she thought, she could see him, she could sketch him, but until she found him, she wouldn't know whether she should jump off the edge of that cliff or scramble back from it.

Glenna Ward was a woman who liked to know.

So, she knew his face, the shape and feel of his body, even the sound of his voice. She knew, without question, he had power. And she believed he had answers.

Whatever was coming, and every portent warned her it was major, he was tied to it. She had a part to play, had known almost since her first breath that she had a part to play. She had a feeling that she was about to take on the role of her lifetime. And the wounded hunk with the clouds of magic and trouble all around him was slated to co-star.

He'd spoken Gaelio, Irish Gaelic. She knew some of it, used the language occasionally in spells, and could even read some in a very rudimentary fashion.

But oddly enough, she'd not only understood everything he'd said in the dream—experience, vision, whatever— she'd been able to speak it herself, like a native.

So somewhere in the past—the good, long past, she determined. And possibly somewhere in Ireland.

She'd done scrying spells and locator spells, using the bloodied bandage she'd brought back with her from that strange and intense visit to . . . wherever she'd been. His blood and her own talent would lead her to him.

She'd expected it to be a great deal of work and effort. Doubled by whatever work and effort would be involved in transporting herself—or at least her essence—to his time and place.

She was prepared to do just that, or at least try. She sat within her circle, the candles lit, the herbs floating on the water in her bowl. Once more she searched for him, focusing on the sketch of his face and holding the cloth she'd brought back with her.

"I seek the man who bears this face, my quest to find his time, his place. I hold his blood within my hand, and with its power I demand. Search and find and show to me. As I will, so mote it be."

In her mind she saw him, brow furrowed as he buried himself in books. Focusing, she drew back, saw the room. Apartment? Dim light, just slanting over his face, his hands.

"Where are you?" she asked softly. "Show me."

And she saw the building, the street.

The thrill of success mixed with absolute bafflement.

The last thing she'd expected was to learn he was in New York, some sixty blocks away, and in the now.

The fates, Glenna decided, were in an all-fired hurry to get things started. Who was she to question them?

She closed the circle, put away her tools and tucked the sketch in her desk drawer. Then she dressed, puzzling over her choices for a bit. What exactly did a woman wear when she went to meet her destiny? Something flashy, subdued, businesslike? Something exotic?

In the end she settled on a little black dress she felt could handle anything.

She traveled uptown by subway, letting her mind clear. There was a drumming in her heart, an anticipation that had been building in her over the past weeks. This, she thought, was the next step to whatever was waiting.

And whatever it was, whatever was coming, whatever would happen next, she wanted to be open to it.

Then she'd make her decisions.

The train was crowded, so she stood, holding the overhead hook and swaying slightly with the movement of the car. She liked the rhythm of the city, its rapid pace, its eclectic musics. All the tones and hues of it.

She'd grown up in New York, but not in the city. The small town upstate had always seemed too limited to her, too closed-in. She'd wanted more, always. More color, more sound, more people. She'd spent the last four of her twenty-six years in the city.

And all of her life exploring her craft.

Something in her blood was humming now, as if it

knew—some part of her knew—she'd been preparing all of her life for these next hours.

At the next station, people filed on, people filed off. She let the sound of them flow over her as she brought the image of the man she sought back into her head.

Not the face of a martyr, she thought. There'd been too much power on him for that. And too much annoyance in him. She'd found it, she could admit, a very interesting mix.

The power of the circle he'd cast had been strong, and so had been whatever hunted him. They chased her dreams, too, those black wolves that were neither animal nor human, but something horribly of both.

Idly, she fingered the pendant she wore around her neck. Well, she was strong, too. She knew how to protect herself.

"She will feed on you."

The voice was a hiss rippling over the back of her throat, icing her skin. Then what spoke moved, seemed to glide and float in a circle around her, and the cold from it had the breath that trembled from between her lips frosting the air.

The other passengers continued to sit or stand, read or chat. Undisturbed. Unaware of the thing that slithered around their bodies like a snake.

Its eyes were red, its eye teeth long and sharp. Blood stained them, dripped obscenely from its mouth. Inside her chest, Glenna's heart tightened like a fist and began to beat, beat, beat against her ribs.

It had human form, and worse, somehow worse, wore a business suit. Blue pinstripes, she noted dully, crisp white shirt and paisley tie.

"We are forever." It swiped a bloody hand over the cheek of a woman who sat reading a paperback novel. Even while red stained her cheek, the woman turned the page and continued to read.

"We will herd you like cattle, ride you like horses, trap you like rats. Your powers are puny and pathetic, and when we're done with you, we'll dance on your bones."

"Then why are you afraid?"

It peeled back its lips in a snarl, and it leapt.

Glenna choked on a scream, stumbled back.

As the train streaked through a tunnel, the thing vanished.

"Watch it, lady." She got an impatient elbow and mutter from the man she'd fallen into.

"Sorry." She gripped the hook again with a hand gone slick with sweat.

She could still smell the blood as she rode the last blocks uptown.

For the first time in her life, Glenna actively feared the dark, the streets, the people who passed by. She had to struggle to not run when the train stopped. Had to suppress the urge to shove and push her way off and race across the platform to the steps leading up.

She walked quickly, and even with the city noises she heard the rapid clip of her heels on the sidewalk and the fearful wheeze of her own breath.

There was a line snaking out from the entrance of the club called Eternity. Couples and singles crammed together hoping to get the signal to go inside. Rather than wait, she walked up to the man on the door. She flashed a smile, did a quick charm.

He passed her through without checking his list or her ID.

Inside was music, blue light and the throb of excitement. For once the press of humanity, the pulse and beat didn't excite her.

Too many faces, she thought. Too many heartbeats. She wanted only one, and the prospect of finding him among so many suddenly seemed impossible. Every bump and jostle as she worked her way into the club jolted through her. And her own fear shamed her.

She wasn't defenseless; she wasn't weak. But she felt both. The thing on the train had been every nightmare. And that nightmare had been sent to her.

For her.

It had known her fear, she thought now. And it had played with it, taunted her until her knees were water and the screams inside her had slashed her mind like razors.

She'd been too shocked, too frightened to reach for the only weapon she held. Magic.

Now anger began to eke through the terror.

She'd told herself she was a seeker, a woman who took risks, valued knowledge. A woman who possessed defenses and skills most couldn't imagine. Yet here she was quivering at the first real whiff of danger. She stiffened her spine, evened her breathing, then headed straight for the huge circular bar.

Halfway across the silver span of the floor she saw him.

The flood of relief came first, then the pride that she'd succeeded in this initial task so quickly. A trickle of interest worked its way through as she veered in his direction.

The guy cleaned up very well.

His hair was carelessly styled rather than ragged, a shining black and shorter than it had been during their first meeting. Then again, he'd been wounded, troubled and in a hell of a fix. He wore black, and it suited him. Just as the watchful, slightly irritable look in those brilliant eyes suited him.

With a great deal of her confidence restored, she smiled and stepped into his path.

"I've been looking for you."

Cian paused. He was accustomed to women approaching him. Not that he couldn't get some enjoyment from it, particularly when the woman was exceptional as this one was. There was a spark in her eyes, jewel green, and a flirtatious hint of amusement. Her lips were full, sensuous and curved; her voice low and husky.

Her body was a good one, and poured into a little black dress that showed a great deal of milky skin and strong muscle tone. He might have amused himself with her for a few moments, but for the pendant she wore.

Witches, and worse, those who played at witchcraft, could be troublesome.

"I enjoy being looked for by beautiful women when I have time to be found." He would have left it at that, moved on, but she touched his arm.

He felt something. And apparently so did she, for her eyes narrowed, and the smile faded.

"You're not him. You only look like him." Her hand tightened on his arm, and he sensed power seeking. "But that's not completely true either. Damn it." She dropped her hand, shook back her hair. "I should've known it wouldn't be so easy."

This time he took her arm. "Let's get you a table." In a
dark, quiet corner, Cian thought. Until he knew who or what
she was.

"I need information. I need to find someone."

"You need a drink," Cian said pleasantly, and steered her
quickly through the crowd.

"Look, I can get my own drink if I want one." Glenna
considered causing a scene, but decided it would probably
get her tossed out. She considered a push of power, but knew
from experience that depending on magic for every irritation
led to trouble.

She glanced around, gauging the situation. The place was
stacked with people on every level. The music was a throb,
heavy on the bass with the female singer purring out the
lyrics in a sensual and feline voice.

Very public, very active, Glenna decided with a lot of
chrome and blue lighting slicking class over sex. What could
he possibly do to her under the circumstances?

"I'm looking for someone." Conversation, she told herself. Keep it conversational and friendly. "I thought you
were him. The light in here isn't the best, but you look
enough alike to be brothers. It's very important I find him."

"What's his name? Maybe I can help you."

"I don't know his name." And the fact that she didn't made
her feel foolish. "And okay, I know how that sounds. But I
was told he was here. I think he's in trouble. If you'd just—"
She started to shove at his hand, found it hard as stone.

What could he do to her in these circumstances? she
thought again. Almost any damn thing. With the first fresh
flicker of panic tickling her throat, she closed her eyes and
reached for power.

His hand flinched on her arm, then his grip tightened. "So,
you're a real one," he murmured, and turned those eyes—as
steely as his grip—on her. "I think we'll take this upstairs."

"I'm not going anywhere with you." Something kin to the
fear she'd felt on the subway worked its way into her. "That
was low wattage. Believe me, you don't want me to up the
amps."

"Believe me." And his voice was silky. "You don't want to piss me off."

He pulled her behind the curve of open, spiral stairs. She planted her feet, prepared to defend herself by any and all means at her disposal. She brought the four-inch spike of her heel down on his instep, slammed a back-fist into his jaw. Rather than wasting her breath on a scream, she began an incantation.

Her breath whooshed out when he lifted her off her feet as if she weighed nothing. Her only satisfaction came from the fact that in thirty seconds, when she finished the spell, he'd be flat on his ass.

That didn't stop her from fighting. She reared back, elbows and feet, and sucked in a breath to add a scream after all.

And the doors on what she saw was a private elevator whisked open.

There he was, flesh and blood. And so like the man currently heaving her over his shoulder she decided she could hate him, too.

"Put me down, you son of a bitch, or I'll turn this place into a moon crater."

W hen the doors of the transportation box opened, Hoyt was assaulted with noise and smells and lights. They all slammed into his system, stunning his senses. He saw through dazzled eyes, his brother with his arms full of struggling woman.

His woman, he realized with yet another jolt. The witch from his dream was half-naked and using language he'd rarely heard even in the seediest public house.

"Is this how you pay someone back for helping you?" She shoved at the curtain of her hair and aimed those sharp green eyes at him. She shifted them, scanned them up and down King, snarled.

"Come on then," she demanded. "I can take all three of you."

As she was currently over Cian's shoulder like a sack of

potatoes, Hoyt wasn't certain how she intended to see the threat through. But witches were tricky.

"You're real then," he stated softly. "Did you follow me?"

"Don't flatter yourself, asshole."

Cian shifted her, effortlessly. "Yours?" he said to Hoyt.

"I couldn't say."

"Deal with it." Cian dropped Glenna back on her feet, caught the fist aimed at his face just before it connected. "Do your business," he told her. "Quietly. Then take off. Keep a lid on the magic. Both of you. King."

He walked off. After a grin and a shrug, King trailed after him.

Glenna smoothed down her dress, shook back her hair. "What the hell's wrong with you?"

"My ribs still pain me a little, but I'm largely healed. Thank you for your help."

She stared at him, then huffed out a breath. "Here's how this is going to work. We're going to sit down, you're going to buy me a drink. I need one."

"I . . . I have no coin in these pants."

"Typical. I'll buy." She hooked an arm through his to make sure she didn't lose him again, then began to wind through the crowd.

"Did my brother hurt you?"

"What?"

He had to shout. How could anyone have a conversation in such noise? There were too many people in this place. Was it some sort of festival?

There were women writhing in what must have been some sort of ritual dance, and wearing even less than the witch. Others sat at silver tables and watched or ignored, drank from clear tankards and cups.

The music, he thought, came from everywhere at once.

"I asked if my brother hurt you."

"Brother? That fits. Bruised my pride for the most part."

She chose the stairs, moving up where the noise wasn't quite so horrific. Still clinging to his arm, she looked right, left, then moved toward a low seat with a candle flickering on the table. Five people were jammed around it, and all seemed to be talking at once.

She smiled at them, and he felt her power hum. "Hi. You really need to get home now, don't you?"

They got up, still chattering, and left the table littered with those clear drinking vessels, some nearly full.

"Sorry to cut their evening short, but I think this takes precedence. Sit down, will you?" She dropped down, stretched out long, bare legs. "God, what a night." She waved a hand in the air, fingered her pendant with the other as she studied his face. "You look better than you did. Are you healed?"

"Well enough. What place are you from?"

"Right to business." She glanced over at the waitress who came to their table to clear it. "I'll have a Grey Goose martini, straight up, two olives. Dry as dust." She cocked a brow at Hoyt. When he said nothing, she held up two fingers.

She tucked her hair behind one ear as she leaned toward him. There were silver coils dangling from her ear in a Celtic knot pattern.

"I dreamed of you before that night. Twice before I think," she began. "I try to pay attention to my dreams, but I could never hold on to these, until the last one. I think in the first, you were in a graveyard, and you were grieving. My heart broke for you, I remember feeling that. Odd, I remember more clearly now. The next time I dreamed of you, I saw you on a cliff, over the sea. I saw a woman with you who wasn't a woman. Even in the dream I was afraid of her. So were you."

She sat back, shuddering once. "Oh yes, I remember that now. I remember I was terrified, and there was a storm. And you . . . you struck out at her. I pushed—I remember I pushed what I had toward you, to try to help. I knew she was . . . she was wrong. Horribly wrong. There was lightning and screams—" She wished actively for her drink. "I woke up, and for an instant, the fear woke with me. Then it all faded."

When he still said nothing, she drew in a breath. "Okay,

we'll stick with me for a while. I used my scrying mirror, I used my crystal, but I couldn't see clearly. Only in sleep. You brought me to that place in the woods, in the circle. Or something did. Why?"

"It was not my work."

"It wasn't mine." She tapped nails painted red as her lips on the table. "You have a name, handsome?"

"I'm Hoyt Mac Cionaoith."

Her smile turned her face into something that all but stopped his heart. "Not from around here, are you?"

"No."

"Ireland, I can hear that. And in the dream we spoke Gaelic, which I don't—not really. But I think it's more than where. It's when, too, isn't it? Don't worry about shocking me. I'm immune tonight."

He waged an internal debate. She'd been shown to him, and she had come within the circle. Nothing that meant harm to him should have been able to come within his protective ring. While he had been told to seek a witch, she was nothing, *nothing* that he'd expected.

Yet she'd worked to heal him, and had stayed with him while the wolves had stalked his ring. She'd come to him now for answers, and perhaps for help.

"I came through the Dance of the Gods, nearly a thousand years in time."

"Okay." She whistled out a breath. "Maybe not completely immune. That's a lot to take on faith, but with everything that's been going on, I'm willing to take the leap." She lifted the glass the waitress set down, drank immediately. "Especially with this to cushion the fall. Run a tab, will you?" Glenna asked and took a credit card out of her purse.

"Something's coming," she said when they were alone again. "Something bad. Big, fat evil."

"You don't know."

"I can't see it all. But I feel it, and I know I'm connected with you on this. Not thrilled about that at this point." She drank some more. "Not after what I saw on the subway."

"I don't understand you."

"Something very nasty in a designer suit," she explained.

"It said she would feed on me. She—the woman on the cliff, I think. I'm going out on a limb here, a really shaky one. Are we dealing with vampires?"

"What is the subway?"

Glenna pressed her hands to her eyes. "Okay, we'll spend some time later bringing you up to date on current events, modes of mass transportation and so on, but right now, I need to know what I'm facing. What's expected of me."

"I don't know your name."

"Sorry. Glenna. Glenna Ward." She held a hand out to him. After a brief hesitation, he took it. "Nice to meet you. Now, what the hell is going on?"

He began, and she continued to drink. Then she held up a hand, swallowed. "Excuse me. Are you saying your brother— the guy who manhandled me, is a vampire?"

"He doesn't feed on humans."

"Oh good. Great. Points for him. He died nine hundred and seventy-odd years ago, and you've come here and now from there and then to find him."

"I am charged by the gods to gather an army to fight and destroy the army the vampire Lilith is making."

"Oh God. I'm going to need another drink."

He started to offer her his, but she waved him away and signaled the waitress. "No, go ahead. You're going to need it, too, I imagine."

He took a testing sip, blinked rapidly. "What is this brew?"

"Vodka martini. You should like vodka," she said absently. "Seems to me they make it from potatoes."

She ordered another drink and some bar food to counteract the alcohol. Calmer now, she listened to the whole of it without interrupting.

"And I'm the witch."

There wasn't just beauty here, he realized. There wasn't just power. There was a seeking and a strength. Some he would seek, he remembered the goddess saying. And some would seek him.

So she had.

"I have to believe you are. You, my brother and I will find the others and begin."

"Begin what? Boot camp? Do I look like a soldier to you?"

"You don't, no."

She propped a chin on her fist. "I like being a witch, and I respect the gift. I know there's a reason this runs in my blood. A purpose. I didn't expect it to be this. But it is." She looked at him then, fully. "I know, the first time I dreamed of you that it was the next step in that purpose. I'm terrified. I'm so seriously terrified."

"I left my family to come here, to do this thing. I left them with only the silver crosses and the word of the goddess that they would be protected. You don't know fear."

"All right." She reached out, laid a hand on his in a kind of comfort he sensed was innate in her. "All right," she repeated. "You've got a lot at stake. But I've got a family, too. They're upstate. I need to make sure they're protected. I need to make sure I live to do what I'm meant to do. She knows where I am. She sent that thing to scare me off. I'm guessing she's a lot more prepared than we are."

"Then prepared is what we'll get. I have to see what you're capable of."

"You want me to audition? Listen, Hoyt, your army so far consists of three people. You don't want to insult me."

"We have four with the king."

"What king?"

"The black giant. And I don't like working with witches."

"Really?" She drew out the word as she leaned toward him. "They burned your kind just as hot as mine. We're kissing cousins, Merlin. And you need me."

"It may be that I do. The goddess didn't say I had to like it, did she? I have to know your strengths and your weaknesses."

"Fair enough," she said with a nod. "And I have to know yours. I already know you couldn't heal a lame horse."

"That's false." And this time insult edged his voice. "It happens I was wounded, and unable to—"

"Mend a couple of broken ribs and a gash on your own palm. So, you won't be in charge of injuries if and when we manage to build this army."

"It's welcome you are to the task," he snapped. "And building the army is what we'll do. It's my destiny."

"Let's hope it's my destiny to get home in one piece." She signed the check, picked up her purse.

"Where are you going?"

"Home. I have a lot to do."

"That's not the way. We must stay together now. She knows you, Glenna Ward. She knows all of us. It's safer we are, and stronger together."

"That may be, but I need things from my home. I have a lot to do."

"They're night creatures. You'll wait until sunrise."

"Orders already?" She tried for flip, but the image of what had circled her in the subway came to her, very clearly.

Now he gripped her hand, held her in her seat and felt the clash of their emotions in the heat that vibrated between their palms. "Is this a game to you then?"

"No. I'm scared. A few days ago I was just living my life. My terms. Now I'm being hunted, and I'm supposed to fight some apocalyptic battle. I want to go home. I need my own things. I need to think."

"It's fear that makes you vulnerable and foolish. Your things will be there in the morning just as they are now."

He was right, of course. Added to it, she wasn't sure she had the bravado or the courage to step back outside into the night. "And just where am I supposed to stay until sunrise?"

"My brother has an apartment upstairs."

"Your brother. The vampire." She flopped back against her seat. "Isn't that cozy?"

"He won't harm you. You have my word on it."

"I'd rather have his, if you don't mind. And if he tries . . ." She held her palm up on the table, focused on it. A small ball of flame kindled just above her hand. "If the books and movies have it right, his type doesn't do well with fire. If he tries to hurt me, I'll torch him, and your army's down by one."

Hoyt merely laid his hand over hers, and the flame became a ball of ice. "Don't pit your skills against mine, or threaten to harm my family."

"Nice trick." She dumped the ice in her empty glass. "Let's put it this way. I have a right to protect myself, from anyone or anything who tries to hurt me. Agreed?"

"Agreed. It will not be Cian." Now he rose, offered his hand. "I will pledge this to you, here and now. I will protect you, even from him, if he means you harm."

"Well then." She put her hand in his, got to her feet. She felt it, knew he did by the way his pupils dilated. The magic, yes, but more. "I guess we've got our first deal."

As they went down, turned toward the elevator, Cian cut across their path. "Hold it. Where do you think you're taking her?"

"I'm going with him," Glenna corrected, "not being taken."

"It's not safe for her to go out. Not until daylight. Lilith already sent a scout after her."

"Check the magic at the door," Cian told Glenna. "She can have the spare room tonight. Which means you get the couch, unless she wants to share."

"He can have the couch."

"Why do you insult her?" Temper sizzled in the words. "She's been sent; she's come here at risk."

"I don't know her," Cian said simply. "And from now on, I expect you to check with me before you invite anyone into my home." He punched in the code for the elevator. "Once you're up, you stay up. I'm locking the elevator behind you."

"What if there's a fire?" Glenna said sweetly, and Cian merely smiled.

"Then I guess you'd better open a window, and fly."

Glenna stepped into the elevator when the doors opened, then laid a hand on Hoyt's arm. Before the doors shut, she flashed Cian that smile again. "Better remember who you're dealing with," she told him. "We may do just that."

She sniffed when the doors shut. "I don't think I like your brother."

"I'm not very pleased with him myself at the moment."

"Anyway. Can you fly?"

"No." He glanced down at her. "Can you?"

"Not so far."

Chapter 5

The voices woke her. They were muted and muffled so that at first she feared she was having another vision. However much she might have prized her art, she also valued sleep—especially after a night of martinis and strange revelations.

Glenna groped for a pillow to put over her head.

Her attitude toward Cian had leveled a bit after she'd gotten a look at the guest room. It boasted a sumptuous bed with lovely soft sheets and enough pillows to satisfy even her love of luxury.

It hadn't hurt that the room was spacious, decked out with antiques and painted the soft, warm green of forest shadows. The bath had been a killer, too, she recalled as she snuggled in. An enormous jet tub in gleaming white dominated a room nearly half the size of her entire loft, with that same rich green for the acre of counters. But it was the wide bowl of sink in hammered copper that had made her purr with delight.

She'd nearly given in to the temptation to wallow in the tub, indulge herself with some of the bath salts and oils housed in heavy crystal jars and arranged with fat, glossy candles on the counter. But images of movie heroines attacked while bathing had her putting that idea on hold.

All in all, the vampire's pied-à-terre—she could hardly call such luxury a den—made mincemeat of her little loft in the West Village.

Though she admired the vampire's taste, it didn't stop her from putting a protective charm on the bedroom door in addition to turning the lock.

Now, she rolled over, shucked the pillow to stare at the ceiling in the dim light of the lamp she'd left on low through the night. She was sleeping in a vampire's guest room. She'd displaced a twelfth-century sorcerer to the sofa. A gorgeous and serious-minded type who was on a mission, and expected her to join in his battle against an ancient and powerful vampire queen.

She'd lived with magic all of her life, was gifted with skills and knowledge most people never dreamed existed in reality. And still, this was one for the books.

She liked her life the way it was. And knew, without a doubt, that she would never have it quite that way again. Knew, in fact, she might lose that life altogether.

But what were her choices? She couldn't very well do nothing, couldn't put a pillow over her head and hide for the rest of her life. It *knew* her, and had already sent an emissary.

If she stayed, pretended none of it had ever happened, it could come for her, any time, anywhere. And she'd be alone.

Would she fear the night now? Would she glance over her shoulder every time she was outside after sunset? Would she wonder if a vampire only she could see would slink onto the subway the next time she rode uptown?

No, that was no way to live at all. The only way to live— the only real choice—was to face the problem, and handle the fear. And to do just that along with joining her powers and resources to Hoyt's.

Knowing sleep was no longer possible, she glanced at the clock, rolled her eyes at the early hour. Then resigned, she climbed out of bed.

* * *

In the living room, Cian ended his night with a brandy, and an argument with his brother.

He had, on occasion, returned to his living quarters at dawn with the sensation of loneliness, a kind of hollowness. He took no woman in the daylight, even with the drapes closed. Sex was, in Cian's mind, a position of vulnerability as well as power. He didn't choose to share that vulnerability when the sun was up.

It was rare for him to have company after sunrise and before dusk. And those hours were often long and empty. But he'd discovered on stepping into his own apartment and finding his brother there, he preferred the long and empty to the crowded and demanding.

"You expect her to stay here until you decide your next move. And I'm telling you that isn't possible."

"How would she be safe otherwise?" Hoyt argued.

"I don't believe her safety is on my list of immediate concerns."

How much had his brother changed, Hoyt thought in disgust, that he wouldn't immediately stand for a woman, for an innocent? "We're all at risk now, everything's at risk now. We have no choice but to stay together."

"I have a choice, and it isn't sharing my quarters with a witch, or with you, for that matter," he added, gesturing with the snifter. "I don't allow anyone in here during the day."

"I was here through yesterday."

"An exception." Cian got to his feet. "And one I'm already regretting. You're asking far too much from one who cares far too little."

"I haven't begun to ask yet. I know what must be done. You spoke of survival. And it's yours at risk now, as much as hers. As mine."

"More, as your redhead might take it into her head to stake me while I sleep."

"She isn't my . . ." Frustrated, Hoyt waved that off. "I would never let her harm you. I swear it to you. In this place, at this time, you're my only family. My only blood."

Cian's face went blank as stone. "I have no family. No blood but my own. The sooner you come to that, Hoyt, accept that, the better you'll be for it. What I do, I do for myself, not for you. Not for your cause, but for me. I said I'd fight with you, and so I will. But for my own reasons."

"What are they then? Give me that at least."

"I like this world." Cian eased down on the arm of a chair as he sipped brandy. "I like what I've carved out of it, and I intend to keep it, and on my own terms—not on Lilith's whimsy. That's worth the fight to me. Added to it, a century of existence has its eras of boredom. I seem to be in one. But I have limits. Having your woman tucked up in my quarters goes beyond them."

"She's hardly my woman."

A lazy smile curved Cian's mouth. "If you don't make her so, you're even slower than I remember in that area."

"This isn't sport, Cian. It's a fight to the death."

"I know more of death than you will ever know. More of blood and pain and cruelty. For centuries I've watched mortals, again and again, teeter close to their own extinction, by their own hand. If Lilith were more patient, she could simply wait them out. Take your pleasures where you find them, brother, for life is long and often tedious."

He toasted with his glass. "Another reason I'll fight. It's something to do."

"Why not join with her then?" Hoyt spat out. "With the one who made you what you are."

"She made me a vampire. I made myself what I am. As for why I align with you and not with her? I can trust you. You'll keep your word, for that's the way you're made. She never will. It's not her nature."

"And what of your word?"

"Interesting question."

"I'd like the answer to it." Glenna spoke from the doorway. She wore the black silk robe she'd found hanging in the closet with a number of other pieces of intimate female attire. "You two can squabble all you like, it's what men do, and siblings. But since my life's on the line, I want to know who I can count on."

"I see you made yourself at home," Cian commented.

"Do you want it back?"

When she angled her head, reached for the tie, Cian grinned. Hoyt flushed.

"Don't be encouraging him," Hoyt said. "If you'd excuse us for a moment—"

"No, I won't. I want the answer to your question. And I want to know if your brother gets a little peckish, he's going to look to me as a snack."

"I don't feed on humans. Particularly witches."

"Because of your deep love of humanity."

"Because it's troublesome. If you feed, you have to kill or word gets around. If you change the prey, you're still risking exposure. Vampires gossip, too."

She thought it over. "Sensible. All right, I prefer sensible honesty to lies."

"I told you he wouldn't harm you."

"I wanted to hear it from him." She turned back to Cian. "If you're concerned about me going after you, I'd give you my word—by why should you trust it?"

"Sensible," Cian returned.

"But your brother's already told me he'd stop me if I tried. He may find that more difficult than he believes, but . . . it would be stupid of me to try to kill you, and alienate him, given the situation we're in. I'm afraid, but I'm not stupid."

"I'd have to take your word for that as well."

Idly, she fingered the sleeve of her robe and sent him a mildly flirtatious smile. "If I'd intended to kill you, I'd have already tried a spell. You'd know if I had. You'd feel it. And if there's no more trust than this between the three of us, we're doomed before we start."

"There you have a point."

"What I want now is a shower, and some breakfast. Then I'm going home."

"She stays." Hoyt stepped between them. When Glenna started to step forward, he merely lifted a hand, and the force of his will knocked her back to the doorway.

"Just one damn minute."

"Be silent. None of us leaves this place alone. None

of us. If we're to band together we start now. Our lives are in each other's hands, and a great deal more than our own lives."

"Don't flick your power at me again."

"Whatever I have to do, I'll do. Understand me." Hoyt shifted his gaze between them. "Both of you. Dress yourself," he ordered Glenna. "Then we'll go get whatever it is you think you need. Be quick about it."

In answer, she stepped back, slammed the door.

Cian let out a short laugh. "You certainly know how to charm the ladies. I'm going to bed."

Hoyt stood alone in the living room and wondered why the gods thought he could save worlds with two such creatures at his side.

She didn't speak, but a man who has sisters knows women often use silence as a weapon. And her silence flew around the room like barbs as she filled some sort of carafe with water from the silver pipe in Cian's kitchen.

Women's fashion might have changed radically in nine hundred years, but he believed their inner workings were very much the same.

And still, much of those remained a mystery to him.

She wore the same dress as the night before, but had yet to don her shoes. He wasn't certain what weakness it spoke to in him that the sight of her bare feet should bring on an unwelcomed tinge of arousal.

She shouldn't have flirted with his brother, he thought with considerable resentment. This was a time of war, not dalliance. And if she intended to stroll about with her legs and arms exposed, she'd just have to . . .

He caught himself. He had no business looking at her legs, did he? No business thinking of her as anything but a tool. It didn't matter that she was lovely. It didn't matter that when she smiled it started something like a low fire in the center of his heart.

It didn't matter—couldn't—that when he looked at her, he wanted to touch.

He busied himself with books, returned her silence with his own and lectured himself on proper behavior.

Then the air began to simmer with some seductive aroma. He shot her a glance, wondering if she was trying some of her women's magic. But her back was to him as she rose on the toes of those lovely bare feet to take a cup from a cupboard.

It was the carafe, he realized, filled now with black liquid, and steaming with an alluring scent.

He lost the war of silence. In Hoyt's experience, men always did.

"What are you brewing?"

She simply poured the black liquid from carafe to cup, then turned, watching him with chilly green eyes over the rim as she sipped.

To satisfy himself, he got up, walked into the kitchen and took a second cup down. He poured the liquid as she had, sniffed—detected no poisons—then sipped.

It was electric. Like a quick jolt of power, both strong and rich. Potent, like the drink—the martini—from the night before. But different.

"It's very good," he said then took a deeper drink.

In response, she skirted around him, crossed the room and went back through the doorway of the guest room.

Hoyt lifted his gaze to the gods. Would he be plagued by bad tempers and sulks from both this woman and his brother? "How?" he asked. "How am I to do what must be done if already we fight among ourselves?"

"While you're at it, why don't you ask your goddess to tell you what she thinks about you slapping at me that way." Glenna came back in, wearing the shoes, and carrying the satchel he'd seen her with the evening before.

"It's a defense against what seems to be your argumentative nature."

"I like to argue. And I don't expect you to flick at me whenever you don't like what I have to say. Do it again, and I'll hit back. I have a policy against using magic as a weapon. But I'll break it in your case."

She had the right of it, which was only more annoying. "What is this brew?"

She heaved a breath. "It's coffee. You've had coffee before, I imagine. The Egyptians had coffee. I think."

"Not the like of this," he replied.

And because she smiled, he assumed the worst of it was over. "I'm ready to go, as soon as you apologize."

He should have known better. Such was the way of females. "I'm sorry I was forced to use my will to stop you from arguing the morning away."

"So, you can be a smart-ass. This once, I'll accept that. Let's get moving." She walked to the elevator, pushed its button.

"Is it the fashion for women of this time to be aggressive and sharp-tongued, or is it only you?"

She glanced back at him over her shoulder. "I'm the only one you have to worry about right now." She stepped into the elevator, held the door. "Coming?"

She'd worked out a basic strategy. First, she was going to have to spring for a cab. Whatever the conversation, however strangely Hoyt might behave, a New York City cabbie would have seen and heard it all before.

Added to that, her courage wasn't quite back up to the level to let her ride the subway again.

As she'd anticipated, the minute they were out of the building, Hoyt stopped. And stared. He looked everywhere, up, down, right, left. He studied the traffic, the pedestrians, the buildings.

No one would pay any attention to him, and if they did, they'd mark him as a tourist.

When he opened his mouth to speak, she tapped a finger on her lips. "You're going to have a million questions. So why don't you just line them up and file them? We'll get to them all eventually. For now, I'm going to hail us a cab. Once we're inside, try not to say anything too outrageous."

Questions might have been scrambling in his mind like ants, but he cloaked himself in dignity. "I'm not a fool. I know very well I'm out of place here."

No, he wasn't a fool, Glenna thought as she stepped to the

curb, held up a hand. And he was no coward either. She'd expected him to gawk, but with having the rush and noise and crowds of the city thrust on him, she'd also expected to see some fear, and there was none. Just curiosity, a dose of fascination and a bit of disapproval.

"I don't like the way the air smells."

She nudged him back when he joined her at the curb. "You get used to it." When a cab cruised up to the curb, she whispered to Hoyt as she opened the door. "Get in the way I do, and just sit back and enjoy the ride."

Inside, she reached over him to pull the door shut and gave the cabbie her address. When the cabbie shot back out into traffic, Hoyt's eyes widened.

"I don't know that much about it," she said under the Indian music pumping from the cabbie's radio. "It's a cab, a kind of car. It runs on a combustible engine, fueled by gasoline, and oil."

She did her best to explain traffic lights, crosswalks, skyscrapers, department stores and whatever else came to mind. She realized it was like seeing the city for the first time herself, and began to enjoy it.

He listened. She could all but see him absorbing and tucking all the information, the sights, the sounds, the smells, away in some internal data bank.

"There are so many." He said it quietly, and the troubled tone had her looking over at him. "So many people," he repeated, staring out the side window. "And unaware of what's coming. How will we save so many?"

It struck her then, a sharp, weighted spear in the belly. So many people, yes. And this was just part of one city in just one state. "We can't. Not all. You never can." She reached for his hand, gripped it tight. "So you don't think of the many, or you'll go crazy. We just take it one at a time."

She took out the fare when the cab pulled over—which made her think of finances, and how she'd handle *that* little problem over the next few months. She reached for Hoyt's hand again when they were on the sidewalk.

"This is my building. If we see anyone inside, just smile

and look charming. They'll just think I'm bringing home a lover."

Shock rippled over his face. "Do you?"

"Now and again." She unlocked the door, then squeezed with him into the tiny anteroom to call for the elevator. With an even tighter squeeze, they started up.

"Do all buildings have these . . ."

"Elevators. No, but a lot of them do." When they reached her apartment, she pulled open the iron gate, stepped inside.

It was a small space, but the light was excellent. Her walls were covered with her paintings and her photographs, and were painted the green of minced onions to reflect the light. Rugs she'd woven herself dotted the floor with bold tones and patterns.

It was tidy, which suited her nature. Her convertible bed was made up as a sofa for the day, plumped with pillows. The kitchen alcove sparkled from a recent scrubbing.

"You live alone. With no one to help you."

"I can't afford help, and I like living alone. Staff and servants take money, and I don't have enough of it."

"Have you no men in your family, no stipend or allowance?"

"No allowance since I was ten," she said dryly. "I work. Women work just as men do. Ideally, we don't depend on a man to take care of us, financially or otherwise."

She tossed her purse aside. "I make my living such as it is selling paintings and photographs. Painting, for the most part for greeting cards like notes, letters, messages people send each other."

"Ah, you're an artist."

"That's right," she agreed, amused that her choice of employment, at least, seemed to meet with his approval. "The greeting cards, those pay the rent. But I sell some of the artwork outright now and then. I like working for myself, too. I make my own schedule, which is lucky for you. I don't have anyone to answer to, so I can take time to do, well, what has to be done."

"My mother is an artist, in her way. Her tapestries are beautiful." He stepped up to a painting of a mermaid, rising up out of a churning sea. There was power in the face, a kind of knowledge that he took as inherently female. "This is your work?"

"Yes."

"It shows skill, and that magic that moves into color and shape."

More than approval, she decided. Admiration now, and she let it warm her. "Thanks. Normally, that kind of thumbnail review would make my day. It's just that it's a very strange day. I need to change my clothes."

He nodded absently, moved to another painting.

Behind him, Glenna cocked her head, then shrugged. She went to the old armoire she used as a closet, chose what she wanted, then carried it into the bathroom.

She was used to men paying a little more attention, she realized as she stripped out of the dress. To the way she looked, the way she moved. It was lowering to be so easily dismissed, even if he did have more important things on his mind.

She changed into jeans and a white tank. Letting the subtle glamour she'd been vain enough to use that morning fade, she did her make-up, then tied her hair back into a short tail.

When she came back, Hoyt was in her kitchen, fiddling with her herbs.

"Don't touch my stuff." She slapped his hand away.

"I was only . . ." He trailed off, then looked deliberately over her shoulder. "Is this what you wear in public?"

"Yes." She turned, and just as deliberately invaded his space. "Problem?"

"No. You don't wear shoes?"

"Not around the house, necessarily." His eyes were so blue, she thought. So sharp and blue against those thick black lashes. "What do you feel when we're like this? Alone. Close."

"Unsettled."

"That's the nicest thing you've said to me so far. I mean, do you feel something? In here?" She laid a fist on her belly, kept her eyes locked on his. "A kind of reaching. I've never felt it before."

He felt it, and a kind of burn in and under his heart as

well. "You haven't broken your fast," he managed, and stepped carefully back. "You must be hungry."

"Just me then," she murmured. She turned to open a cupboard. "I don't know what I'm going to need, so I'm going to take whatever feels right. I'm not traveling light. You and Cian have to deal with that. We should probably leave as soon as possible."

He'd lifted a hand, was on the point of touching her hair, something he'd wanted to do since he'd first seen her. Now he dropped it. "Leave?"

"You don't expect to sit around in New York and wait for the army to come to you? The portal's in Ireland, and we have to assume the battle's to take place in Ireland, or some mystical facet thereof. We need the portal, or at some point we will. So we need to go to Ireland."

He simply stared at her as she loaded bottles and vials into a case not dissimiliar from his own. "Aye, you're right. Of course, you're right. We need to start back. A voyage will take much of the time we have. Oh, Jesus, I'll be sick as six dogs sailing home."

She looked over. "Sailing? We don't have time for the *Queen Mary,* sweetie. We'll fly."

"You said you couldn't."

"I can, if it's in a plane. We'll have to figure out how to get you a ticket. You don't have ID, you don't have a passport. We can do a charm on the ticket agent, the custom's agent." She brushed it away. "I'll work it out."

"A plain what?"

She focused on him, then leaned back against the counter and laughed until her sides ached. "I'll explain later."

"It's not my purpose to amuse you."

"No, it wouldn't be. But it's a nice side pocket. Oh hell, I don't know what to take, what not to take." She stepped back, rubbed her hands over her face. "It's my first apocalypse."

"Herbs, flowers and roots grow in Ireland, and quite well."

"I like my own." Which was foolish, and childish. But still . . . "I'll just take what I consider absolutely essential in this area, then start on books, clothes, and so on. I have to make some calls, too. I've got some appointments that I need to cancel."

With some reluctance, she closed her already loaded case and left it on the counter. She crossed to a large wooden chest in the far corner of the room, and unlocked it with a charm.

Curiosity piqued, Hoyt moved over to study the contents over her shoulder. "What do you keep here?"

"Spell books, recipes, some of my more powerful crystals. Some were handed down to me."

"Ah, then, you're a hereditary witch."

"That's right. The only one of my generation who practices. My mother gave it up when she married. My father didn't like it. My grandparents taught me."

"How could she give up what's inside her?"

"A question I've asked her many times." She sat back on her heels, touching what she could take, and what she couldn't. "For love. My father wanted a simple life, she wanted my father. I couldn't do it. I don't think I could love enough to give up what I am. I'd need to be loved enough to be accepted for what I am."

"Strong magic."

"Yeah." She took out a velvet sack. "This is my prize." From it she lifted the ball of crystal he'd seen her with in the vision. "It's been in my family a long time. Over two hundred and fifty years. Chump change to a man of your years, but a hell of a run to me."

"Strong magic," he repeated, for when she held it in her hands, he could see it pulse, like a heart beating.

"You're right about that." She looked at him over the orb with eyes that had gone suddenly dark. "And isn't it time we used some? Isn't it time we do what we do, Hoyt? She knows who I am, where I am, what I am. It's likely she knows the same about you, about Cian. Let's make a move." She held the crystal aloft. "Lets find out where she's hiding."

"Here and now?"

"Can't think of a better time or place." She rose, jutted her chin toward the richly patterned rug in the room's center. "Roll that up, will you?"

"It's a dangerous step you're after taking here. We should take a moment to think."

"We can think while you're rolling up the rug. I have everything we need for a locator spell, everything we need for protection. We can blind her to us while we look."

He did as she asked and found the painted pentagram under the rug. He could admit that taking a step, any step, felt right and good. But he'd have preferred, very much, to take it alone.

"We don't know if she can be blinded. She's fed on magic blood, and likely more than once. She's very powerful, and very sly."

"So are we. You're talking about going into battle within three months. When do you intend to start?"

He looked at her, nodded. "Here and now then."

She laid the crystal in the center of the pentagram, and retrieved two athames from her chest. She placed these in the circle, then gathered candles, a silver bowl, crystal wands.

"I won't be needing all these tools."

"Fine for you, but I prefer using them. Let's work together, Merlin."

He lifted an athame to study its carving as she ringed the pentagram with candles. "Will it bother you if I work skyclad?"

"Aye," he said without looking up.

"All right, in the spirit of compromise and teamwork, I'll keep my clothes on. But they're restricting."

She removed the band from her hair, filled the silver bowl with water from a vial and sprinkled herbs on it. "Generally I invoke the goddesses when casting the circle, and it seems most appropriate for this. Suit you?"

"Well enough."

"You're a real chatterbox, aren't you? Well. Ready?" At his nod she walked to the opposite curve from him. "Goddesses of the East, of the West, of the North of the South," she began, moving around the circle as she spoke. "We ask your blessing. We call to you to witness and to guard this circle, and all within it."

"Powers of Air, and Water, of Fire and of Earth," Hoyt chanted. "Travel with us now as we go between worlds."

"Night and day, day and night, we call you to this sacred rite. We cast this circle, one times three. As we will, so mote it be."

Witches, he thought. Always rhyming. But he felt the air stir, and the water in the bowl rippled as the candles leapt to flame.

"It should be Morrigan we call on," Glenna said. "She was the messenger."

He started to do so, then decided he wanted to see what the witch was made of. "This is your sacred place. Ask for guidance, and cast your spell."

"All right." She laid down the sacred knife, lifted her hands, palms up. "On this day and in this hour, I call upon the sacred power of Morrigan the goddess and pray she grant to us her grace and prowess. In your name, Mother, we seek the sight, ask you to guide us into the light."

She bent, lifted the crystal into her hands. "Within this ball we seek to find the beast who hunts all mankind, while her eyes to us are blind. Make keen our vision, our minds, our hearts so the clouds within this ball will part. Shield us and show us what we seek to see. As we will, so mote it be."

Mists and light swirled within the glass. For an instant he thought he could see worlds inside it. Colors, shapes, movement. He heard it beat, as his heart beat. As Glenna's heart beat.

He knelt as she did. And saw, as she did.

A dark place, mazed with tunnels and washed by red light. He thought he heard the sea, but couldn't be sure if it was within the glass or just the roaring of power in his own head.

There were bodies, bloodied and torn and stacked like cordwood. And cages where people wept or screamed, or simply sat with dull and deadened eyes. Things moved within the tunnels, dark things that barely stirred the air. Some crawled up the walls like bugs.

There was horrible laughter, high, hideous shrieking.

He traveled with Glenna through those tunnels where the

air stank of death and blood. Down, deep down in the earth, where the stone walls dripped with wet and worse. To a door scribed with ancient symbols of black magicks.

He felt the breath go cold in his body as they passed through.

She slept on a bed fit for a queen, four-posted and wide with sheets that had the sheen of silk and were white as ice. Droplets of blood stained them.

Her breasts were bare above the sheets, and the beauty of her face and form were undiminished since last he'd seen her.

Beside her was the body of a boy. So young, Hoyt thought with a terrible pity. No more than ten years, so pale in death with his cornsilk hair falling over his brow.

Candles were guttering, sending wavering light to flicker over her flesh, and his.

Hoyt gripped the athame, lifted it over his head.

And her eyes opened, stared into his. She screamed, but he heard no fear in it. Beside her the boy opened his eyes, bared fangs and leaped up to skuddle along the ceiling like a lizard.

"Closer," she crooned. "Come closer, sorcerer, and bring your witch. I'll make a pet of her once I drain you dry. Do you think you can *touch* me?"

As she leaped off the bed, Hoyt felt himself flying backward, tearing through air so cold it was shards of ice in his throat.

Then he was sitting within the circle, staring into Glenna's eyes. Hers were dark and wide. There was blood dripping from her nose.

She stanched it with a knuckle while she struggled to get her breath.

"First part worked," she managed. "The blinded part didn't take very well, obviously."

"She has power as well. She's not without skill."

"Have you ever felt anything like that?" she asked him.

"No."

"Neither have I." She allowed herself one hard shudder. "We're going to need a bigger circle."

Chapter 6

Before she packed, Glenna took the time to cleanse the entire loft. Hoyt didn't disagree. She wanted no trace of what they'd touched on, no echoes, no dregs of that darkness in her home.

In the end, she put her tools and books back in the chest. After what she'd seen, what she'd felt, she wasn't going to risk the pick and choose. She was taking the whole lot, along with her travel case, most of her crystals, some basic art supplies, cameras, and two suitcases.

She cast one longing look at the easel standing near the window, and the barely started painting resting on it. If she came back—no *when,* she corrected. When she came back, she would finish it.

She stood beside Hoyt, studying the pile of belongings as he did.

"No comments?" she asked. "No arguments or sarcastic remarks about how I intend to travel?"

"To what end?"

"A wise stand. Now there's the little matter of getting all this out of here, uptown and into your brother's place. At which time, I doubt he'll be as wise as you. But first things first." She toyed with her pendant as she considered. "Do we haul it all by hand, or try a transportation spell? I've never done anything of this scope."

He sent her a bland look. "We'd need three of your cabs and most of what we have left of the day to deal with all of this."

So, he considered the situation as well. "Visualize Cian's apartment," he ordered. "The room where you slept."

"All right."

"Concentrate. Bring it fully into your mind, the details, the shape, the structure."

She nodded, closed her eyes. "I am."

He chose the chest first as he sensed it held the most power. Its magic would aid him in the task. He circled it three times, then reversed, circled again while he said the words, while he opened himself to the power.

Glenna struggled to fix her focus. There was something deeper, richer about his voice, something erotic in the way it spoke the ancient tongue. She felt the heat of what he stirred on her skin, and in her blood. Then a swift and solid punch of air.

When she opened her eyes, the chest was gone.

"I'm impressed." More honestly, she was amazed. She was capable, with considerable preparation and effort, of transporting small, simple objects some distance. But he'd simply and efficiently *poofed* a two-hundred-pound chest.

She could picture him now, in billowing robes on the cliff he'd spoken of in Ireland. Challenging the storm, charging himself with it. And facing what no man should have to face, with faith and with magic.

Her belly tightened with sheer and simple lust.

"Was that Gaelic you were speaking?"

"Irish," he said, so obviously distracted, she didn't speak again.

Once more he circled, focusing now on the cases that contained her photography and art equipment. She nearly yipped a protest, then reminded herself to have faith. Calling on it, she closed her eyes again, brought the guest room back into her mind. Gave him what she could of her own gift.

It took him fifteen minutes to accomplish what she was forced to admit would have taken her hours, if she could have managed it at all.

"Well that was . . . that was something." The magic was still on him, turning his eyes opaque, rippling through the air between them. She felt it like a ribbon wound around both of them, tying them together. Her own arousal was so keen, she had to step back, deliberately break the bond between them.

"No offense, but are you sure they're where we want them?"

He continued to stare at her with those fathomless blue eyes until the heat in her belly grew so strong she wondered it didn't shoot fire from her fingertips.

It was nearly too much, this pressure, this need, the mad beat of it at every pulse. She started to step back again, but he simply lifted a hand and stopped her in her tracks.

She felt the pull, from him, to him, with just enough play for her to resist, to snap that lead and escape. Instead she stood, kept her eyes locked with his as he closed the distance between them with one easy stride.

Then there was nothing easy.

He yanked her to him so that her breath expelled on a quick hitching gasp, and that gasp ended on a moan when their mouths met. The hot, drugging kiss spun through her head, through her body, sizzling in her blood when she clung to him.

Candles she'd left in the room flashed into flame.

At once aggressive and desperate, she dug her hands into his shoulders and plunged headfirst into the storm of sensation. This, this was what she'd craved from the first moment she'd seen him in dreams.

She felt his hands on her hair, her body, her face, and everywhere he touched quivered. No dream now, just need and heat and flesh.

He couldn't stop himself. She was like a feast after the fast, and all he wanted was to gorge. Her mouth was full and soft, and fit so truly to his it was as if the gods had formed it for only that purpose. The power he'd wielded had snapped back on him, inciting an impossible hunger that ached in his belly, in his loins, in his heart and cried out to be sated.

Something burned between them. He'd known it from the first instant, even ill with fever and pain while the wolves stalked beyond his fire. And he feared it nearly as much as he feared what they were fated to face together.

He drew her back, shaken to the bone. What they'd stirred was alive on her face, sultry and tempting. If he accepted and took, what price would they both pay for it?

There was always a price.

"I apologize. I . . . I was caught on the tail of the spell."

"Don't apologize. It's insulting."

Women, was all he could think. "Touching you in that way isn't?"

"If I hadn't wanted you to touch me that way, I'd have stopped you. Oh, don't flatter yourself," she snapped out when she read the expression on his face. "You may be stronger, physically, magically, but I can handle myself. And when I want an apology, I'll ask for one."

"I can't find my balance in this place, or with you." Frustration rippled out from him now, as the magic had. "I'm not liking it, or what I'm feeling for you."

"That's your problem. It was just a kiss."

He caught her arm before she could turn away. "I don't believe, even in this world, that was just a kiss. You've seen what we have to face. Desire is a weakness, one we can't risk. Everything we have must be charged toward what we have to do. I won't risk your life or the fate of the world for a few moments of pleasure."

"I can promise it would be more than a few. But there's no point in arguing with a man who sees desire as a weakness. Let's chalk it up to the moment, and move on."

"I'm not after hurting you," he began with some regret, and she aimed a single, quelling look.

"Apologize again, and you're on your ass." She picked up her keys, her purse. "Put out the candles, would you, and let's go. I want to make sure my things arrived safely, and we've got to arrange for flights to Ireland. And figure out how to smuggle you out of the country."

She grabbed sunglasses from a table, put them on. A great deal of her irritation faded at the baffled expression on his face. "Shades," she explained. "They cut the glare of the sun, and in this case are a sexy fashion statement."

She opened the iron gate, then turned, looked back at her loft, her things. "I have to believe I'll come back here. I have to believe I'll see all this again."

She stepped inside, pushed the button for the ground floor. And left behind much that she loved.

When Cian came out of his room, Glenna was in the kitchen cooking. On their return, Hoyt had taken himself off to the study adjoining the living room, hauling his books with him. Now and again, she felt something ripple out, and assumed he was practicing some spells.

It kept him out of her hair. But it didn't keep him out of her head.

She was careful with men. Enjoying them, certainly, but she didn't share herself recklessly. Which is exactly what she'd done with Hoyt, and she couldn't deny it. It had been reckless, impulsive and apparently a mistake. And though she'd said it had been just a kiss, it had been as intimate an act as she'd ever experienced.

He wanted her, there was no question of that. But he didn't choose to want her. Glenna preferred to be chosen.

Desire wasn't a weakness, not in her mind—but it was a distraction. He was right in that they couldn't afford distractions. That strength of character and good solid sense were two of his appealing traits. But considering her own jumpy system, they were equally irritating ones.

So she cooked, because it kept her busy and settled her down.

When Cian came in looking sleek and sleepy, she was briskly chopping vegetables.

"*Mi casa* is, apparently, *su casa.*"

She kept right on chopping. "I brought some perishables—among other things—from home. I don't know if you eat."

He looked dubiously at the raw carrots and leafy greens.

"One of the advantages of my fate is I don't have to eat my vegetables like a good lad." But he'd scented what was on the stove, and moved to it to sniff at the spicy tomato sauce simmering. "On the other hand, this looks appealing."

He leaned back on the counter to watch her work. "So do you."

"Don't waste your questionable charm on me. Not interested."

"I could work on that, just to get under Hoyt's skin. Might be entertaining. He tries not to watch you. He fails."

Her hand hesitated, then she brought down the knife again. "I'm sure he'll succeed eventually. He's a very determined man."

"Always was, if memory serves. Sober and serious, and as trapped by his gift as a rat in a cage."

"Do you see it that way?" She set down the knife, turned to him. "As a trap. It's not, not for him, not for me. It's a duty, yes. But it's a privilege and a joy as well."

"We'll see how joyful you are when you're in Lilith's path."

"Been there. We did a locator spell at my place. She's holed up in a cave with a series of tunnels. Near the sea, I think. Near, I think, that cliffside where Hoyt faced her. She gave us a good solid blast. We won't be so easy to push next time."

"You're mad as Fat Tuesday, the pair of you." He opened his cold box, took out a bag of blood. His face tightened at the small sound Glenna couldn't quite smother. "You'll have to get used to it."

"You're right. I will." She watched him pour the contents in a thick glass, then set it in the microwave to heat. This time it was a snicker she couldn't smother. "Sorry. But it's just so damn odd."

He studied her, obviously saw no rancor, and relaxed. "Want some wine?"

"Sure, thanks. We need to go to Ireland."

"So I'm told."

"No. Now. As soon as it can be arranged. I've got a passport, but we have to figure out how to get Hoyt out of this country and into another. And we'll need a place to set up, to stay and to, well, train and practice."

"Peas in a pod," Cian muttered, pouring her a glass of wine. "It's not a simple matter, you know, to delegate responsibilities for my businesses, particularly since the man I trust to run the club downstairs is bound and determined to join Hoyt's holy army."

"Look, I spent a lot of my time today packing, transferring my rather limited funds so I could pay the rent on my place through October, cancelling appointments, and handing off a couple of what would be fairly lucrative jobs to an associate. You'll just have to manage."

He retrieved his own glass. "And what is it you do? These fairly lucrative jobs?"

"Greeting card art, of the mystical variety. I paint. And do some photography."

"You any good?"

"No, I suck. Of course, I'm good. The paying photography is mostly weddings. More arty stuff for my own pleasure and the occasional sale. I'm adaptable at keeping the wolf from the door." She lifted her wine. "How about you?"

"Can't survive a millennium otherwise. So, we'll leave tonight."

"Tonight? We can't possibly—"

"Adapt," he said simply and drank.

"We need to check on flights, buy tickets—"

"I have my own plane. I'm a licensed pilot."

"Oh."

"A good one," he assured her. "I've several decades of air time, so you needn't worry on that score."

Vampires who drank blood out of pricey stemware and owned planes. No, what did she have to worry about? "Hoyt doesn't have any identification, no passport, no papers. I can work a charm to get him through Customs, but—"

"No need." He crossed the room, opened a panel on the wall she hadn't detected, and revealed a safe.

Once he'd unlocked it, he took out a lock box, and coming back set it on the counter and flipped the combination.

"He can take his choice," Cian said and pulled out a half a dozen passports.

"Well, wow." She plucked one, opened it, studied the picture. "Handy you look so much alike. The serious lack of mirrors in this place tells me the lore about no reflections hangs true. No problem being photographed?"

"If you're using a reflector camera, you'd have a moment, when the mirror engages when you'd be very puzzled. Then it disengages as you shoot—and there I am."

"Interesting. I brought my cameras. I'd like to try some pictures, when there's time."

"I'll think about it."

She tossed the passport down. "I hope that plane of yours has plenty of cargo space, because I'm loaded."

"We'll manage. I've calls to make, and packing of my own to see to."

"Wait. We don't have a place to stay."

"It won't be a problem," he said as he left the room. "I've something that will suit."

Glenna blew out a breath, looked back at the pot on the stove. "Well, at least we'll get in a good meal first."

It wasn't a simple matter, even with Cian's money and connections laying a path. The luggage and cargo had to be transported the ordinary and laborious way this time. She could see all three of the men she'd hooked her fate with looking for a way to cut down on her load. She cut that route off with a firm: "It all goes"—and left it at that.

She had no idea what Cian had in the single suitcase or the two large metal chests he packed.

She wasn't sure she wanted to know.

She couldn't imagine what they must have looked like, the two tall, dark men, the enormous black man, and the redhead with enough luggage to re-sink the *Titanic*.

She enjoyed the privilege of being female, and left it to the men to do the loading, while she explored Cian's sleek and elegantly appointed private jet.

He wasn't afraid of color, or of spending his money, she

had to give him credit for that. The seats were a deep, rich blue in buttery leather, and generous enough to be comfortable for even a man of King's proportions. The carpet was thick enough to sleep on.

It boasted a small, efficient conference room, two sophisticated bathrooms, and what she initially took to be a cozy bedroom. More than that, she realized when she noted it had no windows, no mirrors, and its own half bath. A safe room.

She wandered into the galley, approved it, and appreciated the fact that Cian had already called ahead to have it stocked. They wouldn't starve on the flight to Europe.

Europe. She trailed her finger over one of the fully reclining seats. She'd always planned to go, to spend as much as a month. Painting, taking photographs, exploring. Visiting the ancient sites, shopping.

Now she was going, and getting there well above the first-class level. But she wouldn't be wandering the hills and the sacred grounds at her leisure.

"Well, you wanted adventure in your life," she reminded herself. "Now you've got it." She closed a hand around the pendant she wore and prayed she'd have not only the strength but also the wits to survive it.

She was seated when the men boarded, and making a show out of enjoying a glass of champagne.

"I popped the cork," she said to Cian. "I hope you don't mind. It seemed appropriate."

"Sláinte." He moved directly to the cockpit.

"Want the two-dollar tour?" she asked Hoyt. "Want to look around?" she explained. "I imagine King's flown in this little beauty before and is thoroughly jaded."

"Beats the hell out of commercial," King agreed, and got himself a beer in lieu of champagne. "The boss knows how to handle this bird." He gave Hoyt a slap on the shoulder. "No worries."

Because he looked far from convinced, Glenna rose and poured another glass of champagne. "Here, drink, relax. We're going to be in here all night."

"In a bird made out of metal and cloth. A flying machine." Hoyt nodded, and because it was in his hand, sipped the bubbling wine. "It's a matter of science and mechanics."

He'd spent two full hours reading of the history and technology of aircraft. "Aerodynamics."

"Exactly." King tapped the beer bottle to Hoyt's glass, then Glenna's. "Here's to kicking some ass."

"You look like you're looking forward to it," Glenna commented.

"Damn straight. Who wouldn't? We get to save the frigging world. The boss? He's been restless the last few weeks. He gets restless, I get restless. Ask me, this is just what the doctor ordered."

"And dying doesn't worry you?"

"Everybody dies." He glanced toward the cockpit. "One way or another. 'Sides, a big bastard like me doesn't go down easy."

Cian strolled in. "We're cleared, boys and girls. Have a seat, strap in."

"Got your back, Captain." King followed Cian back into the cockpit.

Glenna sat, offered a smile as she patted the seat beside hers. She was prepared to soothe Hoyt through his first flight. "You'll need your seat belt. Let me show you how it works."

"I know how it works. I read of it." He studied the metal for a moment, then locked the pieces together. "In the event there is turbulence. Pockets of air."

"You're not the least bit nervous."

"I came through a time portal," he reminded her. He began to play with the control panel, amusement crossing his face when the back reclined, came up again. "I think I'll be enjoying this trip. Bloody shame it's got to be done over water."

"Oh, I nearly forgot." She dug into her purse, pulled out a vial. "Drink this. It'll help. Drink it," she repeated when he frowned at the vial. "It's herbs and some powdered crystals. Nothing harmful. It may help the queasiness."

The reluctance was clear on his face, but he downed it. "You have a heavy hand with the cloves."

"You can thank me when you don't have to use the barf bag."

She heard the engines hum, felt the vibration beneath her. "Spirits of the night, give us wings to take this flight. Hold us safe within your hand until we touch upon the land." She slid her eyes to Hoyt. "It never hurts."

He wasn't ill, but she could see that her potion and his will were fighting a hard battle to keep his system steady. She made him tea, brought him a blanket, then reclined his seat, brought up the footrest herself.

"Try to sleep a little."

Too ill to argue, he nodded, closed his eyes. When she was sure he was as comfortable as she could make him, she moved forward to join the others in the cockpit.

There was music playing. Nine Inch Nails, she recognized. In the co-pilot's seat, King had kicked back and was snoring along with the beat. Glenna looked through the windscreen and felt her heart do a little dance of its own.

There was nothing but the black.

"I've never been in a cockpit before. Awesome view."

"I can kick that one out of here if you want his seat for a bit."

"No. I'm fine. Your brother's trying to sleep. He's not feeling very well."

"He used to turn green crossing the Shannon. I imagine he's sick as a dog by now."

"No, just queasy. I gave him something at takeoff, and he's got an iron will to add to it. Do you want anything?"

He glanced back. "Aren't you the helpful one?"

"I'm too revved up to sleep, too restless to sit. So, coffee, tea, milk?"

"I wouldn't mind the coffee. Thanks for that."

She brewed a short pot, brought him a mug of it. Then stood behind him, staring out into the night sky. "What was he like as a boy?"

"As I told you."

"Did he ever doubt his power? Ever wish he hadn't been given the gift?"

It was a strange sensation, having a woman question him

about another man. Generally if they weren't talking about
themselves they were asking about him, trying to nudge
aside what some of them saw as a curtain of mystery.

"Not that he ever told me. And he would have," Cian said
after a moment. "We were close enough in those days."

"Was there someone—a woman, a girl—for him back
there?"

"No. He looked, and he touched, and he had a few. He's a
sorcerer not a priest. But he never told me of one special to
him. I never saw him look at any of the girls as he looks at
you. To your peril, Glenna, I'd be saying. But mortals are
fools when it comes to love."

"And I'd say if you can't love when you're facing death,
then death's not worth fighting. Lilith had a child with her.
Did he tell you that?"

"He didn't, no. You need to understand there's no sentiment there, no softness. A child is just easy prey, and a sweet
meal."

Her stomach turned, but she kept her voice even. "Eight
or ten years old, I'd say," she continued. "In the bed with her,
in those caves. She'd made him like her. She'd made that
child like her."

"That shocks and angers you, well, that's fine then. Shock
and anger can be strong weapons in the right hand. But remember this. If you see that child, or one like him, put your
pity away, because he'll kill you without thought or mercy
unless you kill him first."

She studied Cian now, that profile that was so like his
brother's, yet so completely his own. She wanted to ask if
he'd ever turned a child, or fed on one. But she was afraid
the answer might be unforgivable, and she needed him.

"Could you do that, destroy a child whatever he'd become?"

"Without thought or mercy." He glanced at her, and she
saw he'd known the other question running in her mind.
"And you're not good to us or yourself if you can't do the
same."

She left him then without a word and went back to stretch
out beside Hoyt. Because the conversation with Cian had

chilled her, she pulled her own blanket up to her throat, curled toward Hoyt's body heat.

And when she slept, finally slept, she dreamed of children, with sunny hair and bloody fangs.

She woke with a start to find Cian leaning over her. A scream clawed up to her throat until she realized he was shaking Hoyt awake.

She pushed at her hair, skimmed her fingers over her face for a quick glamour. They were speaking in low tones and, she realized, in Irish.

"English, please. I can't follow that much, especially with the accents."

Both turned vibrant blue eyes on her, and Cian straightened as she brought her chair up. "I'm telling him we've about an hour flight time left."

"Who's flying the plane?"

"King's got it for the moment. We'll be landing at dawn."

"Good. Great." She barely stifled a yawn. I'll throw some coffee and breakfast together so . . . Dawn?"

"Aye, dawn. I need a good cloud cover. Rain would be a bonus. Can you do this? Otherwise King will land it. He's capable, and I'll be spending the rest of the flight and the day in the back of the plane."

"I said I could do it, and I will."

"We can do it," Glenna corrected.

"Well, be quick about it, will you? I've been singed a time or two and it's unpleasant."

"You're welcome," she muttered when he left them. "I'll get a few things from my travel case."

"I don't need them." Hoyt brushed her aside, got up to stand in the aisle. "This time, it'll be my way. He's my brother, after all."

"Your way then. How can I help?"

"Call the vision to your mind. Clouds and rain. Rain and clouds." He retrieved his staff. "See it, feel it, smell it. Thick and steady, with the sun trapped behind the gloom. Dusky light, light without power or harm. See it, feel it, smell it."

He held his staff in both hands, braced his legs apart for balance, then raised it.

"I call the rain, the black clouds that cover the sky. I call the clouds, fat with rain that streams from the heavens. Swirl and close and lay thick."

She felt it spin, spin out from him, spin out to the air. The plane shook, bucked, trembled, but he stood as if he stood on a floor of granite. The tip of the staff glowed blue.

He turned to her, nodded. "That should do it."

"Well. Okay then. I'll make coffee."

They landed in gloom with the rain like a gray curtain. A little overdone, in Glenna's opinion, and it was going to be a miserable drive from the airport to wherever the hell they were going.

But she stepped off the plane and onto Ireland, and there it was. A connection, instant and surprising even to her. She had a quick sense of memory of a farm—green hills, stone fences and a white house with clothes flapping on a line in a brisk wind. There was a garden in the dooryard with dahlias big as dinner plates and calla lilies white as wishes.

It was gone almost as quickly as it had come. She wondered if it was her memory from another time, another life, or simply a call through her blood. Her grandmother's mother had come from Ireland, from a farm in Kerry.

She had brought her linens and her best dishes—and her magic—to America with her.

She waited for Hoyt to deplane. This would always be home for him, she saw it now in the pleasure that ran over his face. Whether it was a busy airport or an empty field, this was his place. And part, very much a part, she understood now, that he would die to save.

"Welcome home."

"It looks nothing like it did."

"Parts of it will." She took his hand and squeezed. "Nice job with the weather, by the way."

"Well, that at least, is familiar."

King trotted over, wet as a seal. His thick dreads dripped rain. "Cian's arranging for most of the stuff to be delivered by truck. Take what you can carry, or have to have right now. The rest'll be along in a couple hours."

"Where are we going?" Glenna demanded.

"He's got a place here." King shrugged. "So that's where we're going."

They had a van, and even then it was a tight squeeze. And, Glenna discovered, another sort of adventure altogether to sweep along through the pouring rain on wet roads, many of which seemed as narrow as a willow stem.

She saw hedgerows ripe with fuchsia, and those hills of wet emerald rolling up and back into the dull gray sky. She saw houses with flowers blooming in dooryards. Not the one of her quick image, but close enough to make her smile.

Something here had belonged to her once. Now maybe it would again.

"I know this place," Hoyt murmured. "I know this land."

"See." Glenna patted his hand. "I knew some of it would be the same for you."

"No, this place, this land." He pushed up to grab Cian by the shoulder. "Cian."

"Mind the driver," Cian ordered and shook off his brother's hand before turning between the hedgerows and onto a narrow spit of a land that wound back through a dense forest.

"God," Hoyt breathed. "Sweet God."

The house was stone, alone among the trees, and quiet as a tomb. Old and wide, with the jut of a tower and the stone aprons of terraces. In the gloom, it looked deserted and out of its time.

And still there was a garden outside the door, of roses and lilies and the wide plates of dahlia. Foxglove sprang tall and purple among the trees.

"It's still here." Hoyt spoke in a voice thick with emotion. "It survived. It still stands."

Understanding now, Glenna gave his hand another squeeze. "It's your home."

"The one I left only days ago. The one I left nearly a thousand years ago. I've come home."

Chapter 7

It wasn't the same. The furnishings, the colors, the light, even the sound his footsteps made crossing the floor had changed, turning the familiar into the foreign. He recognized a few pieces—some candlestands and a chest. But they were in the wrong places.

Logs had been set in the hearth, but were yet unlit. And there were no dogs curled up on the floor or thumping their tails in greeting.

Hoyt moved through the rooms like a ghost. Perhaps that's what he was. His life had begun in this house, and so much of it had been woven together under its roof or on its grounds. He had played here and worked here, eaten and slept here.

But that was hundreds of years in the past. So perhaps, in a very true sense, his life had ended here as well.

His initial joy in seeing the house dropped away with a weight of sadness for all that he'd lost.

Then he saw, encased in glass on the wall, one of his mother's tapestries. He moved to it, touched his fingers to the glass as she came winging back to him. Her face, her voice, her scent were as real as the air around him.

"It was the last she'd finished before . . ."

"I died," Cian finished. "I remember. I came across it in an auction. That, and a few other things over time. I was able to acquire the house oh, about four hundred years ago now, I suppose. Most of the land as well."

"But you don't live here any longer."

"It's a bit out of the way for me, and not convenient to my work or pleasures. I have a caretaker whom I've sent off until I order him back. And I generally come over once a year or so."

Hoyt dropped his hand, turned. "It's changed."

"Change is inevitable. The kitchen's been modernized. There's plumbing and electricity. Still it's drafty for all that. The bedrooms upstairs are furnished, so take your choices. I'm going up to get some sleep."

He started out, glanced back. "Oh, and you can stop the rain if you've a mind to. King, give me a hand will you, hauling some of this business up?"

"Sure. Very cool digs, if you don't mind a little spooky." King hauled up a chest the way another man might have picked up a briefcase, and headed up the main stairs.

"Are you all right?" Glenna asked Hoyt.

"I don't know what I am." He went to the window, drew back heavy drapes to look out on the rain-drenched forest. "It's here, this place, the stones set by my ancestors. I'm grateful for that."

"But they're not here. The family you left behind. It's hard what you're doing. Harder for you than the rest of us."

"We all share it."

"I left my loft. You left your life." She stepped to him, brushed a kiss over his cheek. She had thought to offer to fix a hot meal, but saw that what he needed most just then was solitude.

"I'm going up, grab a room, a shower and a bed."

He nodded, continued to stare out the window. The rain suited his mood, but it was best to close the spell. Even when he had, it continued to rain, but in a fine, misty drizzle. The fog crawled across the ground, twined around the feet of the rose bushes.

Could they be his mother's still? Unlikely, but they were roses, after all. That would have pleased her. He wondered if in some way having her sons here again, together, would please her as well.

How could he know? How would he ever know?

He flashed fire into the hearth. It seemed more like home with the fire snapping. He didn't choose to go up, not yet. Later, he thought, he'd take his case up to the tower. He'd make it his own again. Instead he dug out his cloak, swirled it on and stepped out into the thin summer rain.

He walked toward the stream first where the drenched foxgloves swayed their heavy bells and the wild orange lilies Nola had particularly loved spread like spears of flame. There should be flowers in the house, he thought. He'd have to gather some before dusk. There had always been flowers in the house.

He circled around, drawing in the scent of damp air, wet leaves, roses. His brother kept the place tended; Hoyt couldn't fault him for that. He saw the stables were still there—not the same, but in the same spot. They were larger than they'd been, with a jut to one side that boasted a wide door.

He found it locked, so opened it with a focused thought. It opened upward to reveal a stone floor and some sort of car. Not like the one in New York, he noted. Not like the cab, or the van they had traveled in from the airport. This was black and lower to the ground. On its hood was a shining silver panther. He ran his hands over it.

It puzzled him that there were so many different types of cars in this world. Different sizes and shapes and colors. If one was efficient and comfortable, why did they need so many other kinds?

There was a long bench in the area as well, and all manner of fascinating-looking tools hanging on the wall or layered in the drawers of a large red chest. He spent some time studying them, and the stack of timber that had been planed smooth and cut into long lengths.

Tools, he thought, wood, machines, but no life. No grooms, no horses, no cats slinking about hunting mice. No litter of wriggling pups for Nola to play with. He closed and locked the door behind him again, moved down the outside length of the stable.

He wandered into the tack room, comforted somewhat by the scents of leather and oil. It was well organized, he saw, just as the stall for the car had been. He ran his hands over a saddle, crouched to examine it, and found it not so different from the one he'd used.

He toyed with reins and bridles, and for a moment missed his mare as he might have missed a lover.

He passed through a door. The stone floor had a slight slope, with two stalls on one side, one on the other. Fewer than there had been, but larger, he noted. The wood was smooth and dark. He could smell hay and grain, and . . .

He moved, quickly now, down the stone floor.

A coal-black stallion stood in the last of three stalls. It gave Hoyt's heart a hard and happy leap to see it. There were still horses after all—and this one, he noted, was magnificent.

It pawed the ground, laid back its ears when Hoyt opened the stall door. But he held up both hands, began to croon softly in Irish.

In response, the horse kicked the rear of the stall and blew out a warning.

"That's all right then, that's fine. Who could blame you for being careful with a stranger? But I'm just here to admire you, to take in your great handsome self, is all I'm about. Here, have a sniff why don't you? See what you think. Ah, it's a sniff I said, not a nip." With a chuckle, Hoyt drew back his hand a fraction as the horse bared his teeth.

He continued to speak softly and stand very still with his hand out while the horse made a show of snorting and pawing. Deciding bribery was the best tack, Hoyt conjured an apple.

When he saw the interest in the horse's eye, he lifted it, took a healthy bite himself. "Delicious. Would you be wanting some?"

Now the horse stepped forward, sniffed, snorted, then nipped the apple from Hoyt's palm. As he chomped it, he graciously allowed himself to be stroked.

"I left a horse behind. A fine horse I'd had for eight years.

I called her Aster, for she had a star shape right here." He stroked two fingers down the stallion's head. "I miss her. I miss it all. For all the wonders of this world, it's hard to be away from what you know."

At length he stepped out of the stall, closed the door behind him. The rain had stopped so he could hear the murmur of the stream, and the plop of rain falling from leaf to ground.

Were there still faeries in the woods? he wondered. Playing and plotting and watching the foibles of man? He was too tired in his mind to search for them. Too tired in his heart to take the lonely walk to where he knew his family must be buried.

He went back to the house, retrieved his case, and walked up all the winding steps to the topmost tower.

There was a heavy door barring his way, one that was deeply scribed with symbols and words of magic. Hoyt ran his fingers over the carving, felt the hum and the heat. Whoever had done this had some power.

Well, he wouldn't be shut out of his own workroom. He set to work to break the locking spell, and used his own sense of insult and anger to heat it.

This was *his* home. And never in his life had a door here been locked to him.

"Open locks," he commanded. "It is my right to enter this place. It is my will that breaks this spell."

The door flew open on a blast of wind. Hoyt took himself and his resentment inside, letting the door slam shut behind him.

The room was empty but for dust and spider webs. Cold, too, he thought. Cold and stale and unused. Once it had carried the scent of his herbs and candlewax, the burn of his own power.

He would have this back at least, as it had been it would be again. There was work to do, and this was where he intended to do it.

So he cleaned the hearth and lit the fire. He dragged up from below whatever suited him—a chair, tables. There was no electricity here, and that pleased him. He'd make his own light.

He set out candles, touched their wicks to set them to burn. By their light he arranged his tools and supplies.

Settled in his heart, in his mind, for the first time in days, he stretched out on the floor in front of the fire, rolled up his cloak to pillow his head, and slept.

And dreamed.

He stood with Morrigan on a high hill. The ground sheered down in steep drops, slicing rolls with shadowy chasms all haunted by the distant blur of dark mountains. The grass was coarse and pocked with rock. Some rose up like spears, others jutted out in gray layers, flat as giant tables. The ground dipped up and down, up again to the mountains where the mists fell into pockets.

He could hear hisses in the mists, the panting breath of something older than time. There was an anger to this place. A wild violence waiting to happen.

But now, nothing stirred on the land as far as his eye could see.

"This is your battleground," she told him. "Your last stand. There will be others before you come here. But this is where you will draw her, and face her with all the worlds in the balance of that day."

"What is this place?"

"This is the Valley of Silence, in the Mountains of Mist, in the World of Geall. Blood will spill here, demon and human. What grows after will be determined by what you, and those with you do. But you must not stand upon this land until the battle."

"How will I come here again?"

"You will be shown."

"We are only four."

"More are coming. Sleep now, for when you wake, you must act."

While he slept the mists parted. He saw there was a maiden standing on that same high ground. She was slim and young with brown hair in a tumble down her back, loose as suited a maiden. She wore a gown of deep mourning, and her eyes showed the ravages of weeping.

But they were dry now, and fixed upon that desolate land,

as his had been. The goddess spoke to her, but the words were not for him.

Her name was Moira, and her land was Geall. Her land, and her heart and her duty. That land had been at peace since the gods had made it, and those of her blood had guarded that peace. Now, she knew, peace would be broken, just as her heart was broken.

She had buried her mother that morning.

"They slaughtered her like a spring lamb."

"I know your grief, child."

Her bruised eyes stared hard through the rain. "Do the gods grieve, my lady?"

"I know your anger."

"She harmed no one in her life. What manner of death is that for one who was so good, so kind?" Moira's hands bunched at her sides. "You cannot know my grief or my anger."

"Others will die even a worse death. Will you stand and do nothing?"

"What can I do? How do we defend against such creatures? Will you give me more power?" Moira held out her hands, hands that had never felt so small and empty. "More wisdom and cunning? What I have isn't enough."

"You've been given all you need. Use it, hone it. There are others, and they wait for you. You must leave now, today."

"Leave?" Stunned, Moira turned to face the goddess. "My people have lost their queen. How can I leave them, and how could you ask it of me? The test must be taken; the gods themselves deemed this so. If I'm not to be the one to stand in my mother's stead, take sword and crown, I still must bide here, to help the one who does."

"You help by going, and this the gods deem so. This is your charge, Moira of Geall. To travel from this world so you might save it."

"You would have me leave my home, my people, and on such a day? The flowers have not yet faded on my mother's grave."

"Would your mother wish you to stand and weep for her and watch your people die?"

"No."

"You must go, you and the one you trust most. Travel to the Dance of the Gods. There I will give you a key, and it will take you where you need to go. Find the others, form your army. And when you come here, to this land, on Samhain, you'll fight."

Fight, she thought. She had never been called to fight, had only known peace. "My lady, am I not needed here?"

"You will be. I tell you to go now where you're needed now. If you stay, you're lost. And your land is lost, as the worlds are. This was destined for you since before your birth. It is why you are.

"Go immediately. Make haste. They only wait for sunset."

Her mother's grave was here, Moira thought in despair. Her life was here, and all she knew. "I'm in mourning. A few days more, Mother, I beg you."

"Stay even one day longer, and this is what befalls your people, your land."

Morrigan waved an arm, parting the mists. Beyond them it was black night with only the silver ripple of light from the cold moon. Screams ripped through the air. Then there was smoke, and the shimmering orange glow of fires.

Moira saw the village overlooked by her own home. The shops and cottages were burning, and those screams were the screams of her friends, her neighbors. Men and women ripped to pieces, children being fed on by those horrible things that had taken her mother.

She watched her own uncle fight, slashing with his sword while blood stained his face and hands. But they leaped on him from above, from below, those creatures with fangs and eyes of feral red. They fell on him with howls that froze her bones. And while the blood washed the ground, a woman of great beauty glided over it. She wore red, a silk gown tightly laced at the bodice and bedecked with jewels. Her hair was uncovered and spilled gold as sunlight over her white shoulders.

In her arms was a babe still swaddled.

While the slaughter raged around her, the thing of great beauty bared fangs, and sank them into the babe's throat.

"No!"

"Hold your grief and your anger here, and this will come." The cold anger in Morrigan's voice pierced through Moira's terror. "All you know destroyed, ravaged, devoured."

"What are these demons? What hell loosed them on us?"

"Learn. Take what you have, what you are and seek your destiny. The battle will come. Arm yourself."

She woke beside her mother's grave, shaking from the horrors she'd seen. Her heart was as heavy as the stones used to make her mother's cairn.

"I couldn't save you. How can I save anyone? How can I stop this thing from coming here?"

To leave all she'd ever known, all she'd ever loved. Easy for gods to speak of destiny, she thought as she forced herself to her feet. She looked over the graves to the quiet green hills, the blue ribbon of the river. The sun was high and bright, sparkling over her world. She heard the song of a lark, and the distant lowing of cattle.

The gods had smiled on this land for hundreds of years. Now there was a price to be paid, of war and death and blood. And her duty to pay it.

"I'll miss you, every day," she said aloud, then looked over to her father's grave. "But now you're together. I'll do what needs to be done, to protect Geall. Because I'm all that's left of you. I swear it here, on this holy ground before those who made me. I'll go to strangers in a strange world, and give my life if my life is asked. It's all I can give you now."

She picked up the flowers she'd brought with her, and laid some on each grave. "Help me do this thing," she pleaded, then walked away.

He was waiting for her on the stone wall. He had his own grief, she knew, but had given her the time she'd needed alone. He was the one she trusted most. The son of her mother's brother—the uncle she'd seen cut down in the vision.

He jumped lightly to his feet when she approached, and simply held open his arms. Going into them, she rested her head on his chest. "Larkin."

"We'll hunt them. We'll find them and kill them. What-ever they are."

"I know what they are, and we will find them, kill them. But not here. Not now." She drew back. "Morrigan came to me, and told me what must be done."

"Morrigan?"

At the suspicion on his face she was able to smile a little. "I'll never understand how someone with your skills doubts the gods." She lifted a hand to his cheek. "But will you trust me?"

He framed her face, kissed her forehead. "You know I will."

As she told him what she'd been told, his face changed again. He sat on the ground, shoving a hand through his mane of tawny hair. She'd envied his hair as long as she'd lived, mourning the fact that she'd been given ordinary brown. His eyes were tawny as well, gilded she'd always thought, while hers were gray as rain.

He'd been gifted with more height, as well as other things she envied.

When she was finished, she drew a long breath. "Will you go with me?"

"I'd hardly let you go alone." His hand closed over hers, firm and steady. "Moira, how can you be sure this vision wasn't simply your heartbreak?"

"I know. I can only tell you that I know what I saw was real. But if it's nothing more than grief, we'll only have wasted the time it takes to go to the dance. Larkin, I need to try."

"Then we'll try."

"We tell no one."

"Moira—"

"Listen to me." Urgently, she gripped his wrists. "Your father would do his best to stop us. Or to come with us if he believed me. This isn't the way, it isn't my charge. One, the goddess told me. I was to take only one, the one I trusted most. It can only be you. We'll write it down for him. While we're gone, he'll rule Geall, and protect it."

"You'll take the sword—" Larkin began.

"No. The sword isn't to leave here. That was a sacred oath, and I won't be the one to break it. The sword remains until I return. I don't take my place until I lift it, I don't lift it until I've earned my place. There are other swords. Arm yourself, she said, so see that you do. Meet me in an hour. Tell no one."

She squeezed his hands now. "Swear to me on the blood we share. On the loss we share."

How could he deny her when tears were still on her cheeks? "I swear it to you. I'll tell no one." He gave her arms a quick rub in comfort. "We'll be back by supper, I wager, in any case."

She hurried home, across the field and up the hill to the castle where her blood had reigned over the land since it was created. Those she passed bowed their heads to her to show their sympathy, and she saw tears glimmer.

And she knew when they dried, many would look to her for guidance, for answers. Many would wonder how she would rule.

So did she.

She crossed the great hall. There was no laughter here now, no music. Gathering the burdensome skirts of her gown, she climbed the steps to her chamber.

There were women nearby, sewing, tending to children, speaking in low voices so it sounded like doves cooing.

Moira went quietly by, and slipped into her room. She exchanged her gown for riding clothes, laced on her boots. It felt wrong to put off her mourning garb so quickly, so easily, but she would travel more swiftly in the tunic and tewes. She bound her hair back in a braid and began to pack.

She would need little but what was on her back, she decided. She would think of this as a hunting trip—there, at least, she had some skill. And so she got out her quiver and her bow, a short sword and lay them on the bed while she sat to write a message to her uncle.

How did you tell a man who'd stood in as father for so many years that you were taking his son into a battle you didn't understand, to fight what was impossible to comprehend, in the company of men you didn't know?

The will of the gods, she thought, her mouth tight as she wrote. She wasn't certain if she followed that or simply her own rage. But go she would.

I must do this thing, she continued in a careful hand. *I pray you will forgive me for it, and that I go only for the sake of Geall. I ask that if I don't return by Samhain, you lift the sword and rule in my place. Know that I go for you, for Geall, and that I swear by my mother's blood, I will fight to the death to defend and protect what I love.*

Now I leave what I love in your hands.

She folded the letter, heated the wax and sealed it.

She put on the sword, shouldered her quiver and bow. One of the women bustled out as she left her chambers.

"My lady!"

"I wish to ride out alone." Her voice was so sharp, her manner so curt that there was nothing but a gasp behind her as she strode away.

Her belly shook, but she didn't pause. When she reached the stables, she waved the boy away and saddled her mount herself. She looked down at him, his soft, young face bursting with freckles.

"When the sun sets, you're to stay inside. This night and every night until I tell you. Do you heed me?"

"Aye, my lady."

She wheeled her horse, kicked her heels lightly at its flanks, riding off at a gallop.

She would not look back, Moria thought. She would not look back at home, but forward.

Larkin was waiting for her, sitting loose in the saddle while his horse cropped grass.

"I'm sorry, it took longer."

"Women always take longer."

"I'm asking so much of you. What if we never get back?"

He clicked to his horse, walking it beside hers. "Since I don't believe we're going anywhere, I'm not worried." He sent her an easy smile. "I'm just indulging you."

"I'd feel nothing but relief if this is nothing more than that." But once again she urged her horse to the gallop. Whatever was waiting, she wanted to meet it quickly.

He matched her pace as they rode, as they had so often, over the hills that sparkled in the sunlight. Buttercups dotted the fields with yellow, giving swarms of butterflies a reason to dance in the air. She watched a hawk circle overhead, and some of the heaviness lifted from her.

Her mother had loved to watch the hawk. She'd said it was Moira's father, there to look down on them while he flew free. Now she prayed her mother flew free as well.

The hawk circled over the ring of stones, and raised its cry.

Nerves made her queasy so she swallowed hard.

"Well, we made it this far." Larkin shook back his hair. "What do you suggest?"

"Are you cold? Do you feel the cold?"

"No. It's warm. The sun's strong today."

"Something's watching." She shivered even as she dismounted. "Something cold."

"There's nothing here but us." But when he jumped down from his horse, Larkin laid a hand on the hilt of his sword.

"It sees." There were voices in her head, whispers and murmurs. As if in a trance, she took her bag from the saddle. "Take what you need. Come with me."

"You're acting considerably strange, Moira." With a sigh, Larkin took his own bag, tossing it over his shoulder as he caught up with her.

"She can't enter here. Never. No matter what her power, she can never enter this circle, never touch these stones. If she tries she'll burn. She knows, she hates."

"Moira . . . your eyes."

She turned them on him. They were nearly black, and they were depthless. And when she opened her hand, there was a wand of crystal in it. "You are bound, as I am bound, to do this thing. You are my blood." She took her short sword, cut her palm, then reached for his.

"Well, bollocks." But he held out his hand, let her slice across the palm.

She sheathed the knife, gripped his bloody hand with hers. "Blood is life, and blood is death," she said. "And here it opens the way."

With his hand in hers, she stepped into the circle.

"Worlds wait," she began, chanting the words that swirled in her head. "Time flows. Gods watch. Speak the words with me."

Her hand throbbed in his as they repeated the words.

The wind swirled, whipping the long grass, snapping their cloaks. Instinctively, Larkin put his free arm around her, folding her into him as he tried to use his body as a shield. Light burst, blinding them.

She gripped his hand, and felt the world spin.

Then the dark. Damp grass, misty air.

They still stood within the circle, on that same rise. But not the same, she realized. The forest beyond wasn't quite the same.

"The horses are gone."

She shook her head. "No. We are."

He looked up. He could see the moon swimming behind the clouds. The dying wind was cold enough to reach his bones. "It's night. It was barely midday and now it's night. Where the bloody hell are we?"

"Where we're meant to be, that's all I know. We need to find the others."

He was baffled, and unnerved. And could admit that he hadn't thought beyond the moment. That would stop now, for now he had only one charge. To protect his cousin.

"What we're going to do is look for shelter and wait for sunrise." He tossed her his pack, then started to stride out of the circle. As he walked, he changed.

The shape of his body, the sinew, the bone. In place of skin a pelt, tawny as his hair, in place of hair a mane. Now a stallion stood where the man had been.

"Well, I suppose that would be quicker." Ignoring the knots in her belly, Moira mounted. "We'll ride the way that would be toward home. I think that makes the most sense— if any of this does. Best not gallop, in case that way is different from what we know."

He set off in a trot, while she scanned the trees and the moonstruck hills. So much the same, she thought, but with subtle differences.

There was a great oak where none had been before, and the murmur of a spring in the wrong direction. Nor was the road the same. She nudged Larkin off it, in the direction where home would be if this were her world.

They moved into the trees, picking their way now carefully, following instinct and a rough path.

He stopped, lifted his head as if scenting the air. His body shifted under her as he turned. She felt muscles bunch.

"What is it? What do you—"

He flew, risking low branches, hidden rocks as he broke into a strong gallop. Knowing only he'd sensed danger, she lowered her body, clung to his mane. But it came like lighting, flying out of the trees as if it had wings. She had time to shout, time to reach for her sword before Larkin reared up, striking the thing with both hooves.

It screamed, tumbled off into the dark.

She would have urged him back into a gallop, but he was already shaking her off, already turning back into a man. They stood back-to-back now, swords drawn.

"The circle," she whispered. "If we can get back to the circle."

He shook his head. "They've cut us off," he replied. "We're surrounded."

They came slowly now, slinking out of the shadows. Five, no six, Moira saw as her blood chilled. Their fangs gleamed in the shivering moonlight.

"Stay close," Larkin told her. "Don't let them draw you away from me."

One of the things laughed, a sound that was horribly human. "You've come a long way to die," it said.

And leaped.

Chapter 8

Too restless to sleep, Glenna wandered the house. It was big enough, she supposed, to accommodate an army—certainly large enough to keep four relative strangers comfortable and afford some privacy. There were high ceilings—gorgeous with ornate plaster work—and steps that spiraled or curved to more rooms. Some of those rooms were small as cells, others spacious and airy.

Chandeliers were iron, the style intricate and artful and leaning toward the Gothic. They suited the house more than anything contemporary, or even the elegance of crystal.

Intrigued by the look, she went back for a camera. While she wandered, she paused when the mood struck, framed in a portion of ceiling, or a light. She spent thirty minutes alone on the dragons carved into the black marble of the fireplace in the main parlor.

Wizards, vampires, warriors. Marble dragons and ancient houses secluded in deep woods. Plenty of fodder for her art, she thought. She could very well make up the hit to her income when she got back to New York.

Might as well think positive.

Cian must have spent a great deal of time and money refurbishing, modernizing, decorating, she decided. But then, he had plenty of both. Rich colors, rich fabrics, gleaming antiques gave the house a sense of luxury and style. And yes, she thought, the place just sat here, year after year, empty and echoing.

A pity, really. A waste of beauty and history. She deplored waste.

Still, it was lucky he had it. Its location, its size, and she supposed, its history made it the perfect base.

She found the library and nodded in approval. It boasted three staggered tiers of books, towering to the domed ceiling where another dragon—stained glass this time—breathed fire and light.

There were candlestands taller than a man, and lamps with jeweled shades. She didn't doubt the lake-sized Oriental rugs were the genuine articles and possibly hundreds of years old.

Not only a good base, she mused, but an extremely comfortable one. With its generous library table, deep chairs and enormous fireplace, she deemed this the perfect war room.

She indulged herself by lighting the fire and the lamps to dispel the gloom of the gray day. From her own supply, she gathered crystals, books, candles, arranging them throughout the room.

Though she wished for flowers, it was a start. But more was needed. Life didn't run on style, on luck, or on magic alone.

"What're you up to, Red?"

She turned, saw King filling the doorway. "I guess we could call it nesting."

"Hell of a nest."

"I was thinking the same. And I'm glad you're here. You're just the man I need."

"You and every other woman. What've you got in mind?"

"Practicalities. You've been here before, right?"

"Yeah, a couple times."

"Where are the weapons?" When his eyebrows shot up, she spread her arms. "Those pesky items required for fighting wars—or so I've heard, since this would be my first war. I know I'd feel better if I had a couple of howitzers handy."

"Don't think the boss runs to those."

"What does he run to?"

He considered. "What you got going in here?"

She glanced toward the crystals. "Just some things I've set around for protection, courage, creativity and so on. This struck me as a good place to strategize. A war room. What?" she said when his lips curved in a wide grin.

"Guess you're on to something." He walked over to a wall of books, ran his big fingers along the carved trim.

"You're not going to tell me there's a . . . secret panel," she finished with a delighted laugh when the wall swiveled out.

"Place is full of 'em." King pushed the wall completely around before she could peek through the gap. "I don't know as he'd want you poking around in the passages. But you said weapons." He gestured. "You got weapons."

Swords, axes, maces, daggers, scythes. Every manner of blade hung gleaming on the exposed wall. There were crossbows, long bows, even what she thought was a trident.

"That's just a little bit scary," she declared, but stepped forward to take down a small dagger.

"Little advice," King began. "You use something like that, whatever's coming for you is going to have to get real close before it does you any good."

"Good point." She replaced the dagger, took down a sword. "Wow. Heavy." She replaced it, took down what she thought would be termed a foil. "Better."

"You got any idea how to use that?"

"Hack, hack, hack, jab, jab?" She gave it a testing swing, found herself surprised she liked the feel of it. "Okay, no. Not a clue. Someone will have to teach me."

"Do you think you could slice through flesh with that?" Cian spoke as he came in the room. "Strike bone, spill blood?"

"I don't know." She lowered the sword. "I'm afraid I'm going to have to find out. I saw what she was, what she did, what she has with her. I'm not going into this with only potions and spells. And I'm sure as hell not going to stand there and go *eek* if she tries to bite me."

"You can wound them with that, slow them down. But you won't kill, you won't stop them unless you use it to cut off the head."

With a grimace she studied the slender blade, then resigned, put it back, took down the heavier sword.

"Swinging that around takes a great deal of strength."

"Then I'll get strong, strong enough."

"Muscle's not the only kind of strength you'll need."

She kept her gaze level. "I'll get strong enough. You know how to use this. You and Hoyt, and you," she said to King. "If you think I'm going to sit back, stirring a cauldron when it comes time to fight, think again. I wasn't brought here so I could have men protect me. I wasn't given this gift to be a coward."

"Me," King said with that wide grin in place again, "I like a woman with grit."

Gripping the hilt with both hands, she sliced the air with the blade. "So. When's my first lesson?"

Hoyt descended the stairs. He tried not to mourn what was changed, what was gone. He would get back, back to his true home, back to his family, and his life.

He would see the torches flaming on the walls again, smell his mother's roses in the garden. And he would walk the cliffs beyond his own cottage in Chiarrai again, and know the world was free of the vermin that sought to destroy it.

He'd needed rest, that was all. Rest and solitude in a place he knew and understood. Now he would work, and he would plan. He was done with this sensation of being swept away into what he couldn't understand.

Darkness had fallen, and those lights—those strange, harsh lights that came from electricity rather than fire—illuminated the house.

It irritated him that he found no one about, and could scent no supper cooking from the direction of the kitchen. It was time to be busy, and time the rest understood it was necessary to take the next steps.

A sound made him pause, then hiss out a breath. He followed the sound of clashing steel at a run. Then he swung toward where a doorway had been and cursed when he found sheer wall. He sprinted around it, and burst into the library where he saw his brother slashing a sword toward Glenna.

He didn't think; didn't hesitate. He punched his power toward Cian, and sent his sword spinning away to clatter on the floor. With her forward motion unblocked, Glenna sliced Cian's shoulder.

"Well, shit." Cian flicked a hand at the sword even as Glenna pulled it back in horror.

"Oh God! Oh my God. Is it bad? How bad?" She dropped her sword to rush forward.

"Back!" With another sweep of power, Hoyt had Glenna tumbling back and landing on her ass. "You want blood?" Hoyt plucked up Glenna's discarded sword. "Come then, get mine."

King grabbed a sword from the wall, slapped the blade against Hoyt's. "Back off, magic boy. Now."

"Don't interfere," Cian said to King. "Step away." Slowly, Cian picked up his own sword, met Hoyt's eyes. "You tempt me."

"Stop it! Stop it this minute. What the hell's wrong with you?" Regardless of the blades, Glenna pushed between the brothers. "I've stabbed him, for God's sake. Let me see."

"He attacked you."

"He did not. He was giving me a lesson."

"It's nothing." With his gaze still burning into Hoyt's, Cian nudged Glenna aside. "Shirt's ruined, and it's the second I've trashed on your account. If I'd wanted her blood, I wouldn't take it with a sword, waste it. But for yours, I could make an exception."

Glenna's breath wanted to heave, the words wanted to babble. But if she knew anything about men, she knew it would take only a flick of a finger to have these two spilling each other's blood.

Instead she spoke sharply—annoyed female to foolish boys. "It was a mistake, an accident on all sides. I appreciate you coming to the rescue," she said to Hoyt. "But I didn't, and don't need the white horse. And you—." She jabbed a finger at Cian. "You know very well what it must have looked like to him, so take it down a little. And you." She rounded on King. "You can just stop standing over there adding to it."

"Hey! All I did was—"

"Add more trouble," she interrupted. "Now go, get some bandages."

"I don't need them." Cian walked back to replace his sword. "I heal quickly, which is something you need to bear in mind." He held out a hand for King's sword. The glance Cian gave him might have been affectionate, Glenna thought. Or proud. "Unlike our irritated witch, I appreciate the gesture."

"No big." King handed Cian the sword, then sent Glenna a kind of sheepish shrug.

Unarmed now, Cian turned back to his brother. "You couldn't beat me with a sword when I was human. You damn well couldn't take me now."

Glenna put a hand on Hoyt's arm, felt the muscles quiver. "Put it down," she said quietly. "This needs to stop." She ran her hand down his arm to his wrist, then took the sword.

"The blade needs cleaning," Cian commented.

"I'll take care of it." King stepped away from the wall. "I'll toss something together for dinner while I'm at it. Got my appetite worked up."

Even after he walked out, Glenna thought there was so much testosterone in the room she couldn't have hacked through it with one of Cian's battleaxes.

"Can we move on?" she said briskly. "I thought we could use the library for our war room. And considering the weapons in here, and the books on magic, warfare, vampires and demons, it seems appropriate. I've got some ideas—"

"I bet you do," Cian mumbled.

"The first . . ." She moved to the table, picked up her crystal ball.

"Did you learn nothing the first time?" Hoyt demanded.

"I don't want to look for her. We know where she is. Or was." She wanted to change the mood. If there had to be tension, she thought, at least they could use it constructively.

"Others are coming, that's what we keep being told. There will be others. I think it's time we find some of them."

He'd planned to do exactly that, but could hardly say so now without looking foolish. "Put that down. It's too soon to use it after the last time."

"I've cleansed and recharged it."

"Regardless." He turned to the fire. "We'll do this my way."

"A familiar refrain." Cian stepped over to a cabinet, took out a heavy decanter. "Have at it then, the pair of you. I'm having a brandy. Elsewhere."

"Please stay." Glenna offered a smile, and there was both apology and cajolery in it. "If we find someone, you should be here to see. We need to decide what to do. All of us need to decide. In fact, I should go get King, so the four of us can do this."

Hoyt ignored them, but found it wasn't quite as simple to ignore the little prick that might have been jealousy. Teaching her swordplay and her fretting over the slightest scratch.

He spread his hands, and began to focus on the fire, using his annoyance to mix the heat.

"A nice thought." Cian nodded toward Hoyt. "But it seems he's already started."

"Well, for— All right then, all right. But we should cast a circle."

"I don't need one for this. Witches are forever casting circles, spinning rhymes. That's why true sorcery eludes them."

When Glenna's mouth dropped open, Cian grinned at her, added a wink. "Always been full of himself. Brandy?"

"No." Glenna set down her ball, folded her arms. "Thank you."

The fire snapped, rose higher and began to snap greedily at the logs.

He used his own tongue, the language of his birth and blood to draw the fire into a dance. Some part of him knew he was showing off, drawing out the moment and the drama.

With a billow of smoke, a hiss of flame, the images began to form in the flames. Shadows and movement, shapes and silhouettes. Now he forgot all but the magic and the purpose, all but the need and the power.

He felt Glenna move closer—in body and in mind. In magic.

In the flames, the shapes and silhouettes became.

A woman on horseback, her hair in a long braid down her back, a quiver of arrows over her shoulder. The horse was gold and sleek, and moved at a powerful, even reckless gallop through the dark forest. There was fear on the woman's face, and a steely determination along with it as she rode low, one hand clutched in the flying mane.

The man that wasn't a man leapt out of the forest, and was struck away. More took shape, sliding out of the dark, moving to surround.

The horse quivered, and in a sudden shimmer of light was a man, tall and lean and young. He and the woman stood back-to-back, blades drawn. And the vampires came for them.

"It's the road leading to the dance." Cian sprang toward the weapons, grabbed a sword and a two-headed ax. "Go in with King," he ordered Glenna as he raced for the window. "Stay here. Let no one in. No one and nothing."

"But—"

He threw up the window and seemed . . . seemed to *fly* out of it.

"Hoyt—"

But he was already grabbing a sword, a dagger. "Do as he says."

He was out the window himself, nearly as quickly as his brother. Glenna didn't hesitate. She followed.

He made for the stables, throwing his power ahead of him to open the doors. When the stallion charged out, Hoyt held up his hands to stop him. It was no time for niceties.

"Go back," he shouted at Glenna.

"I'm going with you. Don't waste time arguing. I'm in this, too." When he grabbed a handful of mane and sprang onto the horse's back, she tossed back her head. "I'll follow on foot."

He cursed her, but held down his hand for her to grip. The horse reared as King charged the stables. "What the hell's going on?"

"Trouble," Glenna shouted back. "On the road to the dance." When the horse reared again, she wrapped her arms tight around Hoyt. "Go!"

In the clearing, Moira fought, but no longer for her life. There were too many, and they were too strong. She believed she would die here. She fought for time, each precious moment of breath.

There was no room or time for her bow, but she had her short sword. She could hurt them, *did* hurt them. If her blade pierced flesh, they shrieked, and some fell back. But they rose again and came again.

She couldn't count them, no longer knew how many Larkin battled. But she knew if she fell, they would have him. So she fought to stand, fought just to hold on.

Two came at her, and with her breath sobbing out she hacked at one. His blood gushed out in a horrible scream as those red eyes rolled back to white. To her horror one of his fellows fell on him and began to drink. But still another got past her guard and sent her flying. It pounced on her like a mad dog with greedy fangs and red eyes.

She heard Larkin shout her name, heard the terror in it as she struggled. Those fangs grazed her throat, and the burn was beyond belief.

Something came out of the night, some dark warrior with sword and axe. What was on her was hurled away. Her dazed eyes watched him cleave the axe down, behead the thing. It screamed and flashed, and turned to dust.

"Take their head," the warrior shouted to Larkin, then turned burning blue eyes on her. "Use your arrows. Wood through the heart."

Then his sword began to sing and slice.

She gained her feet, yanked an arrow out of her quiver. Tried to steady her blood-slicked hand to notch it on the bow. Rider coming, she thought dimly when she heard the thunder of hoofbeats.

Another came for her, a girl younger than herself. Moira shifted, but there was no time to shoot. The girl leaped, and the arrow impaled her. There was nothing left but dust.

The horseman jumped down, sword already swinging.

They would not die, Moira thought as sweat dripped into her eyes. They would not die tonight. She notched an arrow, let it fly.

The three men had formed a triangle, and were beating the things back. One slithered through, crouched to charge the horse where a woman sat watching the battle. Moira scrambled forward, trying to find a clear shot, but could only call out a warning.

The second warrior spun around, sword raised as he prepared to attack. But the woman reared back the horse, so its hooves flashed out to strike the thing down.

When the sword sliced through its neck, there was nothing left but blood and dust.

In the silence, Moira sank to her knees, fighting for breath and against a terrible sickness. Larkin dropped down beside her, running his hands over her body, her face. "You're hurt. You're bleeding."

"Not bad. Not bad." Her first battle, she thought. And she was alive. "You?"

"Nicks, scratches. Can you get up? I'll carry you."

"I can get up, yes, and no, you won't carry me." Still kneeling, she looked up at the man who'd come out of the dark. "You saved my life. Thank you. I think we've come to find you, but I'm grateful you found us instead. I'm Moira, and we've come through the dance from Geall."

He simply looked at her for what seemed like the longest moment. "We need to get back, and inside. It isn't safe here."

"Larkin is my name." He held out a hand. "You fight like a demon."

"True enough." Cian clasped hands briefly. "Let's get them back," he said to Hoyt, and glanced toward Glenna. "The two of you helped yourself to my horse. Good thinking as it turned out. She can ride up with Glenna."

"I can walk," Moira began only to find herself lifted off her feet and onto the horse.

"We need to move," Cian said briskly. "Hoyt, take point, and you stay beside the women. I'm behind you."

Hoyt laid a hand on the stallion's neck as he passed, and glanced up at Glenna. "You've a steady seat."

"I've been riding since I was four. Don't think about trying to leave me behind again." Then she turned on the horse to look over her shoulder at Moira. "I'm Glenna. Nice to meet you."

"It's the pure truth I can't think of anyone in my life it's been nicer to meet." As the horse moved forward, Moira risked a look back. She couldn't see the warrior. He seemed to have melted into the dark.

"What is his name? The one who came on foot?"

"That would be Cian. Hoyt's up ahead. They're brothers, and there's a great deal to explain on all sides. But one thing's for damn sure, we just survived our first battle. And we kicked some vampire ass."

Moira bided her time. Under normal circumstances she would have considered herself a guest, and behaved accordingly. But she knew that was far from the case. She and Larkin were soldiers now, in what was a very small army.

It may have been foolish, but she was relieved not to be the only woman.

Inside the manor house, she sat in a wondrous kitchen. A huge man with skin dark as coal worked at a stove, though she didn't think he was a servant.

He was called King, but she understood this wasn't his rank. He was a man, like the others. A soldier like her.

"We'll patch you up," Glenna told her. "If you want to clean up first, I can show you upstairs."

"Not until we're all here."

Glenna cocked her head. "All right then. I don't know about the rest of you, but I want a drink."

"I'd kill for one," Larkin said with a quick smile. "Actually, it seems I have. I didn't believe you, not really." He laid a hand on Moira's. "I'm sorry."

"It's all right, it's no matter. We're alive, and where we're meant to be. That's what matters." She looked up as the door opened. But it was Hoyt who came in, not the one called Cian. Still she got to her feet.

"We haven't thanked you properly for coming to help us. There were so many. We were losing until you came."

"We've been waiting for you."

"I know. Morrigan showed you to me. And you," she said to Glenna. "Is this Ireland?"

"It is, yes."

"But—"

Moira merely laid a hand on Larkin's shoulder. "My cousin believes Ireland is a fairy tale, even now. We come from Geall, that which was made by the gods from a handful of Ireland, to grow in peace and to be ruled by the descendent of the great Finn."

"You're the scholar."

"Well, she loves her books, that's for certain. Now this is fine," Larkin said after a sip of wine.

"And the one of many shapes," Hoyt added.

"That'd be me, all right."

When the door opened again, Moira felt relief rush through her like a tide.

Cian flicked a glance at her, then at Glenna. "She needs tending to."

"Wouldn't budge until the gang was all here. Why don't you finish your wine, Larkin? Moira, come on upstairs with me."

"I have so many questions."

"We all do. Let's talk over dinner." Glenna took Moira's hand, drew her out.

Cian poured himself a drink, dropped down at the table. There was blood soaked through his shirt. "Do you usually bring your woman into strange places?"

Larkin took another gulp of wine. "She wouldn't be my woman, but my cousin, and fact of it is, she brought me. Had a vision or a dream or something mystical or other—which isn't that unusual for her. Fanciful sort, she is. But she was bound and determined to do this thing, and I couldn't have stopped her. Those things out there, some came to Geall. They killed her mother."

He took another deep drink. "We buried her this morning, if time's the same here. Ripped her to pieces is what they did. Moira saw it."

"How did she survive to tell it?"

"She doesn't know. At least—well, she won't really speak of it. Not as yet."

Upstairs, Moira washed in the shower as Glenna had showed her. The sheer pleasure of it helped ease her aches and hurts, and she considered the heat of the water nothing short of miraculous.

When the blood and sweat had been washed away, she put on the robe Glenna left her, then came out to find her new friend waiting in the bedchamber.

"No wonder we speak of Ireland like a fairy tale. It seems like one."

"You look better. Some color in your cheeks. Let's have a look at that wound on your neck."

"It burns, considerable." Moira touched her fingers to it. "It's hardly more than a scratch."

"It's still a vampire bite." Examining it closely, Glenna pursed her lips. "Not a puncture though, or just barely, so that's good. I've got something that should help."

"How did you know where to find us?"

"We saw you in the fire." Glenna poked into her case for the right balm.

"You're the witch."

"Mmm-hmm. Here we are."

"And the one called Hoyt is the sorcerer."

"Yes. He's not from this world either—or not from this time. It looks like they're getting us from all over hell and back. How does that feel?"

"Cool." Moira let out a sigh as the balm eased the burn. She raised her eyes to Glenna's. "Lovely, thanks. And Cian, what manner of man is he?"

Glenna hesitated. Full disclosure, she decided. Honesty and trust had to be bywords of their little battalion. "He's a vampire."

Going pale again, Moira pushed to her feet. "Why would you say that? He fought them, he saved my life. He's even now down in the kitchen, inside the house. Why would you call him a monster, a demon?"

"I didn't, because I don't consider him either. He's a vampire, and has been one for over nine hundred years. The one who made him is called Lilith, and she's the one we need to worry about. He's Hoyt's brother, Moira, and he's pledged to fight just like the rest of us."

"If what you say . . . He isn't human."

"Your cousin changes into a horse. I'd say that makes him something more than human, too."

"It's not the same."

"Maybe not. I don't have the answers. I do know Cian didn't ask for what happened to him all those years ago. I know he's helped us get here, and he was the first one out of the house to fight for you when we saw you in the fire. I know how you're feeling."

In her mind Moira saw what had been done to her mother, heard the screams, smelled the blood. "You couldn't know."

"Well, I know I didn't trust him initially either. But I do now. Completely. And I know we need him to win this. Here. I brought you some clothes. I'm taller than you, but you can just roll up the pants until we get you something that fits better. We'll go down, have a meal, talk some of this through. And see what goes."

It seemed they would eat in the kitchen, like family or like servants. Moira wondered if she could eat at all, but found her appetite huge. The chicken was fried juicy and crisp with heaps of potatoes and snap beans.

The vampire ate little.

"We're gathered," Hoyt began, "and must gather more at some point yet to be known. But it was to start with us, and so it has. Tomorrow we'll begin to train, to learn. Cian, you know best how to fight them. You'll be in charge. Glenna and I will work on the magicks."

"I need to train, too."

"Then you'll be busy. We'll need to find our strengths, and our weaknesses. We need to be ready when the final battle takes place."

"In the world of Geall," Moira said, "in the Valley of Silence, in the Mountains of Mist. On the sabbot of Samhain." Avoiding Cian's eyes she looked at Hoyt. "Morrigan showed me."

"Aye." He nodded. "I saw you there."

"When the time comes, we'll go through the dance again, and march to the battleground. It's five days' walk, so we'll need to leave in good time."

"Are there those in Geall who'll fight with us?"

"Any and all will fight. Any and all would die to save our home, and the worlds." The burden of it weighed down on her. "I have only to ask."

"You have a lot of faith in your fellow man," Cian commented.

She looked at him now, forced herself to meet his eyes. Blue, she thought, and beautiful. Would they go demon-red when he fed?

"So I do. And in my countrymen, and in humankind. And if I did not, I would order it so. For when I return to Geall, I must go to the Royal Stone, and if I'm worthy, if I'm the one as there is no other, I will pull the sword from that sheath. And I will be queen of Geall. I won't see my people slaughtered by what made you what you are. Not like lambs. If they die, they'll die in battle."

"You should know that the little skirmish you came through tonight was nothing. It was nothing. What were there? Eight, ten of them? There'll be thousands." He got to his feet. "She's had nearly two thousand years to make her army. Your farmers will have to do more than beat their plowshares into swords to survive."

"Then they will."

He inclined his head. "Be ready to train hard, and not tomorrow. Starting tonight. You forget, brother, I sleep days."

He left them with that.

Chapter 9

Glenna signalled to Hoyt, and left the others to King. She glanced back toward the kitchen, down toward the hall. She had no idea where Cian had gone.

"We need to talk. In private."

"We need to work."

"I won't argue with that, but you and I need to go over some things. Alone."

He frowned at her, but nodded. If she wanted privacy, there was one place he could be sure of it. He lead the way up the stairs, wound his way up to his tower.

Glenna wandered the room, studied his work areas, his books and tools. She went to each narrow window, opened the glass that had been put there since his day, closed it again.

"Nice. Very nice. Are you going to share the wealth?"

"What is your meaning?"

"I need a place to work—more, I'd say you and I need a place to work together. Don't give me that look." She waved a hand at him as she walked over to shut the door.

"What look would that be?"

"The 'I'm a solitary sorcerer and don't care for witches'

look. We're stuck with each other, and with the rest. Somehow, God knows, we have to become a unit. Because Cian's right."

She walked back to one of the windows, looked out into the moonstruck dark. "He's right. She'll have thousands. I never looked that far, never thought that big—though, Jesus, what's bigger than an apocalypse? But of course, she'll have thousands. We have a handful."

"It's as it was told to us," he reminded her. "We're the first, the circle."

She turned back, and though her eyes stayed level, he saw the fear in them. And the doubt. "We're strangers, and far from ready to join hands in a circle and chant some unity spell. We're uneasy and suspicious of each other. Even resentful when it comes to you and your brother."

"I don't resent my brother."

"Of course, you do." She pushed at her hair, and now he saw frustration as well. "You drew a sword on him a couple of hours ago."

"I thought he—"

"Yes, yes, and more gratitude for rushing to my rescue."

Her dismissive tone insulted his chivalry, and put his back up. "You're bloody welcome."

"If you actually save my life at some point, my gratitude will be sincere, I promise you. But defending the damsel was only part of it, and answering that was only part of why he very nearly fought you. You know it, I know it, and so does he."

"That being the case, there's no need for you to babble on about it."

She stepped forward. He saw with some satisfaction his wasn't the only back up now. "You're angry with him for letting himself be killed, and worse, changed. He's angry with you for dragging him into this, and forcing him to remember what he was before Lilith got her fangs into him. All of that's a waste of time and energy. So, we either have to get past those emotions, or we have to use them. Because as it stands, as we stand, she's going to slaughter us, Hoyt. I don't want to die."

"If you're afraid—"

"Of course I'm afraid. Are you stupid? After what we've seen and dealt with tonight, we'd be morons not to be afraid." She pressed her hands to her face, struggled to even her breathing again. "I know what has to be done, but I don't know how to do it. And neither do you. None of us do."

She dropped her hands, went to him. "Let's you and I be honest here. We have to depend on each other, have to trust each other, so let's be honest. We're a handful—with power, yes, with skills—but a handful against untold numbers. How do we survive this, much less win?"

"We gather more."

"How?" She lifted her hands. "How? In this time, in this place, Hoyt, people don't believe. Anyone who goes around talking openly about vampires, sorcerers, apocalyptic battles and missions from gods is either considered eccentric—best case—or put in a padded cell."

Needing the contact, she brushed a hand down his arm. "We have to face it. There's no cavalry coming to the rescue here. We *are* the cavalry."

"You give me problems, but no solutions."

"Maybe." She sighed. "Maybe. But you can't find solutions until you outline the problems. We're ridiculously outnumbered. We're going up against creatures—for lack of a better word—that can only be killed in a limited number of ways. They are controlled or led or driven by a vampire of enormous power and, well, thirst. I don't know much about warfare, but I know when the odds aren't in my favor. So we have to even the odds."

She spoke the kind of cold-blooded sense he couldn't deny. The fact that she would say it was, in his mind, another kind of courage. "How?"

"Well, we can't go out and cut off thousands of heads, it's just not practical. So we find the way to cut off the head of the army. Hers."

"If it were so simple, it would already be done."

"If it were impossible, we wouldn't be here." Frustrated, she rapped a fist on his arm. "Work with me, will you?"

"I haven't a choice in that."

Now there was hurt, just the shadow of it in her eyes. "Is it really so distasteful to you? Am I?"

"No." And more than a shadow of shame in his. "I'm sorry. No not distasteful. Difficult. Distracting. You're distracting, the way you look, the way you smell, the way you are."

"Oh." Her lips curved up slowly. "That's interesting."

"I don't have time for you, in that way."

"What way? Be specific." It wasn't fair, she knew, to tease and to tempt. But it was a relief to simply be human.

"Lives are at stake."

"What's the point of living without feeling? I feel for you. You stir something in me. Yes, it's difficult, and it's distracting. But it tells me I'm here, and that being afraid isn't all there is. I need that, Hoyt. I need to feel more than afraid."

He lifted a hand to brush his fingers over her cheek. "I can't promise to protect you, but only to try."

"I'm not asking you to protect me. I'm not asking you for anything—yet—more than truth."

He kept his hand on her face, bringing his other up to join it in framing her as he lowered his lips. Hers parted for him, offering. So he took, needing as she did, to feel and to know.

To be human.

It was a slow simmering in the blood, a lazy tightening of muscle, a flutter of pulse—hers and his.

So easy, he thought, so easy to sink into the warm and the soft. To be surrounded by her in the dark and let himself forget, for a moment, for an hour, all that lay before them.

Her arms slid around him, linking his waist as she shifted up on her toes to meet his mouth more truly. He tasted her lips and her tongue, and the promise of them. This could be his. And he wanted to believe it more than he'd ever believed anything.

Her lips moved on his, forming his name—once, then twice. A sudden spark flared, simmer to sizzle. The heat of it rippled over his skin, burned into his heart.

Behind them, the fire that had gone to embers flared up like a dozen torches.

He drew her back, but his hands still lingered on her cheeks. He could see the fire dance in her eyes.

"There's truth in that," he whispered. "But I don't know what it is."

"Neither do I. But I feel better for it. Stronger." She looked toward the fire. "We're stronger together. That means something."

She stepped back. "I'm going to bring my things up here, and we'll work together and find out what it means."

"You think lying together is the answer?"

"It may be, or may be one of them. But I'm not ready to lie with you yet. My body is," she admitted. "But my mind isn't. When I give myself to someone, it's a commitment for me. A big one. Both of us have committed quite a bit already. We'll both have to be sure we're ready to give more."

"Then what was this?"

"Contact," she said quietly. "Comfort." She reached a hand for his. "Connection. We're going to make magic together, Hoyt, serious magic. That's as intimate to me as sex. I'm going to get what I need, bring it up."

Women, he thought, were powerful and mystical creatures even without witchcraft. Add that dose of power and a man was at a serious sort of disadvantage.

Wasn't her scent still wrapped around him, and the taste of her still on his lips? Women's weapons, he decided. Just as slipping away was a kind of weapon.

He'd do well to arm himself against that sort of thing.

She intended to work here in his tower, alongside him. There was good, strong sense in that. But how was a man supposed to work when his thoughts kept drifting to a woman's mouth, or her skin, her hair, her voice?

Perhaps he'd be wise to make use of a barrier, at least temporarily. He moved to his worktable and prepared to do just that.

"Your potions and spells will have to wait," Cian said from the doorway. "And so will romance."

"I don't follow your meaning." Hoyt continued to work.

"I passed Glenna on the stairs. I know when a woman's had a man's hands on her. I could smell you on her. Not that I blame you," Cian added lazily as he strolled into and around the room. "That's a very sexy witch you have there.

Desirable," he added at his brother's stony look. "Alluring. Bed her if you like, but later."

"Who I bed, and when, is nothing to you."

"Who, certainly not, but when's another matter. We'll use the great hall for combat training. King and I have already begun to set up. I don't intend to end up with a stake through my heart because you and the redhead are too busy to train."

"It won't be a problem."

"I don't intend to let it be. The newcomers are unknown entities. The man fights well enough with a sword, but he's protective of his cousin. If she can't stand up in battle, we need to find another use for her."

"It's your job to see that she can, and will, stand up in battle."

"I'll work her," Cian promised. "And the rest of you. But we'll need more than swords and stakes, more than muscle."

"We'll have it. Leave that to me. Cian," he said before his brother could leave the room. "Did you ever see them again? Do you know how they fared, what became of them?"

He didn't have to be told his brother spoke of their family. "They lived and they died, as humans will."

"Is that all they are to you?"

"Shadows are what they are."

"You loved them once."

"My heart beat once as well."

"Is that the measure of love? A heartbeat?"

"We can love, even we can love. But to love a human?" Cian shook his head. "Only misery and tragedy could follow. Your parents sired what I was. Lilith made what I am."

"And do you have love for her?"

"For Lilith." His smile was slow, thoughtful. And humorless. "In my fashion. But don't worry. It won't stop me from destroying her. Come down, and we'll see what you're made of."

"Two hours' hand-to-hand, every day," Cian announced when they were gathered. "Two hours' weapons training, every day. Two hours' endurance, and two on martial arts. I'll work you here at night. King will take over in the daylight when you can train outdoors."

"We need time for study and strategy as well," Moira pointed out.

"Then make it. They're stronger than you, and more vicious than you can imagine."

"I know what they are."

Cian merely looked at her. "You think you do."

"Had you ever killed one before tonight?" she demanded.

"I have, more than one."

"In my world those that would kill their own kind are villains and outcasts."

"If I hadn't, you'd be dead."

He moved so quickly no one had a chance to react. He was behind Moira's back, an arm around her waist. And a knife at her throat. "Of course, I wouldn't need the knife."

"You're not to touch her." Larkin laid a hand on the hilt of his own knife. "You're not to put your hands on her."

"Stop me," Cian invited, and tossed his knife aside. "I've just snapped her neck." He laid his hands on either side of Moira's head, then gave her a little nudge that sent her careening into Hoyt. "Avenge her. Attack me."

"I won't attack the man who fought at my back."

"I'm not at your back now, am I? Show some spine, or don't the men of Geall have any?"

"We've plenty." Larkin drew his knife, crouched. Began to circle.

"Don't play at it," Cian taunted. "I'm unarmed. You have the advantage. Use it—quickly."

Larkin lunged—feinted, then slashed. And found himself flat on his back, with his knife skittering over the floor.

"You never have the advantage over a vampire. First lesson."

Larkin shook back his hair and grinned. "You're better than they were."

"Considerably." Amused, Cian held down a hand, helped Larkin to his feet.

"We'll start with some basic maneuvers, see what you're made of. Choose an opponent. You have one minute to take that opponent down—bare-handed. When I call switch, choose another. Move fast, and hard. Now."

He watched his brother hesitate and the witch turn into him, using her body to shift him off-balance, then hooking her foot behind his to send him down.

"Self-defense training," Glenna announced. "I live in New York."

While she was grinning, Hoyt swept her feet out from under her. Her ass hit the floorboards, hard. "Ouch. First request, we get pads for the floor."

"Switch!"

They moved, they maneuvered, grappled. And it was more game and competition than training. Even so, Glenna thought, she was going to have her share of bruises. She faced off with Larkin, sensed he would hold back. So she sent him a flirtatious smile, and when the laugh lit his eyes, flipped him over her shoulder.

"Sorry. I like to win."

"Switch."

The bulk of King filled her vision, and she looked up, up, until she met his eyes. "Me, too," he told her.

She went with instinct, a movement of her hands, a rapid chant. When he smiled blankly, she touched his arm. "Why don't you sit down?"

"Sure."

When he obeyed, she glanced over, saw Cian watching her. And flushed a little. "That was probably against the rules—and it's unlikely I'd be able to pull it off in the heat of battle, but I think it should count."

"There are no rules. She's not the strongest," he called out. "She's not the fastest. But she's the most clever of the lot of you. She uses wile and she uses wit as much as muscle and speed. Get stronger," he said to Glenna. "Get faster."

For the first time he smiled. "And get a sword. We'll start on weapons."

By the end of the next hour, Glenna was dripping sweat. Her sword arm ached like a bad tooth from shoulder to wrist. The thrill of the work, of actually doing something tangible had long since faded into a bitter exhaustion.

"I thought I was in good shape," she complained to Moira. "All those hours of pilates, of yoga, of weights—and I might as well be speaking to you in tongues."

"You're doing well." And Moira herself felt weak and clumsy.

"I'm barely standing. I do regular exercise, hard physical training, and this is turning me into a wimp. And you look beat."

"It's been a very long, very hard day."

"That's putting it mildly."

"Ladies? If I could trouble you to join us. Or would you rather have a seat and discuss fashion?"

Glenna set down her water bottle. "It's nearly three in the morning," she said to Cian. "A dangerous time for sarcasm."

"And prime time for your enemy."

"That may be, but not all of us are on that same clock just yet. And Moira and Larkin have traveled a hell of a long way today and dealt with a very nasty welcome. We need to train, you're absolutely right. But if we don't rest we're not going to get strong, and we're sure as hell not going to get fast. Look at her," Glenna demanded. "She can barely stay upright."

"I'm fine," Moira said quickly.

Cian gave her a long look. "Then we can blame fatigue for your sloppy swordsmanship and poor form."

"I do well enough with a sword." When she reached for it, blood in her eye, Larkin stepped up. He slapped a hand on her shoulder, and squeezed.

"Well enough she does, so she proved earlier tonight. But the blade wouldn't be my cousin's weapon of choice."

"Oh?" A wealth of boredom was contained in the single syllable.

"She's a decent hand with a bow."

"She can give us a demonstration tomorrow, but for now—"

"I can do it tonight. Open the doors."

The tone of command had Cian's brow winging up. "You don't rule here, little queen."

"Nor do you." She strode over, picked up bow and quiver. "Will you open the doors, or will I?"

"You're not to go out."

"He's right, Moira," Glenna began.

"I won't have to. Larkin, if you would."

Larkin moved to the doors and threw them open to the wide terrace beyond. Moira notched an arrow as she moved to the threshold. "The oak, I think."

Cian moved to her side as the others crowded in. "Not much of a distance."

"She wouldn't be meaning the near one," Larkin said and gestured. "But that one there, just to the right of the stables."

"Lowest branch."

"I can barely see it," Glenna commented.

"Can you?" Moira demanded of Cian.

"Perfectly."

She lifted the bow, steadied, sighted. And let the arrow fly.

Glenna heard the whiz, then a faint thunk as the arrow hit home. "Wow. Got ourselves a Robin Hood."

"Nicely shot," Cian said in mild tones, then turned to walk away. He sensed the movement even before he heard his brother's sharp command.

When he turned, Moira had another arrow ready, and aimed at him.

He sensed King prepare to rush forward, and held up a hand to stop him. "Be sure to hit the heart," he advised Moira. "Otherwise you'll just annoy me. Let it be," he snapped to Hoyt. "It's her choice."

The bow trembled a moment, then Moira lowered it. Lowered her eyes as well. "I need sleep. I'm sorry, I need sleep."

"Of course you do." Glenna took the bow from her, set it aside. "I'll take you down, get you settled." Glenna aimed a look at Cian every bit as sharp as the arrow as she led Moira from the room.

"I'm sorry," Moira said again. "I'm ashamed."

"Don't be. You're overtired, overworked. Over everything. We all are. And it's barely begun. A few hours' sleep is what we all need."

"Do they? Do they sleep?"

Glenna understood what she meant. The vampires. Cian. "Yes, it seems they do."

"I wish it was morning so I could see the sun. They crawl back into their holes with the sun. I'm too tired to think."

"Then don't. Here, let's get you undressed."

"I lost my pack in the woods, I think. I don't have a night-dress."

"We'll figure that out tomorrow. You can sleep naked. Do you want me to sit with you awhile?"

"No. Thank you, no." Tears welled up and were willed back. "I'm being a child."

"No. Just an exhausted woman. You'll be better in the morning. Good night."

Glenna debated going back up, then simply turned toward her own room. She didn't give a damn if the men thought she was copping out, she wanted sleep.

The dreams chased her, through the tunnels of the vampire's cave where the screams of the tortured were like slashing knives in her mind, into her heart. Everywhere she turned in the labyrinth, each time she raced into the dark opening like a mouth waiting to devour her, the screams followed.

And worse than the screams, even worse, was the laughter.

The dreams hunted her along the rocky shore of a boiling sea where red lightning hacked black sky, black sea. There the wind tore at her, there the rocks pierced up out of the ground to stab at her hands, her feet until both were bloody.

Into the dense woods that smelled of blood and death, where the shadows were so thick she could feel them brushing over her skin like cold fingers.

She could hear what craved her coming with the papery snap of wings, the slithery slide of snakes, the sly scrape of claw on earth.

She heard the wolf howl, and the sound was hunger.

They were everywhere she was, and she had nothing but her empty hands and pounding heart. Still she ran blindly, the scream trapped in her burning throat.

She burst out of the trees and onto a cliff above a raging sea. Below her, waves lashed at rocks that rose up, sharp as razors. Somehow in her terror she'd run in a circle, and was back above the cave that held something even death feared.

The wind whipped at her, and power sang in it. His power, the hot, clean power of the sorcerer. She reached for it, strained toward it. But it slipped through her shaking fingers and left her nothing but herself.

When she turned, Lilith stood, regal in red, her beauty luminous against the velvet black. At each side was a black wolf, quivering for the kill. Lilith stroked her hands over their backs, hands that glittered with rings.

And when she smiled, Glenna felt a terrible pull inside her own belly. A deep and terrible yearning.

"The devil or the deep blue." With a laugh, Lilith snapped her fingers for the wolves to sit. "The gods never give their servants decent choices, do they? I have better."

"You're death."

"No, no, no. I'm life. That's where they lie. They're death, flesh and bone moldering in the dirt. What do they give you these days? Seventy-five, eighty years? How small, how limiting."

"I'll take what I'm given."

"Then you'd be a fool. I think you're smarter than that, more practical. You know you can't win. You're already tired, already weary, already questioning. I'll offer you a way out, and more. So much more."

"To be like you? To hunt and kill? To drink blood?"

"Like champagne. Oh, the first taste of it. I envy you that. That first heady taste, that moment when everything falls away but the dark."

"I like the sun."

"With that complexion?" Lilith said with a gay laugh. "You'd fry like bacon after an hour on the beach. I'll show you the coolness. The cool, cool dark. It's inside you already, just waiting to be wakened. Can you feel it?"

Because she could, Glenna only shook her head.

"Liar. If you come to me, Glenna, you'll stand by my side. I'll give you life, eternal life. Eternal youth and beauty. Power so beyond what they've given you. You'll rule your own world. I would give you that, a world of your own."

"Why would you?"

"Why not? I'll have so many. And I'd enjoy the company
of a woman such as yourself. What are men, really, but tools
to us? If you want them, you'll take them. This is a great gift
I offer you."

"It's damnation you offer me."

Her laugh was lilting and seductive. "Gods frighten children with talk of hell and damnation. They use it to keep you
bound. Ask Cian if he would trade his existence, his eternity,
his handsome youth and lithe body for the chains and traps
of mortality. Never, I promise you. Come. Come with me,
and I'll give you pleasure beyond pleasure."

When she stepped closer, Glenna held up both hands,
drew what she could out of her chilled blood and struggled
to cast a protective circle.

Lilith simply struck out a hand. The tender blue of her
irises began to redden. "Do you think such puny magic will
hold me? I've drunk the blood of sorcerers, feasted on
witches. They're in me, as you will be. Come willing, and
take life. Fight, and take death."

She moved closer, and the wolves rose to stalk.

Glenna felt the pull, mesmerizing, glorious and dark, a
drawing up in the belly that was elemental. It seemed the
beat of her blood answered that call. Eternity and power,
beauty, youth. All for one moment.

She had only to reach for it.

Triumph lit Lilith's eyes, burned them to red. Fangs
flashed as she smiled.

Tears slid down Glenna's cheeks as she turned, as she
leaped toward the sea and the rocks. As she chose death.

There was a scream ripping through her head when she
shot up in bed. But it wasn't her own, she knew it wasn't her
own. It was Lilith's, a scream of fury.

With her breath sobbing, Glenna scrambled out of bed,
dragging the blanket with her. She ran, trembling from terror
and cold, her teeth chattering with them. She fled down the
hallway as if the demons were still after her. Instinct took
her to the one place, the only place, she felt safe.

Hoyt sprang out of a sound sleep to find his arms full of

naked, weeping woman. He could barely see her in the dim, predawn light, but he knew her scent, her shape.

"What? What's happened?" He started to shove her aside, to reach for the sword beside his bed. But she clung to him like ivy on an oak.

"Don't. Don't go. Hold on. Please, please, hold on."

"You're like ice." He dragged up the blanket, trying to find warmth for her, trying to find his wits. "Have you been outside? Bloody hell. Have you done some spell?"

"No, no, no." She burrowed into him. "She came. She came. Into my head, into my dream. Not a dream. It was real. It had to be real."

"Stop. Stop this." He took a firm grip on her shoulders. "Glenna!"

Her head jerked back, her breath came shuddering out. "Please. I'm so cold."

"Then hush now, hush." His tone and his touch gentled while he brushed tears from her cheeks. He wrapped her more fully in the blanket, then pulled her close. "It was a dream, a nightmare. Nothing more."

"It wasn't. Look at me." She tilted her head up so he could see her eyes. "It wasn't just a dream."

No, he realized. He could see it hadn't been only a dream. "Then tell me."

"She was inside my head. Or . . . she pulled some part of me outside myself. The way it was when you were in the woods, hurt, with wolves outside your circle. Just as real as that. You know that was real."

"Aye, it was real."

"I was running," she began, and told him all of it.

"She tried to lure you. Now think. Why would she do so unless she knew you were strong, unless she knew you could hurt her?"

"I died."

"You didn't, no, you didn't. You're here. Cold." He rubbed her arms, her back. Would he ever be able to warm her again? "But alive, and here. Safe."

"She was beautiful. Alluring. I don't go for women, if you understand, but I was drawn to her. And part of it was sexual. Even in fear, I wanted her. The idea of her touching me, taking me, was compelling."

"It's a kind of trance, nothing more. And you didn't allow it. You didn't listen, you didn't believe."

"But I did listen, Hoyt. And some part of me did believe. Some part of me wanted what she offered. So much wanted. To live forever, with all that power. I thought, inside me, I thought, yes, oh yes, why shouldn't I have it? And turning away from it—I nearly didn't—because turning away from it was the hardest thing I've ever done."

"Yet you did."

"This time."

"Every time."

"They were your cliffs. I felt you there. I felt you there, but I couldn't reach you. I was alone, more alone than I've ever been. Then I was falling, and I was even more alone."

"You're not alone. Here." He pressed his lips to her forehead. "You're not alone, are you?"

"I'm not a coward, but I'm afraid. And the dark . . ." She shuddered, looked around the room. "I'm afraid of the dark."

He cast his mind toward the bedside candle, toward the logs in the hearth, set them all burning. "Dawn's coming. Here, see." He gathered her into his arms, got out of bed with her to carry her to the window. "There now, look east. The sun's rising."

She saw the light of it, a gilding low in the sky. The cold ball inside her began to ease. "Morning," she murmured. "It's nearly morning."

"You won the night, and she lost it. Come, you need more sleep."

"I don't want to be alone."

"You won't be."

He took her back to bed, drew her against him. Because she still trembled, because he could, he passed his hand over her head. And sent her gently into slumber.

Chapter 10

She woke with sunlight sliding over her face, and she woke alone.

He'd snuffed the candles out, but left the fire burning low. Kind of him, she thought as she sat up, drawing the blanket over her shoulders. He'd been very kind and very gentle, and had given her exactly the comfort and security she'd needed.

Still, the wave of embarrassment came first. She'd run to him like a hysterical child fleeing from the monster in the closet. Sobbing, shaking and incoherent. She hadn't been able to handle it, and had looked for someone—for him—to save her. She prided herself on her courage and her wits, and she hadn't been able to stand up to her first showdown with Lilith.

No spine, she thought in disgust, and no real magic. Fear and temptation had smothered them. No, worse, she thought, fear and temptation had frozen them inside her, deep, where she hadn't been able to reach. Now, in the light of day, she could see how foolish she'd been, how stupid, how *easy*. She'd done nothing to protect herself before, during or after. She'd run through the caves, through the woods, on the cliffs because they'd wanted her to run, and she'd let terror block out everything but the desperate need to escape.

It wasn't a mistake she'd make again.

She wasn't going to sit here wallowing either, not over something that was done.

She got up, wrapped herself in the blanket, then peeked out into the corridor. She saw no one, heard nothing, and was grateful. She didn't want to talk to anyone until she'd put herself back together.

She showered, dressed, then took a great deal of care with her makeup. She hung amber drops at her ears for strength. And when she made the bed, she put amethyst and rosemary under her pillow. After choosing a candle from her supplies, she set it beside the bed. When she prepared for sleep that night, she would consecrate the candle with oil to repel Lilith and those like her from her dreams.

She would also make a stake, and get a sword from the weapons supply. She wouldn't be defenseless and open again.

Before she left the room she took a long look at herself in the mirror. She looked alert, she decided, and capable.

She would be strong.

Because she considered it the heart of any home, she went to the kitchen first. Someone had made coffee, and by process of elimination, she figured it had been King. There was evidence someone had eaten. She could smell bacon. But there was no one around, and no dishes in the sink.

It was some small comfort to know whoever had eaten— or at least whoever had cooked—had also tidied up. She didn't like to live in disorder, but neither would she care to be in charge of all things domestic.

She poured herself a cup from the pot, toyed with making some breakfast. But there was enough of the dream left in her that the sensation of being alone in the house was uncomfortable.

Her next choice was the library, which she thought of as the main artery of the heart. And there, with some relief, she found Moira.

Moira sat on the floor in front of the fire, surrounded by

books. Even now she was hunched over one like a student cramming for an exam. She wore a tunic the color of oatmeal with brown pants and her riding boots.

She looked up as Glenna entered, offered a shy smile. "Good morning to you."

"Good morning. Studying?"

"I am." The shyness faded so those gray eyes shined. "This is the most marvelous room, isn't it? We have a great library in the castle at home, but this rivals it."

Glenna crouched, tapped a finger on a book thick as a beam. Carved into its scrolled leather cover was a single word. VAMPYRE.

"Boning up?" she asked. "Studying the enemy?"

"It's wise to know all you can about whatever you can. Not all the books I've read so far agree on all things, but there are some elements on which they do."

"You could ask Cian. I imagine he could tell you whatever you wanted to know."

"I like to read."

Glenna only nodded. "Where did you get the clothes?"

"Oh. I went out this morning, early, found my pack."

"Alone?"

"I was safe enough, as I kept to the bright path. They can't come out in the sunlight." She looked toward the windows. "There was nothing left of the ones that attacked us last night. Even the ash was gone."

"Where is everyone else?"

"Hoyt went up to his tower to work, and King said he would go into the town for supplies now that there are more of us. I've never seen a man so big. He cooked food for us, and there was juice from a fruit. Orange. It was wonderful. Do you think I could take some of the seeds of the orange when we go back to Geall?"

"I don't see why not. And the others?"

"Larkin, I imagine, is still sleeping. He tends to avoid the mornings as if they were the plague. The vampire is in his room, I would think." Moira rubbed her finger over the carved word on the book. "Why does he stand with us? I can find nothing in the books to explain it."

"Then I guess you can't find out everything from books. Is there anything else you need for now?"

"No. Thanks."

"I'm going to grab something to eat, then go up to work. I imagine whenever King gets back, we'll start whatever torture session he has in mind."

"Glenna . . . I wanted to thank you for last night. I was so tired, and upset. I feel so out of my place."

"I know." Glenna put her hand over Moira's. "I think in a way, we all do. Maybe that's part of the plan, taking us out of our place, putting us together so we find ourselves, what there is in us—individually and together—to fight this thing."

She rose. "Until it's time to move, we're going to have to make this our place."

She left Moira to the books and returned to the kitchen. There she found what was left of a loaf of brown bread and slathered butter on a slice. Damned if she'd worry about calories at this point. She nibbled on it as she climbed the stairs to the tower.

The door was closed. She nearly knocked before she reminded herself it was her work area, too, and no longer Hoyt's solitary domain. So she balanced the slice of bread on the mug of coffee, unlatched the door.

He wore a shirt the color of faded denim with black jeans and scarred boots, and still managed to look like a sorcerer. It wasn't just the rich and flowing black hair, she thought, or those intense blue eyes. It was the power that fit him more truly than the borrowed clothes.

Irritation crossed his face first when he glanced at her. She wondered if it was habitual, that quick annoyance at being interrupted or disturbed. Then it cleared, and she found herself being carefully studied.

"So, you're up then."

"Apparently."

He went back to work, pouring some port-colored liquid from a kind of beaker into a vial. "King went for provisions."

"So I'm told. I found Moira in the library, reading, from the looks of it, every book in there."

So, it was going to be awkward, she realized as he continued to work in silence. Better to get past that. "I was going to
apologize for disturbing you last night, but that's just an in-
dulgence on my part." She waited, one beat, then two before
he stopped to look over at her. "So you could tell me not to
worry about it, that of course it was all right. I was frightened and upset."

"That would be true enough."

"It would, and since we both know all that, indulgent. So
I won't apologize. But I will thank you."

"It's of no matter."

"It is, for me, on several levels. You were there when I
needed you, and you calmed me down. Made me feel safe.
You showed me the sun." She set the mug down so her hands
would be free as she crossed to him.

"I jumped into your bed in the middle of the night.
Naked. I was vulnerable, hysterical. I was defenseless."

"I don't think the last is true."

"At that moment it was. It won't be again. You could have
had me. We both know that."

There was a long beat of silence that acknowledged the
simple truth more truly than any words. "And what manner
of man would I be to have taken you at such a time? To have
used your fear for my own needs?"

"A different one from what you are. I'm grateful to the
one you are." She skirted the worktable, rose to her toes to
kiss both of his cheeks. "Very. You gave me comfort, Hoyt,
and you gave me sleep. And you left the fire burning. I won't
forget it."

"You're better now."

"Yes. I'm better now. I was caught off-guard, and I won't
be the next time. I wasn't prepared for her, and I will be the
next time. I didn't take precautions, even the simplest ones
because I was tired." She wandered to the fire he kept burning low. "Sloppy of me."

"Aye. It was."

She cocked her head, smiled at him. "Did you want me?"

He got busy again. "That's not the point."

"I'll take that as a yes, and promise the next time I jump into your bed, I won't be hysterical."

"The next time you jump into my bed, I won't give you sleep."

She choked out a laugh. "Well, just so we understand each other."

"I don't know that I understand you at all, but that doesn't stop the wanting of you."

"It's mutual, on both counts. But I think I'm beginning to understand you."

"Did you come here to work, or just to distract me?"

"Both, I guess. Since I've accomplished the latter, I'll ask what you're working on there."

"A shield."

Intrigued she moved closer. "More science than sorcery."

"They're not exclusive, but joined."

"Agreed." She sniffed at the beaker. "Some sage," she decided, "and clove. What have you used for binding?"

"Agate dust."

"Good choice. What sort of shield are you after?"

"Against the sun. For Cian."

She flicked her gaze to his, but he didn't meet it. "I see."

"We risk attack if we go out at night. He dies if he exposes himself to sunlight. But if he had a shield, we could work and train more efficiently. If he had a shield, we could hunt them by day."

She said nothing for a moment. Yes, she was beginning to understand him. This was a very good man, one who held himself to high standards. So he could be impatient, irritable, even autocratic.

And he loved his brother very much.

"Do you think he misses the sun?"

Hoyt sighed. "Wouldn't you?"

She touched a hand to his arm. A good man, she thought again. A very good man who would think of his brother. "What can I do to help?"

"Maybe I begin to understand you as well."

"Is that so?"

"You have an open heart." Now he looked at her. "An open

heart and a willing mind. They're difficult to resist."

She took the vial from him, set it down. "Kiss me, would you? We both want that, and it makes it hard to work. Kiss me, Hoyt, so we settle down."

There might have been amusement, just a sprinkle of it in his voice. "Kissing will settle us down?"

"Won't know unless we try." She laid her hands on his shoulders, let her fingers play with his hair. "But I know, right this minute, I can't think of anything else. So do me a favor. Kiss me."

"A favor then."

Her lips were soft, a yielding warmth under his. So he was gentle, holding her, tasting her the way he'd yearned to the night before. He stroked a hand down her hair, down the length of her back so the feel of her mingled in his senses with her flavor and her scent.

What was inside him opened, and eased.

She skimmed her fingers over the strong edge of his cheekbone and gave herself completely to the moment. To the comfort and the pleasure, and the shimmer of heat flowing under both.

When their lips parted, she pressed her cheek to his, held there a moment. "I feel better," she told him. "How about you?"

"I feel." He stepped back, then brought her hand to his lips. "And I suspect that I'll be needing to be settled again. For the good of the work."

She laughed, delighted. "Anything I can do for the cause."

They worked together for more than an hour, but each time they exposed the potion to sunlight, it boiled.

"A different incantation," Glenna suggested.

"No. We need his blood." He looked at her over the beaker. "For the potion itself, and to test it."

Glenna considered. "You ask him."

There was a thud at the door, then King pushed it open. He wore camo pants and an olive green T-shirt. He'd tied his dreadlocks back into a thick, fuzzy tail. And looked, Glenna thought, like an army all by himself.

"Magic hour's over. Fall in outside. Time to get physical."

If King hadn't been a drill sergeant in another life, karma was missing a step. Sweat dripped into Glenna's eyes as she attacked the dummy Larkin had fashioned out of straw and wrapped in cloth. She blocked with her forearm as she'd been taught, then plunged the stake into the straw.

But the dummy kept coming, flying on the pulley system King had rigged, and knocked her flat on her back.

"And you're dead," he announced.

"Oh, bullshit. I staked it."

"Missed the heart, Red." He stood over her, huge and pitiless. "How many chances you figure you're going to get? You can't get the one in front of you, how are you going to get the three coming at your back?"

"All right, okay." She got up, brushed herself off. "Do it again."

"That's the spirit."

She did it again, and again, until she despised the straw dummy as much as she had her tenth-grade history teacher. Disgusted, she swung around, picked up a sword with both hands, and hacked the thing to pieces.

When she was done, there was no sound but her own labored breathing and Larkin's muffled laugh.

"Okay." King rubbed his chin. "Guess he's pretty damn dead. Larkin, you want to put together another one? Let me ask you something, Red."

"Ask away."

"How come you didn't just tear into the dummy with magic?"

"Magic takes focus and concentration. I think I could use some in a fight—I think I could. But most of me is channelled into handling the sword or the stake, particularly since I'm not used to handling either. If I wasn't centered, I could just send my own weapon flying out of my hand, missing the mark. It's something I'll work on."

She glanced around to make sure Hoyt wasn't anywhere within earshot. "Generally, I need tools, chants, certain rituals.

I can do this." She opened her palm, focused, and brought out the ball of fire.

Curious, he poked at it. And snatched back his singed finger, sucked on it. "Hell of a trick."

"Fire is elemental, like air, earth, water. But if I pulled this out during a battle, tossed it at an enemy, it might hit one of us instead, or as well as."

He studied the shimmering ball with his odd eyes. "Like pointing a gun if you don't know how to shoot. Can't be sure who's going to get the bullet. Or if you'd just end up shooting yourself in your own damn foot."

"Something like that." She vanished the fire. "But it's nice to have it in reserve."

"You go ahead, take a break, Red, before you hurt somebody."

"No argument." She sailed into the house, intending to drink a gallon of water and put together some food. She nearly walked straight into Cian.

"Didn't know you were up and around."

He stood back from the sunlight that filtered through the windows, but she saw he had a full view of the outdoor activities.

"What do you think?" she asked him. "How are we doing?"

"If they came for you now, they'd snack on you like chicken at a picnic."

"I know. We're clumsy, and there's no sense of unity. But we'll get better."

"You'll need to."

"Well, you're full of cheer and encouragement this afternoon. We've been at it over two hours, and none of us is used to this kind of thing. Larkin's the closest King's got to a warrior, and he's green yet."

Cian merely glanced at her. "Ripen or die."

Fatigue was one thing, she thought, and she would deal with the sweat and the effort. But now she was flat-out insulted. "It's hard enough to do what we're doing without one of us being a complete asshole."

"Is that your term for realist?"

"Screw it, and you with it." She stalked around the kitchen, tossed some fruit, some bread, some bottled water into a basket. She hauled it out, ignoring Cian as she passed by.

Outside she dumped the basket on the table King had carried out to hold weapons.

"Food!" Larkin pounced like a starving man. "Bless you down to the soles of your feet, Glenna. I was wasting away here."

"Since it's been two hours for certain since you last stuffed your face," Moira put in.

"The master of doom doesn't think we're working hard enough, and equates us to chicken at a picnic for the vampires." Glenna took an apple for herself, bit in. "I say we show him different."

She took another bite, then whipped around toward the newly stuffed dummy. She focused in, visualized, then hurled the apple. It flew toward the dummy, and as it flew it became a stake. And that stake pierced cloth and straw.

"Oh, that was fine," Moira breathed. "That was brilliant."

"Sometimes temper gives the magic a boost."

The stake slid out again, and splatted as an apple to the ground. She sent Hoyt a look. "Something to work out."

"We need something to unify us, to hold us together," she told Hoyt later. She sat in the tower, rubbing balm into bruises while he pored through the pages of a spellbook. "Teams wear uniforms, or have fight songs."

"Songs? Now we should sing? Or maybe just find a bloody harper."

Sarcasm, she decided, was something the brothers shared as well as their looks. "We need something. Look at us, even now. You and I up here, Moira and Larkin off together. King and Cian in the training room, devising new miseries for us all. It's fine and good to have the whole of the team split into smaller teams, working on their own projects. But we haven't become a whole team yet."

"So we drag out the harp and sing? We've serious work to do, Glenna."

"You're not following me." Patience, she reminded herself. He'd worked as hard as she had today, and was just as tired. "It's about symbolism. We have the same foe, yes, but not the same purpose." She walked to the window, and saw how long the shadows had grown, and how low the sun hung in the sky.

"It'll be dark soon." Her fingers groped for her pendant. It struck her then, so simple, so obvious.

"You were looking for a shield for Cian, because he can't go out in the day. But what about us? We can't risk going out after sundown. And even inside, we know she can get to us, get inside us. What about *our* shield, Hoyt? What shields us against the vampire?"

"The light."

"Yes, yes, but what symbol? A cross. We need to make crosses, and we need to put magic into them. Not only shield, but weapon, Hoyt."

He thought of the crosses Morrigan had given him for his family. But even his powers, even combined with Glenna's, fell short of the gods.

Still . . .

"Silver," he mumbled. "Silver would be best."

"With red jasper, for night protection. We need some garlic, some sage." She began going through her case of dried herbs and roots. "I'll start on the potion." She grabbed one of her books, began flipping through. "Any idea where we can get our hands on the silver?"

"Aye."

He left her, went down to the first level of the house and into what was now the dining room. The furnishings were new—to him, at least. Tables of dark, heavy wood, chairs with high backs and ornate carving. The drapes that were pulled over the windows were a deep green, like forest shadows, and made of a thick and weighty silk.

There was art, all of them night scenes of forests and glades and cliffs. Even here, he thought, his brother shunned the light. Or did he prefer the dark, even in paintings?

Tall cupboards with doors of rippled glass held crystal and pottery in rich jewel tones. Possessions, he thought, of a man of wealth and position, who had an eternity of time to collect them.

Did any of the things mean anything to Cian? With so much, could any single thing matter?

On the larger server were two tall candlestands of silver, and Hoyt wondered if they did—or if they had, at least.

They had been his mother's.

He lifted one, and had the image of her—clear as lake water—sitting at her wheel and spinning, singing one of the old songs she loved while her foot tapped the time.

She wore a blue gown and veil, and there was ease and youth in her face, a quiet contentment that covered her like soft silk. Her body was heavy with child, he saw that now. No, he corrected, heavy with children. Himself and Cian.

And on the chest beneath her window stood the two candlestands.

"They were a gift from my father on the day of my wedding, and of all the gifts given, I prized them most. One will go to you one day, and one to Cian. And so this gift will be passed down, and the given remembered whenever the candle is lit."

He comforted himself that he needed no candle to remember her. But the stand weighed heavy in his hands as he took it up to the tower.

Glenna looked up from the cauldron where she mixed her herbs. "Oh, it's perfect. And beautiful. What a shame to melt it down." She left her work to get a closer look. "It's heavy. And old, I think."

"Aye, it's very old."

She understood then, and felt a little pang in her heart. "Your family's?"

His face, his voice, were carefully blank. "It was to come to me, and so it has."

She nearly told him to find something else, something that didn't mean so much to him. But she swallowed the words. She thought she understood why he had chosen as he had. It had to cost. Magic asked a price.

"The sacrifice you're making will strengthen the spell. Wait." She pulled a ring from the middle finger of her right hand. "It was my grandmother's."

"There's no need."

"Personal sacrifice, yours and mine. We're asking a great deal. I need some time to write out the spell. Nothing in my books is quite right, so we'll need to amend."

When Larkin came to the door they were both deep in books. He glanced around the room and kept to his side of the threshold. "I'm sent to fetch you. The sun's set, and we're going into evening training."

"Tell him we'll be there when we're done," Glenna said. "We're in the middle of something."

"I'll tell him, but I'm thinking he won't like it." He pulled the door shut and left them.

"I've nearly got it. I'm going to draw out what I think they should look like, then we'll both visualize. Hoyt?"

"It must be pure," he said to himself. "Conjured with faith as much as magic."

She left him to it and began to sketch. Simple, she thought, and with tradition. She glanced over, saw he was sitting, eyes closed. Gathering power, she assumed, and his thoughts.

Such a serious face, and one, she realized, she'd come to trust completely. It seemed she'd known that face forever, just as she knew the sound of his voice, the cadence of it.

Yet the time they'd had was short, just as the time they would have was no more than a handful of grains in the sand of an hourglass.

If they won—no when, when they won—he'd go back to his time, his life, his world. And she to hers. But nothing would ever be the same. And nothing would ever really fill the void he'd leave behind.

"Hoyt."

His eyes were different when they met hers. Deeper and darker. She pushed the sketch toward him. "Will this do?"

He lifted it, studied. "Yes, but for this."

He took the pencil from her, added lines on the long base of the Celtic cross she'd drawn.

"What is it?"

"It's ogham script. Old writing."

"I know what ogham is. What does it say?"

"It says light."

She smiled, nodded. "Then it's perfect. This is the spell. It feels right to me."

He took that in turn, then looked at her. "Rhymes?"

"It's how I work. Deal with it. And I want a circle. I'll feel better with one."

Because he agreed he rose, to cast it with her. She scribed fresh candles with her bolline, watched him light them.

"We'll make the fire together." He held out his hand for hers.

Power winged up her arm, struck the heart of her. And the fire, pure and white, shimmered an inch above the floor. He hefted the cauldron, set it on the flames.

"Silver old and silver bright." He set the candlestand in the cauldron. "Go to liquid in this light."

"As we stand in the sorcerer's tower," Glenna continued, adding the jasper, the herbs, "we charge this flame to free your power." She dropped in her grandmother's ring.

"Magicks from the sky and sea, from air and earth we call to thee. We your servants beg this blessing, shield us in this time of testing. We answer your charge with head, heart and hand to vanquish the darkness from the land. So we call you three times three to shield those who serve you faithfully.

"Let this cross shine light to night."

As they chanted the last line, three times three, silver smoke rose from the cauldron, and the white flames beneath it grew brighter.

It flooded her, light and smoke and heat, filled her as her voice rose with his. Through it, she saw his eyes, only his eyes locked on hers.

In her heart, in her belly, she felt it heat and grow. Stronger, more potent than anything she'd ever known. It swirled in her as with his free hand, he threw the last of the jasper dust into the cauldron.

"And each cross of silver a shield will be. As we will, so mote it be."

The room exploded with light, and the force of it shook

the walls, the floor. The cauldron tumbled over, spilling liquid silver into the flame.

The force nearly sent Glenna to the ground, but Hoyt's arms came around her. He spun his body around to shield hers from the sudden spurting flames and roaring wind.

Hoyt saw the door fly open. For an instant, Cian was framed in the doorway, drowned in that impossible light. Then he vanished.

"No! No!" Dragging Glenna with him, Hoyt broke the circle. The light shrank in on itself, swallowed itself and was gone with a crash like thunder. Through the ringing in his ears he thought he heard shouting.

Cian lay on the floor bleeding, his shirt half burned away and still smoking.

Hoyt dropped to his knees, his fingers reaching for a pulse before he remembered there would be none in any case. "My God, my God, what have I done?"

"He's badly burned. Get the shirt off of him." Glenna's voice was cool as water, and just as calm. "Gently."

"What happened? What the hell did you do?" King shoved Hoyt aside. "Son of a bitch. Cian. Jesus Christ."

"We were finishing a spell. He opened the door. There was light. It was no one's fault. Larkin," Glenna continued, "help King carry Cian to his room. I'll be right there. I have things that will help."

"He's not dead." Hoyt said it quietly, staring down at his brother. "It's not death."

"It's not death," Glenna repeated. "I can help him. I'm a good healer. It's one of my strengths."

"I'll help you." Moira stepped up, then eased her body toward the wall as King and Larkin lifted Cian. "I have some skill."

"Good. Go with them. I'll get my things. Hoyt. I can help him."

"What did we do?" Hoyt stared helplessly at his hands. Though they still vibrated from the spell, they felt empty and useless. "It was beyond all I've done."

"We'll talk about it later." She gripped his hand, pulled him into the tower room.

The circle was burned into the floor, scorched in a pure white ring. In its center glinted nine silver crosses with a circle of red jasper at the joining.

"Nine. Three times three. We'll think about all this later. I think we should let them stay there for now. I don't know, let them set."

Ignoring her, Hoyt crossed the circle, picked one up. "It's cool."

"Great. Good." Her mind was already on Cian, and what would have to be done to help him. She grabbed her case. "I have to get down, do what I can for him. It wasn't anyone's fault, Hoyt."

"Twice now. Twice I've nearly killed him."

"This is my doing as much as yours. Are you coming with me?"

"No."

She started to speak, then shook her head and rushed out.

In the lavish bedchamber, the vampire lay still on the wide bed. His face was that of an angel. A wicked one, Moira thought. She sent the men out for warm water, for bandages, and mostly to get them out from underfoot.

Now she was alone with the vampire, who lay on the wide bed. Still as death.

She would feel no heartbeat should she lay her hand on his chest. There would be no breath to fog a glass if she were to hold one to his lips. And he would have no reflection.

She'd read these things, and more.

Yet, he'd saved her life, and she owed him for that.

She moved to the side of the bed, and used what little magic she had to try to cool his burned flesh. Queasiness rose up and was fought down. She'd never seen flesh so scorched. How could anyone—anything—survive such wounds?

His eyes flashed open, searing blue. His hand clamped on her wrist. "What are you doing?"

"You're hurt." She hated to hear the tremor in her voice, but her fear of him—alone with him—was so huge. "An

accident. I'm waiting for Glenna. We'll help you. Lie still."
She saw the instant the pain woke in him, and some of her
fear died. "Lie quiet. I can cool it a little."

"Wouldn't you rather I burn in hell?"

"I don't know. But I know I don't want to be the one who
sends you. I wouldn't have shot you last night. I'm ashamed
I let you believe I would. I owe you my life."

"Go away, and we'll call it quits."

"Glenna's coming. Is it cooling a little?"

He simply closed his eyes; and his body trembled. "I
need blood."

"Well, you won't be having mine. I'm not that grateful."

She thought his lips curved, just the slightest bit. "Not
yours, though I'll bet it's tasty." He had to catch the breath
the pain stole. "In the case across the room. The black case
with the silver handle. I need blood to— I just need it."

She left him to open the case, then swallowed revulsion
when she saw the clear packs that held dark red liquid.

"Bring it over, toss it and run, whatever you want, but I
need it now."

She brought it quickly, then watched him struggle to sit
up, to tear the pack open with his burned hands. Saying nothing, she took the pack, opened it herself, spilling some.

"Sorry." She gathered her strength, then used an arm to
brace him, using her free hand to bring the pack to his lips.

He watched her as he drank, and she made herself look
back into his eyes without flinching.

When he'd drained it dry, she laid his head down again
before going into the bath for a cloth. With it she wiped his
mouth, his chin.

"Small but valiant, are you?"

She heard the edge in his tone, and some return of its
strength. "You haven't a choice because of what you are. I
haven't one because of what I am." She stepped back when
Glenna hurried into the room.

Chapter 11

"Do you want something for the pain?" Glenna coated thin cloth with balm.

"What have you got?"

"This and that." She laid the cloth gently on his chest. "I'm so sorry, Cian. We should have locked the door."

"A locked door wouldn't have stopped me from coming in, not in my own house. You might try a sign next time, something along the lines . . . Bugger it!"

"I know, sorry, I know. It'll be better in a minute. A sign?" she continued, her voice low and soothing as she worked. "Something like: Flammable Magicks. Keep out."

"Wouldn't hurt." He felt the burn not just on the flesh, but down into the bone, as if the fire had burst inside him as well as out. "What the hell were you doing in there?"

"More than either of us were expecting. Moira, coat more cloth, would you. Cian?"

"What?"

She simply looked at him, deeply, her hands hovering just above the worst of the burns. She felt the heat, but not the release. "It won't work unless you let it," she told him. "Unless you trust me and let go."

"A high price for a bit of relief, adding that you're part of what put me here."

"Why would she hurt you?" Moira continued to coat the cloth. "She needs you. We all do, like it or not."

"One minute," Glenna said. "Give me one minute. I want to help you; you need to believe that. Believe me. Look at me, into my eyes. Yes, that's right."

Now it came. Heat and release, heat and release. "There, that's better. A little better. Yes?"

She'd taken it, he realized. Some of the burn, just for an instant, into herself. He wouldn't forget it. "Some. Yes, some. Thanks."

She applied more cloth, turned back to her case. "I'll just clean the cuts and treat the bruises, then give you something to help you rest."

"I'm not looking for rest."

She shifted back, eased down on the bed intending to clean the cuts on his face. Puzzled, she laid her fingers on his cheek, turned his head. "I thought these were worse."

"They were. I heal quickly from most things."

"Good for you. How's the vision?"

He turned those hot blue eyes on her. "I see you well enough, Red."

"Could have a concussion. Can you get concussions? I imagine so," she said before he could answer. "Are you burned anywhere else?" She started to lower the sheet, then flicked him a wicked glance. "Is it true what they say about vampires?"

It made him laugh, then hiss as the pain rippled back. "A myth. We're hung just as we were before the change. You're welcome to look for yourself, but I'm not hurt in that area. It caught me full on the chest."

"We'll preserve your modesty—and my illusions." When she took his hand the amusement faded from his face. "I thought we'd killed you. So did he. Now he's suffering."

"Oh, *he's* suffering, is he? Maybe he'd like to switch places with me."

"You know he would. However you feel or don't about him, he loves you. He can't turn that off, and he hasn't had all the time that you've had to step back from brotherhood."

"We stopped being brothers the night I died."

"No, you didn't. And you're deluding yourself if you believe that." She pushed off the bed. "You're as comfortable as I can make you. I'll come back in an hour and work on you some more."

She gathered her things. Moira slipped out of the room ahead of her, and waited. "What did that to him?"

"I'm not entirely sure."

"You need to be. It's a powerful weapon against his kind. We could use it."

"We weren't controlling it. I don't know that we can."

"If you could," Moira insisted.

Glenna opened the door to her room, carried her case inside. She wasn't ready to go back to the tower. "It controlled us, as far as I can tell. It was huge and powerful. Too powerful for either of us to handle. Even together—and we were linked as closely as I've been with anyone—we couldn't harness it. It was like being inside the sun."

"The sun's a weapon."

"If you don't know how to use a sword, you're just as likely to cut off your own hand as someone else's."

"So you learn."

Glenna lowered to the bed, then held out a hand. "I'm shaky," she said, watching it tremble. "There are places inside my body I didn't know I had shaking like my hand is."

"And I'm badgering you. I'm sorry. You seemed so steady, so calm when you were treating the vampire."

"He has a name. Cian. Start using it." Moira's head snapped back as if she'd been slapped, and her eyes widened at the whip in Glenna's tone. "I'm sorry about your mother. Sick and sorry, but he didn't kill her. If she'd been murdered by a blond man with blue eyes, would you go around hating all men with blond hair and blue eyes?"

"It's not the same, not nearly the same."

"Close enough, especially in our situation."

Sheer stubbornness hardened Moira's face. "I fed him blood, and gave what little I could to ease him. I helped you treat his burns. It should be enough."

"It's not. Wait," Glenna ordered as Moira spun around to leave. "Just wait. I *am* shaking, and short-tempered with it. Just wait. If I seemed calm before it's because that's the way it works for me. Handle the crisis, then fall apart. This is the falling apart portion of our program. But what I said goes, Moira.

"Just as what you said in there goes. We need him. You're going to have to start thinking of him, and treating him like a person instead of a thing."

"They tore her to pieces." Moira's eyes filled even as the defense of defiance crumbled. "No, he wasn't there, he had no part of it. He lifted his sword for me. I know it, but I can't feel it."

She slapped a hand on her heart. "I can't feel it. They didn't let me grieve. They didn't give me time to mourn my own mother. And now, now that I'm here it's all grief and all rage. All blood and death. I don't want this burden. Away from my people, from everything I know. Why are we here? Why are we charged with this? Why are there no answers?"

"I don't know, which is another non-answer. I'm sorry, so horribly sorry about your mother, Moira. But you're not the only one with grief and rage. Not the only one asking questions and wishing they were back in the life they knew."

"One day you will go back. I never can." She yanked open the door and fled.

"Perfect. Just perfect." Glenna dropped her head into her hands.

In the tower room, Hoyt laid each cross on a cloth of white linen. They were cool to the touch, and though the metal had dimmed somewhat, its light was bright enough to glare into his eyes.

He picked up Glenna's cauldron. It was scorched black. He doubted it could ever be used again—wondered if it was

meant to be. The candles she'd scribed and lit were no more
than puddles of wax on the floor now. It would need to be
cleaned. The entire room should be cleansed before any
other magic was done here.

The circle was etched into the floor now, a thin ring of
pure white. And his brother's blood stained the floor and
walls outside the door.

Sacrifice, he thought. There was always payment for
power. His gift of his mother's candlestand, Glenna's of her
grandmother's ring, hadn't been enough.

The light had burned so fierce and bright, so violently hot.
Yet it hadn't scorched his skin. He held his hand up, examined
it. Unmarked. Unsteady yet, he could admit. But unmarked.

The light had filled him, all but consumed him. It had
twined him so truly with Glenna it had been almost as if
they'd been one person, one power.

That power had been heady and fantastic.

And it had whirled out like the wrath of the gods at his
brother. Struck down the other half of him while the sorcerer
had ridden the lightning.

Now he was empty, hollowed out. What power that remained in him was like lead, heavy and cold, and the lead
was coated thick with guilt.

Nothing to be done now, nothing to do but put order back
into the room. He busied himself, calmed himself, with the basic tasks. When King rushed into the room, he stood still, arms
at his side and took the blow he saw coming full in the face.

He had a moment to think it was like being hit by a battering ram as he was launched back against the wall. Then
simply slid bonelessly to the floor.

"Get up. Get up, you son of a bitch."

Hoyt spat out blood. His vision wavered so he saw several black giants standing over him with ham-sized fists
bunched. He braced a hand on the wall, dragged himself to
his feet.

The battering ram struck again. This time his vision went
red, black, shimmered sickly to gray. King's voice went
tinny in his ears, but he struggled to follow the command to
get back up.

There was a flash of color through the gray, a stream of heat through the iced pain.

Glenna flew into the tower. She didn't bother to shove at King, but rammed her elbow viciously into his midsection, then all but fell on Hoyt to shield him.

"Stop it! Get away from him. Stupid bastard. Oh Hoyt, your face."

"Get away." He could barely mumble the words, and his stomach pitched violently as he pushed at her and tried to rise again.

"Go ahead and throw one. Come on." King spread his arms, then tapped his chin. "I'll give you a free shot. Hell, I'll give you a couple of them, you miserable son of a bitch. It's more than you gave Cian."

"He's gone then. Get away from me." Hoyt shoved at Glenna. "Go ahead," he told King. "Finish it."

Though his fists remained bunched, King lowered them a fraction. The man was barely standing, and blood ran from his nose, his mouth. One eye was already swelling shut. And he just swayed there, waiting to take another hit.

"Is he stupid, or just crazy?"

"He's neither," Glenna snapped. "He thinks he's killed his brother so he'll stand here and let you beat him to death because he blames himself as much as you blame him. And you're both wrong. Cian's not dead. Hoyt, he's going to be fine. He's resting, that's all. He's resting."

"Not gone?"

"You didn't pull it off, and you won't get a second chance."

"Oh, for God's *sake*!" Glenna whirled to King. "Nobody tried to kill anyone."

"Just step away, Red." King jerked a thumb. "I'm not looking to hurt you."

"Why not? If he's responsible, so am I. We were working together. We were doing what we came here to do, *damn* it. Cian came in at the wrong time, it's as simple and as tragic as that. If Hoyt could, and would, hurt Cian like that purposely, do you think you'd be standing there? He'd cut you down with a thought. And I'd help him."

King's bi-colored eyes narrowed, his mouth went grim. But his fists stayed at his side. "Why don't you?"

"It's against everything we are. You couldn't possibly understand. But unless you're brick stupid you should understand that whatever affection and loyalty you feel for Cian, Hoyt feels it, too. And he's felt it since the day he was born. Now get out of here. Just go."

King unbunched his fists, rubbed them on his pants. "Maybe I was wrong."

"A lot of good that does."

"I'm going to check on Cian. If I'm not satisfied, I'm going to finish this."

Ignoring him as he strode out, Glenna turned to try to take some of Hoyt's weight. "Here now, you need to sit down."

"Would you get away from me?"

"No, I won't."

In response, Hoyt merely lowered to the floor.

Resigned, Glenna went for more cloth, poured water from a pitcher into a bowl. "It looks like I'm going to spend the evening mopping up blood."

She knelt beside him, dampening cloth, then gently cleaning blood from his face. "I lied. You are stupid, stupid to stand there and let him pound on you. Stupid to feel guilty. And cowardly, too."

His eyes, bloodied and swollen, shifted to hers. "Have a care."

"Cowardly," she repeated, her voice sharp because there were tears welling at the base of her throat. "To stay up here wallowing instead of coming down to help. Instead of coming down to see what shape your brother was in. Which isn't that much worse than you at this point."

"I'm not in the mood to have you jab at me with words, or flutter about me." He waved her hands away.

"Fine. Just fine." She tossed the cloth back in the bowl so water spewed up and lapped over onto the floor. "Tend to yourself then. I'm tired of every single one of you. Brooding, self-pitying, useless. If you ask me, your Morrigan screwed up royally picking this group."

"Brooding, self-pitying, useless. You forgot your part of the whole. Shrew."

She inclined her head. "That's a weak and old-fashioned term. Today, we just go with bitch."

"Your world, your word."

"That's right. While you're up here wallowing, you might take just a minute to consider this. We did something amazing here tonight." She gestured toward the silver crosses on the table. "Something beyond anything I've ever experienced. The fact that we did, that we could, should, in some way, bring this ridiculous group together. But instead we're all whining in our separate corners. So I guess the magic, and the moment was wasted."

She stormed out just as Larkin jogged up the steps. "Cian's getting up. He says we've wasted enough time and we'll be training an extra hour tonight."

"You can tell him to kiss my ass."

Larkin blinked, then craned his head around the curve of the stairs to watch her stride down. "Sure it's a fine one," he said, but very quietly.

He peeked into the tower room, saw Hoyt sitting on the floor, bleeding.

"Mother of Christ, did she do that?"

Hoyt scowled at him and decided his punishment for the night wasn't quite done. "No. For God's sake, do I look like I could be beaten by a woman?"

"She strikes me as formidable." Though he would have preferred keeping clear of magic areas, he could hardly leave the man sprawled there. So Larkin walked over to Hoyt, crouched. "Well, that's a mess, isn't it? You're coming up a pair of black eyes."

"Bollocks. Give me a hand up, will you?"

Agreeably, Larkin helped him up, gave him a shoulder to lean on. "I don't know what the bleeding hell's going on, but Glenna's steaming, and Moira's locked in her room. Cian looks like the wrath of all the gods, but he's out of bed and saying we're training. King's opened some whiskey and I'm thinking about joining him."

Hoyt touched fingers gingerly to his cheekbone, hissed as

the pain radiated to his face. "Not shattered, there's some
fine luck. She might've done a bit more to help instead of
pounding a lecture on my head."

"Words are a woman's sharpest weapon. From the looks
of you, you could use some of that whiskey."

"I could." Hoyt braced a hand on the table, prayed he'd
regain his balance in a moment. "Do what you can, would
you, Larkin, to get the lot of them together in the training
area. I'll be along."

"Taking my life in my hands, I'm thinking. But all right.
I'll try sweetness and charm with the ladies. They'll either
fall for it, or kick me in the balls."

They didn't kick him, but they didn't come happily.
Moira sat cross-legged on a table, eyes, swollen from
weeping, downcast. Glenna stood in a corner, sulking into a
glass of wine. King stood in his own corner, rattling ice in a
short glass of whiskey.

Cian sat, drumming his fingers on the arm of his chair.
His face was white as bone, and the burns the loose white
shirt didn't cover, livid.

"Music might be nice," Larkin said into the silence. "The
sort you hear at funeral pyres and the like."

"We'll work on form and agility." Cian cast his glance
around the room. "I haven't seen a great deal of that in any
of you so far."

"Is there a point to you being insulting?" Moira asked
wearily. "A point to any of this? Slapping swords and trading punches? You were burned worse than anyone I've ever
seen, and here you are, an hour after, up again. If magic such
as that can't take you down, keep you down, what will?"

"I take it you'd be happier if I'd gone to ash. I'm happy to
disappoint you."

"That's not what she meant." Glenna shoved irritably at
her hair.

"And you interpret for her now?"

"I don't need anyone to speak for me," Moira snapped
right back. "And I don't need to be told what to do every

bleeding hour of every bleeding day. I know what kills them, I've read the books."

"Oh, well then, you've read the books." Cian gestured toward the doors. "Then be my guest. Go right on out and take out a few vamps."

"It'd be better than tumbling about on the floor in here, like a circus," she shot back.

"I'm with Moira on this." Larkin rested a hand on the hilt of his knife. "We should hunt them down, take the offense. We haven't so much as posted a guard or sent out a scout."

"This isn't that kind of war, boy."

Larkin's eyes glittered. "I'm not a boy, and from what I can see it's no kind of war."

"You don't know what you're up against," Glenna put in.

"Don't I? I fought them, killed three with my own hands."

"Weak ones, young ones. She didn't waste her best on you." Cian rose. He moved stiffly and with obvious effort. "Added to that, you had help and were lucky. But if you came across one with some seasoning, with some skill, you'd be meat."

"I can hold my own."

"Hold it with me. Come at me."

"You're hurt. It wouldn't be fair."

"Fair is for women. If you take me down, I'll go out with you." Cian gestured toward the door. "We'll hunt tonight."

Interest brightened Larkin's eyes. "Your word on it?"

"My word. Take me down."

"All right then."

Larkin came in fast, then spun out of reach. He jabbed, feinted, spun again. Cian merely reached out, gripped Larkin around the throat and lifted him off his feet. "You don't want to dance with a vampire," he said and tossed Larkin halfway across the room.

"Bastard." Moira scrambled up, raced to her cousin's side. "You've half strangled him."

"The half's what counts."

"Was that really necessary?" Glenna got to her feet, moved to Larkin to lay her hands on his throat.

"Kid asked for it," King commented, and had her whipping her head around.

"You're nothing but a bully. The pair of you."

"I'm all right, I'm all right." Larkin coughed, cleared his throat. "It was a good move," he said to Cian. "I never saw it coming."

"Until you can, and do, you don't hunt." He eased back, lowered carefully into the chair. "Time to work."

"I'd ask you to wait." Hoyt came into the room.

Cian didn't bother to look at him. "We've waited long enough."

"A bit more. I have things to say. First to you. I was careless, but so were you. I should have barred the door, but you shouldn't have opened it."

"This is my house now. It hasn't been yours for centuries."

"That may be. But courtesy and caution should approach a closed door, particularly when magic is being done. Cian." He waited until his brother's eyes shifted to him. "I would not have had you hurt. That's for you to believe or not. But I would not have had you hurt."

"I don't know if I can say the same." Cian gestured with his chin toward Hoyt's face. "Did your magic do that?"

"It's another result of it."

"Looks painful."

"So it is."

"Well then, that balances the scales somewhat."

"And this is what we've come to, checks and balances." Hoyt turned to face the room, and the others. "Arguments and resentments. You were right," he said to Glenna. "A great deal of what you said was right, though I swear you talk too much."

"Oh, really?"

"We aren't united, and until we are, we're hopeless. We could be training and preparing every hour of every day of the time we have left, and never win. Because—this is what you said—we have a common enemy, but not a common purpose."

"The purpose is to fight them," Larkin interrupted. "To fight them, and kill them. Kill them all."

"Why?"

"Because they're demons."

"So is he." Hoyt laid a hand on the back of Cian's chair.

"But he fights with us. He doesn't threaten Geall."

"Geall. You think of Geall, and you," he said to Moira, "of your mother. King's here with us because he follows Cian, and in my way, so do I. Cian, why are you here?"

"Because I don't follow. You or her."

"Why are you here, Glenna?"

"I'm here because if I didn't fight, if I didn't try, everything we have and are and know, every one of us, could be lost. Because what's inside me demands that I be here. And above all, because good needs soldiers against evil."

Oh aye, this was a woman, he thought. She put shame to all of them. "The answer. The single one there is, and she's the only one who knew it. We're needed. Stronger than valor or vengeance, loyalty or pride. We're needed. Can we stand with each other and do this thing? Not in a thousand years and with a thousand more of us to fight. We're the six, the beginning of it. We can't be strangers any longer."

He stepped away from Cian's chair as he reached in his pocket. "Glenna said make a symbol and a shield, a sign of common purpose. That unity of purpose made the strongest magic I've ever known. Stronger than I could hold," he said with a glance at Cian. "I believe they can help protect us, if we remember a shield needs a sword, and we use both with one purpose."

He drew the crosses out so the silver glinted in the light. He stepped to King, offered one. "Will you wear it?"

King set his drink aside, took the cross and chain. He studied Hoyt's face as he looped it around his neck. "You could use some ice on that eye."

"I could use a great deal. And you?" He held a cross out to Moira.

"I'll work to be worthy of it." She sent Glenna a look of apology. "I've done poorly tonight."

"So have we all," Hoyt told her. "Larkin?"

"Not just of Geall," Larkin said as he took the cross. "Or no longer."

"And you." Hoyt started to hand Glenna a cross, then stepped closer, looked into her eyes as he put it around her neck himself. "I think tonight you put us all to shame."

"I'll try not to make a habit of it. Here." She took the last cross, put the chain over his head. Then gently, very gently touched her lips to his battered cheek.

At last, he turned and walked back to Cian.

"If you're about to ask if I'd wear one of those, you're wasting your breath."

"I know you can't. I know you're not what we are, and still I'm asking you to stand with us, for this purpose." He held out a pendant, in the shape of a pentagram much like Glenna's. "The stone in the center is jasper, like the ones in the crosses. I can't give you a shield, not yet. So I'm offering you a symbol. Will you take it?"

Saying nothing, Cian held out a hand. When Hoyt poured pendant and chain into it, Cian shook it lightly, as if checking the weight. "Metal and stone don't make an army."

"They make weapons."

"True enough." Cian slipped the chain over his head. "Now if the ceremony's finished, could we bloody well get to work?"

Chapter 12

Seeking solitude and occupation, Glenna poured a glass of wine, got out a pad of paper and a pencil, and sat down at the kitchen table.

An hour, she thought, of quiet, where she could settle down, make some lists. Then maybe she would sleep.

When she heard someone approaching, her back went up. In a house this size, couldn't everyone find some place else to be?

But King came in, and stood, shifting his weight, digging his hands into his pockets.

"Well?" was all she said.

"Ah, sorry about breaking on Hoyt's face."

"It's his face, you should apologize to him."

"We know where we stand. Just wanted to clear it with you." When she said nothing, he scratched the top of his head through his thick hair, and if a man of six six and two hundred and seventy pounds could squirm, King squirmed.

"Listen, I run up, and that light's blasting, and he's lying there bleeding and burning. Guy's my first sorcerer," King continued after another pause. I've only known him like a week. I've known Cian since . . . a really long time, and I owe him pretty much everything."

"So when you found him hurt, naturally, you assumed his brother tried to kill him."

"Yeah. Figured you had a part in it, too, but I couldn't beat hell out of you."

"I appreciate the chivalry."

The sting in her tone made him wince. "You sure got a way of cutting a man down to size."

"It would take a chain saw to cut you down to size. Oh, stop looking so pitiful and guilty." With a sigh, she scooped back her hair. "We screwed up, you screwed up, and we're all goddamn sorry about it. I suppose you want some wine now. Maybe a cookie."

He had to grin. "I'll take a beer." He opened the refrigerator, got one out. "I'll pass on the cookie. You're a butt-kicker, Red. Quality I admire in a woman—even if it's my butt getting the boot."

"I never used to be. I don't think."

She was also pretty and pale, and had to be dog tired. He'd worked her, all of them, damned hard that afternoon, and Cian had put them through the wringer tonight.

Sure she'd bitched a little, King thought now. But not nearly as much as he'd expected. And when it came down to it, Hoyt was right. She'd been the only one who'd known the answer to what the hell they were doing here.

"That stuff Hoyt was talking about, what you said, it makes a lot of sense. We don't straighten up, we're easy pickings." He popped the cap off the beer, swallowed half the bottle in one long gulp. "So I will if you will."

She looked at the enormous hand he held out, then placed hers in it. "I think Cian's lucky to have someone who'll fight for him. Who'd care enough to."

"He'd do the same for me. We go back."

"That kind of friendship usually takes time to form, to solidify. We're not going to have that kind of time."

"Guess we'd better take some shortcuts then. We cool now?"

"I'd say we're cool now."

He polished off the beer, then dumped the empty bottle in a can under the sink. "Heading up. You ought to do the same. Get some sleep."

"I will."

But when he left her alone, she was bruised and tired and restless, so Glenna sat alone in the kitchen with her glass of wine and the lights on full to beat back the dark. She didn't know the time and wondered if it mattered any longer.

They were all becoming vampires—sleeping through most of the day, working through most of the night.

She fingered the cross around her neck as she continued to write her list. And she felt the press of the night against her shoulder blades like cold hands.

She missed the city, she decided. No shame in admitting it. She missed the sounds of it, the colors, the constant thrum of traffic that was a heartbeat. She yearned for its complexity and simplicity. Life was just life there. And if there was death, if there was cruelty and violence, it was all so utterly human.

The image of the vampire on the subway flashed into her mind.

Or she'd once had the comfort of believing it was human.

Still, she wanted to get up in the morning and wander down to the deli for fresh bagels. She wanted to set her easel in the slash of morning light and paint, and have her strongest concern be how she was going to pay her Visa bill.

All of her life the magic had been in her, and she'd thought she'd valued and respected it. But it had been nothing to this, to know that it was in her for this reason, for this purpose.

That it could very well be the death of her.

She picked up her wine, then jolted when she saw Hoyt standing in the doorway.

"Not a good idea to go creeping around in the dark, considering the situation."

"I wasn't sure I should disturb you."

"Might as well. Just having my own private pity party. It'll pass," she said with a shrug. "I'm a little homesick. Small potatoes compared to how you must feel."

"I stand in the room I shared with Cian when we were boys and feel too much, and not enough."

She rose, got a second glass, poured wine. "Have a seat." She sat down again, set the wine on the table. "I have a brother," she told him. "He's a doctor, just starting. He has a whiff of magic, and he uses it to heal. He's a good doctor, a good man. He loves me, I know, but he doesn't understand me very well. It's hard not to be understood."

How could it be, he wondered, that there had never been a woman in his life other than family he could speak to about anything that truly mattered. And now, with Glenna, he knew he could, and would, talk with her of anything. And everything.

"It troubles me, the loss of him, of what we were to each other."

"Of course it does."

"His memories of me—Cian's—are faded and old while mine are fresh and strong." Hoyt lifted his glass. "Yes, it's difficult not to be understood."

"What I am, what's in me, I used to feel smug about it. Like it was a shiny prize I held in my hands, just for me. Oh, I was careful with it, grateful for it, but still smug. I don't think I ever will be again."

"With what we touched tonight, I'm doubting either of us could be smug again."

"Still, my family, my brother, didn't understand—not fully—that smugness or that prize. And they won't understand—not fully—the price I'm paying for it now. They can't."

She reached out, laid a hand over Hoyt's. "He can't. So, while our circumstances may be different, I understand the loss you're talking about. You look terrible," she said more lightly. "I can help ease that bruising a little more."

"You're tired. It can wait."

"You didn't deserve it."

"I let it take control. I let it fly out of me."

"No, it flew away from us. Who can say if it wasn't meant to." She'd bundled her hair up to train, to work, and now pulled out the pins so it fell, messily, just short of her shoulders.

"Look, we learned, didn't we? We're stronger together than either of us could have anticipated. What we're responsible for now is learning how to control it, channel it. And believe me, the rest of them will have more respect now, too."

He smiled a little. "That sounds a bit smug."

"Yeah, I guess it does."

He drank some wine and realized he was comfortable for the first time in hours. Just sitting in the bright kitchen with night trapped outside the glass, with Glenna to talk with.

Her scent was there, just on the edges of his senses. That earthy, female scent. Her eyes, so clear and green, showed some light bruising of fatigue on the delicate skin beneath them.

He nodded toward the paper. "Another spell?"

"No, something more pedestrian. Lists. I need more supplies. Herbs and so forth. And Moira and Larkin need clothes. Then we need to work out some basic household rules. So far it's been up to me and King for the most part. The cooking, that is. A household doesn't run itself, and even when you're preparing for war, you need food and clean towels."

"There are so many machines to do the work." He glanced around the kitchen. "It should be simple enough."

"You'd think."

"There used to be an herb garden. I haven't walked the land, not really." Put it off, he admitted. Put off seeing the changes, and what remained the same. "Cian might have had one planted. Or I could bring it back. The earth remembers."

"Well, that can go on the list for tomorrow. You know the woods around here. You should be able to tell me where to find the other things I need. I can go out in the morning and harvest."

"I knew them," he said half to himself.

"We need more weapons, Hoyt. And eventually more hands to wield them."

"There will be an army in Geall."

"We hope. I know a few like us, and Cian—it's likely he knows some like him. We may want to start enlisting."

"More vampires? Trusting Cian's been difficult enough.

As for more witches, we're still learning each other, as we learned tonight. We were to start with those we have. We've barely begun. But weapons. We can make them as we made the crosses."

She picked up her wine again, drank, breathed out slowly. "Okay. I'm game."

"We'll take them with us when we go to Geall."

"Speaking of. When and how?"

"How? Through the dance. When? I can't know. I have to believe we'll be told when it's time. That we'll know when it's time."

"Do you think we'll ever be able to get back? If we live? Do you think we'll be able to get back home?"

He looked over at her. She was sketching, her eyes on her pad, her hand steady. Her cheeks were pale, he noted, from fatigue and stress. Her hair was bright and bold, swinging forward as she dipped her head.

"Which disturbs you most?" he wondered. "Dying or not seeing your home again?"

"I'm not entirely sure. Death is inevitable. None of us get out of that one. And you hope—or I have—that when the time comes you'll have courage and curiosity, and so face it well."

Absently, she tucked her hair behind her ear with her left hand while her right continued to sketch. "But that's always been in the abstract. Until now. It's hard to think about dying, harder to think about it knowing I might not see home again, or my family. They won't understand what happened to me."

She glanced up. "And I'm preaching to the choir."

"I don't know how long they lived. How they died. How long they looked for me."

"It would help to know."

"Aye, it would." He shook it off, angled his head. "What do you draw there?"

She pursed her lips at the sketch. "It seems to be you." She turned it around, nudged it toward him.

"Is this how you see me?" His voice sounded puzzled, and not entirely pleased. "So stern."

"Not stern. Serious. You're a serious man. Hoyt McKenna." She printed the name on the sketch. "That's how it would be written and said today. I looked it up." She signed the sketch with a quick flourish. "And your serious nature is very attractive."

"Serious is for old men and politicians."

"And for warriors, for men of power. Knowing you, being attracted to you, makes me realize what I knew before you were boys. Apparently, I like much older men these days."

He sat, looking at her, with the sketch and the wine between them. With worlds between them, he told himself. And still he'd never felt closer to anyone. "To sit here like this with you, in the house that's mine, but not, in a world that's mine, but not, you're the single thing I want."

She rose, moved to him, put her arms around him. He rested his head just under her breasts, listened to her heart.

"Is it comfort?" she asked.

"Yes. But not only that. I have such a need for you. I don't know how to hold it inside me."

She lowered her head, closing her eyes as she rested her cheek on his hair. "Let's be human. For what's left of tonight, let's be human, because I don't want to be alone in the dark." She framed his face, lifted it to hers. "Take me to bed."

He took her hands as he got to his feet. "Such things haven't changed in a millennium, have they?"

She laughed. "Some things never change."

He kept her hand in his as they walked from the kitchen. "I haven't bedded many women—being a serious man."

"I haven't been bedded by many men—being a sensible woman." At the door to her room she turned to him with a quick, wicked smile. "But I think we'll manage."

"Wait." He brought her to him before she could open the door, and laid his lips on hers. She felt warmth, and an underlying shimmer of power.

Then he opened the door.

He'd lighted the candles, she saw. Every one of them, so the room was full of gilded light and soft scent. The fire burned as well, a low red simmer.

It touched a place in her heart even as it rippled anticipation over her skin.

"A very nice start. Thank you." She heard the click of the key in the lock, pressed a hand to her heart. "I'm nervous. All of a sudden. I've never been nervous about being with someone. Not even that first time. That smugness again."

He didn't mind her nerves. In fact, they added an edge to his own arousal. "Your mouth. This fullness here." He traced a fingertip over her bottom lip. "I can taste it in my sleep. You distract me, even when you're not with me."

"That annoys you." She reached up to link her arms around his neck. "I'm so glad."

She eased toward him, watching his gaze drop to her mouth, linger before it came back to hers. Felt his breath mix with her breath, and his heart beat against her heart. They held there, one endless moment, then their lips met. And they sank into each other.

Nerves fluttered in her belly again, a dozen velvet wings that swept against desire. And still that shimmer of power was like a hum in the air.

Then his hands were in her hair, sweeping it back from her face in a gesture of urgency that had her shuddering in anticipation of what was to come. And his mouth left hers to roam her face, to find that throbbing pulse in her throat.

She could drown him. He knew it even as he took more. This outrageous need for her could take him under, somewhere he'd never been. He knew, wherever that was, he would take her with him.

He molded the shape of her with his hands, steeped himself in it. She found his mouth again, avidly. He heard the shudder of her breath as she stepped back. The candlelight washed over her as she reached up, began to unbutton her shirt.

She wore something white and lacy beneath it that seemed to hold her breasts like an offering. There was more white lace when her pants slid down her hips, an alluring triangle that rode low on her belly, high on her legs.

"Women are the canniest creatures," he mused out loud, and reached out to skim a fingertip over the lace. When she trembled, he smiled. "I like these clothes. Are you always wearing these under the others?"

"No. It depends on my mood."

"I like this mood." He took his thumbs, brushed them up over the lace on her breasts.

Her head fell back. "Oh God."

"That pleasures you. What of this?" He did the same with the lace that sat snug below her belly, and watched the arousal slide over her face.

Soft skin, delicate and smooth. But there was muscle under it. Fascinating. "Just let me touch. Your body is beautiful. Just let me touch."

She reached back, gripped the bedpost. "Help yourself."

His fingers skimmed over her, made her skin quiver. Then pressed and made her moan. She could feel her own bones going to liquid, and her muscles to putty as he explored her. She gave herself to it, to the slow, enervating pleasure that was both triumph and surrender.

"Is this the fastener then?"

She opened heavy eyes as he fiddled with the front hook of her bra. But when she started to undo it, he brushed her hands aside.

"I'll figure it out on my own in a minute. Ah yes, there it is." As he unhooked it, her breasts spilled out and into his hands. "Clever. Beautiful." He lowered his head to them, tasted soft, warm flesh.

He wanted to savor; he wanted to rush.

"And the other part? Where is the fastener?" He ran his hands down her.

"They don't—" And over her. Her breath caught, a half cry as her fingers dug into his shoulders.

"Aye, look at me. Just like that." He skimmed his hands over the lace, under it. "Glenna Ward, who is mine tonight."

And she came where she stood, her body exploding and her eyes trapped by his.

Her head went limp on his shoulder as she shuddered, shuddered. "I want you on me, I want you in me." She dragged at the sweatshirt he wore, drawing it up and away. Now she found muscle and flesh with her hands, with her lips. Now the power seeped back into her as she pulled him with her onto the bed.

"Inside me. Inside me."

Her mouth crushed hungrily to his, hips arching and offering. He fought with the rest of his clothes, struggled to devour more of her as the heat pumped off them both.

When he plunged into her, the fire roared, and the candle flames shot up like arrows.

Passion and power whipped through them, spurring them on toward madness. Still she locked herself around him, stared at him even as tears glazed her eyes.

A wind stirred her hair, bright as fire against the bed. He felt her gather beneath him, tighten like a bow. When the light burst through him, he could only breathe her name.

She felt alight, as if whatever they had ignited between them burned still. She wondered she didn't see beams of its gilded light shooting out of her fingertips.

In the hearth, the fire had settled down to a quiet simmer; another afterglow. But the heat that had bloomed from it, and from them, dewed her skin. Even now her heart moved at a gallop.

His head rested there, on her heart, and her hand on his head.

"Have you ever . . ."

His lips brushed her breast, lightly. "No."

She combed her fingers through his hair. "Neither have I. Maybe it was because it was the first time, or because some of what we made earlier was still stored up."

We're stronger together. Her own words echoed in her mind.

"Where do we go from here?"

When he lifted his head, she shook hers. "An expression," she explained. "And it doesn't matter now. Your bruises are gone."

"I know. Thank you."

"I don't know that I did it."

"You did. You touched my face when we joined." He took

her hand, brought it to his lips. "There's magic in your hands, and in your heart. And still your eyes are troubled."

"Just tired."

"Do you want me to leave you?"

"No, I don't." And wasn't that the problem? "I want you to stay."

"Here then." He shifted, bringing her with him, tucking up sheet and blanket. "I have a question."

"Mmm."

"You have a brand, here." He traced his fingers over the small of her back. "A pentagram. Are witches marked so in this time?"

"No. It's a tattoo—my choice. I wanted to wear a symbol of what I am, even when I was skyclad."

"Ah. I mean no disrespect to your purpose, or your symbol, but I found it . . . alluring."

She smiled to herself. "Good. Then it performed its secondary purpose."

"I feel whole again," he said. "I feel myself again."

"So do I."

But tired, he thought. He could hear it in her voice. "We'll sleep awhile."

She tilted her head up so their eyes met. "You said when you took me to bed you wouldn't give me any sleep."

"This once."

She rested her head on his shoulder, but didn't close her eyes, even when he dimmed the candles. "Hoyt. Whatever happens, this was precious."

"For me as well. And for the first time, Glenna, I believe not only that we must win, but that we can. I believe that because you're with me."

Now she closed her eyes for just a moment, on the pang just under her heart. He spoke of war, she thought. And she'd spoken of love.

She woke to rain, and his warmth. Glenna lay, listening to the patter, absorbing the good, natural feel of a man's body beside hers.

She'd had to lecture herself during the night. What she had with Hoyt was a gift, one that should be treasured and appreciated. There was no point in cursing because it wasn't enough.

And what good did it do to question why it had happened? To wonder if whatever was driving them to the battleground had brought them together, had ignited that passion and need, and yes, love, because they were stronger with it?

It was enough to feel; she'd always believed that. And only doubted it now because she felt so much.

It was time to go back to being practical, to enjoy what she had when she had it. And to do the job at hand.

She eased away from him, started to get out of bed. His hand closed around her wrist.

"It's early, and raining. Come, stay in bed."

She looked over her shoulder. "How do you know it's early. There's no clock in here. Got a sundial in your head?"

"Sure a lot of good it would do as it's pouring rain. Your hair's like the sun. Come back to bed."

He didn't look so serious now, she noted, not with his eyes sleepy and his face shadowed by a night's growth of beard. What he looked was edible.

"You need a shave."

He rubbed a hand over his face, felt the stubble. Rubbed his hand over again, and the stubble was gone. "Is that better for you, *a stór?*"

She reached over, flicked a finger down his cheek. "Very smooth. You could use a decent haircut."

He frowned, scooped a hand through his hair. "What would be wrong with my hair?"

"It's gorgeous, but it could use a little shaping. I can take care of that for you."

"I think not."

"Oh, don't trust me?"

"Not with my hair."

She laughed and rolled over to straddle him. "You trust me with other, and more sensitive parts of you."

"A different matter entirely." His hands walked up and

cupped her breasts. "What's the name of the garment you wore over your lovely breasts last night?"

"It's called a bra, and don't change the subject."

"Sure I'm happier discussing your breasts than my hair."

"Aren't you cheerful this morning."

"You put a light in me."

"Sweet talker." She picked up a hank of his hair. "Snip, snip. You'll be a new man."

"You seem to like the man I am well enough."

Her lips curved as she lifted her hips. And lowered them to take him into her. The candles that had guttered out sparked. "Just a trim," she whispered, leaning over him to rub her lips to his. "After."

He learned the considerable pleasure of showering with a woman, then the fascinating pleasure of watching one dress.

She rubbed creams into her skin, and different ones over her face.

The bra, and what she called panties, were blue today. Like a robin's egg. Over these she pulled rough pants and the short, baggy tunic she called a sweatshirt. On it were words that spelled out WALKING IN A WICCAN WONDERLAND.

He thought the outer clothes made what she wore beneath a kind of marvelous secret.

He felt relaxed and very pleased with himself. And balked when she told him to sit on the lid of the toilet. She picked up scissors, snapped them together.

"Why would a man of sense allow a woman to come near him with a tool like that?"

"A big, tough sorcerer like you shouldn't be afraid of a little haircut. Besides, if you don't like it when I'm done, you can change it back."

"Why are women always after fiddling with a man?"

"It's our nature. Indulge me."

He sighed, and sat. And squirmed.

"Be still, and it'll be done before you know it. How do you suppose Cian deals with grooming?"

He rolled his eyes up, over, to try to see what she was doing to him. "I wouldn't know."

"No reflection must make it a chore. And he always looks perfect."

Now Hoyt slid his eyes toward hers. "You like the way he looks, do you?"

"You're almost mirror images, so it's obvious I do. He has that slight cleft in his chin and you don't."

"Where the faeries pinched him. My mother used to say."

"Your face is a little leaner, and your eyebrows have more of an arch. But your eyes, those mouths and cheekbones—the same."

He watched hair fall into his lap, and inside the mighty sorcerer, his belly trembled. "Jesus, woman, are you shearing me bald?"

"Lucky for you I like long hair on a man. At least I do on you." She dropped a kiss on the top of his head. "Yours is like black silk, with just a little wave. You know, in some cultures, when a woman cuts a man's hair it's a vow of marriage."

His head jerked, but she'd anticipated the reaction and moved the scissors. Her laugh, full of fun and teasing, echoed off the bathroom walls. "Joking. Boy, are you easy. Almost done."

She straddled his legs, standing with hers apart, and her breasts close to his face. He began to think a haircut wasn't such a hardship after all.

"I liked the feel of a woman."

"Yes, I seem to recall that about you."

"No, what I'm meaning is I liked the feel of a woman when I had one. I'm a man, have needs like any other. But it never occupied so much of my mind as it does with you."

She set the scissors aside, then combed her fingers through his damp hair. "I like occupying your mind. Here, have a look."

He stood, studied himself in the mirror. His hair was shorter, but not unreasonably. He supposed it fell in a more pleasing shape—though it had seemed fine to him before she'd gone after it.

Still, she hadn't sheared him like a sheep, and it pleased her.

"It's well enough, thank you."

"You're welcome."

He finished dressing, and when they went downstairs they found all but Cian in the kitchen.

Larkin was scooping up scrambled eggs. "Good morning to you. The man here has a magician's hands with eggs."

"And my shift at the stove's over," King announced. "So if you want breakfast, you're on your own."

"That's something I wanted to talk about." Glenna opened the refrigerator. "Shifts. Cooking, laundry, basic house-keeping. It needs to be spread out among all of us."

"I'm happy to help," Moira put in. "If you'll show me what to do and how to do it."

"All right, watch and learn. We'll stick with the bacon and eggs for this morning." She got to work on it with Moira watching her every move.

"I wouldn't mind more, while you're about it."

Moira glanced at Larkin. "He eats like two horses."

"Hmm. We're going to need regular supplies." She spoke to King now. "I'd say that falls to you or me, as these three can't drive. Both Larkin and Moira are going to need clothes that fit. If you draw me a map, I can make the next run."

"There's no sun today."

Glenna nodded at Hoyt. "I have protection, and it may clear up."

"The household needs to run, as you said, so you can draw up your plans. We'll follow them. But as to other mat-ters, you have to follow. I think no one goes out alone, out of doors, into the village. No one goes out unarmed."

"Are we to be under siege then, held in by a shower of rain?" Larkin stabbed the air with his fork. "Isn't it time we showed them we won't let them set the terms?"

"He has a point," Glenna agreed. "Cautious but not cowed."

"And there's a horse in the stable," Moira added. "He needs to be tended."

The fact was Hoyt had intended to do so himself, while

the others were busy elsewhere. He wondered now if what he'd told himself was responsibility and leadership was just another lack of trust.

"Larkin and I will tend to the horse." He sat when Glenna put plates on the table. "Glenna needs herbs and so do I, so we'll deal with that as well. Cautious," he repeated. And began to devise how it could be done while he ate.

He strapped on a sword. The rain was a fine drizzle now, the sort he knew could last for days. He could change that. He and Glenna together could bring out sun bright enough to blast the sky.

But the earth needed rain.

He nodded to Larkin, opened the door.

They moved out together, splitting right and left, back-to-back to gauge the ground.

"Be a miserable watch in this weather if they just sit and wait," Larkin pointed out.

"We'll stay close together in any case."

They crossed the ground, searching for shadows and movement. But there was nothing but the rain, the smell of wet flowers and grass.

When they reached the stables, the work was routine for both of them. Mucking out, fresh straw, grain and grooming. Comforting, Hoyt thought, to be around the horse.

Larkin sang as he worked, a cheery air.

"I've a chestnut mare at home," he told Hoyt. "She's a beauty. It seemed we couldn't bring the horses through the dance."

"I was told to leave my own mare behind. Is it true about the legend? The sword and the stone, and the one who rules Geall? Like the legend of Arthur?"

"It is, and some say it was fashioned from it." As he spoke, Larkin poured fresh water in the trough. "After the death of the king or queen, the sword is placed back in the stone by a magician. On the day after the burial, the heirs then come, one by one, and try to take it out again. Only one will succeed, and rule all of Geall. The sword is kept in the great hall for all to see, until that ruler dies. And so it is repeated, generation after generation."

He wiped his brow. "Moira has no brothers, no sisters. She must rule."

Intrigued, Hoyt stopped to glance over. "If she fails, would it come to you?"

"Spare me from that," Larkin said with feeling. "I've no wish to rule. Bloody nuisance if you're asking me. Well, he's set, isn't he?" He rubbed the stallion's side. "You're a handsome devil, that's the truth. He needs exercise. One of us should ride him out."

"Not today, I think. But you're right in that. He needs a run. Still, he's Cian's, so it's for him to say."

They moved to the door, and as before, stepped out together. "That way." Hoyt gestured. "There was an herb garden, and may still be. I haven't walked that way as yet."

"Moira and I have. I didn't see one."

"We'll have a look."

It sprang off the roof of the stables, so quickly Hoyt had no chance to draw his sword. And the arrow struck it dead in the heart while it was still in the air.

Ash flew as a second leaped. And a second arrow shot home.

"Would you let us have one for the sport of it!" Larkin shouted to Moira.

She stood in the kitchen doorway, a third arrow already notched. "Then take the one coming from the left."

"For me," Larkin shouted at Hoyt.

It was twice his size, and Hoyt started to protest. But Larkin was already charging. Steel struck steel. It clashed and it rang. Twice he saw the thing step back when Larkin's cross glinted at him. But he had a reach, and a very long sword.

When Hoyt saw Larkin slip on the wet grass, he lunged forward. He swung the sword at the thing's neck—and met air.

Larkin leaped up, flipped the wooden stake up, caught it neatly. "I was just throwing him off balance."

"Nicely done."

"There may be more."

"There may be," Hoyt agreed. "But we'll do what we came to do."

"I've got your back then, if you've mine. God knows Moira's got them both. This hurt it," he added, touching the cross. "Gave it some trouble anyway."

"They may be able to kill us, but they won't be able to turn us while we wear them."

"Then I'd say that's a job well done."

Chapter 13

There was no herb garden with its creeping thyme and fragrant rosemary. The pretty knot garden his mother had tended was now a gently rolling span of cropped green grass. It would be a sunny spot when the sky cleared, he knew. His mother had chosen it, though it hadn't been just outside the kitchen as was more convenient, so her herbs could bask in the light.

As a child he'd learned of them from her, of their uses and their beauty, while sitting by her as she weeded and clipped and harvested. She'd taught him their names and their needs. He'd learned to identify them by their scents and shapes of the leaves, by the flowers that bolted from them if she allowed it.

How many hours had he spent there with her, working the earth, talking or just sitting in silence to enjoy the butterflies, the hum of bees?

It had been their place, he thought, more than any other.

He'd grown to a man and had found his place on the cliff in what was now called Kerry. He'd built his stone cabin, and found the solitude he'd needed for his own harvest, for his magic.

But he'd always come back home. And had always found pleasure and solace with his mother here, in her herb garden.

Now, he stood over where it had been as he might have a grave, mourning and remembering. A flare of anger lit in him that his brother would let this go.

"This what you're looking for then?" Larkin studied the grass, then tracked his eyes through the rain, toward the trees. "Doesn't seem to be anything left of it."

Hoyt heard a sound, pivoted as Larkin did. Glenna walked toward them, a stake in one hand, a knife in the other. Rain beaded her hair like tiny jewels.

"You're to stay in the house. There could be more of them."

"If there are, there are three of us now." She jerked her head toward the house. "Five as Moira and King have us covered."

Hoyt looked over. Moira was in the near window, her arrow notched, her bow pointed downward. In the doorway to the left, King stood with a broadsword.

"That ought to do it." Larkin sent his cousin a cheeky grin. "Mind you don't shoot one of us in the arse."

"Only if I'm aiming for it," she called back.

Beside Hoyt, Glenna studied the ground. "Was it here? The garden?"

"It was. Will be."

Something was wrong, she thought, very wrong, to have put that hard look on his face. "I have a rejuvenation spell. I've had good luck with it, healing plants."

"I won't need it for this." He stabbed his sword in the ground to free his hands.

He could see it, just as it had been, and honed that image clear into his mind as he stretched out his arms, spread his hands. This, he knew, would come from his heart as much as from his art. This was tribute to the one who had given him life.

And because of it, would be painful.

"Seed to leaf, leaf to flower. Soil and sun and rain. Remember."

His eyes changed, and his face looked carved from stone.

Larkin started to speak, but Glenna tapped a finger to her lips to stop him. There should be no voice, no words now, she knew, but Hoyt's. Power was already thickening the air.

She couldn't help with the visualization as Hoyt hadn't described the garden to her. But she could focus on scent. Rosemary, lavender, sage.

He repeated the incantation three times, his eyes darkening further, his voice rising with each repetition. Beneath their feet, the ground shuddered lightly.

The wind began to lift, then swirl, then blow.

"Rise up! Return. Grow and bloom. Gift from the earth, from the gods. For the earth, for the gods. Airmed, oh ancient one, release your bounty. Airmed, of the *Tuatha de Danaan,* feed this earth. As once this was, let it return."

His face was pale as marble, his eyes dark as onyx. And the power flowed out of him onto, into, the trembling ground.

It opened.

Glenna heard Larkin suck in his breath, heard her own heartbeat rise up to drum in her ears. The plants rose up, leaves unfurling, blooms bursting. The thrill spun into her, released itself of a laugh of pure delight.

Silvery sage, glossy needles of rosemary, tumbling carpets of thyme and camomile, bay and rue, delicate spears of lavender, and more spread out of the ground and into the misting rain.

The garden formed a Celtic knot, she saw, with narrow loops and pathways to make harvesting easier.

As the wind died, as the earth stilled, Larkin blew out a long breath. "Well, that's some damn fine farming."

She laid a hand on Larkin's shoulder. "It's lovely, Hoyt. Some of the prettiest magic I've ever seen. Blessed be."

He pulled his sword out of the ground. The heart that had opened to make the magic was sore as a bruise. "Take what you need, but be quick. We've been out long enough."

She used her bolline, and worked with efficiency, though she wished she could linger, just enjoy the work.

The scents surrounded her. And what she harvested, she knew, would be only more powerful for the manner of their becoming.

The man who'd touched her in the night, who'd held her in the morning had more power than any she'd ever know. Any she'd ever imagined.

"This is something I miss in the city," she commented. "I do a lot of windowsill pots, but it's just not the same as real gardening."

Hoyt said nothing, simply watched her—bright hair sparkling with rain, slim white hands brushing through the green. It closed a fist over his heart, just one quick squeeze and release.

When she stood, her arms full, her eyes laughing with the wonder of it, that heart tipped in his breast and fell as if a arrow had pierced it.

Bewitched, he thought. She had bewitched him. A woman's magic always aimed first for the heart.

"I can get quite a bit done with these." She tossed her head to swing back her damp hair. "And have enough left to season a nice soup for dinner."

"Best take them in then. We've movement to the west." Larkin nodded toward the west edge of the woods. "Just watching for now."

Bewitched, Hoyt thought again as he turned. He'd forgotten his watch, spellbound by her.

"I count half a dozen," Larkin continued, his voice cool and steady. "Though there may be more hanging back. Hoping to lure us, I'm thinking, into going after them. So they'll be more, aye, more hanging back to cut us down as we come."

"We've done what we need for the morning," Hoyt began, then thought better of it. "But no point letting them think they've pushed us back inside. Moira," he said, lifting his voice enough to carry to her, "can you take one out at this distance?"

"Which one would you like?"

Amused, he lifted a shoulder. "Your choice. Let's give them a bit of something to think about."

He'd barely uttered the words when the arrow flew, and a second so quickly after he thought he imagined it. There were two screams, one melding into the next. And where there had been six there were four—and those four rushed back into the cover of the woods.

"Two would give them more than a bit to think about." With a grim smile, Moira readied another arrow. "I can wing a few back into the woods, drive them back more if you like."

"Don't waste your wood."

Cian stepped to the window behind her. He looked rumpled and mildly irritated. Moira automatically stepped aside. "Wouldn't be wasted if they struck home."

"They'll move on for now. If they were here for more than a nuisance, they'd have charged while they had the numbers."

He walked past her to the side door, and out.

"Past your bedtime, isn't it?" Glenna said.

"I'd like to know who could sleep through all this. Felt like a bleeding earthquake." He studied the garden. "Your work, I assume," he said to Hoyt.

"No." The bitterness from the wound inside him eked out. "My mother's."

"Well, next time you've a bit of landscaping in mind, let me know so I don't wonder if the house is coming down on my ears. How many did you take out?"

"Five. Moira took four." Larkin sheathed his sword. "The other was mine."

He glanced back toward the window. "The little queen's racking up quite the score."

"We wanted to test the waters," Larkin told him, "and see to your horse."

"I'm grateful for that."

"I'm thinking I could take him out for a run now and again, if you wouldn't mind it."

"I wouldn't, and Vlad could use it."

"Vlad?" Glenna repeated.

"Just my little in joke. If the excitement's over, I'll be going back to bed."

"I need a word with you." Hoyt waited until Cian met his eyes. "Privately."

"And would this private word require standing about in the rain?"

"We'll walk."

"Suit yourself." Then he smiled at Glenna. "You look rosy this morning."

"And damp. There are plenty of dry, private places inside, Hoyt."

"I want the air."

There was a moment of humming silence. "He's a slow one. She's waiting to be kissed, so she'll worry less about you getting your throat ripped out because you want a walk in the rain."

"Go inside." Though he wasn't entirely comfortable with the public display, Hoyt took Glenna's chin in his hand, kissed her lightly on the lips. "I'll be fine enough."

Larkin drew his sword again, offered it to Cian. "Better armed than not."

"Words to live by." Then he leaned down, gave Glenna a quick, cocky kiss himself. "I'll be fine, as well."

They walked in silence, and with none of the camaraderie Hoyt remembered they'd shared. Times, he mused, they'd been able to know the other's mind without a word spoken. Now his brother's thoughts were barred to him, as he imagined his were to Cian.

"You kept the roses, but let the herb garden die. It was one of her greatest pleasures."

"The roses have been replaced, I can't count the times, since I acquired the place. The herbs? Gone before I bought the property."

"It's not property as the place you have in New York. It's home."

"It is to you." Hoyt's anger rolled off Cian's back like the rain. "If you expect more than I can or will give, you'll be in a constant state of disappointment. It's my money that bought the land and the house that sits on it, and mine that goes to maintaining both. I'd think you'd be in a better humor this morning, after romping with the pretty witch last night."

"Careful where you step," Hoyt said softly.

"I've good footing." And he couldn't resist treading on tender ground. "She's a prime piece, and no mistake. But I've had a few centuries more experience with women than you. There's more than lust in those striking green eyes of hers. She sees a future with them. And what, I wonder, will you do about that?"

"It's not your concern."

"Not in the least, no, but it's entertaining to speculate, particularly when I haven't a woman of my own to divert me at the moment. She's no round-heeled village girl happy with a roll in the hay and a trinket. She'll want and expect more of you, as women, particularly clever women, tend to."

Instinctively he glanced up, checking the cloud cover. Irish weather was tricky, he knew, and the sun could decide to spill out along with the rain. "Do you think if you survive these three months, satisfy your gods, to ask them for the right to take her back with you?"

"Why does it matter to you?"

"Not everyone asks a question because the answer matters. Can't you see her, tucked into your cottage on the cliffs in Kerry? No electricity, running water, no Saks around the corner. Cooking your dinner in a pot on the fire. Likely shorten her life expectancy by half given the lack of health care and nutrition, but well then, anything for love."

"What do you know of it?" Hoyt snapped. "You're not capable of love."

"Oh, you'd be wrong about that. My kind can love, deeply, even desperately. Certainly unwisely, which it appears we have in common. So you won't take her back, for that would be the selfish thing. You're much too holy, too pure for that. And enjoy the role of martyr too much as well. So you'll leave her here to pine for you. I might amuse myself by offering her some comfort, and seeing as we share a resemblance, I wager she'll take it. And me."

The blow knocked him back, but not down. He tasted blood, the gorgeous burn of it, then swiped a hand over his bleeding mouth. It had taken longer than he'd assumed it would to bait his brother.

"Well now, that's been a long time coming, for both of us." He tossed his sword aside as Hoyt had. "Let's have a go then."

Cian's fist moved so fast it was only a blur—a blur that had stars exploding in front of Hoyt's eyes. And his nose fountaining blood. Then they charged each other like rams.

Cian took one in the kidneys, and a second strike had his ears ringing. He'd forgotten Hoyt could fight like the devil when provoked. He ducked a jab and sent Hoyt down with a kick to the midsection. And found himself on his ass as his brother slashed out his legs and took his feet out from under him.

He could have been up in a fingersnap, ended it, but his blood was hot. And heated, preferred a grapple.

They rolled over the ground, punching, cursing while the rain soaked them through to the skin. Elbows and fists rammed into flesh, cracked against bone.

Then Cian reared back with a hiss and flash of fangs. Hoyt saw the burn sear into his brother's hand, in the shape of his cross.

"Fuck me," Cian muttered and sucked on burned flesh and welling blood. "I guess you need a weapon to best me."

"Aye, fuck you. I don't need anything but my own fists." Hoyt reached up, had nearly yanked off the chain. Then dropped his hand when he realized the utter stupidity of it.

"This is fine, isn't it?" He spat out the words, and some blood with it. "This is just fine. Brawling like a couple of street rats, and leaving ourselves open to anything that comes. If anything had been nearby, we'd be dead."

"Already am—and speak for yourself."

"This isn't what I want, trading blows with you." Though the fight was still on his face as he swiped blood from his mouth. "It serves nothing."

"Felt good though."

Hoyt's swollen lips twitched, and the leading edge of his temper dulled. "It did, that's the pure truth. Holy martyr, my ass."

"Knew that would get under your skin."

"Sure you always knew how to get there. If we can't be brothers, Cian, what are we?"

Cian sat as he was, absently rubbing at the grass and bloodstains on his shirt. "If you win, you'll be gone in a few months. Or I'll see you die. Do you know how many I've seen die?"

"If time's short, it should be more important."

"You know nothing of time." He got to his feet. "You want to walk? Come on then, and learn something of time."

He walked on through the drenching wet so that Hoyt was forced to fall in beside him.

"Is it all still in your hands? The land?"

"Most of it. Some was sold off a few centuries ago—and some was taken by the English during one of the wars, and given to some crony of Cromwell."

"Who is Cromwell?"

"Was. A right bastard, who spent considerable time and effort burning and raping Ireland for the British royals. Politics and wars—gods, humans and demons can't seem to get by without them. I convinced one of the man's sons, after he'd inherited, to sell it back to me. At quite a good price."

"Convinced him? You killed him."

"And what if I did?" Cian said wearily. "It was long ago."

"Is that how you came by your wealth? Killing?"

"I've had nine hundred years and more to fill the coffers, and have done so in a variety of ways. I like money, and I've always had a head for finance."

"Aye, you have."

"There were lean years in the beginning. Decades of them, but I came around. I traveled. It's a large and fascinating world, and I like having chunks of it. Which is why I don't care for the notion of Lilith pulling her own sort of Cromwell."

"Protecting your investment," Hoyt said.

"I am. I will. I earned what I have. I'm fluent in fifteen languages—a handy business asset."

"Fifteen?" It felt easier now, the walking, the talking. "You used to butcher even Latin."

"Nothing but time to learn, and more yet to enjoy the fruits. I enjoy them quite a bit."

"I don't understand you. She took your life, your humanity."

"And gave me eternity. While I may not be particularly grateful to her as it wasn't done for my benefit, I don't see the point in spending that eternity sulking about it. My existence is long, and this is what you and your kind have."

He gestured toward a graveyard. "A handful of years, then nothing but dirt and dust."

There was a stone ruin overcome by vines sharp with thorns and black with berries. The end wall remained and rose in a peak. Figures had been carved into it like a frame, and had been buffed nearly smooth again by time and weather.

Flowers, even small shrubs forced their way through the cracks with feathery purple heads drooping now, heavy from the rain.

"A chapel? Mother spoke of building one."

"And one was built," Cian confirmed. "This is what's left of it. And them, and the ones who came after. Stones and moss and weeds."

Hoyt only shook his head. Stones had been plunged into the ground or set upon it to mark the dead. Now he moved among them, over uneven ground where that ground had heaved, time and again, and the tall grass was slick with wet.

Like the carving on the ruin, the words etched into some of the stones were worn nearly smooth, and the stones bloomed with moss and lichen. Others he could read; names he didn't know. Michael Thomas McKenna, beloved husband of Alice. Departed this earth the sixth of May, eighteen hundred and twenty-five. And Alice, who'd joined him some six years after. Their children, one who'd left the world only days after coming into it, and three others.

They'd lived and died this Thomas, this Alice, centuries after he'd been born. And nearly two centuries before he stood here, reading their names.

Time was fluid, he thought, and those who passed through it so fragile.

Crosses rose up, and rounded stones tilted. Here and there weedy gardens grew over the graves as if they were tended by careless ghosts. And he felt them, those ghosts with every step he took.

A rose bush, heavy with rich red blooms grew lushly behind a stone no taller than his knees. Its petals were sheened like velvet. It was a quick strike to the heart, with the dull echoing pain behind it.

He knew he stood at his mother's grave.

"How did she die?"

"Her heart stopped. It's the usual way."

At his sides, Hoyt's fists bunched. "Can you be so cold, even here, even now?"

"Some said grief stopped it. Perhaps it did. He went first." Cian gestured to a second stone. "A fever took him around the equinox, the autumn after . . . I left. She followed three years after."

"Our sisters?"

"There, all there." He gestured at the grouping of stones. "And the generations that followed them—who remained in Clare, in any case. There was a famine, and it rotted the land. Scores died like flies, or fled to America, to Australia, to England, anywhere but here. There was suffering, pain, plague, pillage. Death."

"Nola?"

For a moment Cian said nothing, then he continued in a tone of deliberate carelessness. "She lived into her sixties—a good, long life for that era for a woman, a human. She had five children. Or it might've been six."

"Was she happy?"

"How could I say?" Cian said impatiently. "I never spoke to her again. I wasn't welcome in the house I now own. Why would I be?"

"She said I would come back."

"Well, you have, haven't you?"

Hoyt's blood was cool now, and ekeing toward cold. "There's no grave for me here. If I go back, will there be? Will it change what's here?"

"The paradox. Who's to say? In any case, you vanished, or so it's told. Depending on the version. You're a bit of a legend in these parts. Hoyt of Clare—though Kerry likes to claim you as well. Your song and story doesn't reach as high as a god, or even that of Merlin, but you've a notch in some guidebooks. The stone circle just to the north, the one you used? It's attributed to you now, and called Hoyt's Dance."

Hoyt didn't know whether to be embarrassed or flattered. "It's the Dance of the Gods, and it was here long before me."

"So goes truth, particularly when fantasy's shinier. The caves beneath the cliffs where you tossed me into the sea? It's said you lie there, deep beneath the rock, guarded by faeries, under the land where you would stand to call the lightning and the wind."

"Foolishness."

"An amusing claim to fame."

For a time they said nothing, just stood, two men of striking physical similarity, in a rainy world of the dead.

"If I'd gone with you that night, as you asked me, ridden out with you, to stop as you said at the pub in the village. A drink and a tumble . . ." Hoyt's throat went hot as he remembered it. "But I had work on my mind and didn't want company. Not even yours. I had only to go, and none of this would be."

Cian slicked back his dripping hair. "You take a lot on yourself, don't you? But then, you always did. If you'd gone, it's likely she'd have had us both—so it's true enough, none of this would be."

What he saw on Hoyt's face brought the fury rushing back into him. "Do I ask for your guilt? You weren't my keeper then or now. I stand here as I did centuries ago, and barring bad luck—or my own idiocy in letting you drag me into this thing and the serious risk of a stake through the heart, I'll stand here again centuries after. And you, Hoyt, food for the worms. So which of us has destiny smiled on?"

"What is my power if I can't change that one night, that one moment? I'd have gone with you. I'd have died for you."

Cian's head whipped up, and on his face was the same hot temper it had held in battle. "Don't put your death, or your regrets, on me."

But there was no answering anger in Hoyt. "And you would have died for me. For any one of them." He spread his arms to encompass the graves.

"Once."

"You are half of me. Nothing you are, nothing that was done changes that. You know it as I know it. Even more than blood, more than bone. We are, beneath all that, what we ever were."

"I can't *exist* in this world feeling this." Emotion swirled now, into his face, his voice. "I can't grieve for what I am, or for you. Or for them. And damn you, goddamn you for bringing me back to it."

"I love you. It's bound in me."

"What you love is gone."

No, Hoyt thought, he was looking at the heart of what he'd loved. He could see it in the roses his brother had planted over their mother's grave.

"You're standing here with me and the spirits of our family. You're not so changed, Cian, or you would not have done this." He touched the petals of a rose over his mother's grave. "You could not have done it."

Cian's eyes were suddenly ageless, filled with the torment of centuries. "I've seen death. Thousands upon thousands. Age and sickness, murder and war. I didn't see theirs. And this was all I could do for them."

When Hoyt moved his hand, the petals of an overblown rose spilled down and scattered on his mother's grave. "It was enough."

Cian looked down at the hand Hoyt held out to him. He sighed once, deeply. "Well, damn to us both then," he said and clasped hands with his brother. "We've been out long enough, no point in tempting fate any longer. And I want my bed."

They started back the way they'd come.

"Do you miss the sun?" Hoyt wondered. "Walking in it, feeling it on your face?"

"They've found it gives you cancer of the skin."

"Huh." Hoyt considered it. "Still, the warmth of it on a summer morning."

"I don't think about it. I like the night."

Perhaps it wasn't the time to ask Cian to allow him to do a little experimental bloodletting.

"What do you do in these businesses of yours? And with your leisure? Do you—"

"I do as I please. I like to work; it's satisfying. And makes play more appealing. And it's not possible to catch up on several centuries during a morning's walk in the rain, even if

I were inclined." He rested the sword on his shoulder. "But likely you'll catch your death from it, and spare me the questions in any case."

"I'm made of stronger stuff than that," Hoyt said, cheerfully now, "as I proved when I bashed your face not long ago. You've a fine bruise on your jaw."

"It'll be gone quicker than yours, unless the witch intervenes again. In any case, I was holding back."

"Bollocks to that."

The shadows that always fell on him when he visited that graveyard began to lift. "If I'd come at you full, we'd be digging your grave back there."

"Let's go again, then."

Cian slanted Hoyt a look. Memories, the pleasure of them so long suppressed, crept back on him. "Another time. And when I'm finished pounding you, you won't be up to romping with the redhead."

Hoyt grinned. "I've missed you."

Cian stared ahead as the house peeked through the trees. "The bloody hell of it is I've missed you, too."

Chapter 14

With a crossbow armed and ready by her side, Glenna kept watch from the tower window. She'd considered the fact that she'd had very little practice with that particular weapon, and that her aim could be called into serious question.

But she couldn't just sit up there, unarmed and wringing her hands like some helpless female. If the damn sun would come out, she wouldn't have to worry. More than that, she thought with a little hiss, if the McKenna boys hadn't wandered off—obviously to snarl at each other in private—she wouldn't have these images in her head of them being ripped to pieces by a pack of vampires.

Pack? Herd? Gang?

What did it matter? They still had fangs and a bad attitude.

Where had they *gone*? And why had they been out, exposed and vulnerable, so long?

Maybe the pack/herd/gang had already ripped them to shreds and dragged their mutilated bodies off to . . . And oh, God, she wished she could turn off the video in her head for five damn minutes.

Most women just worried about their man getting mugged or run over by a bus. But oh no, *she* had to get herself tangled up with a guy at war with blood-sucking fiends.

Why couldn't she have fallen for a nice accountant or stockbroker?

She had thought of using her skill and the crystal to look for them. But it seemed . . . intrusive, she decided. And rude.

But if they weren't back in ten minutes, she was going to say screw manners and find them.

She hadn't thought through, not completely, the emotional turmoil Hoyt was experiencing, what he missed, and what he risked. More than the rest of them, she decided. She was thousands of miles away from her family, but not hundreds of years. He was in the home where he'd grown up, but it was no longer his home. And every day, every hour, was another reminder of that.

Bringing back his mother's herb garden had hurt him. She should have thought of that, too. Kept her mouth shut about what she'd needed and wanted. Just made a damn list and gone out to find or buy supplies.

She glanced back at some of the herbs she'd already bundled and hung to dry. Small things, everyday things could cause the most pain.

Now he was out there somewhere, in the rain, with his brother. The vampire. She didn't believe Cian would attack Hoyt—or didn't want to believe it. But if Cian were angry enough, pushed hard enough, could he control what must be natural urges?

She didn't know the answer.

Added to that, no one could be sure more of Lilith's forces were out and about, just waiting for another chance.

It was probably silly to worry. They were two men of considerable power, men who knew the land. Neither of them were solely dependent on swords and daggers. Hoyt was armed, and he wore one of the crosses they'd conjured, so he was hardly defenseless.

And it proved a point, didn't it, the two of them being out, moving freely? It proved they wouldn't be held under siege.

No one else was worried, particularly. Moira was back in

the library, studying. Larkin and King were in the training area doing a weapon inventory. She was, undoubtedly, worked up about nothing.

Where the *hell* were they?

As she continued to scan, she spotted movement. Just shadows in the gloom. She grabbed the crossbow, ordered her fingers to stop shaking as she positioned it and herself in the narrow window.

"Just breathe," she told herself. "Just breathe. In and out, in and out."

That breath came out on a whoosh of relief when she saw Hoyt, Cian beside him. Trooping along, she noted, dripping wet, as if they had all the time in the world, and not a care in it.

Her brows drew together as they came closer. Was that blood on Hoyt's shirt, and a fresh bruise spreading under his right eye?

She leaned out, bumped the stone sill. And the arrow shot out of the bow with a deadly twang. She actually squealed. She'd hate herself for it later, but the purely female sound of shock and distress ripped out of her as the arrow sliced air and rain.

And landed, just a few inches short of the toe of Hoyt's boot.

Their swords were out, a blur of steel, as they pivoted back-to-back. Under other circumstances she would have admired the move, the sheer grace and rhythm of it, like a dance step. But at the moment, she was caught between mortification and horror.

"Sorry! Sorry!" She leaned out farther, waved her arm frantically as she shouted. "It was me. It got away from me. I was just . . ." Oh hell with it. "I'm coming down."

She left the weapon where it was, vowing to take a full hour of practice with it before she shot at anything but a target again. Before she set off in a run, she heard the unmistakable sound of male laughter. A quick glance showed her it was Cian, all but doubled over with it. Hoyt simply stood, staring up at the window.

As she swung down the stairs, Larkin came out of the training room. "Trouble?"

"No, no. Nothing. Everything's fine. It's nothing at all." She could actually feel the blood rise up to heat her cheeks as she dashed for the main floor.

They were coming in the front door, shaking themselves like wet dogs as she sprinted down the last steps.

"I'm sorry. I'm so sorry."

"Remind me not to piss you off, Red," Cian said easily. "You might aim for my heart and shoot me in the balls."

"I was just keeping watch for you, and I must've pulled the trigger by mistake. Which I wouldn't have done if the two of you hadn't been gone so damn long and had me so worried."

"That's what I love about women." Cian slapped his brother's shoulder. "They damn near kill you, but in the end it's your own fault. Good luck with that. I'm going to bed."

"I need to check your burns."

"Nag, nag, nag."

"And what happened? Were you attacked? Your mouth's bleeding—yours, too," she said to Hoyt. "And your eye's damn near swollen shut."

"No, we weren't attacked." There was a world of exasperation in his voice. "Until you nearly shot me in the foot."

"Your faces are all banged up, and your clothes are filthy—ripped. If you weren't . . ." It came to her, when she saw the expressions on their faces. She had a brother of her own, after all. "You punched each other? *Each other?*"

"He hit me first."

She gave Cian a look that would have withered stone. "Well, that's just fine, isn't it? Didn't we go through all this yesterday? Didn't we talk about in-fighting, how destructive and useless it is?"

"I guess we're going to bed without our supper."

"Don't get smart with me." She jabbed a finger into Cian's chest. "I'm here worried half sick, and the two of you are out there wrestling around like a couple of idiot puppies."

"You nearly put an arrow in my foot," Hoyt reminded her. "I think we're quits on foolish behavior for one day."

She only hissed out a breath. "Into the kitchen, both of you. I'll do something about those cuts and bruises. Again."

"I'm having my bed," Cian began.

"Both of you. Now. You don't want to mess with me at the moment."

As she sailed off, Cian rubbed a finger gently on his split lip. "It's been a long while, but I don't recall you having a particular fondness for bossy women."

"I didn't, previously. But I understand them well enough to know we might as well be after letting her have her way on this. And the fact is, my eye's paining me."

When they came in, Glenna was setting what she needed out on the table. She had the kettle on the boil, and her sleeves rolled up.

"Do you want blood?" she said to Cian, with enough frost in the words to have him clearing his throat.

It amazed him that he actually felt chagrined. It was a sensation he hadn't felt in . . . too long to remember. Obviously living so closely with humans was a bad influence.

"The tea you're making will do, thanks."

"Take off your shirt."

There was a smart comment on the tip of his tongue, she could all but see it. He proved himself a wise man by swallowing it.

He stripped it off, sat.

"I'd forgotten about the burns." Hoyt examined them now. There was no longer any blistering, and they'd gone down to a dull, ugly red. "If I'd remembered," he said as he sat across from Cian, "I'd have put more blows into your chest."

"Typical," Glenna said under her breath, and was ignored.

"You don't fight altogether the way you used to. You use your feet more, and elbows." And Hoyt could still feel the aching result of them. "Then there's that leaping off the ground."

"Martial arts. I have black belts in several of them. Master status," Cian explained. "You need to put more time into training."

Hoyt rubbed his sore ribs. "And so I will."

Weren't they chummy all of a sudden? Glenna thought. What was it about men that made them decide to be pals after they'd smashed their fists into each other's faces?

She poured hot water into the pot, and while it steeped came to the table with her salve.

"I would've said three weeks to heal with what I can do, considering the extent of the burns." She sat, slicked salve on her fingers. "I'm amending that to three days."

"We can be hurt, and seriously. But unless it's a killing blow, we heal—and quickly."

"Lucky for you, especially as you've got a mass of nice bruising to go with the burns. But you don't regenerate," she continued as she applied the salve. "If, say, we were to cut off one of their arms, it wouldn't grow back."

"There's a gruesome and interesting thought. No. I've never heard of anything like that happening."

"Then if we can't get to the heart or the head, we can go for a limb."

She went to the sink to wash the salve from her hands, and make cold packs for the bruising. "Here." She handed one to Hoyt. "Hold that on your eye."

He sniffed at it, then complied. "You shouldn't have worried."

Cian winced. "Bad tact. Wiser to say: 'Ah, my love, we're sorry we worried you. We were selfish and inconsiderate, should likely be flogged for it. We hope you'll forgive us.' Thicken the brogue a bit as well. Women are fools for brogues."

"Then kiss her feet, I suppose."

"Actually, you aim for the ass. Ass kissing is a tradition that never goes out of style. You'll need patience with him, Glenna. Hoyt's still working on the learning curve."

She brought the tea to the table, then surprised them both when she laid a hand on Cian's cheek. "And you're going to teach him how to deal with the modern woman?"

"Well, he's a bit pitiful, is all."

Her lips curved as she lowered her head, brushed them over Cian's. "You're forgiven. Drink your tea."

"Just that easy?" Hoyt complained. "He gets a pat on the cheek and a kiss with it? You didn't nearly put an arrow into him."

"Women are a constant mystery." Cian spoke quietly.

"And one of the wonders of the world. I'll take this up with me." He got to his feet. "I'm wanting some dry clothes."

"Drink all of it." Glenna spoke without turning as she took up another bottle. "It'll help."

"I will then. Let me know if he doesn't learn fast enough to suit you. I wouldn't quibble with being second choice."

"That's just his way," Hoyt told her when Cian left the room. "A kind of teasing."

"I know. So you made friends again while you were bloodying each other."

"It's true enough I hit him first. I spoke to him of our mother, and the garden, and he was cold. Even though I could see what was under that cold, I . . . well, I lashed out, and . . . After, he took me to where our family's buried. And there you have it."

She turned now, and all the pity in her heart swirled into her eyes. "It must've been hard for both of you to be there."

"It makes it real to me, that as I sit here now, they're gone. It didn't seem real before. Not solid and real."

She moved to him, dabbed her tincture on his facial bruises. "And for him, to have lived all this time with no family at all. Another cruelty of what was done to him. To all of them. We don't think of that do we, when we talk about war, and how to destroy them? They were people once, just like Cian."

"They mean to kill us, Glenna. Every one of us that has a heartbeat."

"I know. I know. Something drained them of humanity. But they were human once, Hoyt, with families, lovers, hopes. We don't think of that. Maybe we can't."

She brushed the hair back from his face. A nice accountant, she thought again. A stockbroker. How ridiculous, how ordinary. She had, right here, the amazing.

"I think fate put Cian here, this way, so we understand there's a weight to what we're doing. So that we know, at the end of the day, we've done what we had to do. But not without cost."

She stepped back. "That'll have to do. Try to keep your face from walking into any more fists."

She started to turn, but he took her hand, rising as he drew her back to him. His lips took hers with utter tenderness.

"I think fate put you here, Glenna, to help me understand it's not just death and blood and violence. There's such beauty, such kindness in the world. And I have it." He wrapped his arms around here. "I have it here."

She indulged herself, letting her head rest on his shoulder. She wanted to ask what they'd have when it was over, but she knew it was important, even essential, to take each day as it came.

"We should work." She drew back. "I've got some ideas about creating a safe zone around the house. A protected area where we can move around more freely. And I think Larkin's right about sending out scouts. If we can get to the caves during the day, we might be able to find something out. Even set traps."

"Your mind's been busy."

"I need to keep it that way. I'm not as afraid if I'm thinking, if I'm doing."

"Then we work."

"Moira might be able to help once we have a start," Glenna added as they left the kitchen. "She's reading everything she can get her hands on, so she'd be our prime data source—information," she explained. "And she has some power. It's raw and untrained, but it's there."

While Glenna and Hoyt closed themselves in the tower and the house was quiet, Moira pored over a volume on demon lore in the library. It was fascinating, she thought. So many different theories and legends. She considered it her task to pick them apart for truth.

Cian would know it, or some of it, she concluded. Centuries of existence was plenty of time to learn. And anyone who filled such a room with books sought and respected knowledge. But she wasn't ready to ask him—wasn't sure she would ever be.

If he wasn't like the creatures she read of, those that sought human blood night after night—and thirsted not just for that blood, but the kill—what was he? Now he prepared to make war against what he was, and she didn't understand it.

She needed to learn more, about what they fought, about Cian, about all the others. How could you understand, and then trust, what you didn't know?

She made notes, copious notes, on the paper she'd found in one of the drawers of the big desk. She loved the paper, and the writing instrument. The pen, she corrected, that held the ink inside its tube. She wondered if she could smuggle some of the paper and pens back to Geall.

She closed her eyes. She missed home, and the missing was like a constant ache in her belly. She'd written down her wish, sealed the paper, and would leave it among her things for Larkin to find if it came to pass.

If she died on this side, she wanted her body taken back to Geall for burial.

She continued to write with thoughts circling in her head. There was one she kept coming back to, nibbling at. She would have to find a way to ask Glenna if it could be done— if the others would agree to it, if it could.

Was there a way to seal off the portal, to close the door to Geall?

With a sigh, she looked toward the window. Was it raining in Geall now, too, or was the sun shining on her mother's grave?

She heard footsteps approach, and danced her fingers over the hilt of her dagger. She let them fall away when King came in. For reasons she couldn't name, she felt easier with him than the others.

"Got something against chairs, Shorty?"

Her lips twitched. She liked the way words rumbled out of him, like rocks down a stony hill. "No, but I like sitting on the floor. It is time for more training?"

"Taking a break." He sat in a wide chair, a huge mug of coffee in his hand. "Larkin could go all damn day. Up there now, practicing some katas."

"I like the katas. It's like dancing."

"Just make sure you're doing the leading if you're dancing with a vampire."

Idly, she turned the page of a book. "Hoyt and Cian fought."

King took a drink. "Oh yeah? Who won?"

"I think neither. I saw them coming back, and from their faces and limps, it seemed to be a draw."

"How do you know they were fighting with each other? Maybe they were attacked."

"No." She traced her fingers over words. "I hear things."

"You got big ears, Shorty."

"So my mother always said. They made peace between them—Hoyt and his brother."

"That eliminates a complication—if it lasts." Given their personalities, King figured a full truce between the brothers had the life expectancy of a fruit fly. "What do you expect to find out in all these books?"

"Everything. Sooner or later. Do you know how the first vampire came to be? There are different versions in the books."

"Never thought about it."

"I did—do. One is like a love story. Long ago, when the world was young, demons were dying out. Before, long before that, there were more. Scores of them, walking the world. But man grew stronger and smarter, and the time of the demons was passing."

Because he was a man who enjoyed stories, he settled back. "Kind of an evolution."

"A change, yes. Many demons went beneath the world, to hide or to sleep. There was more magic then, because people didn't turn from it. Man and the faeries forged an alliance to wage war on the demons, to drive them under for once and all. There was one who was poisoned, and slowly dying. He loved a mortal woman, and this was forbidden even in the demon world."

"So man doesn't have a lock on bigotry. Keep going," he said when she paused.

"So the dying demon took the mortal woman from her home. He was obsessed with her, and his last wish was to mate with her before his end."

"Not so different from men in that area then."

"I think, perhaps, all living creatures crave love and plea-sure. And this physical act that represents life."

"And guys want to get off."

She lost her rhythm. "Get off what?"

He nearly spewed coffee, choked instead. He waved a hand at her as his laugh rumbled out. "Don't mind me. Fin-ish the story."

"Ah . . . Well, he took her deep into the forest and had his way with her, and she, like a woman under a spell, wanted his touch. To try to save his life, she offered her blood to him. So she was bitten, and drank his blood in turn, as this was another kind of mating. She died with him, but she did not cease to exist. She became the thing we call vampyre."

"A demon for love."

"Aye, I suppose. In vengeance against men, she hunted them, fed from them, changed them, to make more of her kind. And still she grieved for her demon lover, and killed herself with sunlight."

"Doesn't quite hit *Romeo and Juliet,* does it?"

"A play. I saw the book of it here, on the shelf. I haven't yet read it." It would take years to read all the books in such a room she thought as she toyed with the end of her braid.

"But I read another tale of the vampyre. It tells of a de-mon, mad and ill from a spell even more evil than it, thirst-ing wildly for human blood. He fed, and the more he fed, the more mad he became. He died after mixing his blood with a mortal, and the mortal became vampyre. The first of its kind."

"I guess you like the first version better."

"No, I like truth better, and I think the second is the truth. What mortal woman would love a demon?"

"Led a sheltered life back in your world, haven't you? Where I come from people fall for monsters—or what oth-ers consider monsters—all the time. Ain't no logic with love, Shorty. It just is."

She tossed her braid behind her back in a kind of shrug. "Well, if I love, I won't be stupid about it."

"Hope I'm around long enough to see you eat those words."

She closed the book, drew up her legs. "Do you love someone?"

"A woman? Been close a few times, and that's how I know I didn't make it all the way to the bull's-eye."

"How do you know?"

"When you hit the center, Shorty, you're down for the count. But it's fun shooting for it. Gonna take a special woman to get past this." He tapped a finger to his face.

"I like your face. It's so big and dark."

He laughed so hard he nearly spilled his coffee. "You got that one right."

"And you're strong. You speak well and you cook. You have loyalty to your friends."

That big dark face softened. "Want to apply for the position of love of my life?"

She smiled back at him, at ease. "I'm thinking I'm not your bull's-eye. If I'm to be queen, I must marry one day. Have children. I hope it won't be only duty, but that I find what my mother found in my father. What they found in each other. I'd want him to be strong, and loyal."

"And handsome."

She moved her shoulders, because she did hope that as well. "Do women here only look for beauty?"

"Couldn't say, but it don't hurt. Guy looks like Cian, for instance, he's got to beat them off with sticks."

"Then why is he lonely?"

He studied her over the rim of his mug. "Good question."

"How did you come to meet him?"

"He saved my life."

Moira wrapped her arms around her legs and settled in. There was little she liked more than a story. "How?"

"I was in the wrong place at the wrong time. Bad neighborhood in East L.A." He drank again, lifted a shoulder in a half shrug. "See, my old man took off before I was born, and my old lady had what we'll call a little problem with illegal substances. O.D.'d. Overdosed. Took too much of some bad shit."

"She died." Everything in her mourned for him. "I'm sorry."

"Bad choices, bad luck. You gotta figure some people come into the world set on tossing their life into the shitter. She was one of them. So I'm on the street, doing what I can to get by, and keep out of the system. I'm heading to this place I know. It's dark, steaming hot. I just wanted a place to sleep for the night."

"You had no home."

"I had the street. A couple of guys were hanging out on the stoop, probably waiting to make a score. I got my bad attitude on. Need to get by them to get where I want to go. Car rolls up, blasts at them. Drive-by," he said. "Like an ambush. I'm caught in it. Bullet grazes my head. More coming, and I know I'm going to be dead. Somebody grabs me, pulls me back. Things got blurry, but it felt like I was flying. Then I was someplace else."

"Where?"

"Fancy hotel room. I'd never seen anything like it outside of movies." He crossed his big, booted feet as he remembered. "Big-ass bed, big enough for ten people, and I'm lying on it. Head hurts like a mother, which is why I don't figure I'm dead and this is heaven. He comes out of the bathroom. Got his shirt off, and a fresh bandage on his shoulder. Got himself shot dragging me out of the cross fire."

"What did you do?"

"Nothing much, guess I was in shock. He sits down, studies me like I'm a frigging book. 'You're lucky,' he said, 'and stupid.' He's got that accent. I'm figuring he must be some rock star or something. The way he looks, the fancy voice, the fancy room. Truth is, I thought he was a perv, and he was going to want me to . . . Let's just say I was scared shitless. I was eight."

"You were a child?" Her eyes widened. "You were just a child?"

"I was eight," he repeated. "Grow up like I did, you aren't a kid long. He asks me what the hell I was doing out there, and I give him some sass. Trying to get some of my own back. He asks if I'm hungry, and I shoot back something like I ain't going to . . . perform any sexual favors for a goddamn meal. Orders a steak dinner, a bottle of wine, some soda pop.

And he tells me he isn't interested in buggering young boys. If I've got someplace I'd rather be, I should go there. Otherwise I can wait for the steak."

"You waited for the steak."

"Fucking A." He gave her a wink. "That was the start of it. He gave me food, and a choice. I could go back to where I'd been—no skin off his—or I could work for him. I took the job. Didn't know the job meant school. He gave me clothes, an education, self-respect."

"Did he tell you what he was?"

"Not then. Not long after though. I figured he was whacked, but I didn't much care. By the time I realized he was telling the truth, literal truth, I would've done anything for him. The man I was setting to be died on the street that night. He didn't turn me," King said quietly. "But he changed me."

"Why? Did you ever ask him why?"

"Yeah. That'd be for him to tell."

She nodded. The story itself was enough to think about.

"Break's about over," he announced. "We can get an hour's workout in. Toughen up that skinny ass of yours."

She grinned. "Or we could work with the bow. Improve that poor aim of yours."

"Come on, smart-ass." He frowned, glanced toward the doorway. "You hear something?"

"Like a knocking?" She shrugged, and because she tarried to straighten the books, was several paces behind him out of the room.

Glenna trotted down the steps. What little progress they were making she could leave to Hoyt for the time being. Someone had to see about the evening meal—and since she'd put her name on the list, she was elected. She could toss together a marinade for some chicken, then go back up for another hour.

A good meal would set the tone for a team meeting.

She'd just drop by the library, yank Moira away from the books for a cooking lesson while she was at it. Maybe it was sexist to put the only other woman next on the KP list, but she had to start somewhere.

The knock on the door made her jolt, then pass a nervous hand through her hair.

She nearly called up the stairs for Larkin or King, then shook her head. Talk about sexist. How was she going to fare in serious battle if she couldn't even open the door herself on a rainy afternoon?

It could be a neighbor, dropping by to pay a courtesy call. Or Cian's caretaker, stopping by to make sure they had everything they needed.

And a vampire couldn't enter the house, couldn't step over the threshold, unless she asked it in.

A highly unlikely event.

Still, she looked out the window first. She saw a young woman of about twenty—a pretty blonde in jeans and a bright red sweater. Her hair was pulled back into a tail that swung out of the back of a red cap. She was holding a map—seemed to be puzzling over it as she chewed on a thumbnail.

Someone's lost, Glenna thought, and the sooner she got her on her way and away from the house, the better for everyone.

The knock sounded again as she turned from the window.

She opened the door, careful to keep to her side of the threshold.

"Hello? Need some help?"

"Hello. Thank you, yes." There was relief, and a heavy dose of French in the woman's voice. "I am, ah, lost. *Excusez-moi,* my English, is not so good."

"That's okay. My French is fairly nonexistent. What can I do for you?"

"Ennis? *S'il vovs plaît?* May you tell me how the road it goes to Ennis?"

"I'm not sure. I'm not from around here myself. I can look at the map." Glenna watched the woman's eyes as she held out a hand for it—her fingertips on her side of the door. "I'm Glenna. *Je suis* Glenna."

"Ah, *oui. Je m'apelle* Lora. I am in holiday, a student."

"That's nice."

"The rain." Lora held out a hand so rain drops splattered it. "I am lost in it, I think."

"Could happen to anyone. Let's have a look at your map, Lora. Are you by yourself?"

"Pardon?"

"Alone? Are you alone?"

"Oui. Mes amies—my friends—I have friends in Ennis, but I turn bad. Wrong?"

Oh no, Glenna thought. I really don't think so. "I'm surprised you could see the house from the main road. We're so far back."

"Sorry?"

Glenna smiled brilliantly. "I bet you'd like to come in, have a nice cup of tea while we figure out your route." She saw the light come into the blonde's baby blue eyes. "But you can't, can you? Just can't step through the door."

"Je ne comprendrez pas."

"Bet you do, but in case my Spidey sense is off today, you need to go back to the main road, turn left. Left," she repeated and started to gesture.

King's shout behind her had her spinning around. Her hair swung, the tips of it going beyond the doorway. There was an explosion of pain as her hair was viciously yanked, as her body flew out of the house and hit the ground with a bone-wracking thud.

There were two more, and they came out of nowhere. Instinct had Glenna reaching for her cross with one hand, kicking out blindly with her feet. Movement was a blur, and she tasted blood in her mouth. She saw King slicing at one with a knife, holding it off while he shouted at her to get up, to get into the house.

She stumbled to her feet in time to see them surround him, closing in. She heard herself screaming, and thought— hoped—she heard answering shouts from the house. But they would be too late. The vampires were on King like dogs.

"French bitch," Glenna spat out, and charged the blonde. Her fist cracked bone, and there was satisfaction in that, and the sudden spurt of blood. Then she was once more hur-dling back, and this time when she hit, her vision went gray.

She felt herself being dragged, struggled. It was Moira's voice buzzing in her ear.

"I have you. I have you. You're back inside. Lie still."

"No. King. They've got King."

Moira was already dashing out, dagger drawn. As Glenna pushed herself up, Larkin vaulted over her and through the door.

Glenna gained her knees, then swayed to her feet. Sick-ness burned its acrid taste at the base of her throat as she once more stumbled to the door.

So fast, she thought dully, how could anything move that fast? As Moira and Larkin gave chase, they bundled the still struggling King into a black van. They were gone before she got out of the house.

Larkin's body shimmered, shuddered, and became a cougar. The cat flashed after the van and out of sight.

Glenna went to her knees on the wet grass, and retched.

"Get inside." Hoyt grabbed her arm with his free hand. In his other was a sword. "Inside the house. Glenna, Moira, get inside."

"It's too late," Glenna cried, while tears of horror spilled out of her eyes. "They have King." She looked up, saw Cian standing behind Hoyt. "They took him. They took King."

Chapter 15

"In the house," Hoyt repeated. As he started to drag Glenna inside, Cian shoved past him and flew toward the stables.

"Go with him." Glenna struggled past the tears and pain. "Oh, God, go with him. Hurry."

Leaving her, shaking and bleeding, was the hardest thing he'd ever done.

The door where the black machine sat was open. His brother tossed weapons carelessly inside.

"Will this catch them?" Hoyt demanded.

Cian barely spared him a glance with eyes rimmed red. "Stay with the women. I don't need you."

"Need or not, you have me. How the bloody hell do I get inside this thing?" He fought with the door, and when it opened, folded himself inside it.

Cian said nothing, only got behind the wheel. The machine let out a vicious roar, seemed to quiver like a stallion poised to run. And then they were flying. Stones and sod spewed into the air like missiles. Hoyt caught a glimpse of Glenna in the doorway, holding the arm he feared might be broken.

He prayed to all the gods he'd see her again.

She watched him go, and wondered if she'd sent her lover to his death. "Get all the weapons you can carry," she told Moira.

"You're hurt. Let me see to you."

"Get the weapons, Moira." She turned, her face fierce and bloodied. "Or do you intend for us to stay here like children while the men do the fighting?"

Moira nodded. "Do you want blade or bow?"

"Both."

Glenna went quickly to the kitchen, gathered bottles. Her arm was screaming, so she quickly did what she could to block the pain. This was Ireland, she thought grimly, and that should mean plenty of churches. In the churches would be holy water. She carried the bottles, along with a butcher knife and a bundle of garden stakes to the van.

"Glenna." With a longbow and crossbow slung over her shoulders, two swords in her hand, Moira crossed to the van. She put the weapons inside, then held up one of the silver crosses by its chain.

"This was up in the training room. I think it must be King's. He has no protection."

Glenna slammed the cargo door. "He has us."

Hedgerows and hills were no more than a blur through the gray curtain of rain. Hoyt saw other machines—cars, he reminded himself—traveling the wet road, and the edges of a village.

He saw cattle in fields, and sheep, and the ramble of stone fences. He saw nothing of Larkin, or the car that held King.

"Can you track them in this?" he asked Cian.

"No." He spun the wheel, sent up a flood of water. "They'll take him to Lilith. They'll keep him alive." He had to believe it. "And take him to Lilith."

"The caves?" Hoyt thought how long it had taken him to travel from his cliffs to Clare. But that had been on horseback, and he'd been wounded and feverish. Still the journey would take time. Too much time.

"Alive? Cian, why will they take him alive?"

"He'd be a prize to her. That's what he is, a prize. He's alive. She'd want the kill for herself. We can't be that far behind them. Can't be. And the Jag's faster than the bloody van they have him in."

"He won't be bitten. The cross will stop that."

"It won't stop a sword or an arrow. A fucking bullet. Guns and bows aren't the weapons of choice," he said almost to himself. "Too remote. We like close kills, and some tradition with it. We like to look in the eyes. She'll want to torture him first. Wouldn't want it to be quick." His hands tightened on the wheel enough to bruise the leather. "Should buy us some time."

"Night's coming."

What Hoyt didn't say, and they both knew, was there would be more of them at night.

Cian swung around a sedan at a speed that had the Jag fishtailing on the slick road, then the tires bit in and he shot forward again. A flash of headlights in his eyes blinded him, but didn't slow him down. He had a moment to think: bloody tourists as the oncoming car edged him over. Branches of hedgerows scraped and rattled over the side and windows of the Jag. Loose gravel spat out like stone bullets.

"We should've caught up with them by now. If they took another route, or she's got another hole . . ." Too many options, Cian thought, and pushed for more speed. "Can you do anything? A locator spell?"

"I haven't any . . ." He slapped a hand to the dash as Cian shot around another curve. "Wait." He gripped the cross he wore, pushed power into it. And bearing down, brought its light into his mind.

"Shield and symbol. Guide me. Give me sight."

He saw the cougar, running through the rain, the cross lashing like a silver whip around its throat.

"Larkin, he's close. Fallen behind us. Keeping to the fields. He's tiring." He searched, feeling with the light as if it were fingers. "Glenna—and Moira with her. They didn't stay in the house, they're moving. She's in pain."

"They can't help me. Where's King?"

"I can't find him. He's in the dark."

"Dead?"

"I don't know. I can't reach him."

Cian slammed on the brakes, wrenched the wheel. The Jag went into a sickening spin, revolving closer and closer to the black van that sat across the narrow road. There was a scream of tires and a dull thud as metal slapped metal.

Cian was out before the motion stopped, sword in hand. When he wrenched open the door of the van he found nothing. And no one.

"There's a woman here," Hoyt called out. "She's hurt."

Cursing, Cian rounded the van, yanked open the cargo doors. There was blood, he saw—human blood by its scent. But not enough for death.

"Cian, she's been bitten, but she's alive."

Cian glanced over his shoulder. He saw the woman lying on the road, blood seeping from the punctures in her neck. "Didn't drain her. Not enough time. Revive her. Bring her around," Cian ordered. "You can do it. Do it fast. They've taken her car, switched cars. Find out what she was driving."

"She needs help."

"Goddamn it, she'll live or she won't. Bring her around."

Hoyt laid his fingertips on the wounds, felt the burn. "Madam. Hear me. Wake and hear me."

She stirred, then her eyes flew open, the pupils big as moons. "Rory! Rory. Help me."

Roughly, Cian shoved Hoyt aside. He had some power of his own. "Look at me. Into me." He bent close until her eyes were fixed on him. "What happened here?"

"A woman, the van. Needed help, we thought. Rory stopped. He got out. He got out and they . . . Oh God, sweet God. Rory."

"They took your car. What kind of car was it?"

"Blue. BMW. Rory. They took him. They took him. No room for you. They said no room and threw me down. They laughed."

Cian straightened. "Help me get this van off the road. They were smart enough to take the keys."

"We can't leave her like this."

"Then stay with her, but help me move this bloody van."

Fury had Hoyt spinning around, and the van jumped three feet across the road.

"Nice work."

"She could die out here. She did nothing."

"She won't be the first or the last. It's war, isn't it?" Cian shot back. "She's what they call collateral damage. Good strategy this," he mumbled, and took stock. "Slow us down and switch to a faster car. I won't be catching them now before they reach the caves. If that's where they're going."

He turned toward his brother, considered. "I may need you now after all."

"I won't leave an injured woman on the side of the road like a sick dog."

Cian stepped back to his car, flipped open the center compartment and took out a mobile phone. He spoke into it briefly. "It's a communication device," he told Hoyt as he tossed the phone back into storage. "I've called for help—medical and the garda. All you'll do now by staying is get yourself hauled in, and asked questions you can't answer."

He popped the hood, took out a blanket and some flares. "Put that over her," he instructed. "I'll set these up. He's bait now," Cian added as he set the flares to light. "Bait as much as a prize. She knows we're coming. She wants us to."

"Then we won't disappoint her."

With no hope of cutting off the raiding party before they reached the caves, Cian drove more cautiously. "She was smarter. More aggressive, and more willing to lose troops. So she has the advantage."

"We'll be outnumbered, greatly."

"We always would have been. At this point, she may be willing to negotiate. To take a trade."

"One of us for King."

"You're all the same to her. A human's a human, so you have no particular value in this. You perhaps, because she respects and covets power. But she'd want me more."

"You're willing to trade your life for his?"

"She wouldn't kill me. At least not right away. She'd want to use her considerable talents first. She'd enjoy that."

"Torture."

"And persuasion. If she could bring me over to her side, it would be a coup."

"A man who trades his life for a friend doesn't turn and betray him. Why would she think otherwise?"

"Because we're fickle creatures. And she made me. That gives her quite a bit of pull."

"No, not you. I'd believe you'd trade yourself for King, but I don't think she'd believe it. You'll have to offer me," Hoyt said after a moment.

"Oh, will I?"

"I've been nothing to you for hundreds of years. He's more to you than me. She'd see that. A human for a sorcerer. A good exchange for her."

"And why should she think you'd give yourself for a man you've known for, what a week?"

"Because you'd have a knife to my throat."

Cian tapped his fingers on the steering wheel. "It could work."

The rain had passed into dreary moonlight by the time they reached the cliffs. They rose high above the road, jutted out to cast jagged shadows over the toiling sea.

There was only the sound of the water lashing rock, and the hum of the air that was like the breath of gods.

There was no sign of another car, of human or of creature.

Along the seaside of the road was a rail. Below it was rocks, water and the maze of caves.

"We lure her up." Cian nodded toward the edge. "If we go down to her, we're trapped, with the sea at our backs. We go up, make her come to us."

They started the climb, over slippery rocks and soggy grass. At the headland stood a lighthouse, its beam lancing out into the dark.

The both sensed the attack before the movement. The thing sprang out from behind the rocks, fangs bared. Cian merely pivoted, led with his shoulder, and sent it tumbling down to the road. For the second, he used the stake he'd hitched in his belt.

Then he straightened, turned to the third who appeared more cautious than his fellows.

"Tell your mistress Cian McKenna wants to speak with her."

Vicious teeth gleamed in the moonlight. "We'll drink your blood tonight."

"Or you'll die hungry, and by Lilith's hands because you failed to deliver a message."

The thing melted away, and down.

"There may be more waiting above," Hoyt commented.

"Unlikely. She'd be expecting us to charge the caves, not head to high ground for a hostage negotiation. She'll be intrigued, and she'll come."

So they climbed, then walked the slope to higher ground, and the point where Hoyt had once faced Lilith, and the thing she'd made of his brother.

"She'll appreciate the irony of the spot."

"It feels as it did." Hoyt tucked his cross out of sight under his shirt. "The air. The night. This was my place once, where I could stand and call power with a thought."

"You'd best hope you still can." Cian drew his knife. "Get on your knees." He flicked the point at Hoyt's throat, watched the dribble of blood from the thin slice. "Now."

"So, it comes to choices."

"It always comes to choices. You would have killed me here, if you could."

"I would have saved you here, if I could."

"Well, you did neither, did you?" He slid the knife from Hoyt's sheath, made a V with the blades to hold at his brother's throat. "Kneel."

With the cold edge of the blade on his flesh, Hoyt got to his knees.

"Well, what a handsome sight."

Lilith stepped into the moonlight. She wore emerald green robes with her hair long and loose to spill over her shoulders like sunbeams.

"Lilith. It's been a very long time."

"Too long." The silk rustled as she moved. "Did you come all this way to bring me a gift?"

"A trade," Cian corrected. "Call your dogs off," he said quietly. "Or I kill him, then them. And you have nothing."

"So forceful." She gestured with her hand toward the vampires creeping in at the sides. "You've seasoned. You were hardly more than a pretty puppy when I gave you the gift. Now look at you, a sleek wolf. I like it."

"And still your dog," Hoyt spat out.

"Ah, the mighty sorcerer brought low. I like that, too. You marked me." She opened her robes to show Hoyt the pentagram branded over her heart. "It gave me pain for more than a decade. And the scar never fades. I owe you for that. Tell me, Cian, how did you manage to bring him here?"

"He thinks I'm his brother. It makes it easy."

"She took your life. She's lies and death."

Over Hoyt's head, Cian smiled. "That's what I love about her. I'll give you this one for the human you took. He's useful to me, and loyal. I want him back."

"But he's so much bigger than this one. So much more to feast on."

"He has no power. He's an ordinary mortal. I give you a sorcerer."

"Yet you covet the human."

"As I said, he's of use to me. Do you know how much time and trouble it takes to train a human servant? I want him back. No one steals from me. Not you, not anyone."

"We'll discuss it. Bring him down. I've done quite a bit with the caves. We can be comfortable, have a little something to eat. I've a very Rubenesque exchange student on tap—Swiss. We can share. Oh, but wait." She let out a musical laugh. "I've heard you dine on pigs' blood these days."

"You can't trust everything you hear." Deliberately Cian lifted the knife he'd used to cut Hoyt, flicked his tongue over the bloodied blade.

That first taste of human after so long a fast reddened his eyes, churned his hunger. "But I haven't lived so long to be stupid. This is a one-time offer, Lilith. Bring the human to me, and take the sorcerer."

"How can I trust you, my darling boy? You kill our kind."

"I kill what I like when I like. As you do."

"You aligned yourself with them. With humans. Plotted against me."

"As long as it amused me. It's become boring, and costly. Give me the human, take this one. And, as a bonus, I'll invite you into my home. You can have a banquet on the others."

Hoyt's head jerked, and the blade bit. He cursed, in Gaelic now, with low and steady violence.

"Smell the power in that blood." Lilith crooned it. "Gorgeous."

"Another step, and I cut the jugular, waste it all."

"Would you?" She smiled, beautifully. "I wonder. Is that what you want?" She gestured.

At the edge of the cliff where the lighthouse stood, Cian could see King slumped between two vampires.

"He's alive," she said lightly. "Of course, you only have my word for it, as I have yours that you'd hand that one to me, like a pretty present all wrapped in shiny paper. Let's play a game."

She held her skirts out, twirled. "Kill him, and I give you the human. Kill your brother, but not with the knives. Kill him as you're meant to kill. Take his blood, drink him, and the human is yours."

"Bring me the human first."

She pouted, brushed fussily at her skirts. "Oh, very well." She lifted one arm high, then the other. Cian eased the knives from Hoyt's throat as they began to drag King forward.

They dropped him, and with a vicious kick sent him over the edge.

"Oops!" Lilith eyes's danced with merriment as she pressed a hand to her lips. "Butterfingers. I guess you'll have to pay me back now and kill that one."

With a wild roar, Cian charged forward. And she rose up, spreading her robe like wings. "Take them!" she shouted. "Bring them to me." And was gone.

Cian switched grips on the knives as Hoyt sprang up, yanking free the stakes shoved into the back of his belt.

Arrows flew, slicing through air and hearts. Before Cian could strike the first blow, a half a dozen vampires were dust, blown out to sea by the wind.

"More are coming." Moira shouted from the cover of trees. "We need to go. We need to go now. This way. Hurry!"

Retreat was bitter, a vile taste burning the back of the throat. But the choice was to swallow death. So they turned from battle.

When they reached the car, Hoyt reached for his brother's hand. "Cian—"

"Don't." He slammed in, watched the others leap into the van. "Just don't."

The long drive home was full of silence, of grief and of fury.

Glenna didn't weep. It went too deep for tears. She drove in a kind of trance, her body throbbing with pain and shock, her mind numb with it. And knowing it was cowardice, huddled there.

"It wasn't your fault."

She heard Moira's voice, but couldn't respond to it. She felt Larkin touch her shoulder, she supposed in comfort. But was too numb to react. And when Moira climbed in the back with Larkin to give her solitude, she knew only vague relief.

She turned into the woods, carefully maneuvered the narrow lane. In front of the house where the lights burned, she shut off the engine, the lights. Reached for the door.

It flew open, and she was wrenched out, held inches above the ground. Even then, she felt nothing, not even fear as she saw the thirst in Cian's eyes.

"Tell me why I shouldn't break your neck and be done with it."

"I can't."

Hoyt reached them first, and was flicked away with a careless backward swipe.

"Don't. He's not to blame. Don't," she said now to Hoyt before he could charge again. "Please don't." And to Larkin.

"Do you think that moves me?"

She looked into Cian's eyes again. "No. Why should it? He was yours. I killed him."

"It wasn't her doing." Moira shoved Cian's arm, but didn't budge him an inch. "She isn't to blame for this."

"Let her speak for herself."

"She can't. Can't you see how badly she's hurt? She wouldn't let me tend her before we followed you. We need to get inside. If we're attacked now, we all die."

"If you harm her," Hoyt said quietly. "I'll kill you myself."

"Is that all there is?" Glenna's words were a weary whisper. "Just death? Is that all there'll ever be again?"

"Give her to me." Hoyt cupped his arms, drew her out of Cian's grasp. He murmured to her in Gaelic as he carried her into the house.

"You'll come, and you'll listen." Moira closed a hand around Cian's arm. "He deserves that."

"Don't tell me what he deserves." He wrenched free of her with a force that knocked her back two steps. "You know nothing of it."

"I know more than you think." She left him to follow Hoyt into the house.

"I couldn't catch them." Larkin stared at the ground. "I wasn't fast enough, and I couldn't catch them." He yanked open the cargo doors, unloaded weapons. "I can't turn into one of these." He slammed the doors again. "It has to be alive, what I become. Even the cougar couldn't catch them."

Cian said nothing, and went inside.

They had Glenna on the sofa in the main parlor. Her eyes were closed, her face pale, her skin clammy. Against the pallor, the bruising along her jaw and cheek was livid. Blood had dried at the corner of her mouth.

Hoyt gently tested her arm. Not broken, he thought with relief. Badly wrenched, but not broken. Trying not to jar her, he removed her shirt to discover more bruising over her shoulder, her torso, running down to her hip.

"I know what to get," Moira said and dashed off.

"Not broken." Hoyt's hands hovered over her ribs. "It's good there's nothing broken."

"She's fortunate her head's still on her shoulders." Cian

went directly to a cabinet, took out whiskey. He drank straight from the bottle.

"Some of the injuries are inside her. She's badly injured."

"No less than she deserves for going out of the house."

"She didn't." Moira hurried back in, carrying Glenna's case. "Not the way you're meaning."

"You don't expect me to believe King went out, and she leaped to his defense?"

"He came out for me." Glenna opened eyes glassy from the pain. "And they took him."

"Quiet," Hoyt ordered. "Moira, I need you here."

"We'll use this." She selected a bottle. "Pour it on the bruising." After handing him the bottle, she knelt, rested her hands lightly on Glenna's torso.

"What power I can claim I call now to ease your pain. Warmth to heal and harm none, to take away the damage done." She looked entreatingly at Glenna. "Help me. I'm not very good."

Glenna laid her hand over Moira's, closed her eyes. When Hoyt laid his on top for a triad, Glenna sucked in a breath, let it out on a moan. But when Moira would have yanked her hand away, Glenna gripped it tight.

"Sometimes healing hurts," she managed. "Sometimes it has to. Say the chant again. Three times."

As Moria obeyed, sweat sprang onto Glenna's skin, but the bruising faded a little, going the sickly tones of healing.

"Yes, that's better. Thanks."

"We'll have some of that whiskey here," Moira snapped.

"No. I'd better not." Trying for steady breaths, Glenna pushed up. "Help me sit. I need to see how bad it is now."

"Let's see about this." Hoyt skimmed his fingers over her face. And she grabbed his hand. The tears came now, couldn't be stopped.

"I'm so sorry."

"You can't blame yourself, Glenna."

"Who else?" Cian countered, and Moira shoved up to her feet.

"He wasn't wearing the cross." She dug in her pocket, held it up. "He took it off upstairs and left it behind."

"He was showing me some moves. Wrestling," Larkin explained. "And it got in his way, he said. He must have forgotten about it."

"He never meant to go outside, did he? And wouldn't have but for her."

"He was mistaken." Moira laid the cross on the table. "Glenna, he needs to know the truth. The truth is less painful."

"He thought, he must have thought I was going to let her in, or step out. I wasn't. But I was being cocky, so what's the difference? Smug. He's dead because of it."

Cian took another drink. "Tell me why he's dead."

"She knocked on the door. I shouldn't have answered, but I saw it was a woman. A young woman with a map. I wasn't going out, or asking her in, I swear that to you. She said she was lost. She spoke with an accent, French. Charming, really, but I knew . . . I felt. And I couldn't resist toying with her. God, oh God," she said as more tears spilled. "How stupid. How vain."

She took a deep breath. "She said her name was Lora."

"Lora." Cian lowered the bottle. "Young, attractive, French accent?"

"Yes. You know her."

"I do." He drank again. "I do, yes."

"I could see what she was. I don't know how, but I knew. I should have just shut the door on her. But on the chance I was wrong, I thought I should give her directions and get her moving. I'd just started to when King shouted, and he came running down the hall. I turned around. I was startled, I was careless. She got some of my hair. She pulled me outside by it."

"It was so fast," Moira continued. "I was behind King. I barely saw her move—the vampyre. He went out after them, and there were more. Four, five more. It was like lightning strikes."

Moira poured herself a shot of whiskey, downed it to smooth the raw edge of her nerves. "They were on him, all of them, and he shouted for Glenna to get inside. But she got up instead, she got up and ran to help him. It knocked her back, the female of them, like she was a stone in a sling. She tried to help him, even though she was hurt. Maybe she was careless, but so was he."

Moira picked up the cross again. "And it's a terrible price he paid for it. A terrible price he paid for defending a friend."

With Hoyt's help, Glenna got to her feet. "I'm sorry isn't enough. I know what he meant to you."

"You couldn't possibly."

"I think I do, and I know what he meant to the rest of us. I know he's dead because of me. I'll live with that all of my life."

"So will I. And it's my bad luck that I'll live a great deal longer than you."

He took the whiskey bottle when he walked out.

Chapter 16

In the moment between wake and sleep, there was candlelight, and the bliss of nothing. Easy warmth and sheets scented with lavender, and floating on the comfort of nothing.

But the moment passed, and Glenna remembered.

King was dead, hurled into the sea by monsters with the same carelessness of a boy tossing a pebble into a lake.

She'd gone upstairs alone, by her own request, to seek the solitude and oblivion of sleep.

Watching the candle flicker, she wondered if she would ever be able to sleep in the dark again. If she would ever be able to see night coming and not think their time was coming with it. To walk in the moonlight without fear? Would she ever know that simplicity again? Or would even a rainy day forever send chills down her spine?

She turned her head on the pillow. And she saw him silhouetted by the silver light that slid through the window that overlooked his herb garden. Keeping watch in the night, she thought, over her. Over them all. Whatever burdens they all bore, his were heavier. And still he'd come to stand between her and the dark.

"Hoyt."

She sat up as he turned, and she held out her hands to him.

"I didn't want to wake you." He crossed to her, took her hands while studying her face in the dim light. "Are you in pain?"

"No. No, it's gone under, at least for now. I have you and Moira to thank for that."

"You helped yourself as much as we did. And sleep will help as well."

"Don't go. Please. Cian?"

"I don't know." He sent a troubled look toward the door. "Closed in his rooms with the whiskey." Looking at her, he brushed back her hair, turning her face to take a closer study at the bruising. "We're all using what we can tonight, so the pain goes under."

"She would never have let him go. She would never have released King. No matter what we'd done."

"No." He eased down to sit on the side of the bed. "Cian must have known that somewhere inside him, but he had to try. We had to try."

By pretending to be a bargaining chip, she thought, remembering Hoyt's explanation of what they'd seen on the cliffs.

"Now we all know there can be no bargaining in this," he continued. "Are you strong enough to hear what I have to say?"

"Yes."

"We've lost one of us. One of the six we were told we needed to fight this battle, to win this war. I don't know what it means."

"Our warrior. Maybe it means we all have to become warriors. Better ones. I killed tonight, Hoyt—more from luck than skill—but I destroyed what had once been human. I can and will do it again. But with more skill. Every day with more skill. She took one of us, and she thinks it'll make us weak and frightened. But she's wrong. We'll show her she's wrong."

"I'm to lead this battle. You have great skill in magicks. You'll work in the tower on weapons, shields, spells. A protective circle to—"

"Whoa, wait." She held up a hand. "Am I getting this? I'm consigned to the tower, what like Rapunzel?"

"I don't know this person."

"Just another helpless female waiting to be rescued. I'll work on the magicks, and I'll work harder and longer. Just like I'll train harder and longer. But what I won't do is sit up in the tower day and night with my cauldron and crystals, writing spells while the rest of you fight."

"You had your first battle today, and it nearly killed you."

"And gave me a lot more respect for what we're up against. I was called to this, just like the rest of us. I won't hide from it."

"Using your strengths isn't hiding. I was given the charge of this army—"

"Well, let me slap some bars on you and call you Colonel."

"Why are you so angry?"

"I don't want you to protect me. I want you to value me."

"Value you?" He shoved to his feet so the red shimmer from the fire washed over his face. "I value you almost more than I can bear. I've lost too much already. I've watched my brother, the one who shared the womb with me, taken. I've stood over the graves of my family. I won't see you cut down by these things—you, the single light for me in all of this. I won't risk your life again. I won't stand over your grave."

"But I can risk your life? I can stand over your grave?"

"I'm a man."

He said it so simply, the way an adult might tell a child the sky is blue, that she couldn't speak for ten full seconds. Then she plopped back against the pillows. "The only reason I'm not working on turning you into a braying jackass this very moment is I'm giving you some slack due to the fact you come from an unenlightened age."

"Un . . . unenlightened?"

"Let me clue you in to mine, Merlin. Women are equals. We work, we go into combat, we vote, and above all, we make our own decisions regarding our own lives, our own bodies, our own minds. Men don't rule here."

"I've never known a world where men rule," he muttered. "In physical strength, Glenna, you're not equal."

"We make up for it with other advantages."

"However keen your minds, your wiles, your bodies are more fragile. They're made to bear children."

"You just gave me a contradiction in terms. If men were responsible for childbearing, the world would've ended a long time ago, with no help from a bunch of glory-seeking vampires. And let me point out one little fact. The one causing this whole mess is a female."

"Somehow that should be my point."

"Well, it's just not. So forget it. And the one who brought us together is also female, so you're way outnumbered. And I have more ammo, but this ridiculous conversation is giving me a headache."

"You should rest. We'll talk more of this tomorrow."

"I'm not going to rest, and we're not going to talk about this tomorrow."

His single light? he thought. Sometimes she was a beam searing straight into his eyes. "You are a contrary and exasperating woman."

"Yes." Now she smiled, and once more held out her hands. "Sit down here, would you? You're worried about me, and for me. I understand that, appreciate that."

"If you would do this thing for me." He lifted her hands to his lips. "It would ease my mind. Make me a better leader."

"Oh, that's good." She drew her hands away to poke him gently in the chest. "Very good. Women aren't the only ones with wiles."

"Not wile, but truth."

"Ask me for something else, and I'll try to give it to you. But I can't give you this, Hoyt. I worry for you, too, and about you. For all of us. And I question what we can do, what we're capable of. And I wonder why in all the world—the worlds—we're the ones who have to do this thing. But none of that changes anything. We are the ones. And we've lost a very good man already."

"If I lose you . . . Glenna, there's a void in me at the very thought of it."

Sometimes, she knew, the woman had to be stronger. "There are so many worlds, and so many ways. I don't think we could ever lose each other now. What I have now is more than I've ever had before. I think it makes us better than we were. Maybe that's part of why we're here. To find each other."

She leaned into him, sighed when his arms encircled her. "Stay with me. Come lie with me. Love me."

"You need to heal."

"Yes." She drew him down with her, touched her lips to his. "I do."

He hoped he had the tenderness in him that she needed. He wanted to give her that, the magic of it.

"Slowly then." He brushed kisses over her cheek. "Quietly."

He used just his lips, skimming kisses over her mouth, her face, her throat. Warm and soothing. He brushed away the thin gown she wore to trace those easy kisses over her breasts, over her bruises. In comfort and with care.

Soft as birds' wings, lips and fingertips to ease her mind and her body, and to stir them.

And when their eyes met, he knew more than he'd ever known. Held more than he'd ever owned.

He lifted her up onto a pillow of air and silver light, making magic their bed. Around the room, the candles came to life with a sound like a sigh. And the light they shed was like melted gold.

"It's beautiful." She took his hands as they floated, closed her eyes on the sumptuous joy of it. "This is beautiful."

"I would give you all I have, and still it wouldn't be enough."

"You're wrong. It's everything."

More than pleasure, more than passion. Did he know what he made of her when he touched her like this? Nothing they faced, no terror or pain, no death or damnation could overcome this. The light inside her was like a beacon, and it would never be dark again.

Here was life at its sweetest and most generous. The taste of him was a balm to her soul even as his touch roused desires. Steeped in him, she lifted her arms, turned up her palms. Rose petals, white as snow, streamed down like rain.

She smiled when he slipped into her, when they moved together, silky and slow. Light and air, scent and sensation surrounded the rise and fall of bodies and hearts.

Once more their fingers meshed, once more their lips met. And as they drifted together, love healed them both.

I n the kitchen, Moira puzzled over a can of soup. No one had eaten, and she was determined to make some sort of meal should Glenna awake. She'd managed the tea, but she'd been shown how to conquer that.

She'd only watched King open one of the cylinders with the little machine that made the nasty noise. She'd tried and failed three times to make it work, and was seriously considering getting her sword and hacking the cylinder open.

She had a little kitchen magic—precious little, she admitted. Glancing around to be sure she was alone, she pulled what she had together, and visualized the can open.

It shimmied a bit on the counter, but remained stubbornly whole.

"All right, one more time then."

She bent down, studied the opener that was attached to the underside of the cupboard. With the proper tools she could take it apart, find out how it worked. She loved taking things apart. But if she had the proper tools, she could just open the bloody cylinder in the first place.

She straightened, shook her hair back, rolled her shoulders. Muttering to herself, she tried once again to do the deed. This time, when the machine whirled, the can revolved. She clasped her hands together in delight, then bent close again to watch it work.

It was so clever, she thought. So much here was clever. She wondered if she'd ever be allowed to drive the van. King had said he'd teach her how it was done.

Her lips trembled at the thought of it, of him, and she pressed them hard together. She prayed his death had been quick, and his suffering brief. In the morning, she would put up a stone for him in the graveyard she and Larkin had seen when they'd been walking.

And when she returned to Geall, she would erect another, and ask the harper to write a song for him.

She emptied the contents into a pot, and set in the burner, turning it on as Glenna had showed her.

They needed to eat. Grief and hunger would make them weak, and weakness would make them easier prey. Bread, she decided. They would have some bread. It would be a simple meal, but filling.

She turned toward the pantry, then stumbled back when she saw Cian in the doorway. He leaned against the wall, the nearly empty whiskey bottle dangling from his fingers.

"Midnight snack?" His teeth showed white with his smile. "I've a fondness for them myself."

"No one's eaten. I thought we should."

"Always thinking, aren't you, little queen? Mind's always going."

He was drunk, she could see that. Too much whiskey had dulled his eyes and thickened his voice. But she could also see the pain. "You should sit before you fall over."

"Thanks for the kind invitation, in my own bloody house. But I just came down for another bottle." He shook the one he held. "Someone appears to have made off with this one."

"Drink yourself sick if you want to be stupid about it. But you might as well eat something. I know you eat, I've seen you. I've gone to the trouble to make it."

He glanced at the counter, smirked. "You opened a tin."

"I didn't have time to kill the fatted calf. So you'll make do."

She turned around to busy herself, then went very still when she felt him behind her. His fingers skimmed the side of her throat, light as a moth's wings.

"I'd have thought you tasty once upon a time."

Drunk, angry, grieving, she thought. All of those made him dangerous. If she showed him her fear, he'd only be more so. "You're in my way."

"Not yet."

"I don't have time for drunkards. Maybe you don't want food, but Glenna needs it, for healing strength."

"I'd say she's feeling strong enough." Bitterness edged his tone as he glanced up. "Didn't you see the lights brighten a bit ago?"

"I did. I don't know what that has to do with Glenna."

"It means she and my brother are having a go at each other. Sex," he said when she looked blank. "A bit of naked, sweaty sex to top off the evening. Ah, she blushes." He laughed, moved closer. "All that pretty blood just under the skin. Delicious."

"Stop."

"I used to like when they trembled, the way you are. It makes the blood hotter, and it adds to the thrill. I'd nearly forgotten."

"You smell of the whiskey. This is hot enough now. Sit down, and I'll make a bowl for you."

"I don't want the fucking soup. Wouldn't mind that hot, sweaty sex, but likely I'm too drunk to manage it. Well then, I'll just get that fresh bottle, and finish the job."

"Cian. Cian, people turn to each other for comfort when death's come. It isn't disrespect, but need."

"You don't want to lecture me on sex. I know more of it than you could ever imagine. Of its pleasures and its pain and its purposes."

"People turn to drink as well, but it's not as healthy. I know what he was to you."

"You don't."

"He talked to me, more than the others, I think, because I like to listen. He told me how you found him, all those years ago, what you did for him."

"I amused myself."

"Stop it." The tone of command, bred into her bones, snapped into her voice. "Now it's disrespect you're showing for a man who was a friend to me. And he was a son to you. A friend and a brother. All of that. I want to put a stone up for him tomorrow. It could wait until sunset, until you could go out and—"

"What do I care for stones?" he said, and left her.

*   *   *

Glenna was so grateful for the sun she could have wept. There were clouds, but they were thin and the beams burst through them to toss light and shadows on the ground.

She hurt still, heart and body. But she would deal with it. For now, she took one of her cameras and she stepped outside to let the sun bathe her face. Charmed by the music of it, she walked to the stream. Then just laid down on its bank and basked.

Birds sang, pouring joy into air that was fragrant with flowers. She could see foxglove dancing lightly in the breeze. For a moment she felt the earth beneath her sigh and whisper with the pleasure of a new day.

Grief would come and go, she knew. But today there was light, and work. And there was still magic in the world.

When a shadow fell over her, she turned her head, smiled at Moira.

"How are you this morning?"

"Better," Glenna told her. "I'm better. Sore and stiff, maybe a little wobbly yet, but better."

She turned a bit more to study Moira's tunic and rough pants. "We need to get you some clothes."

"These do well enough."

"Maybe we'll go into town, see what we can find."

"I have nothing to trade. I can't pay."

"That's what Visa's for. It'll be my treat." She lay flat, closed her eyes again. "I didn't think anyone else was up."

"Larkin's taken the horse for a run. It should do both of them good. I don't think he slept at all."

"I doubt any of us did, really. It doesn't seem real does it, not in the light of day with the sun showering down and the birds singing?"

"It seems more real to me," Moira said as she sat. "It shows what we have to lose. I have a stone," she continued, brushing her hand through the grass. "I thought when Larkin comes back we could go to where the graves are, make one for King."

Glenna kept her eyes closed, but reached out a hand for Moira's. "You have a good heart," she told her. "Yes, we'll make a grave for King."

* * *

Her injuries prevented her from training, but it didn't stop Glenna from working. She spent the next two days preparing food, shopping for supplies, researching magic.

She took photographs.

More than busy work, she told herself. It was practical, and organizational. And the photos were—would be—a kind of documentation, a kind of tribute.

Most of all it helped keep her from feeling useless while the others worked up a sweat with swords and hand-to-hand.

She learned the roads, committing various routes to memory. Her driving skills were rusty, so she honed them, maneuvering the van on snaking roads, skimming the hedgerows on turns, zooming through roundabouts as her confidence built.

She pored through spell books, searching for offense and defense. For solutions. She couldn't bring King back, but she would do everything in her power to safeguard those who were left.

Then she got the bright idea that every member of the team should be able to handle the van. She started with Hoyt.

She sat beside him as he drove the van at a creeping pace up and down the lane.

"There are better uses for my time."

"That may be." And at this rate, she thought, they'd be a millennium before he got over five miles an hour. "But every one of us should be able to take the wheel if necessary."

"Why?"

"Because."

"Do you plan to take this machine into battle?"

"Not with you at the wheel. Practicalities, Hoyt. I'm the only one who can drive during the day. If something happens to me—"

"Don't. Don't tempt the gods." His hand closed over hers.

"We have to factor it. We're here, and where we are is remote. We need transportation. And, well, driving gives all of us a kind of independence, as well as another skill. We should be prepared for anything."

"We could get more horses."

The wistfulness in his voice had her giving him a bolstering pat on the shoulder. "You're doing fine. Maybe you could try going just a little bit faster."

He shot forward, spitting gravel from the tires. Glenna sucked in a breath and shouted: "Brake! Brake! Brake!"

More gravel flew when the van came to an abrupt halt.

"Here's a new word for your vocabulary," she said pleasantly. "Whiplash."

"You said to go faster. This is go." He gestured toward the gas pedal.

"Yeah. Well. Okay." She drew in a fresh breath. "There's the snail, and there's the rabbit. Let's try to find the animal in between. A dog, say. A nice, healthy golden retriever."

"Dogs chase rabbits," he pointed out, and made her laugh. "That's good. You've been sad. I've missed your smile."

"I'll give you a big, toothy one if we come through this lesson in one piece. We're going to take a big leap, go out on the road." She reached up and closed her hand briefly over the crystal she'd hung from the rearview. "Let's hope this works."

He did better than she'd expected, which meant no one was maimed or otherwise injured. Her heart got a serious workout from leaping into her throat, then dropping hard into her belly, but they stayed on the road—for the most part.

She liked watching him calculate the turns, his brows knit, his eyes intense, his long fingers gripping the wheel as though it were a lifeline in a storm-tossed sea.

Hedgerows closed them in, green tunnels dotted with blood-red drops of fuchsia, then the world would open up into rolling fields, and the dots were white sheep or lazy spotted cows.

The city girl in her was enchanted. Another time, she thought, another world, and she could have found a great deal to love about this place. The play of light and shadows on the green, the patchwork of fields, the sudden sparkle of water, the rise and tumble of rocks that formed ancient ruins.

It was good, she decided, to look beyond the house in the forest, to look and love the world they were fighting to save.

When he slowed, she glanced over. "You have to keep up your speed. It can be as dangerous to go too slow as too fast. Which applies, now that I think about it, to pretty much anything."

"I want to stop."

"You need to pull over to the shoulder—the side of the road. Put the signal on, like I showed you, and ease over." She checked the road herself. The shoulder was narrow, but there was no traffic. "Put it in park. That's all the way up. Good. So— What?" she said when he pushed his door open.

She pulled off her seat belt, grabbed the keys—and her camera as an afterthought—then hurried after him. But he was already halfway across a field, moving quickly toward what was left of an old stone tower.

"If you wanted to stretch your legs or empty your bladder, you just had to say so," she began, huffing a bit as she caught up to him.

The wind danced through her hair, blowing it back from her face. As she touched his arm, she felt the muscles there gone rigid. "What is it?"

"I know this place. People lived here. There were children. The oldest of my sisters married their second son. His name is Fearghus. They farmed this land. They . . . they walked this land. Lived."

He moved inside to what she saw now must have been a small keep. The roof was gone, as was one of the walls. The floor was grass and starry white flowers, the dung of sheep.

And the wind blew through, like ghosts chanting.

"They had a daughter, a pretty thing. Our families hoped we would . . ."

He laid his hand against a wall, left it there. "Just stone now," he said quietly. "Gone to ruin."

"But still here, Hoyt. Still here, a part of it. And you,

remembering them. What we're doing, what we have to do, won't it mean they had the very best chance to live a long, full life? To farm the land and walk it. To live."

"They came to my brother's wake." He dropped his hand. "I don't know how to feel."

"I can't imagine how hard this is for you. Every day of it. Hoyt." She laid her hands on his arms, waiting for his eyes to meet hers. "Part of it stands, what was yours. It stands in what's mine. I think that matters. I think we need to find the hope in that. The strength in it. Do you want some time here? I can go back, wait for you in the van."

"No. Every time I falter, or think I can't bear what's been asked of me, you're there." He bent, plucked one of the little white flowers. "These grew in my time." He twirled it once, then tucked it into her hair. "So, we'll carry hope."

"Yes, we will. Here." She lifted her camera. "It's a place that cries for pictures. And the light's gorgeous."

She moved off to choose her angles. She'd make him a present of one, she decided. Something of her to take with him. And she'd make a copy of the same shot for her loft.

Imagine him studying the photo while she studied hers. Each of them remembering standing there on a summer afternoon with wildflowers waving in a carpet of grass.

But the idea of it hurt more than it warmed.

So she turned the camera on him. "Just look at me," she told him. "You don't have to smile. In fact—" She clicked the shutter. "Nice, very nice."

Inspired, she lowered the camera. "I'm going to set it up on timer, take one of us together. She looked around for something to set the camera on, wished she'd thought to bring a tripod.

"Well, I'll have to mix a little something in." She framed him in. Man and stone and field. "Air be still and heed my will. Solid now beneath my hand, steady as rock upon the land. Hold here what I ask of thee. As I will, so mote it be."

She set the camera on the platter of air, engaged the timer. Then dashed to Hoyt. "Just look at the camera." She slipped an arm around his waist, pleased when he mirrored the gesture. "And if you can manage a little smile . . . one, two . . ."

She watched the light blink. "There we are. For posterity."

He walked with her when she retrieved the camera. "How do you know how it will look when you take it out of the box?"

"I don't, not a hundred percent. I guess you could say it's another kind of hope."

She looked back at the ruin. "Do you need more time?"

"No." Time, he thought, there would never be enough of it. "We should go back. There's other work to do."

"Did you love her?" Glenna asked as they started back across the field.

"Who?"

"The girl? The daughter of the family who lived here."

"I didn't, no. A great disappointment that was to my mother, but not—I think—to the girl. I didn't look for a woman in that way, for marriage and family. It seemed . . . It seemed to me that my gift, my work, required solitude. Wives require time and attention."

"They do. Theoretically, they also give it."

"I wanted to be alone. All of my life it seemed I never had enough of it, the solitude and the quiet. And now, now I'm afraid I may always have too much."

"That would be up to you." She stopped to look back at the ruins a last time. "What will you tell them when you go back?" Even saying it tore little pieces from her heart.

"I don't know." He took her hand so they stood together, looking at what was, imagining what had been. "I don't know. What will you tell your people when this is done?"

"I think I probably won't tell them anything. Let them think as I told them when I called before I left that I took an impulsive trip to Europe. Why should they have to live with the fear of what we know?" she said when he turned to her. "We know what goes bump in the night is real, we know that now, and it's a burden. So I'll tell them I love them, and leave it at that."

"Isn't that another kind of alone?"

"It's one I can handle."

This time she got behind the wheel. When he got in beside her, he took one last look at the ruin.

And, he thought, without Glenna, the alone might swallow him whole.

Chapter 17

It plagued him, the idea of going back to his world. Of dying in this one. Of never seeing his home again. Of living in it the rest of his life without the woman who'd given new meaning to it.

If there was a war to be fought with sword and lance, there was another raging inside him, battering the heart he'd never known could yearn for so much.

He watched her from the tower window as she took pictures of Larkin and Moira sparring, or posed them in less combative stances.

Her injuries had healed enough that she no longer moved stiffly, or tired as quickly. But he would always remember how she'd looked on the ground, bleeding.

Her manner of dress no longer seemed strange to him, but proper and so right for who she was. The way she moved in the dark pants and white shirt, her fiery hair pinned messily atop her head seemed the essence of grace to him.

In her face, he'd found beauty and life. In her mind, intelligence and curiosity. And in her heart both compassion and valor.

In her, he realized, he'd found everything he could want, without ever knowing he'd been lacking.

He had no right to her, of course. They had no right to each other beyond the time of the task. If they lived, if the worlds survived, he would go back to his while she remained in hers.

Even love couldn't span a thousand years.

Love. His heart ached at the word so that he pressed his hand to it. This was love then. The gnawing, the burning. The light and the dark.

Not just warm flesh and murmurs in the candlelight, but pain and awareness in the light of day. In the depths of the night. To feel so much for one person, it eclipsed all else.

And it was terrifying.

He was no coward, Hoyt reminded himself. He was a sorcerer by birth, a warrior by circumstance. He had held lightning in the palm of his hand and called the wind to launch it. He'd killed demons, and twice had faced their queen.

Surely, he could face love. Love couldn't maim him or kill him, or strip him of power. What level of cowardice was it then, for a man to shrink back from it?

He strode out of the room, down the stairs, moving with the rush of impulse. He heard music as he passed his brother's door—something low and brooding. He knew it as the music of grief.

And knew, too, if his brother was stirring, so might others of Cian's kind be stirring. Sunset was close.

He moved quickly through the house, into the kitchen where something simmered on the stove, and out the back.

Larkin was amusing himself, shimmering into a gold wolf while Glenna called out her delight and moved around him with the little machine that took the pictures. The camera, he reminded himself.

He shaped back into a man, and hefting his sword assumed a haughty pose.

"You look better as the wolf," Moira told him.

He raised his sword in mock attack and chased after her. Their shouts and laughter were so opposed to his brother's music, Hoyt could only stand in wonder.

There was still laughter in the world. Still time, and need, for play and fun. There was still light even as the darkness crept closer.

"Glenna."

She turned, the humor still dancing in her eyes. "Oh, perfect! Stand right there. Just there, with the house behind you."

"I want to—"

"Ssh. I'm going to lose the light soon. Yes, yes, just like that. All aloof and annoyed. It's wonderful! I wish there was time to go back in and get your cloak. You were made to wear one."

She changed angles, crouched down, shot up at him. "No, don't look at me. Look off, over my head, think deep thoughts. Look into the trees."

"Wherever it is I look, I still see nothing but you."

She lowered her camera for a moment, with pleasure blooming in her cheeks. "You're just trying to distract me. Give me that Hoyt look, just for a minute. Off into the trees, the serious sorcerer."

"I want to speak with you."

"Two minutes." She changed angles, kept shooting, then straightened. "I want a prop," she muttered, and studied the weapons on the table.

"Glenna. Would you go back with me?"

"Two minutes," she repeated, debating between long sword and dagger. "I need to go in and check the soup anyway."

"I don't mean back into the bloody kitchen. Will you go with me?"

She glanced over, automatically lifting her camera, framing his face and capturing the intensity of it. A good meal, she thought, another solid night's sleep, and she'd be ready for full training by the next morning.

"Where?"

"Home. To my home."

"What?" She lowered the camera, felt her heart do a quick, hard jump. "What?"

"When this is done." He kept his eyes on hers as he

closed the distance between them. "Will you come with me? Will you be with me? Belong to me?"

"Back with you? To the twelfth century?"

"Yes."

Slowly, carefully, she set the camera down. "Why do you want me?"

"Because all I see is you, all I want is you. I think if I have to live five minutes in a world without you in it, it would be eternity. I can't face eternity without seeing your face." He brushed his fingers over her cheek. "Without hearing your voice, without touching you. I think if I was sent here to fight this war, I was sent here to find you as well. Not just to fight with me. To open me. Glenna."

He gathered her hands in his, brought them to his lips. "In all this fear and grief and loss, I see you."

She kept her eyes on his as he spoke, searching. When the words were done, she touched a hand to his heart. "There's so much in there," she said quietly. "So much, and I'm so lucky to be part of it. I'll go with you. I'll go with you anywhere."

The joy of it spread inside him, warmed as he touched his fingertips to her cheek again. "You would give up your world, all you know? Why?"

"Because I've thought of living five minutes without you, and even that was eternity. I love you." She saw his eyes change. "Those are the strongest words in any magic. I love you. With that incantation, I already belong to you."

"Once I speak it, it's alive. Nothing can ever kill it." Now he framed her face. "Would you have me if I stayed here with you?"

"But you said—"

"Would you have me, Glenna?"

"Yes, of course, yes."

"Then we'll see which world is ours when this is done. Wherever, whenever it is, I will love you in it. You." He touched his lips to hers. "And only you."

"Hoyt." Her arms came hard around him. "If we have this, we can do anything."

"I haven't said it yet."

She laughed, rained kisses over his cheeks. "Close enough."

"Wait." He drew her back, just an inch. Those vivid blue eyes locked with hers. "I love you."

A single beam of light shot out of the sky, washed over them, centered them in a circle of white.

"So it's done," he murmured. "Through this life and all the ones to come, I'm yours. And you're mine. All that I am, Glenna."

"All that I'll be. I pledge that to you." She held close again, pressed her cheek to his. "Whatever happens, this is ours."

She tipped back her head so their lips could meet. "I knew it would be you," she said softly, "from the moment I walked into your dream."

They held each other in the circle of light, held close while it bathed them. When it faded, and twilight oozed over the day, they gathered the rest of the weapons, and took them into the house together.

Cian watched them from his bedroom window. Love had flashed and shimmered around them in a light that had all but burned his skin, seared his eyes.

And it had pressed against a heart that hadn't beat in nearly a thousand years.

So his brother had fallen, he thought, for the single blow against which there was no shield. Now they would live their short and painful lives within that light.

Perhaps it would be worth it.

Then he stepped back into the shadows of his room, and the cool dark.

When he came down, it was full dark, and she was in the kitchen alone. Singing at the sink, Cian noted, in an absent and happy voice. The sort, he decided, that a fanciful person would say had little pink hearts spilling out from between her lips with the tune.

She was loading the dishwasher—a homey chore. And the kitchen smelled of herbs and flowers. Her hair was bundled up, and now and then her hips moved with the rhythm of the song.

Would he have had a woman like that if he'd lived? he wondered. One who'd sing in the kitchen, or stand in the light, looking at him with her face alive with love?

He'd had women, of course. Scores of them. And some had loved him—to their loss, he supposed. But if their faces had been alive with that love, those faces were a blur to him now.

And love was a choice he had eliminated from his life.

Or had told himself he had. But the fact was he had loved King, as a father does a son, or a brother a brother. The little queen had been right about that, and damned her for it.

He had given his love and his trust to a human, and as humans were wont to do, it had died on him.

Saving this one, he thought now as Glenna set dishes in the rack. Another thing humans had a habit of doing was sacrificing themselves for other humans.

It was, or had been, a trait that had intrigued him often enough. Easier to understand, in his circumstances, their habit on the other side of the coin—of killing each other.

Then she turned, and jolted. The dish she held slipped out of her hands and shattered on the tiles.

"God. I'm sorry. You startled me."

She moved quickly—and jerkily, he noted, for a woman of easy grace. She took the broom and dustpan from the closet, and began to sweep the shards.

He hadn't spoken to her, nor to any of the others, since the night of King's death. He'd left them to train themselves, or do as they pleased.

"I didn't hear you come in. The others finished dinner. They—they went up to do some training. I had Hoyt out for an hour or so today. Um, driving lesson. I thought . . ." She dumped the shards, turned again. "Oh God, say *something*."

"Even if you live, you're from two different worlds. How will you resolve it?"

"Did Hoyt speak to you?"

"He didn't have to. I have eyes."

"I don't know how we'll resolve it." She put the broom away. "We'll find a way. Does it matter to you?"

"Not in the least. It's of interest to me." He got a bottle of wine from the counter rack, studied the label. "I've lived among you for a considerable amount of time. Without interest, I'd have died of boredom long ago."

She steadied herself. "Loving each other makes us stronger. I believe that. We need to be stronger. So far, we haven't done very well."

He opened the wine, got down a glass. "No, you haven't done very well, particularly."

"Cian," she said as he turned to go. "I know you blame me for King. You have every right to—to blame me and to hate me for it. But if we don't find a way to work together, to mesh, he won't just be the only one of us to die. He'll just be the first."

"I beat him to that by a few hundred years." He tipped the glass toward her in a kind of salute, then walked out with the bottle.

"Well, that was useless," Glenna muttered, and turned back to finish the dishes.

He would hate her, she thought, and likely hate Hoyt as well because Hoyt loved her. Their team was fractured even before it had a genuine chance to become a unit.

If they had time, nothing but time, she would let it lie, wait until Cian's resentment cooled, began to fade. But they didn't have that luxury of wasting any more of the precious little time they'd been given. She'd have to find a way to work around it, or him.

She dried her hands, flung the cloth down.

There was a thump outside the back door, as if something heavy had fallen. Instinctively she stepped back, reached for the sword braced against the counter, and one of the stakes lying on it.

"They can't get in," she whispered, and even the whisper shook. "If they want to spy on me while I'm cleaning up the kitchen, so what?"

But she wished she and Hoyt had had better luck devising a spell to create a protected area around the house.

Still, she couldn't let it frighten her, wouldn't let it. She certainly wasn't going to open the door again to have a chat with something that wanted to rip her throat out.

But there came a kind of scratching, low on the door. And a moan. And the hand gripping the sword went damp with sweat.

"Help me. Please."

The voice was weak, barely audible through the wood. But she thought . . .

"Let me in. Glenna? Glenna? In the name of God, let me in before they come."

"King?" The sword clattered on the floor as she leaped toward the door. Still, she held the stake in a firm grip.

Fool me once, she thought, and kept well out of reach as she opened the door.

He lay on the stones just outside, his clothes bloody and torn. More blood had dried on the side of his face, and his breathing was a thin wheeze.

Alive, was all she could think.

She started to crouch down, pull him inside, but Cian was beside her. He shoved her aside, lowered down himself. Laid a hand on King's battered cheek.

"We need to get him in. Hurry, Cian! I've got things that can help."

"They're close. Tracking me." He groped blindly for Cian's hand. "I didn't think I'd make it."

"You have. Come inside now." He gripped King under the arms, dragged him into the kitchen. "How did you get away?"

"Don't know." King sprawled on the floor, eyes closed. "Missed the rocks. Thought I'd drown, but . . . I got out, got out of the water. Hurt pretty bad. Passed out, don't know how long. Walked, walked all day. Hid at night. They come at night."

"Let me see what I can do for him," Glenna began.

"Close the door," Cian told her.

"Did everybody make it? Did everybody . . . thirsty."

"Aye, I know." Cian gripped his hand, looked into his eyes. "I know."

"We'll start with this." Glenna mixed something briskly in a cup. "Cian, if you'd go get the others. I could use Hoyt and Moira. We'll want to get King into bed, make him comfortable."

She bent to him as she spoke, and the cross around her neck dangled down, swung toward King's face.

He hissed like a snake, bared fangs and skuddled back.

Then to Glenna's horror, he got to his feet. And grinned.

"You never told me how it felt," he said to Cian.

"Words fall short. It needs to be experienced."

"No." Glenna could only shake her head. "Oh God, no."

"You could've taken me here a long time ago, but I'm glad you didn't. I'm glad it was now, when I'm in my prime."

King circled around as he spoke, blocking the door out of the kitchen. "They hurt me first. Lilith—she knows amazing ways to give pain. You know you don't stand a chance against her."

"I'm sorry," Glenna whispered. "I'm sorry."

"Don't be. She said I could have you. Eat you or change you. My choice."

"You don't want to hurt me, King."

"Oh yes, he does," Cian said easily. "He wants the pain in you nearly as much as he wants your blood in his throat. It's how he's made. Had she already given you the gift before they threw you off the cliff?"

"No. I was hurt though, hurt bad. Could hardly stand. They had a rope around me when they tossed me off. If I lived, she'd give me the gift. I lived. She'll take you back," he said to Cian.

"Yes, I know she will."

Glenna looked from one to the other. Trapped, she realized, between them. He'd known—she saw that now. Cian had known what King was before he'd let him in the house.

"Don't do this. How can you do this? To your brother."

"I can't have him," King told Cian. "Neither can you. She wants Hoyt herself. She wants to drink him, the sorcerer. With his blood, she'll ascend even higher. Every world there is will be ours."

The sword was too far away, and she no longer had the stake. She had nothing.

"We're to take Hoyt and the other female to her, alive. This one, and the boy? They're ours if we want them."

"I haven't drunk human blood for a very long time." Cian reached over, trailed a fingertip down the nape of Glenna's neck. "This one, I'd think, would be heady."

King licked his lips. "We can share her."

"Yes, why not?" He tightened his grip on Glenna, and when she fought, when she sucked in her breath, he laughed. "Oh aye, scream for help. Bring the others on down to save you. It'll save us the trip up."

"Rot in hell. I'm sorry for what happened to you," she said to King as he moved toward her. "Sorry for any part I played in it. But I won't make it easy for you."

She used Cian as a brace, swung up her legs and kicked out. She knocked King back a few steps, but he only laughed and moved toward her again.

"They let them run in the caves. So we can chase them. I like when they run. When they scream."

"I won't scream." She rammed back with her elbows, kicked out again.

She heard the rush of footsteps, and thought only, No! So screamed after all as she kicked and struggled.

"The cross. I can't get past the fucking cross. Knock her out!" King demanded. "Get it off her. I'm hungry!"

"I'll fix it." He tossed Glenna aside as the others rushed into the room.

And looking into King's eyes, drove the stake he'd had at his back into his friend's heart.

"It's all I could do for you," he told him, and tossed the stake aside.

"King. Not King." Moira dropped to her knees beside the dust. Then she laid her hands on it, spoke in a voice choked with tears. "Let what he was, the soul of him and the heart, be welcomed in a world again. The demon that took him is dead. Let him have light to find his way back."

"You won't raise a man from a pile of ash."

She looked up at Cian. "No, but maybe free his soul so it can be reborn. You didn't kill your friend, Cian."

"No. Lilith did."

"I thought . . ." Glenna still shook as Hoyt helped her to her feet.

"I know what you thought. Why shouldn't you?"

"Because I should have trusted you. I've said we aren't a unit, but I didn't understand I'm as much to blame for that as any. I didn't trust you. I thought you'd kill me, but you chose to save me."

"You're wrong. I chose to save him."

"Cian." She stepped toward him. "I caused this. I can't—"

"You didn't, no. You didn't kill him, you didn't change him. Lilith did. And sent him here to die once more. He was new, and not yet used to his skin. Injured as well. He couldn't have taken all of us, and she knew it."

"She knew what you would do." Hoyt moved to his brother's side, laid a hand on his shoulder. "And what it would cost you."

"In her way, she couldn't lose. So she'd think. I don't kill him, he takes at least one of you—maybe the lot if I turn. If I go the other way, destroy him, it costs me . . . oh quite a bit, quite a lot indeed."

"The death of a friend," Larkin began, "is a hard death. We all feel it."

"I believe you do." He looked down to where Moira still knelt on the floor. "But it comes to me first because he was mine first. She did this to him not because of you," he said to Glenna. "But because of me. I could've blamed you, and did, if she'd just killed him. Clean. But for this, it's not yours. It's hers and it's mine."

He walked over to pick up the stake he used, studied the killing point. "And when it comes time, when we face her, she's mine. If any of you step up to do the killing blow, I'll stop you. So you see, she miscalculated. I owe her for this, and I'll give her death for it."

Now, he picked up the sword. "We train tonight."

She trained, going one-on-one with Larkin, sword to sword. Cian had paired Moira with Hoyt, and stood back, or moved around them as steel clashed. He called out insults, which Glenna assumed was his style of motivation.

Her arm ached, and her still tender ribs throbbed. While sweat dribbled down her back, into her eyes, she continued to push. The pain, the effort, helped block out the image of King in the kitchen, moving toward her with fangs ready.

"Keep your arm up," Cian shouted at her. "If you can't hold a shagging sword properly you won't last five minutes. And stop dancing with her, for Christ's sake, Larkin. This isn't a bloody nightclub."

"She isn't fully healed," Larkin snapped back. "And what the hell's a nightclub?"

"I need to stop." Moira lowered her sword, wiped her sweaty brow with the back of her free hand. "Rest for a moment."

"You don't." Cian spun toward her. "Do you think you're doing her a favor, asking to rest? Do you think they'll be agreeable to a bloody time out just because your pal here needs to catch her breath?"

"I'm fine. There's no need to snap at her." Glenna struggled to catch her breath, to will some strength back into her legs. "I'm fine. Stop holding back," she told Larkin. "I don't need to be coddled."

"She needs to be looked at." Hoyt gestured Larkin back. "It's too soon for her to train like this."

"That isn't for you to say," Cian pointed out.

"I am saying it. She's exhausted, and she's in pain. And that's enough."

"I said I'm fine, and can speak for myself. Which, though he enjoys being a bastard, is what your brother pointed out. I don't need or want you to speak for me."

"Then you'll have to grow accustomed to it, because so I will when you need it."

"I know what I need and when I need it."

"Maybe the two of you will just talk the enemy to death," Cian said dryly.

Out of patience, Glenna thrust at Cian with her sword. "Come on. Come on then, you and me. You won't hold back."

"No." He tapped his blade to hers. "I won't."

"I said enough." Hoyt slashed his sword between them, and his fury sent a ripple of fire down the steel.

"Which one of us would you like to take on?" Now, Cian's tone was like silk. And his eyes darkened with a dangerous pleasure when Hoyt pivoted toward him.

"Should be interesting," Larkin said, but his cousin stepped in.

"Wait," she said. "Just wait. We're upset, all of us. Tired out, and overheated like horses at too long a gallop on top of it. It serves no purpose to hurt each other. If we won't rest, then at least, let's have the doors open. Have some air."

"You want the doors open?" Everything about him suddenly genial, Cian cocked his head. "A bit of air's what you're wanting? Sure we'll have ourselves some fresh air."

He strode to the terrace doors, threw them open. Then in a move fast as a fingersnap, reached out into the dark. "Come in, won't you?" he said and yanked a pair of vampires through the doorway.

"Plenty to eat here." He wandered to the table as both of them leapt up, drew swords. With the tip of his own he speared an apple from the bowl. Then leaned back against the wall, plucking it off to have a bite.

"Let's see what you can do with them," he suggested. "It's two against one, after all. You may just have a shot at surviving."

Hoyt pivoted, instinctively putting Glenna behind him. Larkin was already moving in, flashing his sword. His opponent blocked the slash easily, punched out with its free hand and sent Larkin flying halfway across the room.

It turned, rushed Moira. The first strike hit her sword, and the force knocked her down, sent her skidding over the floor. She groped desperately for her stake as it flew—seemed to fly—through the air toward her.

Glenna buried her terror, dug out her fury. She shot her power out—the first learned, the last lost—and brought the fire. The vampire burst into flames midair.

"Nicely done, Red," Cian commented, and watched his brother battle for his life.

"Help him. Help me."

"Why don't you?"

"They're too close to risk the fire."

"Try this." He tossed her a stake, took another bite of apple.

She didn't think, couldn't think, as she ran forward. As she plunged the stake into the back of the vampire who'd beaten Hoyt to his knees.

And missed the heart.

It howled, but there seemed to be more pleasure than pain in it. It turned, lifted its sword high. Both Moira and Larkin charged, but Glenna saw her death. They were too far away, and she had nothing left.

Then Hoyt sliced his sword through its neck. Blood splattered her face before there was dust.

"Fairly pitiful, but effective enough all in all." Cian wiped his hands. "Now pair off. Playtime's over."

"You knew they were out there." Moira's hand, still holding the stake, trembled. "You knew."

"Well, of course, I knew they were out there. If you'd use your brains, or at least some of your senses, you'd have known it as well."

"You'd have let them kill us."

"More to the point, you nearly let them kill you. You." He gestured at Moira. "Stood there, letting the fear soak you, scent you. You." And now Larkin. "You charged in without using your head, and nearly lost it for the trouble. As for you," he said to Hoyt. "Protecting the womenfolk may be chivalrous, but you'll both die—with your honor intact, of course. While Red, at least, used her head initially—and the power your bloody gods gave her—she then fell apart, and stood meekly waiting to be dead."

He stepped forward. "So, we'll work on your weaknesses. Which are legion."

"I've had enough." Glenna's voice was hardly more than a whisper. "Enough of blood and death, enough for one night. Enough." She dropped the stake and walked out.

"Leave her be." Cian waved a hand when Hoyt turned to follow. "For Christ's sake, an ounce of brain would tell you she wants only her own company—and a strong, dramatic exit like that deserves to stand. Let her have it."

"He's right." Moira spoke quickly. "As much as it pains

me to say it. She needs the quiet." She walked over to pick up the sword that had been knocked out of her hand. "Weaknesses." She nodded her head, faced Cian. "Very well then. Show me."

Chapter 18

Hoyt expected to find her in bed when he came in. He'd hoped she'd be sleeping, so that he could put her under more deeply and work on her injuries.

But she was standing by the window in the dark.

"Don't turn on the light," she said with her back to him. "Cian was right, there are more outside still. If you pay attention, you can sense them. They move like shadows, but there's movement—more a sense of movement. They'll go soon, I think. To whatever hole they burrow in during the day."

"You should rest."

"I know you say that because you're concerned, and I'm calm enough now not to take your head off for it. I know I behaved poorly upstairs. I don't really care."

"You're tired, as I am. I want to wash, and I want to sleep."

"You have your own room. And that was uncalled for," she continued before he could speak. Now she turned. Her face seemed very pale in the dark, pale against the dark robe she wore. "I'm not as calm as I thought. You had no right, no right, to stand in front of me up there."

"Every right. Love gives me the right. And even without that, if a man doesn't shield a woman from harm—"

"Stop right there." She held up a hand, palm out, as if to block his words. "This isn't about men and women. It's about humans. The seconds you took to think of me, to worry for me could have cost you your life. We can't spare it, neither of us. Any of us. If you don't trust that I can defend myself—that all of us can, we're nowhere."

That her words made sense didn't matter a whit as far as he was concerned. He could still see the way that monster had leaped on her. "And where would you be if I hadn't destroyed that thing?"

"Different. A different matter." She moved closer now so that he could scent her, the lotions she used on her skin. So utterly female.

"This is foolishness, and a waste of time."

"It's not foolish to me, so listen up. Fighting with and protecting fellow soldiers is one thing, a vital thing. We all have to be able to count on each other. But to brush me back from battle is another. You have to understand and accept the difference."

"How can I, when it's you, Glenna? If I lost you—"

"Hoyt." She gripped his arms, a kind of impatient comfort. "Any or all of us might die in this. I'm fighting to understand and accept that. But if you die, I won't live with the responsibility of knowing it was for me. I won't do it."

She sat on the side of the bed. "I killed tonight. I know how it feels to end something. To use my power to do that, something I never thought I'd do, need to do." She held out her hands to study them. "I did it to save another human being, and still it weighs on me. I know that if I'd done it with stake or sword I'd accept it more easily. But I used magic to destroy."

She lifted her face to his, and the sorrow was deep in her eyes. "This gift was always so bright, and now there's a darkness in it. I have to understand and accept that, too. And you have to let me."

"I accept your power, Glenna, and what you can and will do with it. I think all of us would be better served by it if you worked solely on the magicks."

"And left the bloody work to you? Off the front line, out of harm's way, stirring my cauldron?"

"Twice this night I nearly lost you. So you'll do as I say."

It took a moment to find her voice. "Well, in a pig's eye. Twice this night I faced death, and I survived."

"We'll discuss this further tomorrow."

"Oh no, oh no, we won't." She flicked out a hand, slammed the door to the bathroom inches before he reached it.

He whirled back, a man obviously at the end of his tether. "Don't slap your power out at me."

"Don't slap your manhood out at me. And that didn't come out the way I meant it." Because there was laughter tickling the back of her throat right along with the temper, she took a breath. "I won't snap to, Hoyt, when you order it, any more than I expect you will for me. You were frightened for me, and oh boy, do I understand that, because I was frightened for me. And for you, for all of us. But we have to get past it."

"How?" he demanded. "How is that done? This love is new for me, this need and this terror that goes with it. When we were called for this, I thought it would be the hardest thing I'd ever done. But I was wrong. Loving you is harder, loving you and knowing I could lose you."

All of her life, she thought, she'd waited to be loved like this. What human didn't? "I never knew I could feel so completely for anyone. This is new for me, too, hard and scary and new. And I wish I could say you won't lose me. I wish I could. But I know the stronger I am, the better chance I have of staying alive. The stronger each one of us is, the better chance we have of surviving this. Of winning."

She stood again. "I looked at King tonight, a man I'd come to like quite a lot. I looked at what they'd made of him. What they made of him wanted my blood, my death, would have rejoiced in it. Seeing that, knowing that, hurt beyond the believing of it. He was a friend. He became a friend so quickly."

Her voice trembled, so that she had to turn away, move back to the window and the dark. "There was a part of me, even as I tried to save myself, that saw what he had been—the man who'd cooked with me, sat with me, laughed with me. I couldn't use my powers against him, couldn't pull it out of me to do that. If Cian hadn't . . ." She turned back now, straight and slim.

"I won't be weak again. I won't hesitate a second time. You have to trust me for that."

"You called out for me to run. Would you say that was putting yourself in front of me in battle?"

She opened her mouth, closed it again. Cleared her throat. "Seemed like the thing to do at the time. All right, all right. Point made and taken. We'll both work on it. And I've some ideas on weaponry that might be helpful. But before we put this, and ourselves to bed, I want to cover one more thing."

"I don't find myself at all surprised."

"Fighting with your brother over me isn't something I appreciate or consider flattering."

"It wasn't only about you."

"I know that. But I was the catalyst. And I'm going to have a word with Moira about it, too. Of course, her idea of distracting Cian from us changed the entire scope of things."

"It was madness for him to bring those things into the house. His own temper and arrogance could have cost us lives."

"No." She spoke quietly now, and with absolute certainty. "He was right to do it."

Stunned, he gaped at her. "How can you say so? How can you defend him?"

"He made a very big and illuminating point, one we won't be able to forget. We won't always know when they'll come, and we have to be ready to kill or be killed every minute, every day. We weren't, not really. Even after King, we weren't. If there'd been more of them, the odds more even, it might've been a very different story."

"He stood by, did nothing."

"Yes, he did. Another point. He's the strongest of us, and the smartest in these circumstances. It's up to us to work toward closing that gap. I have some ideas, at least for the two of us."

She came to him, rising on her toes to brush her lips over his cheek. "Go ahead, wash up. I want to sleep on it. I want to sleep with you."

She dreamed of the goddess, of walking through a world of gardens, where birds were bright as the flowers, and the flowers like jewels.

From a high black cliff, water the color of liquid sapphire tumbled down to strike a pool clear as glass where gold and ruby fish darted.

The air was warm and heavy with fragrance.

Beyond the gardens was a silver sickle of beach where the turquoise water lapped its edges gently as a lover. There were children building sparkling castles of sand, or splashing in the foamy surf. Their laughter carried on the air like the birdsong.

Rising from the beach were steps of shimmering white with diamonds of ruby red along their edges. High above them were houses, painted in dreamy pastels, skirted with yet more flowers, with trees that dripped blossoms.

She could hear music drifting down from the tall hill, the harps and flutes singing of joy.

"Where are we?"

"There are many worlds," Morrigan told her as they walked. "This is just another. I thought you should see that you fight for more than yours, or his, or the world of your friends."

"It's beautiful. It feels . . . happy."

"Some are, some are not. Some demand a hard life, full of pain and effort. But it is still life. This world is old," the goddess said, her robes flowing as she opened her arms. "It earned this beauty, this peace, through that pain and that effort."

"You could stop what's coming. Stop her."

Her bright hair dancing in the wind, she turned to Glenna. "I have done what I can to stop it. I have chosen you."

"It's not enough. Already we've lost one of us. He was a good man."

"Many are."

"Is this how fate and destiny work? The higher powers? So coldly?"

"The higher powers bring laughter to those children, they bring the flowers and the sun. Love and pleasures. And yes, death and pain. It must be so."

"Why?"

Morrigan turned, smiled. "Or it would all mean so little. You are a gifted child. But the gift has weight."

"I used that gift to destroy. All of my life I've believed, been taught, I *knew* what I had, what I was, could never harm. But I used it to harm."

Morrigan touched Glenna's hair. "This is the weight, and it must be carried. You were charged to strike at evil with it."

"I won't be the same again," Glenna stated, looking out to sea.

"No, not the same. And you're not ready. None of you. You're not yet whole."

"We lost King."

"He isn't lost. He's only moved to a different world."

"We're not gods, and we grieve for the death of a friend. The cruelty of it."

"There will be more death, more grieving."

Glenna closed her eyes. It was harder, even harder, to speak of death when she looked at such beauty. "We're just full of good news today. I want to go back."

"Yes, you should be there. She'll bring blood, and another kind of power."

"Who will?" Fear had Glenna jerking back. "Lilith? Is she coming?"

"Look there." Morrigan pointed to the west. "When the lightning strikes."

The sky went black, and the lightning arrowed out of the sky to strike the heart of the sea.

When she whimpered, turned, Hoyt's arms came around her.

"It's dark."

"Nearly dawn." He touched his lips to her hair.

"A storm's coming. She's coming with it."

"Did you dream?"

"Morrigan took me." She pressed closer. He was warm. He was real. "Some place beautiful. Perfect and beautiful. Then the dark came, and the lightning struck the water. I heard them growling in the dark."

"You're here now. Safe."

"None of us are." Her mouth lifted, met his desperately. "Hoyt."

She rose above him, slim and fragrant. White skin against pearled shadows. She took his hands, pressed them to her breasts. Felt his fingers cup her.

Real and warm.

As her heartbeat quickened, the candles around the room began to flicker. In the hearth, the fire woke to simmer.

"There's a power in us." She lowered to him, her lips racing over his face, down his throat. "See it. Feel it. What we make together."

Life, was all she could think. Here was life, hot and human. Here was a power that could strike back the icy fingers of death.

She rose up again, taking him into her, strong and deep. Then bowing back as the thrill washed through her like wine.

He wrapped around her, coming to her so his mouth could take her breast, so he could taste the pounding of her heart. Life, he thought as well. Here was life.

"All that I am." Already breathless, he feasted on her. "This is more. From the first moment, for the rest of time."

She took his face, watched herself in his eyes. "In any world. In all of them."

It poured through her, so fast, so hot, she cried out.

Dawn broke quietly while their passion raged.

"It's the fire," Glenna told him.

They were in the tower, sitting over coffee and scones. She had the door firmly locked, and had added a charm to make certain no one and nothing entered until she was finished.

"It's exciting." His eyes were still sleepy, his body relaxed.

Sex, Glenna thought, could work wonders. She was feeling pretty damn good herself.

"Wake-up sex agrees with you, but I'm not talking about that kind of fire. Or not exclusively. Fire's a weapon, a big one, against what we're fighting."

"You killed one with it last night." He poured more coffee. He was, he realized, developing quite a taste for it. "Effective, and quick, but also—"

"A little unpredictable, yes. If the aim's off, or one of our own is too close—or steps or is shoved in the line, it would be extremely tragic. But . . ." She tapped her fingers against her cup. "We learn to control it, to channel it. That's what we do, after all. Practice, practice. And more, we can use it to enhance the other weapons. The way you did last night, with the fire on the sword."

"I'm sorry?"

"The fire on your sword when you clashed with Cian." She lifted her eyebrows at his blank expression. "You didn't call it, it just came. Passion—in that case anger. Passion, when we're making love. A flame shot down your sword last night, just for an instant. A flaming sword."

She pushed up from the table to pace around the room. "We haven't been able to do anything about creating a protected zone around the house."

"We may yet find the way."

"Tricky, since we have a vampire on the premises. We can't set down a spell to repel vampires without repelling Cian. But yes, in time—if we have the time—we may find a way around that. In the meantime, the fire's not only effective, it's beautifully symbolic. And you bet your gorgeous ass, it'll put the fear of the gods into the enemy."

"Fire takes focus and concentration. A little difficult when you're fighting for your life."

"We'll work on it until it isn't so difficult. You wanted me to work more on magic, and in this case I'm willing. It's time to make ourselves a serious arsenal."

She came back, sat on the table. "When it's time to take this war to Geall, we're going loaded."

She spent the day at it, with him and without him. She buried herself in her own books, and the ones she dragged up from Cian's library.

When the sun set, she lit candles for work light and ignored Cian's banging on the door. She closed her ears to his curses, and his shouts that it was bloody well time for training.

She *was* training.

And she'd come out when she was damn good and ready.

The woman was young, and fresh. And very, very alone.

Lora watched from the shadows, gleefully pleased with her luck. To think she'd been annoyed when Lilith had sent her out with a trio of foot soldiers on a simple scouting mission. She'd wanted to hit one of the outlying pubs, have some fun, have a feast. How long did Lilith expect them to keep to the caves, lying low, picking off the occasional tourist?

The most fun she'd had in *weeks* had been smacking that witch around, and stealing the black man right from under the noses of that tedious, holy brigade.

She wished they could have based somewhere, *anywhere* but in this dreary place. Somewhere like Paris or Prague. Somewhere so full of people she could pluck them like plums. Somewhere full of sound and heartbeats, and the smell of flesh.

She would swear there were more cows and sheep than people in this stupid country.

It was boring.

But now, there was this interesting possibility.

So pretty. So unfortunate.

This one would be a good candidate for the change as well as a quick snack. It would be fun to have a new companion, a woman particularly. One she could train, and play with.

A new toy, she decided, to stave off this endless ennui, at least until the real fun began.

Where, she wondered, had the pretty thing been going after dark in her little car? Such bad luck to have a puncture on this quiet country road.

Nice coat, too, Lora thought as she watched the woman haul out the jack and spare. They were close enough to the same size that she could have the coat as well as what was in it.

All that lovely warm blood.

"Bring her to me." She gestured at the three who stood with her.

"Lilith said we weren't to feed until—"

She whirled, fangs glinting, eyes burning red. And the vampire who'd once been a man of two hundred and twenty pounds of muscle when alive, backed off hurriedly.

"You question me?"

"No." She was here, after all—and he could smell her hunger. Lilith was not.

"Bring her to me," Lora repeated, tapping him on the chest, then wagging that finger playfully in front of his face. "And no tasting. I want her alive. It's time I had a new playmate." Her lips moved over her fangs in a pretty pout. "And try not to damage the coat. I like it."

They moved out of the shadows and onto the road, three males who'd been ordinary in life.

They scented human. And female.

Their hunger, always waiting, woke—and only the fear of Lora's reprisal prevented them from charging like wolves.

She glanced over as they approached. She smiled, quick and friendly as she straightened from her crouch at the side of the car, and raked a hand through short, dark hair that left her throat and neck exposed in the gloomy light.

"I was hoping someone would come along."

"Must be your lucky night." The one Lora had chastised grinned.

"I'll say. Dark, deserted road like this, middle of nowhere. Whew. It's a little scary."

"It can get scarier."

They spread out in a triangle to close her in with the car at her back. She took a step back, eyes going wide, and they growled low in the throat.

"Oh God. Are you going to hurt me? I don't have much money, but—"

"Money's not what we're after, but we'll take that, too."

She still held the tire iron, and when she lifted it, the one closest to her laughed. "Stay back. Just keep away from me."

"Metal's not a big problem for us."

He charged toward her, hands lifted toward her throat. And exploded into dust.

"No, but the pointy end of this is." She wagged the stake she'd held behind her back.

She lunged, kicking one aside with a flashing foot to the belly, blocking a blow with her forearm then leading with the stake. She let the last one come to her, let the momentum of his rage and hunger rush him forward. She swung the tire iron full at his face. She was on him in an instant when he landed on the road.

"Metal's a little problem after all," she said. "But we'll finish up with this."

She staked him, rose. Dusted off her coat. "Damn vampires."

She started back to her car, then stopped, her head lifting like a dog scenting the air.

She spread her legs, shifted her grip on the tire iron, on the stake. "Don't you want to come out and play?" she called out. "I can smell you out there. These three didn't give me much action, and I'm revved."

The scent began to fade. In moments, the air was clear again. She watched, and waited, then with a shrug hooked the stake into the sheath on her belt. When she finished changing the tire, she glanced up at the sky.

Clouds had rolled over the moon, and in the west thunder grumbled. "Storm's coming, she murmured.

In the training room, Hoyt landed hard on his back. He felt every bone in his body rattle. Larkin pounced, then brought the blunted stake down to tap Hoyt's heart.

"I've killed you six times already tonight. You're off your game." He cursed lightly when he felt the blade at his throat.

Moira eased it back, then leaned over him to give him an upsidedown smile. "He'd be dust, that's certain, but you'd be bleeding all over what's left."

"Well, if you're going to come at a man from behind—"

"They will," Cian reminded him, giving Moira one of his rare nods of approval. "And more than one. You make your kill, you move on. Quick, fast and in a bloody hurry."

He vised his hands on Moira's head, feigned giving it a twist. "Now the three of you are dead because you spend too much time talking. You need to handle multiple opponents, whether it's sword, stake or bare hands."

Hoyt stood, shook himself off. "Why don't you demonstrate for us?"

Cian lifted his brows at the irritable challenge. "All right then. All of you, on me. I'll try not to hurt you more than is necessary."

"Bragging. That would be talking, wouldn't it?" Larkin crouched into fighting stance.

"It would be, in this case, stating the obvious." He picked up the blunted stake, tossed it to Moira. "What you want to do here is anticipate each other's moves, as well as mine. Then . . . So you decided to join the party."

"I've been working on something. Making progress." Glenna touched the hilt of the dagger she'd strapped to her waist. "I needed to step away from it awhile. What's the drill here?"

"We're going to kick Cian's arse," Larkin told her.

"Oh. I'll play. Weapons?"

"Your choice." Cian nodded toward the dagger. "You seem to have yours."

"No, not for this." She moved over, selected another blunted stake. "Rules?"

In answer, Cian shot over, flipped Larkin and sent him tumbling to a pad. "Win. That's the only rule."

When Hoyt moved on him, Cian took the blow, let the momentum of it carry him into the air. He kicked off the wall, revolved, and used his body to knock Hoyt into Moira. And took them both down.

"Anticipate," he repeated, and kicked back almost idly to send Larkin into the air.

Glenna grabbed a cross, held it out as she stepped forward.

"Ah, smart." His eyes went red, just at the rims. Outside the doors, thunder began to grumble. "Shield and weapon, put the enemy in retreat. Except . . ." He lashed out, forearm to forearm and knocked the cross away. But when he spun to dispatch the stake, Glenna dived, going under him.

"Now this one's clever." Cian nodded approval, and for a moment, his face was illuminated by a ripple of lightning against the glass. "She uses her head, her instincts—at least when the stakes—haha—are low."

They circled him now, which he considered a small improvement in their strategy. Not quite a team, not yet an oiled machine, but an improvement.

As they closed in, he could see the need to pounce in Larkin's eyes.

Cian chose what he considered the weakest link, pivoted, and using one hand simply lifted Moira off her feet. When he tossed her, Larkin instinctively shifted to catch her. All Cian needed to do was sweep out a leg, take Larkin off his feet, and both of them went down in a tangle of limbs.

He spun to block his brother, gripped Hoyt's shirt. The solid head-butt had Hoyt stumbling back, giving Cian the instant he needed to wrench the stake from Glenna.

He had her back against him, his arm hooked tight around her neck.

"What now?" he asked the rest of them. "I've got your girl here. Do you back off, leave her to me? Do you come in, risk me snapping her in half? It's a problem."

"Or do they let me take care of myself?" Glenna gripped the chain around her neck, swung the cross back toward Cian's face.

He released her, vaulted clear to the ceiling. He clung there a moment, a dangerous fly, then dropped lightly to his feet.

"Not bad. And still, the four of you have yet to put me down. And if I were to—" There was a burst of lightning as his hand shot out, snatched the flying stake an inch from his own heart. The end was honed to killing point.

"We'd call that cheating," he said mildly.

"Back away from him."

They turned to see the woman step through the terrace doors as another flash of lightning ripped the sky behind her. She was slim in a black leather coat that hit her at the knees. Her dark hair was cut short, showcasing a high forehead and enormous eyes of vivid blue.

She dumped the large sack she carried on the floor, and with another stake in one hand, a two-edged knife in the other, she moved farther into the light.

"Who the hell are you?" Larkin demanded.

"Murphy. Blair Murphy. And I'll be saving your lives tonight. How the hell'd you let one of them in the house?"

"It happens I own it," Cian told her. "This is my place."

"Nice. Your heirs should be celebrating really soon. I said keep back from him," she snapped as both Larkin and Hoyt moved in front of Cian.

"I'd be his heir, as this is my brother."

"He's one of us," Larkin said.

"No. He's really not."

"But he is." Moira held up her hands to show they were empty, and moved slowly toward the intruder. "We can't let you hurt him."

"Looked to me like you were doing a piss-poor job of trying to hurt him when I came in."

"We were training. He's chosen to help us."

"A vampire helping humans?" Those big eyes narrowed in interest, and what might have been humor. "Well, there's always something new." Slowly Blair lowered the stake.

Cian pushed his shields aside. "What are you doing here? How did you come here?"

"How? Aer Lingus. What? Killing as many of your kind as I can manage. Present company, temporarily, excluded."

"How do you know about his kind?" Larkin asked her.

"Long story." She paused to scan the room, eyebrows lifting

thoughtfully at the stockpile of weapons. "Nice stash. There's something about a battle-ax that warms my heart."

"Morrigan. Morrigan said she'd come with the lightning." Glenna touched a hand to Hoyt's arm, then walked to Blair. "Morrigan sent you."

"She said there'd be five. She didn't mention any undead in the crew." After a moment, she sheathed the knife, tucked the stake into her belt. "But that's a god for you. Just gotta be cryptic. Look, it's been a long trip." She picked up her bag, slung the strap over her shoulder. "Got anything to eat around here?"

Chapter 19

"Well I have a lot of questions."

Blair nodded at Glenna as she sampled stew. "Bet you do, and right back at you. This is good." She took another spoonful. "Thanks, and compliments to the chef and all that."

"You're welcome. I'm going to start, if that's okay." Glenna scanned the faces of the rest of the group. "Where did you come from?"

"Lately? Chicago."

"The Chicago in the here and now?"

A smile tugged at Blair's wide mouth. She reached for the hunk of bread Glenna had set out, ripped it in two with nails painted a deep candy pink. "That's the one. In the heartland, Planet Earth. You?"

"New York. This is Moira, and her cousin Larkin. They're from Geall."

"Get out." Blair studied them as she ate. "I always figured that for a myth."

"You don't seem particularly surprised it's not."

"Nothing much surprises me, less now after the visit from the goddess. Heavy stuff."

"This is Hoyt. He's a sorcerer from Ireland. Twelfth-century Ireland."

Blair watched as Glenna reached behind her for Hoyt's hand, the way their fingers smoothly intertwined. "You two paired up?"

"You could say that."

Now she lifted her wine, took a small sip. "That's taking going for older men to a new level, but who could blame you?"

"Your host is his brother, Cian, who was made a vampire."

"Twelfth century?" Blair leaned back, took a good, long look at him, with all the interest but none of the amusement she'd shown when studying Hoyt. "You've got nearly a thousand years? I've never met a vamp who lasted that long. The oldest I ever came across was a couple decades shy of five hundred."

"Clean living," Cian said.

"Yeah, that'll be the day."

"He doesn't drink humans." Since it was there, Larkin got another bowl, spooned up stew for himself. "He fights with us. We're an army."

"An army? Talk about delusions of grandeur. What are you?" she asked Glenna.

"Witch."

"So, we've got a witch, a sorcerer, a couple of refugees from Geall and a vampire. Some army."

"A powerful witch." Hoyt spoke for the first time. "A scholar of remarkable skill and courage, a shape-shifter, and a centuries-old vampire who was made by the reining queen."

"Lilith?" Now Blair set down her spoon. "She made you?"

Cian leaned back against the counter, crossed his ankles. "I was young and foolish."

"And had really bad luck."

"What are you?" Larkin demanded.

"Me? Demon hunter." She picked up her spoon to resume

eating. "I've spent most of my life tracking and dusting his kind."

Glenna angled her head. "What, like Buffy?"

With a laugh, Blair swallowed stew. "No. First, I'm not the only, just the best."

"There are more of you." At that point, Larkin decided he could use some wine as well.

"It's a family thing, has been for centuries. Not all of us, but every generation one or two more of us. My father's one, and my aunt. His uncle was—and like that. I have two cousins on the job now. We fight the fight."

"And Morrigan sent you here," Glenna put in. "Only you."

"I'd have to say yes, since I'm the only one here. Okay, so the last couple of weeks, things have been weird. More undead activity than usual, like they're getting some brass ones. And I'm having these dreams. Portentous dreams go with the package, but I'm having them every time I close my eyes. And sometimes when I'm wide awake. Disturbing."

"Lilith?" Glenna asked.

"She made some appearances—cameos we'll say. Up till then, I figured she was another myth. Anyway, in the dream, I thought I was over here—Ireland. It looked like here anyway. I've been to Ireland before, another family tradition. But I'm on this rise. Barren place, rough ground, deep chasms, wicked rocks."

"The Valley of Silence," Moira interrupted.

"That's what she called it. Morrigan. She said I was needed." Blair hesitated, looked around. "I probably don't have to fill in all the details since you're all here. Big battle, possible apocalypse. Vampire queen forming an army to eliminate humankind. There would be five waiting for me, gathered together. We'd have until Samhain to prepare. Not a lot of time considering, you know—goddess, eternity. But that's how it's laid out."

"So you came," Glenna said. "Just like that?"

"Didn't you?" Blair shrugged. "I was born for this. I've dreamed of that place before, as long as I can remember. Me standing on that rise, watching it rage below. The moon, the fog, the screams. I always knew I'd end up there."

Always assumed she would die there.

"I just expected a little more backup."

"In three weeks we've killed more than a dozen," Larkin said with some annoyance.

"Good for you. I don't keep a tally of kills since I had my first thirteen years ago. But I took out three tonight on the road, on the way here."

"Three?" He held up his spoon. "Alone?"

"There was another. It stayed back. Chasing it down didn't seem like a good way to stay alive, which is the first rule in the family handbook. There might have been more of them, but I only scented the one. You've got more stationed around the perimeter of this place. I had to slip through them to get inside."

She pushed her empty bowl away. "That was really good. Thanks again."

"You're welcome again." Glenna took the bowl to the sink. "Hoyt, can I have a word with you? Excuse us, just for a minute."

She drew him out of the kitchen, toward the front of the house. "Hoyt, she's—"

"The warrior," he finished. "Yes, she's the last of the six."

"It was never King." She pressed her fingers to her mouth as she turned away. "He was never one of the six, and what happened to him—"

"Happened." Hoyt took her shoulders, turned her to face him. "Can't be changed. She's the warrior, and completes the circle."

"We have to trust her. I don't know how we begin to do that. She damned near killed your brother before she bothered to say hello."

"And we have only her word she's who she says she is."

"Well, she's not a vampire. She walked right into the house. Added to that, Cian would know."

"Vampires can have human servants."

"So how do we know? Do we take what she says she is on faith? If she is what she says, she's the last of us."

"We have to be sure."

"It's not like we can check her ID."

He shook his head, not bothering to ask her meaning. "She has to be tested. Upstairs, I think, in the tower. We'll make the circle, and we'll be sure."

When they were gathered upstairs, Blair looked around. "Close quarters. I like things roomier. You're going to want to keep your distance," she warned Cian. "I might stake you, just knee-jerk."

"You can try."

She tapped her fingers on the stake in her belt. There was a ring, a ridged band of silver, on her right thumb. "So, what's all this about?"

"We had no sign you were coming," Glenna began. "Not you specifically."

"So, you're thinking Trojan Horse?"

"It's a possibility we can't dismiss without proof."

"No," Blair agreed, "you'd be stupid just to take my word. And I feel better, actually, knowing you're not stupid. What do you want? My demon hunter's license?"

"You actually have—"

"No." She planted her feet, very like a warrior bracing for battle. "But if you're toying with doing some kind of witchcraft that involves my blood or other bodily fluid, you're out of luck. Line drawn on that."

"Nothing like that. Well, witchcraft, but nothing that requires blood. We're linked, the five of us. By fate, by necessity. And some, yes, by blood. We are the circle. We are the chosen. If you're the last link of that circle, we'll know."

"Otherwise?"

"We can't harm you." Hoyt laid a hand on Glenna's shoulder. "It's against all we are to use power against a human being."

Blair glanced toward the broadsword leaning against the tower wall. "Anything in the rule book about sharp, pointy objects?"

"We won't harm you. If you're Lilith's servant, we'll make you our prisoner."

She smiled, one corner of her mouth rising, then the other. "Good luck with that. All right, let's do it. Like I said, if you'd swallowed everything without a *hmmm,* I'd be more worried about what I'd walked into here. You guys around this white circle, me in it?"

"You know witchcraft?" Glenna asked her.

"I know something about it." She stepped into the circle.

"One of us at each point," Glenna instructed, "to form a pentagram. Hoyt will do the search."

"Search?"

"Of your mind," he assured Blair.

"There are some private things in there, too." Uncomfortable, she moved her shoulders, frowned at Hoyt. "Am I supposed to think of you as my witch doctor?"

"I'm not a witch. It will go more quickly, and without discomfort if you open to this." He lifted his hands, and lit the candles. "Glenna?"

"This is the circle of light and knowledge, formed by like minds, like hearts. Within this circle of light and knowledge no harm will we impart. We seek to link so we may know, within this ring only truth bestow. With mind to mind in destiny, as we will, so mote it be."

The air rippled, and still the candle flames rose straight as arrows. Hoyt held out his hands toward Blair.

"No harm, no pain. Only thoughts within thoughts. Your mind to my mind, your mind to our minds."

Her eyes looked deeply into his, had something flickering in his head. Then they went black, and he saw.

They all saw.

A young girl fighting a monster nearly twice her size. There was blood on her face, and her shirt was torn. They could hear each drawing of her labored breath. A man stood off to the side, and watched the battle.

She was struck to the ground with a vicious backhanded blow, and sprang up. Struck down again. When the thing leaped, she rolled. And stabbed it through the back, into the heart, with a stake.

Slow, the man said. *Sloppy, even for a first kill. You'll need to do better.*

She didn't speak, but the mind inside her mind thought, *I'll do better. I'll do better than anyone.*

Now she was older, and fought beside the man. Ferociously, savagely. The odds were five to two, but it was done quickly. And when it was done, the man shook his head. *More control, less passion. Passion will kill you.*

She was naked, in bed with a young man, moving with him in the low light of the lamp. She smiled as she arched to him, nipped his lip. A diamond winked madly on her finger. Her mind was full of passion, of love, of joy.

And of despair and misery as she sat on the floor in the dark, alone, weeping out the shards of a broken heart. Her finger was bare.

She stood on the rise above the battleground, with the goddess a white shadow beside her.

You were the first to be called, and the last, Morrigan told her. *They're waiting for you. The worlds are in your hands. Take theirs, and fight.*

She thought, *I've been coming toward this all my life. Will it be the end of it?*

Hoyt lowered his hands, brought her slowly back, as he closed the circle. Her eyes cleared, blinked.

"So? Did I pass the audition?"

Glenna smiled at her, then walked to the table, lifted one of the crosses. "This is yours now."

Blair took it, let it dangle. "It's nice. Beautiful craftsmanship, and I appreciate the gesture. But I have my own." She tugged the chain from under her shirt. "Family thing again. Like an heirloom."

"It's lovely, but if you'd—"

"Wait." Hoyt snatched at the cross, stared at it as it lay in his palm. "Where did you get this? Where did it come from?"

"I told you, family. We have seven of them. They've been passed down. You're going to want to let go of that."

When he looked up into her eyes again she narrowed hers. "What's the problem?"

"There were seven, the goddess gave me, on the night she charged me to come here. I asked for protection for my family, the family she ordered me to leave behind. And these were what she gave me."

"That was what, nine hundred years back? It doesn't mean—"

"It's Nola's." He looked over her head to Cian. "I can feel it. This is Nola's cross."

"Nola?"

"Our sister. The youngest." His voice thickened as Cian moved closer to see for himself. "And here, on the back, I inscribed it with her name. She said I'd see her again. And by the gods, I am. She's in this woman. Blood to blood. Our blood."

"There's no question?" Cian said quietly.

"I put this around her neck myself. Look at her, Cian."

"Aye. Well." He looked away again, then moved to the window.

"Forged in the fire of the gods, given by the hand of a sorcerer." Blair breathed deep. "Family legend. My middle name is Nola. Blair Nola Bridgit Murphy."

"Hoyt." Glenna touched his arm. "She's your family."

"I guess you'd be my uncle, a thousand times removed or however it works." She glanced over toward Cian. "And isn't it a kick in the ass? I'm related to a vampire."

In the morning, under a weak and fitful sunlight, Glenna stood with Hoyt in the family graveyard. The storm had soaked the grass, and rain still dripped from the petals of the roses that climbed over his mother's grave.

"I don't know how to comfort you."

He took her hand. "You're here. I never thought I would need anyone to be with me, not the way I need you. It's all so fast, all of this. Loss and gain, discovery, questions. Life and death."

"Tell me about your sister. About Nola."

"She was bright and fair, and gifted. She had sight. She loved animals—had, I think, a special affinity for them. Before I left, there were puppies born to my father's wolfhound. Nola would spend hours in the stables playing with them. And while the world turned, she grew to a woman, had children."

He turned, rested his brow against Glenna's. "I see her in this woman, this warrior who's with us now. And inside of me is another war."

"Will you bring her here? Blair?"

"It would be right."

"You do what's right." She tipped up her head so her lips brushed his. "It's why I love you."

"If we were to marry—"

She took one quick, jerky step back. "Marry?"

"Sure that hasn't changed over the centuries. A man and a woman love, they take vows, make promises. Marriage or handfasting, a tie to bind them to each other."

"I know what marriage is."

"And it disturbs you?"

"Not disturbs, and don't smile at me that way, as if I'm being endearingly stupid. Give me just a minute here." She looked over the stones, toward the sparkling hills beyond. "Yes, people still marry, if they like. Some live together without the ritual."

"You and I, Glenna Ward, we're creatures of ritual."

She looked back at him, felt her stomach jitter. "Yes, we are."

"If we were to marry, would you live here with me?"

It was a second jolt. "Here? In this place, in *this* world?"

"In this place, in this world."

"But . . . don't you want to go back? Need to?"

"I don't think I can go back. Magically, aye, I think it's possible," he said before she could speak. "I don't think I can go back, to what was. To what was home. Not knowing when they'll die. Knowing that Cian is here—that other half of me. I don't think I could go back knowing you would go with me, and pine for what you left here."

"I said I would go."

"Without hesitation," he agreed. "Yet you hesitate at the rite of marriage."

"You caught me off guard. And you didn't actually ask

me," she said with some annoyance. "You more posed a hypothesis."

"If we were to marry," he said a third time, and the humor in his voice had her fighting her own, "would you live with me here?"

"In Ireland?"

"Aye, here. And in this place. It would be a kind of melding of our worlds, our needs. I would ask Cian to let us live in the house, to tend it. It needs people, family, the children we'd make together."

"Leaps and bounds," she murmured. Then took a moment to settle herself, to search herself. Her time, his place, she thought. Yes, it was a loving compromise, could be—would be—a melding of spirits.

"I've always been a confident sort, even as a child. Know what you want, work to get it, then value it once you have it. I've tried not to take anything in my life for granted, or not too much. My family, my gift, my lifestyle."

Reaching out, she brushed her fingers over one of his mother's roses. Simple beauty. Miraculous life.

"But I've learned that I took the world for granted, that it would always be—and that it would roll along, pretty much without my help. I learned otherwise, and that's given me something else to work for, to value."

"Is that a way of saying this isn't the time to speak of marriage and children?"

"No. It's a way of saying I understand the little things—and the big ones—the normal things, life, become only more important when it's all on the line. So . . . Hoyt the Sorcerer."

She touched her lips to his cheek, then the other. "If we were to marry, I would live here with you, and tend this house with you, and make children with you. And I'd work very hard to value all of it."

Watching her, he held up a hand, palm to her. When hers met it, their fingers linked, firm and strong. Light spilled out of their clasped hands.

"Will you marry me, Glenna?"

"Yes."

He cupped the back of her neck, drawing her to him. The kiss spun out, full of promise and possibilities. Full of hope. When her arms came around him, she knew she'd found the strongest part of her destiny.

"We have more to fight for now." He turned his face into her hair. "More to be now."

"Then we will be. Come with me. I'll show you what I'm working on."

She took him with her closer to the house where there were targets set up for archery training. The sound of hoof-beats had her looking over, just in time to see Larkin ride the stallion into the trees.

"I wish he wouldn't ride in the woods. There are so many shadows."

"I doubt they could catch him, if they were lying in wait. But if you asked him," Hoyt said, running a hand down Glenna hair, "he'd keep to the fields."

Her brows lifted in puzzlement. "If I asked?"

"If he knew you worried, he'd give that to you. He's grateful for what you do for him. You feed him," Hoyt said when she frowned.

"Oh. Well, he certainly likes to eat." Glenna looked toward the house. Moira, she imagined, was having her morning session with the books, and Cian would be sleeping. As for Blair, it would take a little time before Glenna learned the newcomer's routine.

"I think we'll have lasagna for dinner. Don't worry." She patted his hand. "You'll like it—and it occurs to me that I'm already tending the house, and the family in it. I never thought of myself as particularly domestic. The things you learn. And now."

She drew her dagger, moving she realized, with complete ease from cookery to weaponry.

The things you learn.

"I worked on this yesterday."

"On the dagger," Hoyt prompted.

"On charming the dagger. I thought I should start small, eventually work up to a sword. We talked about doing something about weapons, but with one thing and the other, we haven't really gotten down to it. Then I thought of this."

He took it from her, skimmed a finger up the edge. "Charmed in what way?"

"Think fire." His gaze moved back to hers. "No, literally," she said as she stepped back a pace. "Think fire. Visualize it, skimming over the blade."

He turned the dagger in his hand, then shifted to a fighting grip. He imagined fire, pictured it coating the steel. But the blade remained cool.

"Are there words to be said?" he asked her.

"No, you just have to want it, to see it. Try it again."

He focused, and got nothing.

"All right, maybe it only works for me—for now. I can refine it." She took it back from him, drew out the image, and pointed the dagger toward the target.

There wasn't so much as a spurt.

"Damn it, it worked yesterday." She took a closer look to make certain she hadn't grabbed the wrong weapon that morning. "This is the right one, I inscribed a pentagram on the hilt. See?"

"Yes, I see it. Perhaps the charm is limited. It wore off."

"I don't see how. I should have to break the charm, and I didn't. I put a lot of time and energy into this, so—"

"What's going on?" Blair strolled out, one hand tucked in the front pocket of her jeans, the other holding a steaming cup of coffee. There was a knife in a sheath at her hip, and the glimmer of moonstones dangling from her ears. "Knife-throwing practice?"

"No. Good morning."

She lifted an eyebrow at the irritation in Glenna's voice. "For some of us anyway. Nice dagger."

"It's not working."

"Let's see." Blair snatched it from Glenna, tested the weight. And sipping coffee, threw it toward the target. It stabbed the bull's-eye. "Works for me."

"Great, so it's got a pointy end, and you've got excellent aim." Glenna stomped toward the target, wrenched out the dagger. "What happened to the magic?"

"Search me. It's a knife, a nice one. It stabs, it hacks, it slices. Does the job. You start counting on magic, you can get sloppy. Then somebody puts that pointy end into you."

"You have magic in your blood," Hoyt pointed out to her. "You should have respect for it."

"Didn't say otherwise. I'm just more comfortable with sharp implements than voodoo."

"Voodoo is a different matter entirely," Glenna snapped. "Just because you can throw a knife doesn't mean you don't need what Hoyt and I can give you."

"No offense—seriously. But I count on myself first. And if you can't fight with that, you should leave the combat to the ones who can."

"You think I can't hit that stupid target?"

Blair sipped more coffee. "I don't know. Can you?"

Riding on insult, Glenna turned, and with curses running through her head flung the knife.

It hit the outer circle. And burst into flame.

"Excellent." Blair lowered her coffee. "I mean your aim's for shit, but the fire show is very cool." She gestured with the mug. "Probably going to need a new target though."

"I was pissed off," Glenna mumbled. "Anger." She turned her excited face to Hoyt's. "Adrenaline. We weren't angry before. I was happy. She pissed me off."

"Always happy to help."

"It's a fine charm, a good weapon." He laid a hand on Glenna's shoulder as the target burned. "How long will the flame last?"

"Oh! Wait." She stepped away, centered herself. Calmed, she put out the fire in her mind. The flame flickered out to smoke.

"It needs work. Obviously, but . . ." She went back to the target, gingerly tested the dagger's hilt. It was warm, but not too hot to touch. "It could give us a real edge."

"Damn straight," Blair agreed. "Sorry about the voodoo crack."

"Accepted." Glenna sheathed the dagger. "I'm going to ask you for a favor, Blair."

"Ask away."

"Hoyt and I need to get to work on this now, but later today . . . Could you teach me to throw a knife like you do?"

"Maybe not like me." Blair grinned. "But I can teach you to throw it better than you do, less like you're shooing pigeons."

"There's more," Hoyt said. "Cian takes charge of the training after sunset."

"A vampire training humans to kill vampires." Blair shook her head. "There's some sort of strange logic in there. Okay, so?"

"We train in the day as well—a few hours. Outside if the sun holds."

"From what I saw last night, you can use all you can get. And don't take insult," Blair added. "I work on it a couple hours a day myself."

"The one in charge of our daylight training . . . we lost him. Lilith."

"Rough. I'm sorry, it's always rough."

"I think you'd be the best to lead that training now."

"Give you guys orders, make you sweat?" Sheer pleasure shone on her face. "Sounds like fun. Just remember you asked when you start to hate me. Where are the others anyway? Daylight shouldn't be wasted."

"I imagine Moira's in the library," Glenna told her. "Larkin took the horse out a little while ago. Cian—"

"I got that part. Okay, I'm going to do a little scouting around, get the lay a little better. We'll get the party started when I get back."

"The trees are thick." Glenna nodded toward the curve of the forest. "You shouldn't go too far in, even during the day."

"Don't worry."

Chapter 20

Blair liked the woods. She liked the smell of them, the look of the big-trunked trees, the play of light and shadow that, for her, made a kind of visual music. The forest floor was carpeted with leaves that had fallen over countless years, and the fairy green of moss. The stream that ran glinting through it only added to that fairy-tale quality. It was slender and curvy, making more music with the water singing over rock.

She'd been to Clare before, had wandered field and forest and hill, and wondered how she'd missed this place if it truly was her beginnings. She supposed she hadn't been meant to find it before, to walk here. To know.

It was now, with these people, in this place.

The witch and the wizard, she mused. They were so full of love, all shiny and new, they all but glistened with it.

Advantage or disadvantage—she'd have to wait and see.

But she knew one thing. She wanted Glenna to make her a fire dagger.

The witch was okay. Great hair, too, and an urban sense of style that showed through even with simple pants and shirts. Lot of smarts going on in there, if Blair was any judge. And she was. She'd gone out of her way to be welcoming, it seemed, the night before. Fixing food, fluffing up the room she'd assigned to Blair.

It was a lot more than she was used to. And it was nice.

The wizard seemed to be on the intense side. Did a lot of watching, didn't have a lot to say. She could respect that. Just as she could, and did, respect the power he wore like skin.

As for the vampire, she was in a holding pattern there. He would be a formidable ally, or foe—and to date, she'd never considered a vamp any kind of ally. Still, she'd seen something in his face when his brother had spoken of Nola. It had been pain.

The other woman was quiet as a mouse. Watchful, oh yeah, and a little on the soft side yet. She hadn't made up her mind about Blair any more than Blair had about her.

And the guy? Larkin. Some serious eye-candy. He had a good, athletic build that should make him an asset in a fight. Boiling with energy, too, she thought. The shape-shifting deal could come in handy, if he was any good at it. She'd have to ask for a demo.

It was a lot—they were a lot—to whip into shape in a very short time. She'd have to be up to it if any of them were going to make it out of this alive.

But for now, it was nice to take a morning stroll through the trees, listening to the water sing, watching the light dance.

She skirted around a rock, cocked her head at what was curled sleeping under its shadow.

"This is your morning wake-up call," she said, and pulled the trigger on the crossbow she carried.

The vampire barely had time to open its eyes.

She retrieved the arrow, set it again.

She took out three more, disturbing another who sprinted off down the path, dodging beams of thin sunlight. Without a clear shot, and unwilling to waste an arrow, she took off after him.

The horse leaped onto the path, a gleaming black beast,

with the gilded god on its back. Larkin sliced down with his sword, and beheaded the fleeing vampire.

"Nice job," she called out.

Through streams of sunlight, Larkin trotted the horse toward her. "What are you doing out here?"

"Killing vampires. You?"

"The horse needed a run. You shouldn't be out here alone, so far from the house."

"You are."

"They couldn't catch this one." He patted Vlad on the neck. "He's the wind. So then, how many have you seen?"

"The four I killed, and yours makes five. There are probably more."

"Four others, you say? Aren't you the busy one. Do you want to hunt them now?"

He looked up to it, but she couldn't be sure. Working with an unknown partner was a good way to die, even if that partner showed a wicked skill with a sword. "That should do it for now. One of them, at least, will run back to Mommy and report we're taking them out of their nests during the day. Should tick her off."

"Tick?"

"Annoy her."

"Ah. Aye, there's that."

"Anyway, we need to do some training so I can see what you're made of."

"You can see?"

"I'm your new sergeant." She could see he wasn't thrilled with that news—and who could blame him? But she held up a hand. "How about a lift, cowboy?"

He reached down, and with a clasp of hands to forearms, she vaulted up behind him.

"How fast will this guy move?" she asked.

"You'd best hold on, and tight."

A tap of his heels sent the horse flying.

Glenna rubbed her thumb and finger together over the cauldron to add another pinch of sulfur to the mix.

"A little at a time," she said absently to Hoyt. "We don't want to overdo it and end up—"

She jerked back as the liquid flashed.

"Mind your hair," Hoyt warned.

She grabbed some pins, bundled it hastily on top of her head. "How's it coming there?"

Inside the metal trough, the dagger continued to burn. "The fire's still unstable. We have to tame it or we'll burn ourselves as well as vampires."

"It's going to work." She took a sword, slid it into the liquid. Stepping back, she held her hands in the smoke and began her chant.

He stopped what he was doing to watch her, to study the beauty that came into her with the magic. What had his life been before she'd come into it? With no one with whom he could fully share what he was, not even Cian? With no one to look into his eyes in a way that made his heart shine?

Fire licked at the edges of the cauldron, shimmied up the sword, and still she stood, in the smoke and the flame. Her voice like music, her power like dance.

When the flames died, she removed the sword with tongs, set it aside to cure and cool.

"Each has to be done separately. I know it's going to take time, days, but in the end . . . what?" she said when she caught him staring at her. "Have I got magic soot all over my face?"

"No. You're beautiful. When will you marry me?"

She blinked in surprise. "I thought after, when it's over."

"No, I don't want to wait. Every day is a day less, and every day is precious. I want us to be married here, in this house. Before long, we'll travel to Geall, and then . . . It should be here, Glenna, in the home we'll make."

"Of course it should. I know your family can't be here, except for Cian and Blair. Neither can mine. But when it's over, Hoyt. When everyone's safe again, I'd like another ritual here, I'd like my family here then."

"A handfasting now, a wedding ceremony after. Would that suit?"

"Perfect. I'd—now? As in *now*? I can't be ready now. I have to . . . do things first. I need a dress."

"I thought you preferred your rituals skyclad."

"Very funny. A few days. Say the coming full moon."

"The end of the first month." He nodded. "It seems right. I want to—what is all that shouting?"

They walked to the window to see Blair going toe-to-toe with Larkin. Moira stood, hands fisted on her hips.

"Speaking of rituals," Glenna commented. "Looks like the head-butting portion of the daily training's started without us. We'd better get down there."

"She's slow and she's sloppy, and slow and sloppy get you dead."

"She's neither," Larkin shot back at Blair. "But her strengths lie in her bow and in her mind."

"Great, she can think a vamp to death. Let me know how that works out. As for the bow, yeah, eye like an eagle, but you can't always kill at a distance."

"I can speak for myself well enough, Larkin. And you—" Moira jabbed a finger at Blair. "I don't care to be spoken to as if I were addle-brained."

"I've got no problem with your brain, but I've got a big one with your sword arm. You fight like a girl."

"So I am."

"Not during training, not during battle. Then you're a soldier, and the enemy doesn't give a rat's ass about your plumbing."

"King had her working on her strengths."

"King's dead."

There was a moment of utter silence that couldn't have been sliced through with Cian's battle-ax. Then Blair sighed. That, she could admit, had been unnecessarily harsh.

"Look, what happened to your pal is terrible. I sure as hell don't want it to happen to me. If you don't want it to happen to you, you'll work on your weaknesses—and you've got plenty. You can play with your strengths on your own time."

She planted her feet as Hoyt and Glenna came to join them. "Did you put me in charge of this?" Blair demanded.

"I did," Hoyt affirmed.

"And we've nothing to say about it?" Fury tightened Larkin's face. "Nothing at all?"

"You don't, no. She's the best for it."

"Because she's your blood."

Blair rounded on Larkin. "Because I can put you on your ass in five seconds flat."

"Sure of that, are you?" He shimmered and changed, and the wolf he became crouched and snarled.

"Excellent," Blair said under her breath, with temper smothered by pure admiration.

"Oh, Larkin, leave off, would you?" Obviously out of patience, Moira slapped a hand at him. "He's only angry because you were rude to me. And you've no cause to be so insulting. It happens I agree with you about working on the weaknesses." And Cian had said the same, Moira recalled. "I'm willing to practice, but I won't be after standing and being berated while I'm about it."

"More flies with honey than vinegar?" Blair said. "I always wondered why the hell anyone would want to catch flies. Look, you and I can paint our toenails and talk about boys when we're off the clock. While I'm training you, I'm the bitch because I want you alive. Does it hurt when you do that?" Blair asked Larkin when he changed back. "Shifting bones and organs and so on?"

"Some actually." He couldn't recall anyone ever asking him. His temper cooled as quickly as it had flared. "But it's fun, so I don't mind so much."

He slung his arm around Moira's shoulder, gave her arm a little rub as he spoke to Hoyt and Glenna. "Your girl here took out four of them in the forest. I took a fifth myself."

"This morning? Five?" Glenna stared at Blair. "How close to the house?"

"Close enough." Blair glanced toward the woods. "Lookouts, I figure, and not very good ones. Caught them napping. Lilith's going to get word of it. She's going to be unhappy."

* * *

It wasn't a matter of killing the messenger; not in Lilith's long-standing opinion. It was a matter of killing it as painfully as possible.

The young vampire who'd foolishly gone back to the nest after Blair's morning foray was now on a slow roast, belly-down, over a simmering fire. The smell wasn't particularly pleasant, but Lilith understood command required certain sacrifices.

She circled him now, careful to keep the hem of her red gown away from the lick of flames. "Why don't we go over this again?" Her voice was melodious, somewhat like a devoted teacher speaking to a favored student. "The human—female—destroyed everyone I'd posted, save you."

"The man." Pain turned the words to guttural rasps. "The horse."

"Yes, yes. I keep forgetting the man and the horse." She stopped to study the rings she wore. "The one who came along after she'd already cut down—what was it now—four of you?"

She crouched down, a spider of stunning beauty, to stare into his red, wheeling eyes. "And she was able to do this because? Wait, wait, I remember. Because you were *sleeping*?"

"They were. The others. I was at post, Majesty. I swear it."

"At post, and yet, this single female human lives. Lives because—do I have this detail correct? Because you ran?"

"Came back . . . to report." Its sweat dripped into the fire, and sizzled. "The others, they ran away. They ran. I came to you."

"So you did." She tapped him playfully on the nose with each word, then rose. "I suppose I should reward your loyalty."

"Mercy. Majesty, mercy."

She turned around with a silky rustle of skirts to smile at the boy who sat cross-legged on the floor of the cave, systematically ripping the heads off a pile of *Star Wars* action figures.

"Davey, if you break all your toys, what will you have to play with?"

His lips moved to pout as he beheaded Anikin Skywalker. "They're boring."

"Yes, I know." She ran a loving hand over his sunny hair. "And you've been cooped up too long, haven't you?"

"Can we go outside now?" He bounced, and his eyes went round and wide at the prospect of a promised treat. "Can we go outside and play? *Please!*"

"Not quite yet. Now don't sulk." She tipped his chin up to peck a kiss on his lips. "What if your face froze like that? Here now, my sweet boy, what if I gave you a brand-new toy?"

Round cheeks bright with temper, he snapped Han Solo in two. "I'm tired of toys."

"But this will be a new one. Something you've never had before." She turned her head, and with her finger still on his chin, turned his until they both looked at the vampire over the fire pit.

And on the spit, seeing their eyes, it began to struggle and thrash. And weep.

"For me?" Davey said brightly.

"All for you, my own dumpling. But you must promise Mama not to get too close to the fire. I don't want you burned, my precious one." She kissed his little fingers before she rose.

"Majesty, I beg you! Majesty, I came back to you."

"I dislike failure. Be a good boy, Davey. Oh, and don't spoil your dinner." She gestured to Lora, who stood quietly by the door.

The screams began before it was closed behind them. And locked.

"The Hunter," Lora began. "It had to be. None of the other women have the skill to—"

A single look from Lilith silenced her. "I haven't given you leave to speak. My fondness for you is all there is between you and the pit. And my affections only go so far."

Lora bowed her head in deference and followed Lilith into the adjoining chamber. "You lost three of my good men. What can you say to that?"

"I have no excuse."

With a nod, Lilith roamed the chamber, idly picking a ruby necklace from the top of a chest. The single thing she missed of life was mirrors. She longed, even after two millennia, to see herself reflected. To be wooed by her own beauty. She had hired—and fed on—countless sorcerers, witches and magicians over the centuries to make it so.

It was her greatest failure.

"You're wise not to offer one. I'm a patient woman, Lora. I've waited more than a thousand years for what's coming. But I won't be insulted. I dislike having these *people* pick and pluck us off like flies."

She threw herself into a chair, tapped her long red nails on its arms. "Speak, then. Tell me about this new one. This Hunter."

"As the seers prophesied, my lady. The warrior of old blood. One of the hunters who has plagued our kind for centuries."

"And you know this because?"

"She was too fast to be a mere human. Too strong. She knew what they were before they moved on her that night, and she was ready. She completes their number. The first stage is set."

"My scholars said the black man was their warrior."

"They were wrong."

"Then what good are they?" Lilith heaved the necklace she still toyed with across the room. "How can I rule when I'm surrounded by incompetence? I want what's due me. I want blood and death and beautiful chaos. Is it too much to ask that those who serve me be accurate on the details?"

For nearly four hundred years Lora had been by Lilith's side. Friend, lover, servant. No one, she was sure, knew the queen better. She poured a glass of wine, carried it to the chair.

"Lilith." She said it gently, offering both it and a kiss. "We've lost nothing important."

"Face."

"No, not even that. They only believe what they've done in these past weeks matters. It's good they do, because it makes them overconfident. And we killed Cian's boy, didn't we?"

"We did." Lilith pouted another moment, then sipped. "There was satisfaction in that."

"And sending him to them only demonstrated your bril-
liance, and your strength. Let them take dozens of the mean-
ingless foot soldiers. We cut their heart."

"You're a comfort to me, Lora." Drinking her wine, Lilith
stroked Lora's hand. "And you're right, of course, you're
right. I'm disappointed, I admit. I so wanted to break their
number, to foil the prophecy."

"But it's better this way, isn't it? And it'll be the sweeter
when you take them all."

"Better, yes, better. And yet . . . I think we need to make a
statement. It would improve my mood, and morale as well. I
have an idea. I'll think it through a bit." She watched the
wine swirl in her glass. "One day, one day soon, this will be
the sorcerer's blood. I'll drink it from a silver cup, and nib-
ble on sugar plums between sips. All that he is will be in me,
and all that I am will make even the gods tremble.

"Leave me now. I need to plan."

As Lora rose to go to the door, Lilith tapped on her glass.
"Oh, and this irritating business has made me hungry. Bring
me someone to eat, will you?"

"Right away."

"Make sure it's fresh." Alone she closed her eyes and began to plot. While she plotted, the screams and squeals from
the next chamber battered the cave walls.

Her lips curved. Who could be blue, she thought, with a
child's laughter ringing in the air?

Moira sat cross-legged on Glenna's bed and
watched Glenna work on the magic little machine
she called a laptop. Moira was desperate to get her hands on
it. There were worlds of knowledge inside, and so far she'd
only been allowed a few peeks.

She'd been promised a lesson, but just at the moment,
Glenna seemed so absorbed—and they only had an hour
free.

So she cleared her throat.

"What do you think of this one?" Glenna asked and
tapped the image of a woman wearing a long white dress.

Angling her head for a better view, Moira studied the screen. "She's very lovely. I was wondering—"

"No, not the model, the dress." Glenna scooted around on the chair. "I need a dress."

"Oh, did something happen to yours?"

"No." With a little laugh Glenna twisted the pendant around her neck. "I need a very special dress. A wedding dress. Moira, Hoyt and I are going to be married. Handfasted. We decided on handfasting, with a wedding ceremony later. After."

"You're betrothed to Hoyt? I didn't know."

"It just happened. I know it might seem rushed, and the timing of it—"

"Oh, but this is wonderful!" Moira sprang up, and in a burst of enthusiasm, threw her arms around Glenna. "I'm so happy for you. For all of us."

"Thanks. For all of us?"

"Weddings, they're bright, aren't they? Bright and happy and human. Oh, I wish we were home so I could have a feast made. You can't make your own wedding feast, and I'm still not very good at the cooking."

"We won't worry about that, not yet. Weddings *are* bright—and happy and human. And I'm human enough to want the perfect dress."

"Well, of course. Why would you want less?"

Glenna let out a long, happy sigh. "Thank God. I've been feeling a little shallow. I should've known all I needed was another girl. Help me, will you? I have a few picked out, and I need to narrow it down."

"I'd love to." Gently, curiously, she tapped the side of the screen. "But . . . how do you get the dress out of the box?"

"We'll get to that, too. I'm going to have to take a few shortcuts. But later, I'll show you how to shop online the conventional way. I want something—I think—along these lines."

While they were huddled, Blair gave the doorjamb a knuckle rack. "Sorry. You got a minute, Glenna? I wanted to talk to you about requisitions and supplies. Figured you were the go-to. Hey. Nice toy."

"One of my favorites. Cian and I are the only ones linked up, so if you need to use—"

"Brought my own, but thanks. Shopping? Nieman's," she said as she moved close enough to see the screen. "Pretty fancy duds for wartime."

"Hoyt and I are getting married."

"No kidding? That's great." She gave Glenna a friendly punch on the shoulder. "Congratulations. So when's the big day?"

"Tomorrow night." When Blair only blinked, Glenna hurried on. "I know how it must seem, but—"

"I think it's terrific. I think it's excellent. Life can't stop. We can't let it. We can't let them make it stop; that's the whole point. Plus, it's great, seriously great, that the two of you found what you've got when everything's so extreme. It's one of the things we're fighting for, right?"

"Yes. Yes, it is."

"Wedding dress?"

"A potential. Blair, thank you."

Blair put a hand on Glenna's shoulder in a gesture that might have been woman-to-woman or soldier-to-soldier. Glenna supposed it was now one and the same.

"I've been fighting for thirteen years. I know better than anyone you need some real, you need things that matter, and that warm you up inside, or you lose the mission. I'll let you get back to it."

"Want to help us shop?"

"Really?" Blair did a little shuffle dance. "Are vampires blood-sucking fiends? I'm so in. One thing, not to put the damper, but how are you going to get the dress here by tomorrow?"

"I've got my ways. And I'd better get started. Would you mind closing the door? I don't want Hoyt coming in while I'm trying them on."

"Trying . . . Sure." Blair obliged while Glenna set several crystals on and around the laptop. She lit candles, then stood back, held her arms out to the side.

"Mother Goddess I ask your grace to bring this garment to this place. Through the air, from there to here, in the light unto my sight a symbol of my destiny. As I will so mote it be."

With a shimmer and flash, Glenna's jeans and T-shirt were replaced by the white gown.

"Wow. A whole new level of shoplifting."

"I'm not stealing it." Glenna's scowled at Blair. "I'd never use my powers that way. I'm trying it on, and when I find the one, I've got another spell to work the sale. It's just to save time, which I don't have."

"Don't get bent. I was just kidding." Sort of. "Will that work for weapons if we need more?"

"I suppose it would."

"Good to know. Anyway, great dress."

"It's lovely," Moira agreed. "Just lovely."

Glenna turned, studied her reflection in the antique cheval glass. "Thank God Cian didn't strip all the mirrors out of this place. It's beautiful, isn't it? I love the lines. But . . ."

"It's not the one," Blair finished, and settled down on the bed with Moira to watch the show.

"Why do you say that?"

"It doesn't light you up. That light, in the gut, in the heart, that just spreads out right to your fingertips. You put on your wedding dress, take one look at yourself in it and you know. The others are just practice."

So it had gotten that far, Glenna thought, remembering the vision of Blair and the engagement ring on her finger. And the image of her weeping in the dark, her hand bare.

She started to comment, then said nothing. A tender area like that required more than camaraderie. It needed true friendship, and they weren't there yet.

"You're right, it's not the one. I've got four more picked out. So we'll try number two."

She hit it on the third, and felt that light glowing. Heard it in Moira's long, wistful sigh.

"And we have a winner." Blair circled her finger. "Do the turn. Oh, yeah, that one's yours."

It was romantic, and simple, Glenna thought. Just as she'd hoped. There was a little float in the long skirt, and the soft sweetheart neckline was framed by two thin straps that left her shoulders bare then ran down her shoulder blades to spotlight her back.

"It's so exactly right." She glanced at the price again, winced. "Well, maxing out my credit card doesn't seem that big a deal considering the possible apocalypse."

"Seize the day," Blair agreed. "You doing a veil, a head-piece?"

"Traditional Celtic handfastings call for a veil, but in this case . . . Just flowers, I think."

"Even better. Soft, earthy, romantic and sexy all rolled into one. Do the deal."

"Moira?" Glenna looked over, saw Moira's eyes were damp and dreamy. "I can see it has your vote, too."

"I think you'll be the most beautiful of brides."

"Well, this was serious fun." Blair got to her feet. "And I agree with the brain trust here—you look outstanding. But you need to wrap it up." She tapped her watch. "The two of you are due in training. You need some major hand-to-hand practice. Why don't you come with me now?" she said to Moira. "We can get started."

"I'll only be a few minutes," Glenna told them, then turned back to study herself in the glass.

From wedding dresses to combat, she thought. Her life had become a very strange ride.

Because he heard the music playing inside, Hoyt knocked on Cian's door a little before sundown. There'd been a time, he remembered, he wouldn't have thought of knocking, when asking permission to enter his brother's chambers wouldn't have been necessary.

A time, he thought, he wouldn't have needed to ask his brother if he could live with his wife in his own home.

Locks clicked and snicked. Cian wore only loose pants and a sleepy expression when he opened the door. "A bit early for me, for visiting."

"I need a private word with you."

"Which, of course, can't wait on my convenience. Come in then."

Hoyt stepped into a room that was pitch black. "Must we speak in the dark?"

"I can see well enough." But Cian switched on a low light beside a wide bed. The covers on the bed gleamed jewel-like in that light, and the sheets carried the sheen of silk. Cian moved to a cold box, took out a packet of blood. "I haven't had breakfast." He tossed the packet into the microwave sitting on top of the box. "What do you want?"

"When this is done, what do you intend to do?"

"As I choose, as always."

"To live here?"

"I think not," Cian said with a half laugh, and took a crystal glass from a shelf.

"Tomorrow night . . . Glenna and I are to be handfasted."

There was a slight hesitation in his rhythm, then Cian set the glass down. "Isn't that interesting? I suppose congratulations are in order. And you intend to take her back, introduce her to the family. Ma, Da, this is my bride. A little witch I picked up a few centuries from now."

"Cian."

"Sorry. The absurdity of it amuses me." He took the package out, broke it open and poured the warmed contents in the glass. "Well, anyway. *Sláinte.*"

"I can't go back."

After the first sip, the first long stare over the rim, Cian lowered the glass. "More and more interesting."

"It's no longer my place, knowing what I know. Waiting for the day to come when I know they'll die. If you could go back, would you?"

Cian frowned into his glass, then sat. "No. For thousands of reasons. But that would be one of them. But that aside, you brought this war to me. Now you take time from it to handfast?"

"Human needs don't stop. They're only keener, it seems, when the end of days threaten."

"It happens that's true. I've seen it countless times. It also happens war brides don't always make reliable wives."

"That's for me and for Glenna."

"It certainly is." He raised his glass, drank some more. "Well then, good luck to you."

"We want to live here, in this house."

"In my house?"

"In the house that was ours. Setting aside my rights, and our kinship, you're a businessman. You pay a caretaker when you're not in residence. You'd no longer have that expense. Glenna and I would tend this place and the land, at no cost to you."

"And how do you propose to make a living? There isn't much demand for sorcerer's these days. Wait, I take it back." Cian laughed, finished off the blood. "You could make a goddamn fortune on television, on the Internet. Get yourself an eight-hundred number, a web site, and off you go. Not your style though."

"I'll find my way."

Cian set the glass aside, looked off into the shadows. "Maybe I hope you do, providing you live, of course. I've no problem with you staying in the house."

"Thanks for that."

Cian shrugged. "It's a complicated life you've chosen for yourself."

"And I intend to live it. I'll let you get dressed."

A complicated life, Cian thought again when he was alone. And it stunned and annoyed him that he could envy it.

Chapter 21

Glenna figured most brides were a little stressed and very busy on their weddings days. But most brides didn't have to fit in sword practice and spells between their facials and pedicures.

At least the pace cut down on the time for the nerves she'd had no idea she'd have. She couldn't squeeze in much of an anxiety attack when she was worried about flower arrangements, romantic lighting and the proper form for beheading a vampire.

"Try this." Blair started to toss the weapon, then obviously changed her mind when Glenna's mouth dropped open. She walked it over. "Battle-ax. More heft than a sword, which would work better for you, I think. You got pretty decent upper body strength, but you'd cut through easier with this than a sword. You need to get used to its weight and its balance. Here."

She walked back, picked up her own sword. "Block me with it."

"I'm not used to it. I could miss, hurt you."

"Believe me, you won't hurt me. Block!" She thrust out,

and more from instinct than obedience, Glenna clanged the axe to the sword.

"Now see, I'd just stab you cheerfully in the back while you're fumbling to turn."

"It's top heavy," Glenna complained.

"It's not. Spread out your grip more for now. Okay, stay forward after the first strike. Come down on the sword, back up at me. Slow. One," she said and thrust. "Two. Again, keep it coming. You want to counter my moves, sure, but what you want is to throw me off balance, to make me counter yours, force me to follow your moves. Think of it as a dance routine where you not only want to lead, but you also really want to kill your partner."

Blair held up a hand, stepped back. "Let me show you. Hey, Larkin. Come be the practice dummy." She tossed him her sword, hilt up, then took the battle-ax. "Take it slow," she told him. "This is a demo."

She nodded. "Attack."

As he moved on her, she called out the steps. "Strike, strike, turn. Thrust up, across, strike. He's good, see?" she said, still calling out to Glenna. "So he's pushing at me while I push at him. So you ad lib as necessary. Turn, kick, strike, strike, pivot. Slice!"

She flipped the dagger strapped to her wrist and swiped it an inch from Larkin's belly. "When his guts are spilling out, you—"

And dodged back from the swipe of what looked like a very large bear claw.

"Wow." She rested the head of her axe on the floor, leaned on the handle. Only his arm had changed shape. "You can do that? Just pieces of you?"

"If I like."

"I bet the girls back home can't get enough of you."

It took him a moment—she'd already turned to go back to Glenna—then he burst into delighted laughter. "Sure that's the truth. But not due to what you're meaning. I prefer my own shape for that kind of sport."

"Bet. Square off with Larkin. I'm going to work with Shorty for a while."

"Don't call me that," Moira snapped.

"Lighten up. I didn't mean anything by it."

Moira opened her mouth, then shook her head. "I'm sorry. That was rude."

"King called her that," Glenna said quietly.

"Oh. Got it. Moira. Resistance training. We're going to pump you up."

"I'm sorry I spoke to you that way."

"Look. We're going to irritate each other a lot before this is done. I don't bruise easily—literally or figuratively. You're going to have to toughen up yourself. Five-pound free weights. You're going to be cut by the time I'm done with you."

Moira narrowed her eyes. "I may be sorry I lashed at you, but I'm not going to let you cut me."

"No, it's an expression. It means . . ." And every other term Blair could think of would be just as confusing. Instead she curled her arm, flexed her biceps.

"Ah." A smile glimmered in Moira's eyes. "Sure I'd like that. All right then, you can cut me."

They worked a full morning. When Blair paused to gulp water from a bottle she nodded at Glenna. "You're coming right along. Ballet lessons?"

"Eight years. Never thought I'd pirouette with a battle-ax, but life's full of surprises."

"Can you do a triple?"

"Not so far."

"Look." Still holding the bottle, Blair whipped her body around three times then shot her leg out to the side, up at a forty-five-degree angle. "That kind of momentum puts a good solid punch in a kick. You need solid to knock one of these things back. Practice. You've got it in you. So." She took another swig. "Where's the groom?"

"Hoyt? In the tower. There are things that need to be done. As important as what we're doing here, Blair," she added when she sensed disapproval.

"Maybe. Okay, maybe. If you come up with more stuff like the fire dagger."

"We've fire charmed a number of the weapons." She

walked to another section of the room, took down a sword to bring it back. "Those that are charmed we've marked. See?"

On the blade near the hilt was a flame, etched into steel.

"Nice. Really. Can I try it?"

"Better take it outside."

"Good point. Okay, we should break for an hour anyway. Grab something to eat. Cross- and longbows, boys and girls, after lunch."

"I'll come with you," Glenna told her. "In case."

Blair used the terrace doors, jogged down to ground level. She glanced at the straw dummy Larkin had hung from a post. You had to give it to the guy, she mused. He had a sense of humor. He'd drawn fangs on the stuffed face and a bright red heart on the chest.

It would be fun to test the fire sword out on it—and a waste of good material. No point burning up Vampire Dummy.

So she began in a fighting stance, her arm arched behind her head, the sword pointing out.

"It's important to control it," Glenna began. "To pull the fire when you need it. If you're just slapping the burning sword around, you could burn yourself, or one of us."

"Don't worry."

Glenna started to speak again, then shrugged. There was nothing and no one to hurt but the air.

Then she watched as Blair began to move, slowly, fluid as water, the sword like an extension of her arm. Yes, a kind of ballet, she thought, a lethal one. But nonetheless compelling. The blade shimmered when the sun struck its edge, but remained cool. Just as Glenna began to assume Blair needed coaching on how to use it, the woman thrust out, and the blade erupted.

"And you're toast. God, I *love* this thing. Will you make me one, out of one of my personal weapons?"

"Absolutely." Glenna lifted her brows as Blair swished the sword through the air and the fire died. "You learn fast."

"Yeah, I do." She frowned, scanning the sky. "Clouds boiling up in the west. Guess we're in for more rain."

"Good thing I planned an indoor wedding."

"Good thing. Let's go eat."

Hoyt didn't come down until late afternoon, and by that time Glenna had given herself permission to take time for herself. She didn't want to do a quick glamour to look her best. She wanted to pamper herself, just a bit.

And she needed flowers to make the circlet for her hair, to make a bouquet. She'd made the facial cream herself, from herbs, so dabbed it on generously as she studied the sky from the bedroom window.

The clouds were moving in now. If she was going to get flowers, she had to get them before the sun was lost and the rain came. But when she opened the door to dash out, Moira and Larkin stood on the other side. He made some sound as his eyes widened, reminding her of the soft green goo on her face.

"It's a female thing, just deal with it. I'm running behind. I haven't got the flowers for my hair yet."

"We . . . Well." Moira brought her hand from behind her back and offered the circlet of white rosebuds with red ribbon braided through it. "I hope it's all right, that it's what you wanted. I know something red's traditional for a handfasting. Larkin and I wanted to give you something, and we don't have anything really, so we did this. But if you'd rather—"

"Oh, it's perfect. It's perfectly beautiful. Oh, *thank* you!" She grabbed Moira in a crushing hug, then turned a beaming smile up to Larkin.

"I've thought it wouldn't be a hardship to have you kiss me," he began, "but just at the moment . . ."

"Don't worry. I'll catch you later."

"There's this as well." He handed her a nosegay of multi-colored roses twined with more red ribbon. "To carry, Moira says."

"Oh God, this is the sweetest thing." Tears dribbled through the cream. "I thought this would be hard without family here. But I have family here, after all. Thank you. Thank you both."

She bathed, scented her hair, creamed her skin. White candles burned as she performed the female ritual of preparing herself for a man. For her wedding, and her wedding night.

She was in her robe, brushing her fingers over the skirt of the dress that hung outside the wardrobe when someone knocked.

"Yes, come in. Unless you're Hoyt."

"Not Hoyt." Blair came in carrying a bottle of champagne nestled in an ice bucket. Behind her, Moira brought in three flutes.

"Compliments of our host," Blair told her. "I gotta say, he's got some class for a vampire. This is prime bubbly we got here."

"Cian sent champagne?"

"Yep. And I'm going to get down to popping this cork before we suit you up."

"I have a wedding party. Oh, you should have dresses. I should've thought of it."

"We're fine. Tonight's all about you."

"I've never had champagne. Blair says I'll like it."

"Guaranteed." Blair gave Moira a quick wink then popped the cork. "Oh, I got something for you. It's not much, seeing as I don't have your style with on-line shopping, but anyway." She dug into her pocket. "I didn't have a box either."

She put the pin in Glenna's hand. "It's a claddaugh. Traditional Irish symbol. Friendship, love, loyalty. I'd've gone for the toaster or salad bowl, but time was limited. And I didn't know where you'd registered."

Another circle, Glenna thought. Another symbol. "It's beautiful. Thank you." She turned, pinned it to the ribbon trailing from her bouquet. "Now I'll carry both of your gifts with me."

"I love sentiment. Especially with champagne." Blair poured three glasses, passed them around. "To the bride."

"And her happiness," Moira added.

"And to the continuity represented by what we do tonight. To the promise of the future it represents. I'm going to get all the teary stuff out before I do my make-up."

"Good plan," Blair agreed.

"I know what I found with Hoyt is right, is mine. I know what we're promising each other tonight is right, is ours. But having you here with me, that's right, too. And it's special. I want you to know it's very special to me, having you share this."

They touched glasses and drank. Moira closed her eyes. "Blair was right. I do like it."

"Told ya. Okay, Moira, let's you and me make ourselves a bride."

Outside the rain splashed down and fog billowed. But in the house was candlelight and the scent of flowers.

Glenna stepped back from the mirror. "Well?"

"You look like a dream," Moira stated. "Like a goddess in a dream."

"My knees are shaking. I bet goddesses don't get shaky knees."

"Take a couple of deep breaths. We'll go down, make sure everything's set up. Including the lucky guy. You're going to blow his socks off."

"Why would she—"

"You know, sweetie," Blair said to Moira as they started for the door. "You're too literal. Start studying contemporary slang while you're buried in books." She pulled open the door, stopped short when she saw Cian. "This is girl territory."

"I'd like a moment with my . . . future sister-in-law."

"It's all right, Blair. Cian. Please come in."

He stepped inside, sent Blair a mild look over his shoulder, then shut the door in her face. Then he turned and took a long look at Glenna. "Well now, you're a vision, aren't you? Truly. My brother's fortune leaps and bounds."

"You probably think this is foolish."

"You'd be wrong. While it may be something I think of as particularly human, it's not one of the things I think of as foolish. Though there are many of those."

"I love your brother."

"Yes, a blind man could see that."

"Thank you for the champagne. For thinking of it."

"My pleasure. Hoyt's ready for you."

"Oh boy." She pressed a hand to her jumpy belly. "I hope so."

Cian smiled at that, stepped closer. "I have something for you. A wedding gift. I thought to put it in your hand as I assume, at least for now, you'd be in charge of the paperwork."

"Paperwork?"

He handed her a thin leather portfolio. After opening it, she sent him a puzzled look. "I don't understand."

"It should be clear enough. It's the deed to this house, the land. It's yours."

"Oh, but we can't. When he asked if we could stay, he only meant—"

"Glenna, I only make grand gestures once every few decades, if the whim happens to strike me. Take it when it's offered. It's more to him than it could ever be to me."

Her throat had filled so she had to wait to speak. "I know what it means to me. It will mean a great deal more to him. I wish you'd give it to him yourself."

"Take it," was all he said, then turned to the door.

"Cian." She set the folder aside, picked up her bouquet. "Would you walk me down? Would you take me to Hoyt?"

He hesitated, then opened the door. Then held out a hand to her.

She heard music as they started down.

"Your handmaidens have been busy. I expected it of the little queen—a lot of sentiment there. But the hunter surprised me."

"Am I shaking? I feel like I'm shaking."

"No." He tucked her hand into his arm. "You're steady as a rock."

And when she stepped into the room filled with candles and flowers, when she saw Hoyt standing in front of the low, gold flames of the fire, she felt steady.

They crossed the room to each other. "I've waited for you," Hoyt whispered.

"And I for you."

She took his hand, scanned the room. It was, as was traditional, madly decked with flowers. The circle had been formed, and the candles lighted, but for the ones they would light during the ritual. The willow wand lay on the table that served as altar.

"I made this for you." He showed her a thick ring of silver, deeply etched.

"One mind," she said, and drew the one she'd made him from her thumb.

They joined hands, walked to the altar. Touched fingers to the candles to light them. After slipping their rings onto the willow wand, they turned to face the others.

"We ask you to be our witnesses at this sacred rite," Hoyt began.

"To be our family as we become one."

"May this place be consecrated for the gods. We are gathered here in a ritual of love."

"Beings of the Air be with us here, and with your clever fingers tie closely the bonds between us." Glenna looked into his eyes as she spoke the words.

"Beings of the Fire be with us here . . ."

And they continued through Water, through Earth, the blessed goddess and laughing god. Her face was luminous as they spoke, as they lit incense, then a red candle. They sipped wine, scattered salt.

She and Hoyt held the wand with the rings gleaming on it between them.

The light grew warmer, brighter as they spoke to each other, the rings under their hands sparkling wildly.

"It is my wish to become one with this man." She slipped the ring from the wand and onto his finger.

"It is my wish to become one with this woman." He mirrored her gesture.

They took the cord from the altar, draped it over their joined hands.

"And so the binding is made," they said together. "Then, as the goddess and the god and the old ones—"

A scream from outside shattered the moment like a rock through glass.

Blair leaped to a window, yanked back the drape. Even her nerves jolted at the vampire's face only inches away behind the glass. But it wasn't that which turned her blood cold; it was what she saw beyond it.

She looked over her shoulders at the others, and said: "Oh, shit."

There were at least fifty, probably more, still in the forest or hidden nearby. Three cages sat on the grass, their occupants bloodied and shackled—and screaming now as they were dragged out.

Glenna shoved her way by to see, then groped behind her for Hoyt's hand. "The blonde one. That's the one who came to the door. When King—"

"Lora," Cian said. "One of Lilith's favorites. I had an . . . incident with her once." He laughed when Lora hoisted a white flag. "And if you believe that, I've all manner of bridges you can buy."

"They have people out there," Moira added. "Injured people."

"Weapons," Blair began.

"Best wait—and see how best to use them." Cian stepped away, and walked to the front door. Wind and rain sliced in when he opened it. "Lora," he called out, almost conversationally. "Why you're good and soaked, aren't you now? I'd ask you and your friends in, but I still have my sanity and my standards."

"Cian, it's been too long. Did you like my present, by the way? I didn't have time to wrap him."

"Taking credit for Lilith's work? That's just sad. And you should tell her she'll pay dearly for it."

"Tell her yourself. You and your humans have ten minutes to surrender."

"Oh? All of ten?"

"In ten minutes, we'll kill the first of these." She grabbed one of the prisoners by the hair. "Pretty, isn't she? Only sixteen. Old enough to know better than to go walking along dark roads."

"Please." The girl wept, and the blood on her neck showed

that something had already tasted her. "Please, God."

"They're always calling for God." With a laugh, Lora threw the girl facedown on the sodden grass. "He never comes. Ten minutes."

"Close the door," Blair said quietly from behind him. "Close it. Okay, give me a minute. One minute to think."

"They'll kill them regardless," Cian pointed out. "Bait is all they are."

"That's not the issue," Glenna snapped. "We have to do something."

"We fight." Larkin drew one of the swords they'd stocked in an umbrella stand near the door.

"Hold your water," Blair ordered.

"We don't surrender, not to the likes of them."

"We fight," Hoyt agreed. "But not on their terms. Glenna, the shackles."

"Yes, I can work that. I'm sure I can."

"We need more weapons from upstairs," Hoyt began.

"I said hold it." Blair grabbed his arm. "You've been in a couple of skirmishes with vampires. That doesn't prepare you. We're not just charging out there and getting cut down like meat. You can work the shackles?"

Glenna drew a breath. "Yes."

"Good. Moira, you're upstairs, bows. Cian, they've probably got guards around the house. Pick a door, start taking them out, quiet as you can manage. Hoyt's with you."

"Wait."

"I know how to do this," she told Glenna. "Are you ready to use that axe?"

"I guess we'll find out."

"Get it. You're up with Moira. They'll have archers too, and they see a hell of lot better in the dark than we do. Larkin, you and me, we're going to create a diversion. Moira, you don't start picking them off until you get the signal."

"What signal?"

"You'll know it. One more thing. Those three out there, they're already gone. All we can do is make a statement. You have to accept that chances are slim to none when it comes to saving any of them."

"We have to try," Moira insisted.

"Yeah, well, that's what we're here for. Let's go."

"Is that one of your trick swords?" Cian asked Hoyt as they approached the east door.

"It is."

"Then keep it well away from me." He touched his finger to his lips, eased open the door. For a moment, there was no sound, no movement but the rain. Then Cian was out, a blur of dark in the dark.

Even as Hoyt stepped out to follow, he saw Cian snap two necks and behead a third. "On your left," Cian said quietly.

Hoyt pivoted and met what came at him with steel, and with fire.

Upstairs, Glenna knelt within the circle she'd cast and chanted. The silver around her throat, on her finger glowed brighter with every heartbeat. Moira crouched to the side of the open doorway, a quiver at her back, a bow in her hand.

Moira glanced back at her. "The shackles."

"No, that was for something else. I'll start that now."

"What was it . . . Oh." Moira looked back into the dark, but now thanks to Glenna, with the vision of a cat. "Oh aye, that's a right good one. They've archers back in the trees. I only see six. I can take six."

"Don't go outside. Don't go out until I'm done here." Glenna fought to clear her mind, calm her heart, and call the magic.

Out of the dark, like vengeance, came a gold horse. And the rider on its back wielded death.

With Larkin at a gallop, Blair swung the torch, striking three that burst into flames and took two more into the blaze with them. Then she heaved it, spinning destruction through the air, and flashed a fiery sword.

"It's now, Glenna!" Moira let the first arrow fly. "It's now!"

"Yes, I've got it. I've got it." She grabbed the ax, and a dagger, at a run.

Moira's arrows were winging as they both sprinted into the rain. And the things that were waiting rushed them.

Glenna didn't think, only acted, only felt. She let her

body move into that dance of life and death, striking, blocking, thrusting. Fire rippled over the blades as she swung.

There were screams, such horrible screams. Human,
vampire, how could she tell? She smelled blood, tasted it;
knew some of it was her own. Her heart beat, a war drum in
her chest so she barely registered the arrow that whizzed by
her head as she plunged fire into what leaped at her.

"They've hit Larkin. They've hit him."

At Moira's shout, Glenna saw the arrow in the foreleg of
the horse. But it ran still like a demon with Blair raging destruction from its back.

Then she saw Hoyt fighting fang and sword to get to one
of the prisoners.

"I have to go help. Moira, there are too many down there."

"Go. I've got this. I'll lower the odds, I promise you."

She charged down, screaming to draw some away from
Hoyt and Cian.

She thought it would be a blur, just madness rushing over
her, and through her. But it was clear in every detail. The faces,
the sounds, the scents, the feel of warm blood and cold rain
running over her. The red eyes, the terrible hunger in them.
And the horrible flash and screaming when fire took them.

She saw Cian break off the end of an arrow that had
found his thigh, and plunge it into the heart of an enemy. She
saw the ring she'd put on Hoyt's finger burn like another fire
as he took two with one blow.

"Get them inside," he shouted to her. "Try to get them inside."

She rolled over the wet grass toward the girl Lora had tor-
mented. She half expected to find her dead. Instead she
found her showing fangs in a grin.

"Oh God."

"Didn't you hear her? He doesn't come."

She pounced, knocking Glenna onto her back, then threw
back her head with the joy of the kill. Blair's sword cut it off.

"You'd be surprised," Glenna returned.

"Inside," Blair shouted. "Back in. That's enough of a goddamn statement." She reached down to help Glenna mount
behind her.

They left the field flaming, and covered with dust.

"How many did we kill?" Larkin demanded as he collapsed on the floor. Blood ran down his leg to puddle on the wood.

"At least thirty—damn good ratio. You've got some speed, Golden Boy." Blair looked straight into his eyes. "Winged you a little."

"It's not altogether too bad. It just—" He didn't scream when she yanked the arrow out. He didn't have the breath to scream. When he got it back, all he could manage was a stream of shaky curses.

"You next," she said to Cian, nodding at the broken arrow protruding from his thigh.

He simply reached down, yanked it out himself. "Thanks all the same."

"I'll get supplies. Your leg's bleeding," Glenna told Blair.

"We're all banged up some. But we're not dead. Well." She sent Cian a cocky grin. "Most of us."

"That never gets tired, does it?" Cian speculated and went for the brandy.

"They weren't human. In the cages." Moira held her shoulder where the tip of an arrow had grazed it.

"No. I couldn't tell from in here. Too many of them to separate the scents. It was smart." Blair nodded, a grim acknowledgment. "A good way to engage us and not waste any of their food supply. Bitch has a brain."

"We didn't get Lora." With his breath still heaving out of his lungs, Hoyt eased down. He had a gash on his side, another on his arm. "I saw her when we were fighting our way back into the house. We didn't get her."

"She's going to be mine. My very special friend." Blair pursed her lips when Cian offered her a brandy. "Thanks."

Standing in the center of them on shaky knees, Glenna took stock. "Blair, get Larkin's tunic off. I need to see the wound. Moira, how bad is your wound?"

"More a scratch, really."

"Then get some blankets from upstairs, some towels. Hoyt." Glenna moved to him, knelt, then just took his hands and buried her face in them. However much she wanted to fall apart, it wasn't time. Not time yet. "I felt you with me. I felt you with me every moment."

"I know. You were with me. *A ghrá*." He lifted her head, pressed his lips to hers.

"I wasn't scared, not while it was happening. I couldn't think to be scared. Then I reached that girl, that young girl and saw what she was. I couldn't even move."

"It's done. For tonight it's done. And we proved a match for them." He kissed her again, long, deep. "You were magnificent."

She laid a hand over the wound on his side. "I'd say we all were. And we proved more than being able to hold our own. We're a unit now."

"The circle is cast."

She let out a long sigh. "Well, it wasn't the handfasting celebration I was looking for." She struggled to smile. "But at least we . . . No, no, damn it, we didn't. We didn't finish. Just hold everything." She shoved at her dripping hair. "I will not let those monsters ruin this for us." She gripped his hand as Moira rushed down with arms loaded with towels and blankets. "Are you all listening? You're still witnesses."

"We got it," Blair said as she cleansed Larkin's wound.

"Your head's bleeding." Cian passed Moira a damp cloth. "Go right ahead," he told Glenna.

"But Glenna, your dress."

She only smiled at Moira. "It doesn't matter. Only this matters. She clasped hands with Hoyt, locked her eyes with his. "As the goddess and the god and the old ones . . ."

Hoyt's voice joined hers. "Are witness to this rite. We now proclaim we're husband and wife."

He reached down, took her face in his hands. "I will love you beyond the end of days."

Now, she thought, now, the circle was truly cast, strong and bright.

And the light glowed warmer, a wash of gold when their lips met, when their lips clung in hope and promise, and in love.

* * *

"So," the old man said, "with the handfasting complete, they tended to their wounds and began the healing. They drank a toast to the love, the true magic, that had come out of dark and out of death."

"Inside the house while the rain fell, the brave rested and prepared for the next battle."

He sat back, picking up the fresh tea a servant had sat beside him. "That is all of the story for today."

The protests were immediate, and passionate. But the old man only chuckled and shook his head.

"There'll be more tomorrow, I promise you, for the story's not finished. Only this beginning. But for now, the sun is out, and so should you be. Haven't you learned from the beginning of the tale that light is to be treasured? Go. When I finish my tea, I'll come out to watch you."

Alone, he drank his tea, watched his fire. And thought of the tale he would tell on the morrow.

Glossary of Irish Words, Characters and Places

a chroi, (ah-REE) Gaelic term of endearment meaning "my heart," "my heart's beloved," "my darling"

a ghrá, (ah-GHRA) Gaelic term of endearment meaning "my love," "dear"

a stór, (ah-STOR) Gaelic term of endearment meaning "my darling"

Aideen, (Ae-DEEN) Moira's young cousin

Alice McKenna, descendant of Cian and Hoyt Mac Cionaoith

An Clar (Ahn-CLAR) modern-day County Clare

Ballycloon (ba-LU-klun)

Blair Nola Bridgitt Murphy, one of the circle of six, the "warrior"; a demon hunter, a descendant of Nola Mac Cionaoith (Cian and Hoyt's younger sister)

Bridget's Well, cemetery in County Clare, named after St. Bridget

Burren, the, a Karst limestone region in County Clare, which features caves and underground streams *cara*, (karu) Gaelic for "friend, relative"

Ceara, one of the village women

Cian (KEY-an) **Mac Cionaoith/McKenna**, Hoyt's twin brother, a vampire, Lord of Oiche, one of the circle of six "the one who is lost"

Cirio, Lilith's human lover

ciunas, (CYOON-as) Gaelic for "silence"; the battle takes place in the Valley of Ciunas—the Valley of Silence

claddaugh, the Celtic symbol of love, friendship, loyalty

Cliffs of Mohr (also Moher), the name given to the ruin of forts in the South of Ireland, on a cliff near Hag's Head "Moher O'Ruan"

Conn, Larkin's childhood puppy

Dance of the Gods, the Dance, the place in which the circle of six passes through from the real world to the fantasy world of Geall

Davey, Lilith, the Vampire Queen's "son," a child vampire

Deirdre (DAIR-dhra) **Riddock**, Larkin's mother

Dervil, (DAR-vel) one of the village women

Eire (AIR-reh), Gaelic for Ireland

Eogan, (O-en) Ceara's husband

Eoin, (OAN) Hoyt's brother-in-law

Eternity, the name of Cian's nightclub, located in New York City

Faerie Falls, imaginary place in Geall

fàilte à Geall, (FALL-che ah GY-al) Gaelic for "Welcome to Geall"

Fearghus, (FARE-gus) Hoyt's brother-in-law

Gaillimh (GALL-yuv) modern-day Galway, the capital of the West of Ireland

Geall, (GY-al), in Gaelic means "promise"; the city in which Moira and Larkin come; the city which Moira will someday rule

Glenna Ward, one of the circle of six, the "witch"; lives in modern-day New York City

Hoyt Mac Cionaoith/McKenna, (mac KHEE-nee) one of the circle of six, the "sorcerer"

Isleen, (Is-LEEN) a servant at Castle Geall

Jarl, (Yarl) Lilith's sire, the vampire who turned her into a vampire

Jeremy Hilton, Blair Murphy's ex-fiance

King, the name of Cian's best friend, whom Cian befriended when King was a child; the manager of Eternity

Larkin Riddock, one of the circle of six, the "shifter of shapes," a cousin of Moira, Queen of Geall

Lilith, the Vampire Queen, aka Queen of the Demons; leader of the war against humankind; Cian's sire, the vampire who turned Cian from human to vampire

Lora, a vampire; Lilith's lover

Lucius Lora's male vampire lover

Malvin villager, soldier in Geallian army

Manhattan, city in New York; where both Cian McKenna and Glenna Ward live

mathair, (maahir) Gaelic word for mother

Michael Thomas McKenna, descendant of Cian and Hoyt Mac Cionaoith

Mick Murphy, Blair Murphy's younger brother

Midir, (mee-DEER) vampire wizard to Lilith, Queen of the Vampires

miurnin, (also sp. miurneach [mornukh]) Gaelic for sweetheart, term of endearment

Moira, (MWA-ra) one of the circle of six, the "scholar"; a princess, future queen of Geall

Morrigan, (Mo-ree-ghan) Goddess of the Battle

Niall, (Nile) a warrior in the Geallian army

Nola Mac Cionaoith Hoyt and Cian's youngest sister,

ogham, (ä-gem) (also spelled ogam) (ä-gem): fifth/sixth century Irish alphabet

oiche (EE-heh) Gaelic for night

Oran (O-ren) Riddock's youngest son, Larkin's younger brother

Phelan, (FA-len) Larkin's brother-in-law

Prince Riddock, Larkin's father, acting king of Geall, Moira's maternal uncle

Region of Chiarrai (kee-U-ree), modern-day Kerry, situated in the extreme southwest of Ireland, sometimes referred to as "the Kingdom"

Samhain, (SAM-en) summer's end, (Celtic festival), the battle takes place on the Feast of Samhain; the feast celebrating the end of summer

Sean Murphy, (Shawn) Blair Murphy's father, a vampire hunter

Shop Street, cultural center of Galway

Sinann, (shih-NAWN) Larkin's sister

sláinte, (slawn-che) Gaelic term for "cheers!"

slán agat, (shlahn u-gut) Gaelic for "good-bye," which is said to person staying

slán leat, (shlahn ly-aht) Gaelic for "good-bye," which is said to the person leaving

Tuatha de Danaan, (TOO-aha dai DON-nan) Welsh Gods

Tynan, (Ti-nin) guard at Castle Geall

Vlad, Cian's stallion

Turn the page for a look at

Dance of the Gods

the second book in the
Circle Trilogy.

Out now from Piatkus.

Chapter 1

⬦

Clare
The first day of September

Through the house, still as a grave, Larkin limped.
The air was sweet, fragrant with the flowers gathered
lavishly for the handfasting rite of the night before.

The blood had been mopped up; the weapons cleaned.
They'd toasted Hoyt and Glenna with the frothy wine, had
eaten cake. But behind the smiles the horror of the night's
battle lurked. A poor guest.

Today, he supposed, was for rest and more preparation. It
was a struggle for him not to be impatient with the training,
with the planning. At least last night they'd fought, he
thought as he pressed a hand to his thigh that ached from an
arrow strike. A score of demons had fallen, and there was
glory in that.

In the kitchen, he opened the refrigerator and took out a
bottle of Coke. He'd developed a taste for it, and had come
to prefer it over his morning tea.

He turned the bottle in his hand, marveling at the clever-
ness of the vessel—so smooth, so clear and hard. But what
was inside it—this was something he'd miss when they returned to Geall.

He could admit he hadn't believed his cousin, Moira, when she'd spoken of gods and demons, of a war for worlds. He'd only gone with her that day, that sad day of her mother's burial, to look after her. She wasn't only blood, but friend, and would be queen of Geall.

But every word she'd spoken to him, only steps away from her mother's grave, had been pure truth. They'd gone to the dance, they'd stood in the heart of that circle. And everything had changed.

Not just the where and when they were, he mused as he opened the bottle and took that first bracing sip. But everything. One moment, they'd stood under the afternoon sun in Geall, then there'd been light and wind, and a roar of sound.

Then it had been night, and it had been Ireland—a place Larkin had always believed a fairy tale.

He hadn't believed in fairy tales, or monsters, and despite his own gift had looked askance at magic.

But magic there was, he admitted now. Just as there was an Ireland, and there were monsters. Those demons had attacked them—springing out of the dark of the woods, their eyes red, their fangs sharp. The form of a man, he thought, but not a man.

Vampire.

They existed to feed off man. And now they banded together under their queen to destroy all.

He was here to stop them, at all and any costs. He was here at the charge of the gods to save the worlds of man.

He scratched idly at his healing thigh and decided he could hardly be expected to save mankind on an empty stomach.

He cut a slab of cake to go with his morning Coke and licked icing from his finger. So far, through wile and guile he'd avoided Glenna's cooking lessons. He liked to eat, that was true enough, but the actual making of food was a different matter.

He was a tall, lanky man with a thick waving mane of tawny hair. His eyes, nearly the same color, were long like his cousin's, and nearly as keen. He had a long and mobile mouth that was quick to smile, quick hands and an easy nature.

Those who knew him would have said he was generous with his time and his coin, and a good man to have at your back at the pub, or in a brawl.

He'd been blessed with strong, even features, a strong back, a willing hand. And the power to change his shape into any living thing.

He took a healthy bite of cake where he stood, but there was too much quiet in the house to suit him. He wanted, needed, activity, sound, motion. Since he couldn't sleep, he decided he'd take Cian's stallion out for a morning run.

Cian could hardly do it himself, being a vampire.

He stepped out of the back door of the big stone house. There was a chill in the air, but he had the sweater and jeans Glenna had purchased in the village. He wore his own boots—and the silver cross Glenna and Hoyt had forged with magic.

He saw where the earth was scorched, where it was trampled. He saw his own hoofprints left in the sodden earth when he'd galloped through the battle in the form of a horse.

And he saw the woman who'd ridden him, slashing destruction with a flaming sword.

She moved through the mists, slow and graceful, in what he would have taken for a dance if he hadn't known the movements, the complete control in them, were another preparation for battle.

Long arms and long legs swept through the air so smoothly they barely disturbed the mists. He could see her muscles tremble when she held a pose, endlessly held it, for her arms were bared in a snug white garment no woman of Geall would have worn outside the bedchamber.

She lifted a leg behind her into the air, bent at the knee, reaching an arm back to grasp her bare foot. The shirt rose up her torso to reveal more flesh.

It would be a sorry man, Larkin decided, who didn't enjoy the view.

Her hair was short, raven black, and her eyes were bluer than the lakes of Fonn. She wouldn't have been deemed a beauty in his world, as she lacked the roundness, the plump sweet curves, but he found the strength of her form appealing, the angles of her face, the sharp arch of brows interesting and unique.

She brought her leg down, swept it out to the side, then dropped into a long crouch with her arms parallel to the ground.

"You always eat that much sugar in the morning?"

Her voice jolted him. He'd been still and silent, and thought her unaware of him. He should've known better. He took a bite of the cake he'd forgotten he held. "It's good."

"Bet." Blair lowered her arms, straightened. "Earlier rising for you than usual, isn't it?"

"I couldn't sleep."

"Know what you mean. Damn good fight."

"Good?" He looked over the burned ground and thought of the screams, the blood, the death. "It wasn't a night at the pub."

"Entertaining though." She looked as he did, but with a hard light in her eyes. "We kicked some vampire ass, and what could be a better way to spend the evening?"

"I can think of a few."

"Hell of a rush, though." She rolled any lingering tension from her shoulders as she glanced at the house. "And it didn't suck to go from a handfasting to a fight and back again—as winners. Especially when you consider the alternative."

"There's that, I suppose."

"I hope Glenna and Hoyt are getting a little honeymoon time in, because for the most part, it was a pretty crappy reception."

With the long, almost liquid gait he'd come to admire, she walked over to the long table they used during daylight training to hold weapons and supplies. She picked up the bottle of water she'd left there and drank deep.

"You have a mark of royalty."

"Say what?"

He moved closer, touched a fingertip lightly to her shoulder blade. There was the mark of a cross like the one around his neck, but in bold and bloody red.

"It's just a tattoo."

"In Geall only the ruler would bear a mark on the body. When the new king or queen becomes, when they lift the sword from the stone, the mark appears. Here." He tapped a hand on his right biceps. "Not the symbol of the cross, but the claddaugh, put there, it's said, by the finger of the gods."

"Cool. Excellent," she explained when he frowned at her.

"I myself have never seen this."

She cocked her head. "And seeing's believing?"

He shrugged. "My aunt, Moira's mother, had such a mark. But she rose to queen before I was born, so I didn't see the mark become."

"I never heard that part of the legend." Because it was there, she swooped a fingertip through the icing of his cake, sucked it off. "I guess everything doesn't trickle down."

"How did you come by yours?"

Funny guy, Blair thought. Curious nature. Gorgeous eyes. Danger, Will Robinson, she thought. That sort of combo just begged for complications. She just wasn't built for complications—and had learned it the hard way. "I paid for it. A lot of people have tattoos. It's like a personal statement, you could say. Glenna's got one." She took another drink, watching him as she reached around to tap herself on the small of the back. "Here. A pentagram. I saw it when we were helping her get dressed for the handfasting."

"So they're for women."

"Not only. Why, you want one?"

"I think not." He rubbed absently at his thigh.

Blair remembered yanking the arrow out of him herself, and that he'd barely uttered a sound. The guy had balls to go with the gorgeous eyes and curious nature. He was no slouch in a fight, and no whiner after the battle. "Leg giving you trouble?"

"A little stiff, a little sore. Glenna's a good healer. Yours?"

She bent her leg back, heel to butt, gave it a testing pull. "It's okay. I heal fast—part of the family package. Not as fast as a vamp," she added. "But demon hunters heal faster than your average human."

She picked up the jacket she'd tossed on the table, put it on against the morning cool. "I want coffee."

"I don't like it. I like the Coke." Then he smiled, easy, charming. "Will you be making yourself the breakfast?"

"In a little while. I've got some things I want to do first."

"Maybe you wouldn't mind making enough for two."

"Maybe." Clever guy, too, she thought. You had to respect his finagling. "You got something going now?"

It took him a moment, but he tried to spend a little time each day with the miraculous machine called the television. He was proud to think he was learning new idioms. "I'm after taking the horse for a ride, then feeding and grooming him."

"Plenty of light today, but you shouldn't head into the woods unarmed."

"I'll be riding the fields. Ah, Glenna, she asked if I'd not ride alone in the forest. I don't like to worry her. Were you wanting a ride yourself?"

"I think I had enough of one last night, thanks to you." Amused, she gave him a light punch in the chest. "You've got some speed in you, cowboy."

"Well, you've a light and steady seat." He looked back out at the trampled ground. "You're right. It was a good fight."

"Damn right. But the next one won't be so easy."

His eyebrows winged up. "And that one was easy?"

"Compared to what's coming, bet your ass."

"Well then, the gods help us all. And if you've a mind to cook eggs and bacon with it, that'd be fine. Might as well eat our fill while we still have stomachs."

Cheery thought, Blair decided as she went inside. The hell of it was, he'd meant it that way. She'd never known anyone so offhand about life and death. Not resigned—she'd been raised to be resigned to it—just a kind of confidence that he'd live as he chose to live, until he stopped living.

She admired the viewpoint.

She'd been raised to know the monster under the bed was real, and was just waiting until you relaxed before it ripped your throat out.

She'd been trained to put that moment off as long as she could stand and fight, to slash and to burn, and take out as many as humanly possible. Because under the strength, the wit and the endless training was the knowledge that some day, some way, she wouldn't be fast enough, smart enough, lucky enough.

And the monster would win.

Still there'd always been a balance to it—demon and hunter, with each the other's prey. Now the stakes had been raised, sky-fricking-high, she thought as she made coffee. Now it wasn't just the duty and tradition that had been passed down through her blood for damn near a millennium.

Now it was a fight to save humankind.

She was here, with this strange little band—two of which, vampire and sorcerer, turned out to be her ancestors—to fight the mother of all battles.

Two months, she thought, until Halloween. Till Samhain, and the final showdown the goddess had prophesied. They'd have to be ready, she decided as she poured the first cup. Because the alternative just wasn't an option.

She carried her coffee upstairs, into her room.

As quarters went, it had it all over her apartment in Chicago where she'd based herself over the last year and a half. The bed boasted a tall headboard with carved dragons on either side. A woman could feel like a spellbound princess in that bed—if she was of a fanciful state of mind.

Despite the fact the place was owned by a vampire, there was a wide mirror, framed in thick mahogany. The wardrobe would have held three times the amount of clothes she'd brought with her, so she used it for secondary weapons, and tucked her traveling wardrobe in the chest of drawers.

The walls were painted a dusky plum, and the art on them woodland scenes of twilight or predawn, so that the room seemed to be in perpetual shadow if the curtains were drawn. But that was all right. She had lived a great deal of her life in the shadows.

But she opened the curtains now so morning spilled in and then sat at the gorgeous little desk to check her e-mail on her laptop.

She couldn't prevent the little flicker of hope, or stop it from dying out as she saw there was still no return message from her father.

Nothing new, she reminded herself and tipped back in the chair. He was traveling, somewhere in South America to the best of her knowledge. And she only knew that much because her brother had told her.

It had been six months since she'd had any contact with him, and there was nothing new about that, either. His duty to her had been, in his opinion, fulfilled years ago. And maybe he was right. He'd taught her, he'd trained her, though she'd never been good enough to merit his approval.

She simply didn't have the right equipment. She wasn't his son. The disappointment he'd felt when it had been his daughter instead of his son who'd inherited the gift was something he'd never bothered to hide.

Softening blows of any sort just wasn't Sean Murphy's style. He'd pretty much dusted her off his hands on her eighteenth birthday.

Now she'd embarrassed herself by sending him a second message when he'd never answered the first. She'd sent that first e-mail before she'd left for Ireland, to tell him something was up, something was twitching, and she wanted his advice.

So much for that, she thought now, and so much for trying again, after her arrival, to tell him what was twitching was major.

He had his own life, his own course, and had never pretended otherwise. It was her own problem, her own lack, that she still coveted his approval. She'd given up on earning his love a long time ago.

She turned off the computer, pulled on a sweatshirt and shoes. She decided to go up to the training room and work off frustration, work up an appetite lifting weights.

The house, she'd been told, had been the one Hoyt and his brother, Cian, had been born in. In the dawn of the twelfth century. It had been modernized, of course, and some additions had been made, but she could see from the original structure the Mac Cionaoiths had been a family of considerable means.

Of course Cian had had nearly a millennium to make his own fortune, to acquire the house again. Though from the bits and pieces she'd picked up, he didn't live in it.

She didn't make a habit out of conversing with vampires—just killing them. But she was making an exception with Cian. For reasons that weren't entirely clear to her, he was fighting with them, even bankrolling their little war party to some extent.

Added to that, she'd seen the way he'd fought the night before, with a ruthless ferocity. His allegiance could be the element that tipped the scales in their favor.

She wound her way up the stone stairs toward what had once been the great hall, then a ballroom in later years. And was now their training room.

She stopped short when she saw Larkin's cousin Moira doing chest extensions with five-pound free weights.

The Geallian wore her brown hair back in a thick braid that reached her waist. Sweat dribbled down her temples, and more darkened the back of the white T-shirt she wore. Her eyes, fog gray, were staring straight ahead, focused, Blair assumed, on whatever got her through the reps.

She was, by Blair's gauge about five-three, maybe a hundred and ten pounds, after you'd dragged her out of a lake. But she was game. Having game held a lot of weight on Blair's scale. What Blair had initially judged as mousiness was, in actuality, a watchfulness. The woman soaked up everything.

"Thought you were still in bed," Blair said as she stepped inside.

Moira lowered the weights, then used her forearm to swipe her brow. "I've been up for a bit. You're wanting to use the room?"

"Yeah. Plenty of room in here for both of us." Blair walked over, selected ten-pound weights. "Not hunkered down with the books this morning."

"I . . ." On a sigh, Moira stretched out her arms as she'd been taught. She might have wished her arms were as sleek and carved with muscle as Blair's, but no one would call them soft any longer. "I've been starting the day here, before I use the library. Usually before anyone's up and about."

"Okay." Curious, Blair studied Moira as she worked her triceps. "And you're keeping this a secret because?"

"Not a secret. Not exactly a secret." Moira picked up a bottle of water, twisted off the cap. Twisted it back on. "I'm the weakest of us. I don't need you or Cian to tell me that—though one or the other of you make a point to let me know it with some regularity."

Something gave a little twist inside Blair's belly. "And that sucks. I'm going to tell you I'm sorry about that, because I know how it feels to get slammed down when you're doing your best."

"My best isn't altogether that good, is it? No, I'm not looking for sorry," she said before Blair could speak. "It's hard to be told you're lacking, but that's what I am—for now. So I come up here in the mornings, early, and lift these bloody things the way you showed me. I won't be the weak one, the one the rest of you have to worry about."

"You don't have much muscle yet, but you've got some speed. And you're a frigging genius with a bow. If you weren't so good with it, things wouldn't have turned out the way, they did last night."

"Work on my weaknesses, and on my strengths, on my own time. That's what you said to me—and it made me angry. Until I saw the wisdom of it. I'm not angry. You're good at training. King was . . . He was more easy on me, I think, because he was a man. A big man at that," Moira added with sorrow in her eyes now. "Who had affection for me, I think, because I was the smallest of us."

Blair hadn't met King, Cian's friend who'd been captured, then killed by Lilith. Then turned, and sent back as a vampire.

"I won't be easy on you," Blair promised.

By the time she'd finished a session with the weights and grabbed a quick shower, Blair had worked up that appetite. She decided to go for one of her favorites, and dug up the makings for French toast.

She tossed some Irish bacon into a skillet for protein, selected Green Day on her MP3 player. Music to cook by.

She poured her second cup of coffee before breaking eggs in a bowl.

She was beating the batter when Larkin strolled in the door. He stopped, stared at her player. "And what is it?"

"It's a—" How to explain? "A way to whistle while you work."

"No, it's not the machine I'm meaning. There are so many of those, I can't keep them all in my brain. But what's the sound?"

"Oh. Um, popular music? Rock—of the hard variety."

He was grinning now, head cocked as he listened. "Rock. I like it."

"Who wouldn't? Not going for eggs, this morning. Doing up French toast."

"Toast?" Disappointment fell over his face, erasing the easy pleasure of the music. "Just cooked bread?"

"Not just. Besides, you get what you get when I'm manning the stove. Or you forage on your own."

"It's kind of you to cook, of course."

His tone was so long-suffering, she had to swallow a laugh. "Relax, and trust me on this, I've seen you chow down, cowboy. You're going to like it as much as Rock, especially after you drown it in butter and syrup. I'll have it going in a minute. Why don't you flip that bacon over?"

"I'm needing to wash first. Been mucking out the stall and such, and I'm not fit yet to touch anything."

She lifted a brow as he strolled right out. She'd seen him slip out of all manner of kitchen duties already. And she had to admit, he was slick about it.

Resigned, she turned the bacon herself, then heated a second skillet. She was about to dunk the first piece of bread when she heard voices. The newlyweds were up, she realized, and added to the batter to accommodate them.

Effortless style. It was something Glenna had in spades, Blair thought. She wandered in wearing a sage green sweater and black jeans with her bold red hair swinging straight and loose. The urban take on country casual, Blair supposed. When you added the pretty flush of a woman who'd obviously had her morning snuggles, you had quite a package.

She didn't look like a woman who would rush a squad of

vampires while she bellowed war cries and swung a battle-ax, but she'd done just that.

"Mmm, French toast? You must have read my mind." As she moved to the coffeepot, Glenna gave Blair's arm an absent stroke. "Give you a hand?"

"No, I got this. You've been taking the lion's share of KP, and I'm better at breakfast than dinner. Didn't I hear Hoyt?"

"Right behind me. He's talking to Larkin about the horse. I think Hoyt's a little put out he didn't get to Vlad before Larkin did. Coffee's good. How'd you sleep?"

"Like I'd been knocked unconscious, for a couple hours." Blair dipped bread, then laid it to sizzle. "Then, I don't know, too restless. Wired up." She slanted Glenna a look. "And nowhere to put the excess energy, like the bride."

"I have to admit, I'm feeling pretty loose and relaxed this morning. Except." Wincing a little, Glenna massaged her right biceps. "My arms feel like I spent half the night swinging a sledgehammer."

"Battle-ax has weight. You did good work with it."

"*Work* isn't the word that comes to mind. But I'm not going to think about it—at least not until I've gorged myself." Turning, Glenna opened a cupboard for plates. "Do you know how often I had a breakfast like this—fried bread, fried meat—before all this started?"

"Nope."

"Never. Absolutely never," she added with a half laugh. "I watched my weight as if the, well, as if the fate of the world depended on it."

"You're training hard." Blair flipped the bread. "You need the fuel, the carbs. If you put on a few pounds, I can guarantee it's going to be pure muscle."

"Blair." Glenna glanced toward the doorway to ensure Hoyt hadn't started in yet. "You've got more experience with this than any of us. Just between you and me, for now, anyway, how did we do last night?"

"We lived," Blair said flatly. She continued to cook, sliding fried bread onto a plate, dunking more. "That's bottom line."

"But—"

"Glenna, I'll tell you straight." Blair turned, leaning back on the counter for a moment while bread sizzled and scented the air. "I've never been in anything like that before."

"But you've been doing this—hunting them—for years."

"That's right. And I've never seen so many of them in one place at one time, never seen them organized that way."

Glenna let out a quiet breath. "That can't be good news."

"Good or bad, it's fact. It's not—never been in my experience—the nature of the beast to live, work, fight in large groups. I contacted my aunt, and she says the same. They're killers, and they might travel, hunt, even live together in packs. Small packs, and there might be an alpha, male or female. But not like this."

"Not like an army," Glenna murmured.

"No. And what we saw last night was a squad—a small slice of an army. The thing is, they're willing to die for her, for Lilith. And that's powerful stuff."

"Okay. Okay," Glenna said as she set the table. "That's what I get for saying I wanted it straight."

"Hey, buck up. We lived, remember? That's a victory."

"Good morning to you," Hoyt said to Blair as he came in. Then his gaze went straight to Glenna.

They shared coloring, Blair thought, she and her however-many-times great-uncle. She, the sorcerer and his twin brother the vampire shared coloring, and ancestry, and now this mission, she supposed.

Fate was certainly a twisty bastard.

"You two sure have the glow on," she said when Glenna lifted her face to meet Hoyt's lips. "Practically need my shades."

"They shield the eyes from the sun, and are a sexy fashion statement," Hoyt returned and made her laugh.

"Have a seat." She turned off the music, then brought the heaping platter to the table. "I made enough for an army, seeing as that's what we are."

"It looks a fine feast. Thank you."

"Just doing my share, unlike some of us who're a little more slippery." She met Larkin's perfectly timed appearance with a shake of her head. "Right on time."

His expression was both innocent and affable. "Is it ready then? It took me a bit longer to get back as I stopped to tell Moira there was food being cooked. And a welcome sight it is."

"You look, you eat." Blair slapped four slices of French toast on a plate for him. "And you and your cousin do the dishes."